The Gaius Realm: Echoes of Choice

J. W. Frederick
T. L. Hughes

CONTENTS

PART 1 – BREAKING POINT

CHAPTER 1 - DREAMS

"I had a weird dream last night. I'll spare you the details because you know my dreams are always crazy. But I wanted to tell you about it because you were in it. I don't know if I've mentioned this before, but in my dreams, it usually isn't there. I don't have to deal with it or even think about it, ya know? And if it is there, I can control it. It's just a part of me, like my hand or arm or whatever. It does what I want, if you can believe that. It doesn't hurt people. When I use it in my dreams, it's just to have fun, to make you laugh, or to help somebody. It doesn't... hurt you in my dreams. And in my dreams, you and I are... we're okay."

My voice fades. I've drifted deeper into my thoughts than I wanted, and I don't like where it's taking me. So I just focus on Leia lying there. She looks so peaceful. But I know better. Even in her sleep, I can feel the anger, fear, and loneliness radiating from her. She feels lost. And as I watch her—unconscious for the 13th day in a row because of me, because of what it did to her—talking about my dreams feels pointless.

Why would she care about my dreams? They don't come true anyway.

And just like that, it stirs again, rising in my chest and pouring into my arms. That electric sensation—hot and cold at the same time, like I'm being pulled apart and squeezed together all at once. I feel powerful, connected to everything around me. I feel more alive than ever while sensing that death is hovering just beyond the limits of my control. I grit my teeth, giving all I have to keep it bottled in. Because what I've learned about this power is that if it gets out, it will do whatever it wants to do.

I can't let that happen. Hasn't it done enough damage already?

Deep breaths, Aiden. Deep breaths. Focus. Talk about something else.

Determined to calm the storm, I take Leia's hand in mine, lifting it to my lips as I scoot closer to her bedside. I kiss her fingers, then lay her hand gently back down. The steady beep of the EKG becomes an anchor for my focus. Listening to its forgettable pace and volume centers my mind in the eye of the hurricane.

I place a hand on her forehead and let my eyes wander over her face. The sunlight streaming through the blinds catches the contours of her cheeks, caressing her in soft, golden light.

This face should be smiling.

"How are they treating you in here?" I ask, my voice low. "Anybody I need to beat up? I saw how that nurse was looking at you earlier. I mean, I can't be mad at him for recognizing how beautiful you are—because you *are* beautiful—but he better just do his job and keep it moving."

I feel her laughter. I can't tell if she's laughing at what I said. I can't tell if she can even hear what I said. But thanks to the one benefit of these powers—the ability to feel the emotions of others—I know she laughed.

She's probably just dreaming about something funny. But, no... I know the feeling of her laughing at me, and this felt just like that. I think. Or maybe I'm just hoping she's laughing at me because that would mean she doesn't hate me. It could mean that maybe—just maybe—if she wakes up, she can forgive me and we can move on like none of this ever happened.

If only I could read minds instead of just feelings!

"Seems like they're working around the clock to bring you back to us," I say, keeping my voice light. "And that's good because Candace called me yesterday saying all I do is mope around with you gone like this. Well, not gone, but, you know... sleeping. She told me to tell you to hurry up and come back because she's tired of seeing me all sad and depressed. I told her to get a life.

"I think you'll be back soon, though. They told me all your vitals look good. Your blood pressure and heart rate are stabilized. You're breathing on your own. Your eyes are reacting to light stimulation. Really, we're just waiting on you to come back from... wherever you are. I wish I knew where that was. I would go there myself and bring you back... You know I would. No matter how far, I'd find a way. Just like I'm going to figure out a way to get these powers under control so that I never push you away like this again."

With those last words, her inner turmoil resurfaces. The sadness in her heart is unbearable... It's a deep, raging sorrow, so intense I feel suffocated by it. The loneliness that engulfed her is so thick that I find myself tempted to step out into the hallway for a moment just to catch my breath. But I refuse to walk out on her.

How could I hurt her like this and then abandon her to suffer by herself? Even as the anger floods in—and I know it's directed at me—I deserve to feel this. I need to feel it. It's my fault. I gotta tough it out and stay with her.

That's when it hits me: this sudden flurry of emotions is confirmation, at least to me, that she can hear me. That's a good thing because there's something I need her to hear.

"Leia, I love you. And I'm so sorry for this. When you come back, we're gonna be okay. I'm not gonna leave you like this. I'll be right here the whole time while you heal. I'll be here... as long as it takes, I'll be—"

"Knock, knock."

I turn to see who just ruined the intimate moment I was trying to create. Dr. Larson stands just inside the doorway, his white lab coat crisp, his thin-framed silver glasses glinting in the late afternoon sunlight. Seeing him makes me instinctively release some of the tension in my core. His presence always projects calmness and comfort, which is impressive for someone in his mid-30's carrying the stress of his job. I can't help but admire him, especially with the compassion I feel in him. It's so real I'm surprised I didn't sense him earlier.

How long has he been standing there?

He smiles warmly and says, "Aiden, how are you doing?"

I give a half-hearted shrug, which communicates all that I care to share.

We don't need to be talking about me.

"How's she doing?"

"Well, that's what I'm here to get a better understanding of." He pauses, his voice steady but cautious. "Like we mentioned before, her body has fully recovered from the injury that caused her coma. Actually, she recovered much faster than normal. Physically speaking, I don't think there's anything else wrong with her. I'm going to run one more test, and if it comes back negative like I expect, then we will have exhausted all the help conventional medicine can provide."

I don't know how to feel about that, so I just blurt out, "Well, doc, if she's fine, why won't she wake up?"

Dr. Larson doesn't flinch at the unintended sarcasm in my voice. His composure holds, calm and compassionate. "I wish I could have said she was fine. Let me clarify... I said conventional medicine may not have anything else to add to her recovery. I don't think this is a physiological problem anymore. But the good news is we have a liaison in ARL's Laosi Integration department, and they've placed Leia's case file in their high-priority review queue."

Laosi integration? So my power hurt Leia on the soul level this time?

"They need me to gather as much information as possible before sending a specialist to assess her condition. That's why I've got one more test to run."

If we have to get an Alma Research Labs specialist to look at Leia, then I did even more damage to her than I thought. I didn't even think it was possible to impact a person's Laosi. I'm surprised I didn't kill her.

Wait, I almost killed Leia because I can't control my stupid powers!?

As if in a trance, I say, "Okay, Doc... I'll leave you to it, then..." I stand up, dazed, look down at Leia, and then turn toward the door.

I walk past Dr. Larson in a mental haze, with just enough awareness to hear him say, "Hey, actually, if you could wait in the waiting room, I'd like to..."

What did I do to you, Leia?

My body switches to autopilot. I've been to this hospital enough times to know how to get to the waiting room without thinking. As I pass the nurses' counter, hear them answering calls, and see patients being wheeled through the sterile white halls, it feels like I'm in another dimension. I see them, but I don't really see them. I can't think about anything except the fact that Leia can't wake up because her soul was damaged—by me.

Of course, Dr. Larson didn't say that explicitly, but that idea is all-consuming. I round the corner and drop onto the royal blue, uncomfortable-as-ever leather couch in the waiting room. The flowers on the coffee table in front of me, the vending machine in the corner, the picture of the rainbow that arched over Sanctuary Hospital for three days—they're all lifeless shades of grey. I don't know or care to know if anyone else is in the room. I rest my elbows on my knees and bury my face in my hands.

I almost killed the love of my life using these stupid powers that I can't get rid of or control. I don't know of anybody else who can't control their abilities. What's wrong with me? Why am I the only one like this?

The floor under my feet trembles at the sound of a low rumble.

It's happening.

I recognize the sensation instantly, but instead of reacting to it, I keep my face buried in my hands. Through the gaps between my fingers, I watch the vending machine slowly sliding toward me, held back only by the cord plugged into the wall. The furniture in the room shifts and slides across the floor.

Not again. Come on, focus, Aiden. Focus!

I close my eyes, trying to will my adrenaline to settle.

If I can't get this under control, somebody's going to get killed. And if my Laosi powers kill someone else, I'll be put to death. I gotta get out of here before I bring this whole hospital down. I'm a threat to everyone here. Who am I kidding? I'm a danger to everybody everywhere. I should just be left alo—

The rumbling stops. I open my eyes and lift my head.

"Wha—" I mumble, looking around. "Where am I?"

The sky above me is overcast, and a cool breeze rustles the tall, purple marsh grass all around. The ground that I find myself sitting on is damp and soggy, adding an awkward discomfort to my lower regions that I try to shake off by standing quickly. I scan the area for clues, taking in the large madron trees with their gray and green trunks, bent in the distinct semi-circle formation their species is known for.

These only grow in Reality. Am I in... Alabast?

The sound of the Kerioth River flowing about 15 yards ahead of me confirms my location just outside of Sanctuary. I squint and shake my head, struggling to accept the fact that my Laosi-Empowered Talent includes teleportation—and that it chose to teleport me here.

Will it be so kind as to take me back? Probably not, but I'll give it a shot.

I shake some mud off my pants, clench my fists and my teeth to concentrate—though it doesn't actually help—and fill my mind with images of the hospital waiting room. I hold my breath, picture myself traveling through space, and brace for reentry. When I open my eyes...

Nothing. I'm still in this godforsaken swamp, which barely shows any signs of the last humans who evacuated decades ago.

I don't know why everyone left, but I feel like I should follow their lead. That's just like my LET—creating problems it won't help me solve. I can teleport to the middle of nowhere but can't get back to where I need to be. My Laosi-Empowered "Talent" is so useless.

I notice how peaceful the river is, though. It flows with an almost hypnotic, neon blue hue. Unless my eyes are playing tricks on me, it's actually glowing.

Interesting. What's causing that glow? Is this the color of Laosi? Or is it what caused the evacuation?

I search for a shallow spot to wade through, but seeing the reflection of Sanctuary City in the river distracts me. I turn my gaze upward, spotting Sheridan Tower, Sanctuary Hospital, and other landmarks of the city. The view reminds me that I was supposed to meet Dr. Larson in the waiting room so he could ask some more questions about Leia.

Maybe I shouldn't go back. If she wakes up, would she even want to see me? I'll probably just find a way to make everything worse if I go back. Like usual. Why do I keep messing everything up?

A jarring sound—like lightning tearing through the sky, a jungle barberyx roaring, and a freight carrier's engine all at once—interrupts my thoughts. I wince and close my eyes. When I open them again, I'm back in the hospital, falling on top of Dr. Larson as he turns the corner into the waiting room.

"Oh! Sorry, doctor... I can—umm... let me get that for you." I lower my gaze as I scramble to pick up his writing tablet. Out of the corner of my eye, I see Dr. Larson's calm composure slip for the first time. His eyes widen. His eyebrows raise. His chest heaves.

I look down again, not yet ready to endure another round of rejection on account of my out-of-control LET. But when he reaches for his notetaking device, the look on his face conveys concern. He places a hand on my shoulder, and his touch makes the compassion I feel from him more tangible.

He motions for me to sit down on the couch as he follows me to it. I sink into the seat, sweating bullets like a kid called to the principal's office. My hands wring themselves without me realizing it, and my eyes stay glued to the floral pattern on the wallpaper in front of me. Dr. Larson sits beside me, his body angled slightly away at first. Then, as he begins to speak, he turns toward me.

"Aiden," he starts, then pauses, clearing his throat. "I told you I thought the final test I was going to perform on Leia would come back negative. That turned out to be the case, and now I think I understand a little bit more about why."

He gestures toward the furniture, causing me to notice how my powers rearranged all of it. The two coffee tables with their blue vases, the three white plastic chairs, and the vending machine are all crowded in a tight semicircle around the couch I was sitting on before I disappeared.

At least nothing's broken—this time.

"Is it safe to assume you did this as well?" he asks.

I hesitate before giving a dry, "Yeah."

Dr. Larson presses his lips together, swallowing as he surveys the scene again.

"Did you... not appreciate the work of our overpaid interior designers? I've always thought this room had some weird feng shui myself, but I can't say I understand your stylistic choices either." He strokes his chin, his eyes narrowing as though he's analyzing an abstract painting at an art gallery.

"I didn't try to... It just happens sometimes."

His tone shifts, the sarcasm vanishing. He turns to face me fully, his expression serious now. "So... you have an active LET, and you can't control it?"

My head drops. I inhale deeply, trying to fill my lungs with enough air to keep out the truth I've avoided admitting. When I finally let the breath go, it takes the last scraps of hope I had for a normal life along with it.

I worked so hard to keep my powers a secret for so long. I had a few slip-ups, but the only people who really knew were my parents, my brother, sister, fiancée, and best friend. I trust Dr. Larson enough to answer his question, but still... where is this going to go once I tell him?

"No... I can't control it."

His expression sharpens with the curiosity of his relentless scientific mind. That curiosity is exactly what I wanted to avoid because I know it leads to a question that I do not want to answer.

"The details of Leia's accident have always been somewhat vague to me," he says slowly, his voice quieter. "Now I understand why. ARL has agreed to send a specialist, but he'll need all the information relevant to Leia's injury in order to diagnose and effectively treat her condition." He pauses, his gaze locking onto mine. "Aiden, I have to ask you—what really happened that night?"

CHAPTER 2 - NIGHTMARE PT. 1

"Personally, I think it's amazing. I really wanna know what else you can do."

I glance over at Leia, raising an eyebrow, dumbfounded. She challenges my skepticism with that look—the one that says, "*I believe in you, and I want you to believe in you, too.*"

Her faith in me unlocks a smile that had been yearning to break through and could no longer be denied. I lean back, interlocking my fingers behind my head as I sit up straight on the ledge circling the top of Sheridan Tower. My red sneakers dangle over the edge as I lightly kick them together, mostly to make sure they stay on my feet.

I hope my shoe doesn't fall off. Eighty-one stories is a long way for a shoe to drop. There are thousands of people down there. I've been worried about killing someone with my powers, but with a shoe? 'Hey, man. I'm sorry to hear about your loss. How'd your brother die?' 'He got hit by a shoe while waiting for the Sanctuary Achievement Week fireworks.' That would be tragic.

The night is clear and beautiful, and a crisp breeze blows by. More refreshing than the wind is the energy from the crowd below that we can feel all the way up here. There's so much light, life, and excitement as people celebrate our nation's holiday week.

"What else I can do? I... think I've done enough," I say.

"Now Aiden, this whole week is about the people of Sanctuary feeling proud of everything we've accomplished since Sanctuary was founded. That includes you." Her voice softens. "You don't have to rain on our week of parades by thinking about ways you've messed up. You've accomplished a lot, too. And you're gonna accomplish even more."

She leans closer, and I slip my arm around her shoulders as she continues. "I think one of these Sanctuary Achievement Week plays could be about you one day... You have so much potential, babe. I wish you could see it like I do."

"Me, too," I say, still bewildered. "Yeah, I don't... because, like... So, you're seeing Day Six, the Sanctuary Today display, the highlight of all our cutting-edge cultural and scientific breakthroughs, proudly presenting Aiden Lore?" I shake my head. "What'd I do? Invent a revolutionary method of finding defective staples just as the paper industry completely disappears from every corner of Tryon?"

Leia elbows me in the ribs, cutting off my deriding laugh.

"Yeah, yeah, okay... but serious question," she says. "If I had an LET that could make your dreams a reality, what would you want to do for a living? Like, all the training taken care of, any salary you want. What would you be?"

"Free of my powers," I mutter.

"Focus," she says, not letting me off the hook. "That's what you want to avoid. But what would you want to pursue?"

"That's a good question... I feel like I should have an answer, but I honestly don't know."

"Well, why not?" she asks, gently placing her hand on my thigh. "I know this isn't the first time you've ever been asked this question."

"Hmm. I guess I never felt like there was room for my answer, so why bother trying to find it?" I say. "You know, when my dad told me his work at ARL was gonna be the Sanctuary Today headline, I couldn't help but wonder how? How did he know what he wanted to do, and how did he get to do it? All the life-changing work and technological advancements he's been a part of in the building we're sitting on... He's basically second in command of the largest corporation in the Sovereign State. And he loves his work! Most people just get jobs doing what they *can* do, not what they *want* to do."

I pause, the memory replaying in my head. "And when I saw him on the display yesterday... It was weird, because I actually saw why people always ask me, 'Are you related to Richard Lore?'"

"You're only just now seeing the resemblance?" Leia teases.

"That's not the point," I say, laughing. "But when I saw it, I just felt... stuck. Does that make sense?"

"You don't need permission to pursue your dreams," Leia says. "I think that's the point of this week. And I think you should talk to your dad about how he got to where he is. Have y'all ever had that conversation? Like, about your career path and all?"

"Nah, we don't really have those kinds of conversations."

A flood of conversations I wish we'd had runs through my mind. The most important conversation we never had rises to the top—the one where I ask why his technology worked for my brother and sister but not for me.

Why don't we have the important conversations? Why doesn't he help me the way he works so hard to help others? Am I past being helped? Am I—

"Aiden?" Leia interrupts, sitting up and tensing.

"What's wrong?"

"Did you hear that?" she asks, looking around nervously.

"Hear what?"

"It was this really high-pitched, like... Do you know what I'm talking about? You didn't hear it?"

"A high-pitched noise? Like, a ringing?"

"Yeah, but more like a hum, I think."

"No, I didn't hear that. Maybe they're cueing up the fireworks? You know how electrical devices make that noise when you turn them on?" I say, more dismissive than I mean to be. Even still, she relaxes and takes another look at the city below.

"You know, I've only been up here one other time in my life," I say, remembering when my dad brought me here for "Bring Your Kids to Work" day 15 years ago. "But this view... it always feels like you're seeing it for the first time."

"Sometimes I forget how big Sanctuary is," Leia says. She looks around and adds, "I bet they put Sheridan Tower in the center of the city on purpose. No matter which direction you look, it's just more Sanctuary as far as the eye can see. I love this view! It's almost as amazing as the man who brought me up here to see it."

"Amazing, huh? If you say so... This view is amazing. You are amazing. Me and these powers, though?" I sigh, shivering gently—not from the breeze, but from the thought of what my powers and I have done.

Leia grins. "Awww, is widdle Aiden chiwwy? I'll keep you warm," she says in a playful, childlike voice, wrapping her arms around my ribs and pulling me closer.

"Get outta here." My first reaction is to push her away, but then I remember we're over eight hundred feet in the air. I stop myself and just give in, enjoying the playful embrace. Eventually, she loosens her grip, but I keep my head resting on her shoulder. Another breeze blows, and her hair brushes against my neck. I pull back and sit up straight, just so I can look at her.

"Okay, I gotta know. How are you doing that?"

"Doing what?" She tenses up and pulls back, suddenly feeling self-conscious.

"How are you making the wind blow your hair perfectly into place like that? Every single strand is exactly where it needs to be. I'm starting to think you're using some Laosi here, too, or something. You got some powers you wanna tell me about?"

"Shut up, Aiden." She balls her fist and playfully jabs me in the thigh.

"I'm serious. I've seen Candace spend two hours trying

to get her hair just right. Meanwhile, you just step outside, make the breeze blow, and voilà! All this time, I thought your beauty was effortless, but here you are, out here manipulating the elements to get the job done. I'm onto you."

She giggles.

"You know you're beautiful, right?" I say. "This view *is* amazing, but I'm really just up here to look at you." I slide about a foot away from her to get a better view of her. I then wave a hand toward the food vendors, street performers, family reunions and so on below and say, "This is all nice and everything, but it's actually distracting me from the real reason I'm here."

Leia squirms because she's terrible at receiving compliments. I consider dragging it out for fun, but I decide to let her off the hook. I kiss her cheek and stroke her hair.

"Oh, wait. Did I mess it up? Do it again. Make the wind blow it back in place."

"You play too much. You know that, right?" She takes a deep breath and rests her hands on her knees. "My power would definitely not be to blow my hair into place. Well, I guess you can't control what powers you get, but I would not want that to be mine."

"Yeah, I don't think that would be your power either. You don't need soul energy to make you more beautiful. You have a beautiful soul already... But what do you think your soul energy would help you do?"

"I don't know, really. But I think it would be to help people."

"Well, that just depends on how you use it, ya know?" I ask.

"That makes sense... But what if I had the power to make food grow so no one went hungry? Or to help sick people recover?"

I smile. "It doesn't surprise me at all that you would want powers you could use to fix the world's biggest problems. But most people's powers flow from themselves or enhance their own abilities. Like, some people can run super fast or see really well or turn invisible. Stuff like that."

"Yeah, I guess that's true." She pauses for a while, then asks, "So... what exactly do *your* powers do?"

"You mean besides hurt the people I care about? Because that's pretty obvious at this point." I sigh, looking away. "Other than that, though, I... don't really know. I don't even like thinking about it. I just want it to go away."

I stare out over Sanctuary City without really looking at anything. I just need something—anything—that isn't my powers to focus on.

"You do more than hurt people, though, Aiden," Leia says. "Think about it. How did we get up here? What made it possible for us to have this moment?"

"Hey, did I ever tell you I hate it when you make irrefutable points like this?" I mutter, conceding.

She presses on. "I want you to say it. How did we get up here? How did we get the best view in town, all alone? Because the last thing I remember, we were hugging right over there." She points down at the last place our feet touched the actual ground.

"Okay, okay. Touché. We were hugging, and then I flew us 800 feet up in the air to the top of Sheridan Tower. My power is the reason we're having this great night. Are you happy now?"

"I am, Aiden. I'm really happy right now," she says warmly.

"But it's so unpredictable. I even thought we might stop flying on the way up and fall five hundred feet to our deaths."

"Those were probably the times when I felt us flying faster."

"Maybe. I don't know."

She sighs, her tone turning serious. "Your powers are so cool to me. It just sucks, ya know? There are over twenty-two million people with Laosi-Empowered Talents, and you're probably the first one in history to complain about having them."

"Hey, what can I say? I'm a one-of-a-kind kinda guy," I say with a smirk.

Her face is unmoved, but her eyes speak volumes. With more passion in her voice, she says, "You are. And you have so much potential to help people, not just hurt them. If you could get your powers under control, you could do so much more with your life, ya know? With LETs like yours... there are so many people who wish they had..."

Her words start to blur as my mind wanders.

That "one-of-a-kind" comment wasn't one of my best jokes. I could've tried harder. She didn't even give a courtesy smirk. Tough crowd. Did she even know I was trying to be funny? I need another way to avoid talking about what I "could be doing." Better yet—

"Oh wow, Leia! Look, look! The fireworks are starting!" I interrupt, pointing at the sky.

Perfect timing. Leia loves fireworks.

As expected, she's immediately caught up in the brilliant blues, reds, silvers, yellows, and greens lighting up the sky. I'm not as into them as she is, but there's something surreal about watching them from this height.

I gently pull her closer, making the moment more intimate. She scoots over, and soon, we're sitting side by side again. I slide my hand under hers, resting them on her thigh and interlocking our fingers. She looks at me with a perfect mix of affection and contentment for a moment before turning back to the sky, enraptured. She doesn't have to say it because she knows I can sense her heart saying, "*I love you, and I love being with you right now*". The feeling all but overwhelms me, so I let my mind wander again.

Okay, maybe it was a little lame to distract her just to avoid another awkward conversation. But now she's happy, and that's all I really care about. The ends justified the means.

My shoulders and abs loosen, and I fall into her a little more.

"Hey, look at that one! It looks like a smiley face! Do you see it?" Leia says, her voice bursting with excitement.

"Hmm? Smiley face? No, where?"

"Right there! Oh, it's fading now."

"Leia, that wasn't a smiley face. That was the Symbol of Sanctuary."

Sing-songy, she replies, "Nope, it was definitely a smiley face."

"A smiley face that just happens to be silver, green, and blue—our national colors?"

"Exactly! Weird, right?"

"You're weird."

"Your face is weird."

"Thank you for that, Leia..."

She takes her eyes off the fireworks just long enough to deliver the final blow: "Anytime." She winks at me.

I chuckle and shake my head, bracing for the finale, which was signaled by that "smiley face" Leia saw. All at once, the entire night sky erupts in a cascade of rainbow colors. Lights dance, patterns shift, and boom after boom reverberates through the air.

Wait, this is the finale. Which means it's almost over. Which means...we have to get down so we can go home. Oh no. Sheridan Tower is locked for the night, so we can't just take the elevator. Flying up here seemed like a great idea at the time, but once again, my talent left us in a bind. Should we call emergency responders? No, because how would we explain how we got up here? Technically, we're trespassing. I've used my LETs to commit a crime. That's a five-year minimum sentence. And Leia's an accomplice. She can't afford that fine! This is bad. I don't know what we're—

"Hey, what's wrong?" Leia asks.

"What? Oh, uh. Nothing..."

"You sure?"

"Yeah, it's just late. I'm getting kinda tired. The show should be wrapping up soon. Let's just enjoy the last little bit."

I always deflect when my mind starts racing, and I shouldn't do that. But when Leia picks up on the fact that I have something on my mind, she gets anxious. Then, stuff gets blown out of proportion, and the next thing you know, there's a hole in the living room wall. I'm not trying to have anything like that happen tonight.

Still, I know she can tell I'm deflecting. I can sense that she feels shut out, and that wasn't what I wanted.

Ugh, she knows me too well sometimes.

She sits up straight, shivering just a little. The temperature has dropped. I let go of her hand and wrap my arms around her. She smiles, grateful for the gesture, even though it isn't really helping. The show is ending anyway, so it doesn't matter.

As the final boom fades and the roaring applause from below fizzles out, Leia looks at me and says, "That was great. I think they outdid last year, for sure. But, then again, maybe I enjoyed it more because of this view. Babe, thank you so much for this. No one's ever done anything like this for me. Your powers made this night unforgettable."

She leans over and kisses me. She takes in the view one last time and says, "Okay. Are you ready to go?"

"Um, yeah... kinda. I mean..." I trail off, my words refusing to form sentences.

She looks confused. Then, she asks, "Hey, so... how are we getting down from here?" Her eyes dart around the roof, searching for our exit.

I sit in silence. I don't have an answer.

Her gaze lands on the stairwell door. "Can we take that?"

I groan. "No, it's locked. They secure everything because of all the classified stuff they work on."

"Well, this is your dad's building. Can't he come and unlock it?"

"He's at a banquet receiving his award right now," I say, sighing.

"Babe... I'm sure that if you called him and told him

you're on top of his building with no way down, he'd leave the banquet in a heartbeat," Leia says with an incredulous half-smile.

"Maybe..." I shrug. "But it's one of those fancy banquets where they make you leave your Solo at the door," I answer.

Plus... I can hear him now: 'Thank you, everyone, for the most prestigious honor our nation awards to any of its citizens. But I gotta run because my helpless son got himself stuck on the roof of our building on tonight of all nights. Be right back!'

"Oh, I see." She nods thoughtfully. She stands up and walks the perimeter of the roof, peering over the edge as she goes.

What is she looking for? This building doesn't have a fire escape.

Noticing I haven't moved, she calls from the other side, "Hey, babe, come here."

I stand carefully and walk over to her. As I approach, she continues gazing down over the edge.

Man, that's a long way down.

"So, what's the plan?" she asks.

"I... don't know yet. But I'm open to suggestions."

"So you didn't have a plan when you brought me up here?"

I sigh. "No, I didn't think that far ahead. It just... kinda happened."

Standing face to face with me, she says, "I think we can get down the same way we got up." She grabs my hands, looking deep into my eyes. I avoid her gaze. "I know what you're thinking, but you can do this."

"Do what? You mean... Oh, you want me to fly us back —"

"You can do it, my love. I know you can. You just have to believe in yourself." She squeezes my hands, her faith in me radiating through her touch.

"Leia, no, I—"

"Just hear me out. When you grabbed me and flew us

up here, I trusted you. It was scary, but I trusted you, and you brought us this far. It was the craziest ride of my life, but we made it. And I'm glad I took it with you because I'll always have this memory. But now you have to get us back down. And you can. You have what it takes. Trust me."

Did she rehearse that little speech? She's actually got me believing in myself.

"You're right... I can do this."

She pulls me in for a hug. "I've watched you, and I know you're capable. I've seen you do amazing things. You can learn to control your powers and use them for good. But you're going to have to dig deeper than ever before. I think you just need a little push."

Her affection and confidence feel kinda—

I wonder what kind of "little push" she—

My body feels warm. Oh, no! Is this Laosi? But it feels diff—

She's holding me tighter now. Why so—

Before I can finish any of these thoughts, Leia takes two quick steps to her left, still holding on to me, and throws us both over the ledge of Sheridan Tower.

CHAPTER 3 - NIGHTMARE PT. 2

"LEIAAAAAAAA!!"

As we tumble over the edge, I reach out frantically, clawing at the ledge for anything to grab onto. My fingers barely manage to find a hold deep enough to support my weight, but grabbing the ledge meant letting go of Leia. Somehow, she managed to grab onto my legs, but her grip is slipping.

"Leia... grab my hand! I'm gonna try to—"

Trusting my left hand more than I should, I reach my right hand down to her. But the look on her face—somber yet hopeful—makes it clear we're thinking the same thing: using my powers is the only way we survive this.

How could you take this kind of gamble?! Why would you put me in this position?

Sweat makes my palm slick, compromising my hold on the ledge. I reach back up with my right hand, giving everything I have to stabilize myself, but it's too late. My grip fails.

Leia and I freefall from the top of tallest building in Sanctuary City.

I close my eyes, unable to watch what I know is coming. But even with my eyes shut, I can sense the ground rushing up to meet us. A few seconds later, at about five hundred feet up, Leia cries out, "Aiden!!"

Her voice is thick with desperation, her limbs flailing wildly as gravity pulls us both down. She looks up at me, reaching not just with her hands but with her heart.

Streamlining my body, I fall faster through the air to

catch up to her. I extend my arms and pull her into a hug. I feel her relax, somehow comforted by the embrace—even though nothing about our situation has changed. I bury my face in her shoulder, trying not to think about the inevitable.

This is it. It's happening so fast. I don't wanna die—not like this! Is it gonna hurt? No! I don't want this!

At fifty feet above ground, a surge of energy explodes out of my core.

BOOOM!!

I'm... We're... not dead?

I hesitate in the stillness before opening my eyes. A pale green bubble, made of translucent, hexagonal plates, surrounds us.

What is that? A force field? I can make force fields?!

The sound of impact between the bubble and the pavement is deafening, louder than anything I've ever heard. But hearing the muffled echoes of the crash makes it all the more unbelievable that I didn't feel the impact at all. As we float in the middle of the sphere, about ten feet in diameter, I notice how quiet, spacious and cozy the inside of this force field is.

As big as this ball is, it feels like there's only room for Leia and me in here.

I look down and see the crater beneath us where the force field cushioned our fall.

How much is that gonna cost the city to repair?

The pride and relief in Leia's heart leave no room to worry about the city's expenses. She exhales a long, shaky breath, trying to release the tension and adrenaline still coursing through her. Her wide eyes meet mine. "I knew you could do it."

She cranes her neck up and kisses me. My mind replays everything that just happened, too busy to enjoy the kiss from her or even kiss back. As I piece it together, the bubble begins to fade from the top down, gently lowering us to the ground.

We land in the crater and stay there for a moment,

dazed. Then, I scramble to my feet, peering above the pavement to see if anyone's nearby. The crowds are gathered only a few blocks away—someone must've heard the crash.

"We gotta get outta here," I mutter to Leia.

Without waiting for her response, I motion for her to follow, and we climb out of the crater. Taking her hand, I lead her toward the carrier station, zigzagging through backstreets to avoid any attention.

When we finally reach the station, I pause to take in the scene. Chatter and laughter fill the air with all the busyness of the national holiday. I push my empathy LET through the crowd, but I don't sense any aggression or suspicion towards us. I pull Leia forward.

"Hey, while we're here, we should get a Sanctuary Achievement Week souvenir!" Leia says brightly, her hopeful tone cutting through the tension.

I shake my head. "I think we need to just go straight home."

"But... it's only 8:00," she says with a hint of protest. "We always do something fun when we come to the station. We could try that new restaurant AJ was raving about. Or stop by the arcade so I can beat you at *Sky Racer* like usual. Who knows? I might even let you win tonight." She winks. "Or we could act like tourists. Or sneak onto the 28th floor."

I chuckle but keep walking toward the pickup area, where a few people wait for carriers arriving one after another. "I do want to see what they're building in place of that junk food buffet. Did I ever tell you that's where I met Devon?"

"This is, like, the ninth time you've told me that," she teases. "But who's counting?"

"Whatever," I say, smirking. "I basically grew up there. But as tempting as that sounds... this was a lot. I think we should just get some rest. Don't you?"

"You're right," she admits. "It was a lot. But it was the best night of my life! I can't tell you how proud I am of you for using your powers the way you wanted to. It was terrifying at some parts, but... if you keep learning to use them like this, I mean... I guess I was so happy about what this could mean for us that I just didn't want the night to end."

Best night of her life?

Our carrier arrives, and Leia and I climb in.

"Where would you like to go?" asks the carrier's AI interface.

"City Sector RL, Apartment Building Q9, Floor 14, please," I reply.

The carrier glides off smoothly. I stare out the window as we pass the familiar streets and landmarks of Sanctuary. Meanwhile, my thoughts keep traveling to places I'm usually careful to avoid. Mindful of the hard-earned lesson learned that letting my mind wander doesn't tend to go well, I double down on my resolve to keep tight reins on my thoughts.

Leia breaks the silence. "Aiden, are you... okay?"

"Hm? Yeah... I think using all that Laosi really took it out of me. I'm just..."

She cuts in gently. "But it seems like more than that. You seem... distant." Her tone is soft, but I sense sadness beneath it.

"I'm sorry. I'm not trying to pull back from you—I know how much you hate that." I sigh. "I just... If my mind goes the wrong way... I just can't let that happen."

"I understand..." Leia says, sighing heavily. "Man, I hate that your powers come between us like this sometimes. I just... I love you, and I want you to be happy. I want *us* to be happy. And I feel like if you—"

"We have arrived!" the AI chirps, entirely too cheerful for the moment. "Please stay seated until the carrier has come to a complete stop."

The metal doors at the base of Leia's apartment building slide open, and the carrier hovers into the loading zone. The platform rises to the 14th floor.

"Please remember to grab all your belongings and enjoy the rest of your evening," the AI announces.

Leia scoffs. "I thought AIs weren't supposed to interrupt

conversations."

The loading zone doors open into the hallway. I step out of the carrier and walk around to open Leia's side.

"I keep telling you you don't have to do that," she says earnestly, trying to coax me into talking.

I'm not trying to avoid you, baby. I promise! I just... can't right now.

The energy inside me still feels volatile, bubbling under the surface, waiting for an excuse to break free. I know Leia just wants me to be present, but all my focus has to be directed to keeping this power from exploding.

"I know... I guess I'm just old-fashioned," I say halfheartedly.

As she steps out, she kisses me on the cheek. "It's okay," she says with a smile. "I'll still keep you, old man."

"You do know you're older than me, right?" I jab back.

We step out of the loading zone, and the whoosh of the closing doors echoes behind us. Walking down the hall, we reach her apartment. She stands in front of the door and says, "Leia Hart and one guest."

The biometric scanner reads her vitals and responds, "Welcome home, Leia."

She walks inside. I do not.

She turns back, puzzled. "You're not coming in?"

"I... wasn't planning to."

"We need to talk," she says firmly.

"Of course we do," I mutter, rolling my eyes.

She sighs and says, "I don't really have a lot to say, but I don't want to end the night with so much distance between us. Tonight was amazing, Babe! I know it was stressful, and you're probably mad at me for what I did. But I only did it because I believed you could get us down safely—and you *did*! Now that it's over, you can talk to me. Just tell me what you're feeling." She walks back to me as if to physically comfort me.

"I see what you're trying to do, Leia, but I just... can't." My voice wavers. "Goodnight, Leia." I turn back toward the carrier.

"Are you mad because I pushed you to learn to control your powers?"

"Mad?!" The word bursts out of me before I can think. "Me being mad isn't the issue. You *almost killed us!*"

"Aiden, please," she whispers, glancing around the hallway. "You're kinda loud. Come inside so we can talk."

Reluctantly, I follow her inside, closing the door behind me. The soft oranges and yellows of the decor blending with pastel pinks and blues set a calm atmosphere, enhanced by the gentle floral fragrance and the hologram of the Beaches of Eternity projected on the wall. It all creates an ambiance that clashes starkly against the tone of the air between us right now.

I sit on the loveseat near the door, avoiding the couch where we usually sit to laugh and talk about the life we can't wait to build together as husband and wife. Leia notices my choice but doesn't comment. Instead, she joins me, her disappointment evident in the way her shoulders drop.

"I hear you loud and clear when you say I almost killed us," she starts, her voice calm but firm. "But tonight was a triumph, Baby! Don't you see? You used your powers twice, and no one got hurt! You took us to the roof, we had an incredible night, and you got us back down safely. And that bubble thingy? Did you know you could do that?"

"Nope. I didn't."

"See? No one got hurt, and you learned something new about your powers."

She's acting like she didn't do anything wrong.

"So... did you learn anything that might help you understand what triggers it?" she asks gently.

"No... I'm actually more confused now than before." I sigh. "I thought there was a pattern because whenever my mind starts racing, my powers usually activate. But when I started flying, it wasn't like the other times."

Leia pauses, then asks cautiously, "I have a theory. Can I

share it?"

I nod, my eyes fixed on the swirls of the rug.

"I think your powers are based on what you want most at the time. Like tonight, you wanted me to enjoy the fireworks, so you took us to the best view. And when we were falling, you wanted to protect me, so you made a force field. Does that make sense?"

It sucks when she feels so uneasy with me.

"So... that time when the energy came out of my hands and did *that*"—I point at the patch of wall she had repaired last month—"I wanted... what? To raise your renter's insurance?" Pointing to the scar on her arm, I add, "Or this, with the knife... You think I was trying to add you to the dinner menu that night?"

"Come on. Don't be like that. It's just a theory. I don't have it all figured out," she pleads, discouraged. "I'm trying to think of ways your powers can help. I know better than anyone how bad it can get when they're out of control. But what if it's not all bad? You did good with your powers tonight."

"And I destroyed part of the road! And with all the cameras there, CLU probably already knows it was me. I'm probably gonna go to jail for property damage. And who knows who we could've landed on!"

Leia shrinks back, her voice barely above a whisper. "I checked before we jumped. I made sure we wouldn't land on anyone."

"But, see... we didn't jump—*you threw us!*"

Maybe I shouldn't be yelling at her.

"I had a plan, and it worked!" she responds desperately. "Don't you see that I'm trying to help you learn how to control your powers?"

"You had no right to force that on me! It's already hard enough without... You just have no idea what it's like to be me!"

Leia wraps her arm around mine, holding it tightly against her. "But I would if you told me. That's all I really want —to hear how you feel. For you to just let it all out, ya know?"

You and I both know you don't want me to let it all out.

"I know it might not seem like that was the best way to handle things... but it worked. Like I said on the rooftop, I knew you just needed a little push, so I pushed you."

"I didn't *ask* to be pushed!" I say adamantly.

"Well, have you been pushing yourself lately?" she counters. "I mean, how else are you gonna learn?"

"Oh, so that's what this is *really* about. Me not learning as fast as you want me to. Stop acting like this is all about supporting me!"

Defiantly, she snaps back, "Okay, yeah, I'm trying to support you *and* protect myself. Is it a problem that I want to feel safe with you? That I want to live with the man I love without being scared he's gonna lose control and hurt me again? That's why I gave you a push."

I sigh, losing the will to fight anymore but still needing to be understood. "But you can't fix me, Leia. That's why I told you about my problem before we fell in love."

No one can fix me.

"You're right. You did tell me," she says softly. "But you also told me you'd do whatever it takes to get better. And I believed you. I thought you'd be better by now."

"Leia, I told you so you could decide whether you'd love me as I am, not need me to get better first."

"I do love you," she replies, her voice trembling. "But that doesn't mean I'm okay with getting hurt! So, yeah, maybe I can't fix you, but I thought you'd love me enough to try harder to get it under control. Sometimes, it feels like maybe you don't love me as much as I thought you did."

"I don't love...? Babe, this has *nothing* to do with how much I love you! You mean the world to me!"

"Then what are you doing to get this under control?"

"Everything I know to do!" I shout, standing up and pacing across the living room floor.

I should leave.

"Well, have you reached out to anyone? Dan and

Timothy have powers like you, and they know your dad. They could help. And you could be using all this potential I see in you to help others like they do."

"Yeah, I reached out," I grumble.

"Oh, you did? I didn't know... when was that?"

"Three months ago."

Her brow furrows. "Well, what'd they say?"

"They said I need to get my powers under control before I can work with them. That I'm 'beyond their scope'. That there's only so much they can do to help me."

"I see..." she says, watching me pace around her floor. She shakes her head and says, "I'm sorry to hear that."

Then, after a beat, she asks, "So, what have you done since then to learn? I remember Jack offered to go with you to Drayda Park to that huge clearing in the middle - you remember? - so you could just, like, practice letting it out. He said he could watch and see if he could help you learn about it. Did you reach out to him, maybe?"

"Well, he's been busy with school and everything, so we haven't had time to meet up."

She sighs, studying me. "I can't imagine how alone you feel with all this."

Finally! Some sympathy instead of judgment.

"But at the same time," she continues, "I'm just... I'm tired of being hurt by the man I love. It's discouraging to see you living so far beneath what you're capable of. You shouldn't have to take a job you hate just to avoid getting worked up. You should be able to do something that shows the whole world how amazing you are. I was trying to help you grow, but... I guess I need to accept that I can't *make* you change."

I stop pacing and glare at her. "You... gambled with my *life.* You wagered me changing against me living. Am I so bad as I am now that you'd rather I die than to remain the same?"

"No, Aiden, that's not... Don't think about it like that. I jumped off with y—"

Her voice fades as I tune her out.

"I think your powers are amazing." Amazing? AMAZING?!

Yeah, it's so amazing to have these powers when everyone wants you to change before they'll accept you. Amazing when people you look up to say they can't help you. It's amazing that advanced treatment—your father's life's work, no less—can't fix you. Amazing to be the black sheep of your family. Amazing when the woman of your dreams feels like you're a threat to her.

So amazing!

What if my powers hadn't activated? What if Leia pushed me and I didn't survive? Would she be happier? I'm sure she'd be safer. Maybe the problem is that I'm still here. Maybe—

The warmth of Leia's hands on my biceps jolts me out of my spiraling thoughts.

"Look," she says softly. "All I'm saying is I want more for you. For us."

Does she not realize how much I want more for us, too?

"I don't think this has to be our life forever," she continues. "I know you didn't like what I did, but... I can't apologize for it. Believe it or not, I pushed you because I believe in you. Because I want us to work."

I exhale slowly. "I get it, Leia. My deepest regret is the pain I've caused you. But I *am* trying to figure this out. Tonight felt... different. When we flew to the roof, and even before the fall, it didn't feel so chaotic. It's hard to explain to someone without powers, but... I think I'm making progress. I just need you to be patient. Can you do that? Please?"

Leia looks away briefly, biting her lip. "This is probably unfair to ask, but... how long should I wait? If I were your sister Candace, would you tell her to keep waiting while her health and safety are at risk?"

"Babe," I say firmly, "you know my powers include empathy. I can literally feel what you're feeling. You don't have to try to put me in your shoes."

Without realizing it, I pull my arm from her grip. "Maybe you shouldn't... be with me, then. Because I don't have an answer. I don't know how long it'll take. But I know I'll do whatever it takes because I believe in us. I believe we're worth fighting for."

"I think we're worth fighting for, too. But this… this has to stop."

Her voice trails off, but the silence speaks louder than anything she could say.

The air in the room feels stuffy and stale as we stand here, looking at each other for what feels like ages. My gaze rolls over every soft curve of her face, searching for any hint of sympathy. I don't see it anymore.

She's more concerned about the pain I've caused her in the past than about what I'm feeling right now. But… can I even blame her?

"You're right," I say, letting out a deep exhale. "This does need to stop. Being in love with someone who doesn't threaten your life isn't too much to ask for."

Although, now we're both guilty of that offense. But will that come up anymore? No… It'll always be about the many ways I failed, the ways I've put her at risk. That's the narrative. These are our roles. I'm the screw-up who needs to be fixed, and she's the compassionate, patient saint.

The air shifts from stale to suffocating.

What was Aiden feeling in that moment? Doesn't matter. What matters is that I've hurt her so many times in the past that nothing else counts. Like I'm some big, bad entronga, claws and teeth out, wrecking everything in my path. And she won't even apologize for almost killing me?! My mistakes are just so big and so unforgivable that the crazy things she does don't even register by comparison. I didn't ask to be like this. And you didn't have to say yes.

"Thank you… for trying to be understanding," Leia says, her tone softening. "I don't hate you, ya know? I don't mind saying it again—I think you and what you can do are amazing."

If I'm so amazing… then why am I not even worth an apology? You took an action that would have killed me, but what I went through isn't even worth an apology?

"I just… feel stuck sometimes…"

Stuck? Do you hate being with me that much?

Wait. Is that—? No. It's activating again! I knew this was a bad idea!

Holding it together as best I can, I manage to say, "Well… if you'd rather one or both of us die than stay with me, then…"

"What? Come on. That's not what I said. Don't twist—"

I'm doing this for your own good, Leia!

"Then I think… maybe you should just leave…" I say, my voice trembling. I want to run out the door, but my feet feel glued to the floor. My breath quickens. Nausea settles into my stomach.

There's so much energy. I don't think I can hold this back! I need something to redirect it to. Fast.

My whole body feels hot, like my skin is burning through my clothes. I'm trying—*trying*—to contain it, but it's desperate to get out.

Resist, Aiden. Please, resist it! Don't think about it. Maybe it'll go away.

"Leave? You know this is my apartment, right?" Leia chuckles, incredulous.

"Leia, just… If you don't want to be with me, then LEAVE!"

I can't resist it anymore.

Suddenly, everything in the room disappears. I can only see Leia and me, standing in an endless black void. Against the backdrop of the infinite darkness, a few ghostly streaks of navy blue, purple, and red energy appear in the distance and then evaporate into nothingness. All else is pitch black.

Despite the void, however, I can see Leia clearly, as if sunlight is shining on her. Or maybe it's more like I can *feel* her presence.

Where are we? Is this real? Am I hallucinating?

Without warning, the energy that had built up inside me erupts in a massive wave, exploding out of my body in every direction. A green blast rushes past Leia, knocking her off her feet.

The living room snaps back into focus. Leia is on the floor, eyes closed, not moving.

What have I done? Is she breathing?

I run over to her and drop down on my knees beside her.

"Leia? Leia, baby... Can you hear me? Leia, please! I'm so sorry!"

Did I kill her?

I grab her limp hand and clutch it to my chest. I can't sense anything—no emotions, nothing. I press my ear to her chest, straining to hear...

A heartbeat. She's alive!

I slide my hand under her head to lift it gently. I turn her face toward me, hoping her eyes will open. Noticing moisture on my palm, I dismiss it as sweat until I see her blood trickling down my arm. I freeze.

The overturned end table—she must've hit it when she fell. She needs help. She needs a hospital.

But that would mean calling for help. Which would mean exposing my LET. That means everyone will know I hurt her with my powers.

No. There has to be another way.

I stumble out of the apartment, leaving the door open behind me. I knock on the third door down the hall.

"Can I help you?" An older man wearing striped pajama pants and a white shirt opens the door, his expression a mix of confusion and irritation.

"Hi, um... Maybe," I stammer, trying to sound casual. "Did you hear a loud thud just now?"

"Who are you? You don't live here, do you?" He sizes me up, scratching his scruffy beard.

"No, sir." I chuckle nervously, trying to lighten the mood. "I'm just here to visit a friend. I got off on the wrong floor... But did you hear—?"

"Yeah, I heard something. So what?"

"Well, I think someone might've gotten hurt. The door to 135 is open, and I heard a scream. Could you... call Emergency Services? I broke my Solo earlier. Dropped it right on the pavement when the fireworks started—can you believe it? Anyway, I think she needs help."

"Who's hurt?"

"Lei—layiiiiing down. The girl on the floor in 135. I think she's hurt." I turn to point to the door that I left open, but I decide against showing this stranger the blood on my hands.

The man's eyes narrow, but after a pause, he says, "Okay. Let me grab my Solo."

"Thank you!" I step back as he shuffles inside.

Once he's out of sight, I slip around the corner. Closing my eyes, I focus on his emotions, tracking his movement toward Leia's apartment. Frustration turns to concern, then urgency, then a mix of fear and compassion.

He found her.

"Hello, um... I found my neighbor unconscious in her apartment... No, like I said, I just found her... I don't know, I just heard a thud and some guy came to my door and asked me to call... Like I said, she's my neighbor. Are you listening to me? Look, just send somebody. She's bleeding out her head and she's unconscious... Yeah, okay, I'll stay here with her."

Leia, I'm so sorry I have to leave you with a stranger. I'll meet you at the hospital. I won't leave you like this again. I'm so sorry.

When you wake up, I'll be right there.

CHAPTER 4 – AWAKENED

"I see."

For the first time since I started telling him the story, I notice how tightly drawn the lines on Dr. Larson's forehead have become.

I just invited him into the worst night of my life. Why did I let him in on this?

My heart rate has slowed, and my palms are no longer clammy. I peek into his emotional state, half-expecting judgment. Instead, I sense concern. Genuine concern. And I kick myself internally for doubting him.

He's actually worried about me. Leia's his patient, sure, but he genuinely seems concerned about me, even though I'm the one who hurt her.

His gaze stays locked on me, a fixed expression of understanding that makes me want to ask, *Can you help me?* But I don't. I can tell he's conflicted about something. I can't pin down what it is. The only thing he's said in response to my entire confession has been, "I see."

What are you thinking, Doc?

After an unbearable silence, he sighs, removes his glasses, and wipes them with a handkerchief from the breast pocket of his lab coat.

"I believe you know," he says finally, "that the ethical code doctors are bound by includes the responsibility to notify the proper authorities of any injury caused by the use of Laosi Empowered Talents. Failure to do so on my part would result in my license to practice being revoked, fines, and possibly imprisonment."

Another sigh. He slips his glasses back on and continues, "I'm really not a fan of having to say this, but I'm going to fulfill my obligation. I don't know what will happen to you once I report it, and that makes this harder. But you have two things in your favor."

He leans forward slightly. "First, it was an accident. I would gladly testify to your unyielding devotion to your fiancée's bedside. How you've come every single day she's been here to check on her, talk to her, and make sure she's not alone. Ever since I mentioned that patients with frequent visitors tend to recover faster, you've spent every moment you could with her. Speaking professionally, I'd say Leia's speedy physical recovery is due in no small part to your presence. Any judge would see that this isn't the behavior of someone who intentionally caused harm with their abilities."

He pauses. "It makes me wonder what kind of relationship you two would have if you could control your abilities."

You don't know how many times I've asked myself that question, doc.

"Secondly," he adds, "your dad is very well-connected in Sanctuary. He sits on boards and rubs elbows with key Laosi policymakers. I'm sure he knows a way to mitigate the legal ramifications of what you've just disclosed. Call him and see what strings he can pull. Being the foremost authority on Laosi in Sanctuary has to count for something."

He sighs again, leaning back slightly. "But that leads me to a very puzzling question, Aiden. Your dad developed the LIST procedure. Yet not only do you still have powers, but they remain out of control. How is...? I assume you've been through the procedure? Knowing you, you've probably studied it by now, right?"

I can't hold his gaze anymore. My eyes drift to the rainbow painting on the wall, tilted just enough to look like it might fall if someone sneezes too hard. I glance at the scattered furniture and decide I should straighten it up. Anything to shift the energy in this room.

I get up and walk to the vending machine, pushing the

cold metal frame back to the wall. All the while, I feel Dr. Larson watching me, waiting for an answer. With a heavy breath, I give him the truth.

"Honestly... I haven't looked into it much. I mean, if the experts can't figure out how to make it work for me, what could I add? I just kinda chalked it up to being incurable. My dad said his people would keep researching, but apparently, no one's found anything yet. So I gave up on it."

"Is it common for the LIST procedure not to work?" he asks, curiosity breaking through his professional tone. "I don't mean to pry, so I hope you'll forgive me. It's just that I was trained to see the soul as being just as integral to healing the body as medicine. I believe that the more we understand Laosi, the more healthcare can advance. But feel free not to answer if you don't feel comfortable doing so."

"I don't think it's common, but there are other cases. From what I've heard, mindset plays a role. Like, if someone likes their Talent but has to undergo LIST for some reason—like joining a sports team or meeting some requirement—it's less likely to work. But no one wants to get rid of their powers more than me. I think there are a couple other variables that affect it as well, but none of them apply to me."

With the vending machine back in place, I start resetting the chairs and tables. Dr. Larson watches me, stroking his chin thoughtfully.

"Fascinating," he says softly. "And tragic. It sounds like a terrible ordeal to live through."

He stands, walks over to me and places a gentle hand on my shoulder, stopping me mid-step.

"Call your dad. Let's keep this from getting worse. Like I mentioned, one of his colleagues is on the way here. He's going to ask questions that I'm obligated to answer truthfully —for my job and for Leia's recovery. Let's give them a heads-up. Tell your dad what you told me. I assume you haven't told him the whole truth; he probably would have gotten involved much sooner if you had."

I nod slightly, the weight of his words settling over me.
What's he gonna think when I call him?

"Okay," he says softly. "Call him. He'll help you sort this out."

"I will."

He gives my shoulder a supportive squeeze, meeting my eyes with a steady, understanding gaze before walking off down the hallway.

Slowly, I pull my Solo from my pocket. The lightweight device feels impossibly heavy in my hand. I place my fingers on opposite quadrants of the glass, activating its computing units.

The screen comes to life, and Lil' A's holographic avatar pops up, nodding at me with his usual smirk.

I thought Solos could gauge moods from your vitals. This guy's way off today... even more than usual.

Maybe I should change these sunglasses and the multicolored beanie on his head. An avatar is supposed to represent you, right? That's a little bit too showy for my taste.

"You got a new Connect message, big guy!" Lil' A chirps.

I swipe past the Games, Marketplace, and Profile tabs to reach Messages. The thread at the top of the list is highlighted in fluorescent green, so I tap it to see who reached out.

Profile ID: TinyTay. Why does that name sound familiar? Last Connection: Played Reign of Terrans *together. Oh yeah! Let's see what he said.*

I tap his name to open the thread, prompting his avatar to read aloud, "Great game! The Coven didn't even know what hit 'em. Next time you're playing *Reign*, look me up. Cool avvy."

Ya know, I think I'll leave Lil' A just the way he is.

Lil' A pops up on the corner of the screen, dusts off his shoulder, pops his collar, and smirks again.

On second thought...

I navigate back to the home screen and glance at the news and weather outlet in the top left. I already know it's a pleasant day outside, so my eyes drift to the vitals display in the bottom left.

Heart rate and blood pressure? Elevated, of course. That tracks, given the call I'm about to make.

I tap the bottom right quadrant, pulling up the synced contacts database. "Call Dad... audio only," I say.

"Calling Richard Lore," Lil' A chirps.

"Hello?"

"Hey, Dad."

"Hey, Aiden. I see you're calling from the hospital. How's Leia? Is she responsive?"

He sounds hopeful, like he's expecting some good news from this call.

I could really use some good news right now.

"No... no, she's not. Well, not really. Kinda. Like, I can tell she hears me—because, you know, the empathy thing—but she's not moving or anything."

"Oh, okay. Well, I'm sure she appreciates you being there with her. So, what's up, son?"

"I take it you haven't heard yet?"

Please don't make me explain this again.

"Heard what?"

"About Leia's condition."

"What, did something change?"

I shift my weight from one foot to the other, then start pacing around the waiting room. After a deep sigh, I finally answer him.

"Well, physically, she's doing great. Everyone's saying her body has almost fully recovered—faster than they expected, honestly. But... she's still not waking up. So they called in a specialist from ARL to check her out. You didn't hear about it?"

"I didn't. I get a lot across my desk, so I might've missed it. What's going on? Why is ARL getting involved?"

I knew he was too busy for me.

"They think... well, they think her coma might not be just physical anymore. They're trying to rule out... if her soul might have been damaged that night or something."

"Hmmm. That's concerning. Let me see who they sent over." The faint *plinks* as he conducts his search drift through the Solo.

It's time to face the music.

"Dad, there's something else I need to tell you... about that night."

"Oh yeah? What's that?"

If I pace any harder, I'll wear through the floor.

I sit down and glance around the room, making sure the furniture is back in place. No distractions left. I wipe my hand across my face, steady myself with a deep breath, and spill it.

"Dad, I know what really happened to Leia that night. And why she won't wake up. It's my fault. I didn't mean to, but I couldn't help it, and now she's in a coma, and they're talking about soul damage... and it just—it got out of control. But I did it."

The *plinks* stop.

My dad clears his throat, his tone more serious now. "Are you talking about... the struggle we've discussed before?"

"Yeah... the struggle."

He won't even call it what it is. Say it with me, Dad: Aiden's LETs are out of control. Why does he downplay it like this is normal?

"I knew that."

"You... you knew? What did...? You knew what?"

"I knew you weren't telling us the whole truth when we got to the hospital. So I figured you were leaving something out about... your struggle."

You knew? So why haven't you said anything in the past two weeks about how much trouble I'm in?

"Oh... Well, I had to tell Dr. Larson because he said the ARL specialist needs the full picture to make the right diagnosis. And once I told him it was my powers that caused this, he said, 'Well, you know I have to report this, right? Call your dad, though, because you're gonna be in some big trouble once CLU finds out.' He thought, with all your connections, you could keep me out of Atheria. Can you help me? What's gonna happen to me? It was an accident. They'll see that, right?"

"It's gonna be okay, son. I have a few calls I can make. I know you didn't mean for any of this to happen."

"No, I didn't. I never wanted to hurt Leia. I just..."

The words fail me. I know he understands, though, and I know he's got my back.

Richard Lore vouching for you practically guarantees you won't end up in maximum security. He knows half the CLU board. He even chaired it for a few years. If he says it's fine, then it'll be fine.

But I can't ignore the elephant in the room.

"Hey, Dad..."

"Yeah, son?"

"How come it didn't work on me? Have you guys found anything? Are there other cases like mine? I mean... what's wrong with me?"

I sense his discomfort, a mix of helplessness and shame. It's so familiar I don't even need my Laosi to feel it through the Solo. We've had this conversation enough times in person for me to know what's coming. I save him the trouble.

"I know you're still looking. I just... I just didn't want you to forget. I don't want to keep hurting Leia, you know?"

"I know. And trust me—we're still looking. You'll be the first to know when we figure out how to make the procedure work for you. Zoe and I are hopeful we're on the cusp of another breakthrough. I want this for you, too. You're a good son, son."

I sigh. "You're a good dad, Dad."

I thought our relationship would have outgrown us saying that by now. I also thought it'd be easier to believe by now.

If I'm such a good son, why does my dad feel so much shame over me?

"So, what should I do now?" I ask.

Calmly, my dad says, "Just go home and try not to worry. You don't need to be there while my colleague examines Leia. I know you're concerned about her, but I don't want you to forget to take care of yourself as well. Try to get some rest. The best way to help Leia now is to provide information. If my colleague calls after he's done examining her, just answer as truthfully as possible. Don't worry about the fallout. I've got some guys I can call and present your case to at CLU, so... you'll be fine. Just go home and get some rest."

"Thanks, Dad," I say, exhaling deeply. "Yeah, I'm beat. I'll tell Leia goodbye and head home."

"They sent Dr. Merit to evaluate Leia," he adds with renewed energy. "He's who I'd have recommended for my future daughter-in-law. She's in good hands. Let me know if you need anything."

"Will do. Thanks again, Dad. Bye."

"Call ended," Lil' A chirps.

I meander through the hospital's hallways back to Leia's room. She's still lying there, peaceful, emotionless. Her consciousness must be at rest. She's probably not even dreaming.

She won't hear me, but I speak anyway.

"Leia, it's me again. Dad's sending a colleague to examine your Laosi. He says you're in good hands. He also told me to go home and take care of myself. I hate leaving you alone, but he's right. I need to rest... So I can be fresh when you wake up. It's been work, hospital, repeat all week. I even dreamed I worked here."

I chuckle softly. No response from Leia.

We both need to rest.

"Okay, my love. I'll see you tomorrow."

I lean down, kiss her forehead, and head for the door. When I reach the threshold, a wave of emotions ripples through her, sharp but fleeting. I glance back, hesitant to leave. But I clench my jaw and walk out, closing the door gently behind me.

Take care of yourself, Aiden.

The elevator takes me to the lobby. I nod at the security guard at the door but skip the usual small talk with her. Resting feels much more urgent than hearing about her grandbaby reaching his most recent developmental milestone.

Stepping outside, I'm greeted by warm spring air.

I pause to let my eyes adjust to the light of the brilliant sky as puffy, white clouds float lazily by. I pause to bathe in the warmth of the setting sun and inhale deeply, savoring the fresh air that reminds me that life is bigger than that hospital room.

I pause to steady myself for the flood I'm about to wade into.

The sidewalk is packed with people and their various feelings. Sanctuary City doesn't pause for anyone.

It would be nice if the festival was still going on or if there was some central focus for everybody. But with this range of emotional experience, we gotta work hard to keep from getting overwhelmed. We know how to handle this, though. Just gotta find something to lock in on.

I overhear a stressed Solo conversation about work deadlines not getting met. I feel the subtle momentary lightness as the anti-gravity propulsion system of a carrier passes by 30 feet above my head. Mouthwatering, savory aromas fill the air from the street vendors serving food to the dinner rush. A med transport's siren wails off in the distance. The monotony of daily life in Sanctuary City becomes a suit of armor for my sanity.

"All right, Aiden. Focus," I murmur, not realizing I've spoken out loud until I see the funny look from a college kid as he walks by.

Is it selfish to detach myself from other people's struggles like this? Maybe. But I can't help everyone, right? Or maybe... anyone.

Turning toward my apartment, I avoid eye contact with everyone by looking up at the flashing billboards above me.

That sandwich looks good. Too bad I'm broke.

A knife that can cut through wood? What kind of spherra are people cooking?

That new Solo customization kiosk might be worth checking out.

Maybe a hoverbike would help me float above all this emoti

—

My thoughts are interrupted by an intense, focused anger that I sense.

It's focused on me?

I look around the crowd for a familiar face, but there are easily one hundred people in front of me and behind me.

Who's mad at me? What did I do this time?

A little girl stares at me as she eats ice cream.

It can't be her. How could anyone be mad while eating ice cream?

A businessman in a burgundy suit bumps into me from behind. He's startled and a little embarrassed, but not mad. A guy just up ahead drops his Solo. A woman with a mismatched purse cuts a glare at me before crossing the road.

Who could it be? And why?

I continue scanning the crowd, the strength of this anger gnawing at me. It's crossing the line into hatred.

Is my safety in jeopardy? Who have I made that mad? The sweaty gym guy with his friends? The girl whose black hoodie covers her eyes? The little boy struggling to tie his loose shoelaces? Someone in that carrier overhead? Who is it?

Don't freak out, Aiden!

My mind races, but I notice something: my LET hasn't activated. My heart is pounding, but my breathing is steady. That's good.

I wonder if regulating my breath is a key to keeping my powers under control?

The anger starts to fade, and I assume the threat has passed.

Weird. It's pretty much gone now.

Still, I'm not reassured enough to rule out the scenic route in case I'm being followed. I'm almost home anyway. I glance up at the clouds and let my mind wander to the jingle for those gross Fruit Beans candies.

Who even buys those? How do you make candy that tastes that bad? Isn't that an oxymoron? Great jingle, though.

Now, fruity Smackers—those were good. Do they still sell them? I haven't seen them anywhere lately.

I reach my high-rise apartment building, concluding an otherwise uneventful walk. The sun dips below the horizon, casting long shadows. I pause, debating if I should run errands or head straight in. My gaze shifts to the eight identical high-rises along the street, each 45 stories tall.

Why did the Sanctuary Housing Authority stick me here? Sure, it's close to work and the hospital, but I'd rather live somewhere like Leia's place. How did she get that assignment? We're the same age, make almost the same money... Well, she makes more. But still. What's their criteria?

"Welcome home, Aiden."

The bioscanner's voice startles me from my thoughts. I've already entered the lobby and walked to the elevator on autopilot.

The elevator whisks me to the 23rd floor. At unit 2304, I press my thumb to the scanner, and the door slides open. The narrow, undecorated corridor leads to my living area. My eyes trace the hunter-green wall, landing on the futon—the perfect place for crashing.

Are those my jeans or Tyrus's? Eh, who cares?

I grab the jeans to toss them aside, but a growl from my stomach interrupts me. I glance toward the kitchen, trying to recall what I left in the fridge the last time I was here three days ago.

Before I can decide on what meal I'll make with the essentials that I keep in stock, a wave of anger and resentment, thick enough to make me cough, hits me out of nowhere.

It's coming from inside my kitchen!?

"Hello?"

My voice echoes. No response.

Who's in my apartment? Leia and Devon are the only ones with keys. Could it be the property manager? Why would he be so mad?

I cross the living room cautiously.

Don't overreact, Aiden. Don't blow up the apartment.

Standing in my kitchen with her back to me is a female wearing blue jeans and a black hoodie. It's the girl from the street!

But how did she get in my home!

She faces the pantry, scanning the countertop like she's deciding where to place something. My kitchen is bare—clean dishes, two pictures of Leia and me, and standard appliances—so I have no idea what she's looking for.

What's so fascinating about a can opener?

"What are you doing in my apartment?"

She spins around, but her expression doesn't match the anger I sensed.

"I, um... Where is the...? You can't just... This isn't... I was... I'm trying to... Can you...?"

Her words tumble out, disjointed, like she's struggling just to form a coherent thought.

What's going on?

I focus my empathy, probing deeper. Fear. Loneliness. And beneath it all, anger.

It's strange. Though I have never seen her in my life before...

"Who are you?" I demand.

She pauses, looking around as if clues to her identity are hidden within my bland wallpaper.

"Who am I? Yeah, who...? Who am I? I am... My name. My name, my name, my name... What...?"

Her demeanor shifts suddenly, and her voice carries a sharp decisiveness as she says, "My name... is Alexi. And this..."

She raises her left hand, fingers straightened. Her body

glows with a dark red aura. Waves of fiery energy ripple around her, condensing into three dagger-like blades aimed at me.

"This is what you deserve!"

"Hey, what are—"

Before I can finish, she mentally propels the daggers into my torso.

"Uuugggh!!"

As soon as they make contact, the daggers unleash a rampage of pain through my body. My muscles seize, and I collapse in the corner of my kitchen. I manage to glance down to gauge my injuries, but there's no blood or puncture wounds.

Her Laosi... targeted my nervous system? How dare she come into my home and do this to me?

My Laosi begins to activate.

Okay, lady... You came looking for a fight. Allow me to give you exactly what you asked for.

I brace myself, allowing—better yet, encouraging—the Laosi to rise.

I'm always holding back to prevent myself from hurting someone or damaging something. But this time? I might actually enjoy unleashing my power at full force. Just remember—you brought this on yourself.

I give in to the Laosi and anticipate the chaotic form it might take. But then, the pain doubles.

"Eeerrggghhkkk!" I choke out, my body twisting and writhing on the floor.

Alexi glares at me from the opposite side of the kitchen, her eyes as menacing as her daggers. She watches me struggle to regain control over myself as the pain reaches dizzying intensity.

I don't know how much more of this I can take!

"Ya know," she says, her voice low and cold, "I think I like you in this position... So *you* can see how it feels."

My breaths come shallow and strained. I can't even yell for help.

She walks toward me, her steps slow and deliberate. The

confusion I sensed before is long gone. Now she moves with clear conviction, carrying out her malicious intent with an eerie calm.

Another dagger forms, and she takes it in her hand, holding it with an airtight grip.

She wants this one to be personal!

She kneels in front of me, her right hand pressing firmly onto the top of my head. Her dark eyes pierce into mine, full of hurt and rage.

"Aiden..." she says, her voice trembling with unrestrained passion. "This is *your* fault. You made me this way!"

She knows my name? What did I do to her? Who is she?!

She drives the final blade straight into my chest.

"AAAHH!!" My body jerks and tenses, waves of agony crashing around through me. Every heartbeat feels like it's pumping shattered glass through my veins. Each breath I take amplifies the pain, like the air I inhale is tearing me apart from the inside.

The electricity coursing through my nerves sends me into uncontrollable spasms. I try to shift, to move—*anything* to lessen the torment. But after writhing on the floor for a few seconds more, my body gives out, completely spent, leaving me paralyzed. In the midst of the most severe suffering I've ever experienced, my body relaxes completely as the bond between my consciousness and my body deteriorates.

Alexi rises, looking down at me with disgust etched across her face. Less aware of the physical pain, her emotions cut into me almost as deeply as her Laosi did: fear, loneliness, sorrow, despair, bitterness...

"I asked you to stop, Aiden. I begged you. But you're just so stubborn. So now..." She pauses, a mix of satisfaction and emptiness washing over her. "Now you get to find out how it feels."

Lady, you got the wrong guy! I scream out internally. *I've never done anything like this to anyone! Who are you? Why did you...*

My vision fades. The last thing I see is a single tear slipping down her cheek as she looks at her trembling hands.

CHAPTER 5 – LUCID

"—ear me? Yo, Aide, can you hear me, bro? Wake up, man! Okay, think, Dev... Let's try..."

My eyes crack open sluggishly. Light filters in as I adjust to a pounding headache and a groggy haze blurring my vision.

Where am I?

The coolness of the darkwood laminate flooring against my skin helps me realize I'm lying down in my kitchen. The open window above the sink reveals a cloudy night sky.

A figure moving by the sink turns the faucet on, pouring water into a glass. As I push myself up against the corner, my eyes focus on Devon turning around with the glass in hand. Relief flashes across his face when he sees I'm awake.

"Yo, you good?"

I shake my head. "Nah, man, not really. I got this pulsating headache, and my body feels like it's chained to the middle of Tryon right now. Can you help me up?"

He steps toward me, then pauses, turning back to the sink. "Oh, yeah... I guess I don't need this anymore." He dumps the water into the sink and sets the glass down.

"What were you gonna do with that water?"

"Oh, uh, I was gonna throw it in your face... to wake you up." His sheepish grin tells me he already knows how bad that sounds.

"Man, you've been watching too much holovision... You were about to drown me!"

We both laugh, and he walks back to help me up. I grip his hand and brace against the navy-blue wall behind me, testing my legs to see if they'll hold me.

Once I'm upright and stable, Devon asks, "What happened, man? Your Solo sent me a distress signal. Your vitals were going crazy, your heart rate went through the roof, and your breathing stopped. So I came as fast as I could, and when I got here, you were laid out on the floor."

"I don't... really know," I admit, rubbing the knot forming on my head. "I must've hit my head pretty hard on the way down. Or maybe I hit my head and that's why I fell? It's all so blurry. How long was I out?"

"At least an hour and 47 minutes. I was at work when the alert came, so I didn't see it for another 15 minutes. But when I saw it was my boy going through it, I dropped everything, and I got here in an hour and a half."

"Devon, there's no way you got from Serenity to my apartment in an hour and a half. That's a nine-hour trip, minimum. How'd you get here so fast?"

"Oh... I portaled," he says casually.

"You *portaled*?! Dude, how much did that cost?"

He smirks. "Listen, Aide. When my boy's in trouble, no expense is to be spared. Money is not an object!" He clasps his hands to his chest in mock sincerity. "Plus, I kinda work for TU now, in the Transit Authority, so... I get two free portals a month."

"Pause. Bruh, you work for Tryon United? *How?*"

Leaning against the counter, Devon runs his fingers through the straight black hair on top of his head, trying to suppress a smirk. "Guess I didn't tell you that, huh? My bad..."

"Man," I say, shaking my head, "I don't know how you do it, but you're the only person I know who has a lifetime full of once-in-a-lifetime opportunities."

We laugh, and he shrugs. "I knew you were gonna say that."

"'Cause it's true!"

"If you say so." He stuffs his hands in his pockets, his voice softening. "Honestly, it never really felt like that before. It felt like I was just living my life, ya know? But this time... this time it does."

It's about time. I wonder if he's even grateful for all the opportunities that just fall into his lap.

"Oh, yeah? Why's that?" I ask.

"They make you feel it. You can't even get the job without passing a college-level exam on the history of Tryon United. They drill this sense of pride into you that you get to be a part of the oldest organization on the planet. Like they're the saviors of Tryon or something."

"Well... they kinda are, right?"

"I mean... yeah," he snickers. "But I don't need my supervisors randomly quizzing me on how many days it's been since the Tryon United Peace Treaty was signed. For the record, it's been 362 years, 4 months, and 10 days. Not that you asked."

I laugh. "So what happens if you don't know?"

"You get sent home for the day."

"Seriously?"

He nods, hopping onto the counter.

"Actually, you wanna sit at the table? You want anything to drink?" I ask as I walk over to the fridge. Looking in, I say, "I got water, vittranus juice... aaand actually just water and vittranus juice."

"Lemme get that vittranus."

"My man," I say, pouring two glasses. I bring them to the table, sitting across from him.

"They act like it's a big deal they ended a world war, established international transportation, and streamlined the global economy. Pssh, that's nothing we haven't done on a weekend."

"At the arcade, you mean? When we were, what, 14 or 15? Yeah, TU's accomplishments are clearly second-rate compared to the exploits of DnA!"

"DNA!" Devon shouts, laughing. "Man, it's been forever since I heard that! Those were the days, my friend."

"Simpler times, for sure. Back then, it was homework. Now it's jobs, bills, and all this other adulting crap," I laugh. "Speaking of, what do you actually do at TU?"

"I'm a monorail coordinator."

"So, logistics?" I ask and take a sip of the tart, green, velvety juice in my cup.

"Pretty much. Arrival times, departures, maintenance schedules, freight weight checks, speeds—stuff like that."

"That... sounds... kinda boring. Not gonna lie," I laugh. "I mean, clearly not more boring than inspecting staples for quality like I do, but still. I guess I expected, or maybe wanted, something more exciting for you."

Devon snickers. "Monorails can be monotonous. But I'd rather do that than portals."

"Really? Why's that?"

"With portals, it's all, 'Is the portal clear? Okay.' Then, you type in the destination command, you check the power levels, barometric pressures, and the time manifold kinematics and press enter."

"Ummm... So for the common folk in the room?" I say, chuckling.

"If something's off, the display turns red. If it's blue, you tap 'Go.' Very boring." He downs half his juice. "At least with monorails, you get stories. Like this one time, a dude legit tried to transport explosives from Serenity to Integrity."

"WHAT?!" I nearly spit out my juice.

"Crazy, right? We're all in there like, 'Um, sir... You do know that the whole reason we regulate transportation is to ensure weapons don't travel from one Sovereign State to another, right?'"

"So, what did he say? Like, what was he thinking?" I ask.

"He said the devices were inert and had some rare material he needed for research. Security wasn't buying it, though—they took him straight to jail. Pretty sure he's never getting out."

"Right! He was trying to smuggle bombs into Integrity? Isn't that where TU's headquarters is?"

"Nah, everybody thinks that because the first carrier station was built there. HQ's actually in Felicity."

"Oh, for real? Either way, people are insane, man," I sigh.

"Yeah, so maybe the job isn't as boring as you think," Devon says with a smirk. "But where I really wanna be is the helijet department. Out of the three, that's the most exciting."

"I bet." I set my empty glass down on the table.

"It's got the most moving parts, the most action, and —c'mon, helijets? Seventy-six passenger aerial transports that can take off from anywhere and hit speeds just below the sound barrier? They can accelerate to max spee—"

"Yo, Devon, heads up—your nerd is showing," I tease.

"You're a hater."

"Oh, absolutely. You know I hate you, right? But seriously, that sounds dope! Where've you been so far? How long you been working for TU? How'd you even land the job?"

"If this was just a social visit, I'd gladly tell you all about it. It's been a long time, my friend."

"Too long."

We bump fists.

Devon says, "Let's focus. You seem a little better, but how are you really feeling? Do you remember what happened?"

"Oh, yeah... Let's see. I remember leaving the hospital after going to see Leia. Right before that I called my dad because I talked to the doctor... Wait. Did you know Leia's in the hospital?"

"No, I didn't... Well, okay, yeah, I did. Your Connect profile kinda made it obvious. But you didn't tell me much. What happened? Your posts were vague, so I figured it was LET-related."

My slumped shoulders answer his question.

"It got out again, didn't it? How's she doing?"

"She's still in a coma." My voice drops. "I... I don't really wanna talk about it right now."

"No worries. DNA back at it for the first time in maybe half a year? No need to kill the mood, homie. You'll tell me when you're ready."

I nod gently. "Thanks."

"For sure. So, what happened after you left the hospital?"

"Yeah, so... I was walking down the street. Saw a candy ad, something about a bike... Someone was mad at me? Oh! Did you see her?"

"Her? Her who?"

"A girl in a black hoodie."

"Nah, I didn't see anybody."

"Was the door open when you got here?"

"No, it was locked. Your scanner unlocked it for me because of the distress signal."

"Hmmm... Dev, you're gonna think I'm crazy, but I swear this girl showed up in my apartment and attacked me. She stabbed me four times with these daggers made of pure Laosi! I've never felt pain like that in my life."

Devon glances down at my torso, then at the floor. "She used an LET against you? That's intense. You know who she was or why she came for you?"

"She said her name was Alexi... I think. And no, she didn't say why. Just that it was my fault and I deserved it."

"You deserved it? Why'd she say that? You ever seen her before?"

"Bruh, I've never seen her in my life. And I have no idea why she said it."

"But when she said it," Devon asks, eyes narrowing, "what did you think about her saying it? What did that make you feel?"

I sigh as I grab our glasses and walk to the sink.

"Dev, have you ever noticed how your little genius moments where you ask the *exact* right question always get on my nerves?" He laughs as I scrub the glasses. "The truth? When she said it, I thought she was probably right."

Dev taps a finger against his lips, staring off for a moment. Finally, he says, "So, let me get this straight: without even knowing what she was blaming you for, you agreed with her. That's... interesting."

"All right, what are you thinking?"

"Well, you obviously went through something serious —I wouldn't be here if you hadn't. But there's no blood, no signs of a struggle, and the door was locked when I got here, so..."

"Yep, you think I'm crazy. I knew it," I say with a laugh.

He chuckles, standing up and following me into the kitchen. "Not crazy. Just exhausted. I checked the records of your vitals on the way here—you haven't been sleeping, and your stress levels are off the charts. I think your body just... crashed. And this encounter with Alexi... I'm thinking that was probably just a dream."

"But wait," I argue, "I saw Alexi on the street *before* she was in my apartment."

"That actually makes more sense," Devon says, leaning against the counter. "How else could a stranger get in without leaving a trace? I think Alexi is your mind's way of personifying your guilt for hurting Leia. That girl you saw on the street became a stand-in for everything you're feeling."

He locks eyes with me, his tone sharpening. "One more question... and it might be kinda tough. Have you ever thought you wished it was *you* in the coma instead of Leia?"

I nod, caught off guard by how he keeps reading me like a book.

"So some random chick—whose name sounds like Leia, but scrambled and an 'X' thrown in—shows up, tells you that you deserve to suffer, and attacks you?" He leans forward, pinning me with his stare. "That's not a coincidence. That's your guilt, bro. That's you punishing yourself."

"Wow, Dev," I say, shaking my head. "You've been back in my life for all of five minutes, and you already got me figured out just like that? I didn't even think about the name thing."

How did he just–?

"But, I mean, I'm no psychoanalytic professional or anything, but this is at least worth thinking through," Devon says, shrugging.

"Hey, man... You can't just be dropping knowledge like that and then act all humble! That made a whole lotta sense, dude. Case closed, huh, Detective?"

Devon laughs, shrugging again. Then he places a hand on my shoulder. "Get some rest, bro. My guess is you'll feel a lot better after that."

"Yeah, that's not a bad id—"

Lil' A interrupts with, "Yo, Aiden! You got a hologram from a new contact. You want me to play it now or wait till later?"

"This dude is so rude!" I say, shaking my head at Devon.

"What'd I do?" Lil' A pipes up, feigning innocence. "I didn't wanna interrupt your little nap, so I'm telling you now. I can't win for losing."

I sigh. "Remind me in an hour."

"Okay, check you later," Lil' A replies cheerfully.

"Wait, Lil' A—who sent the message?"

"It was from a Dr. Merit. Would you like to see the transcript?"

"No, I'll just watch it when I have time."

"Okie doke, boss!"

"That sounds important," Devon says, watching me closely.

"Yeah, that's the specialist they sent in for Leia. Physically, she's doing okay, but they're still trying to figure out why she hasn't woken up yet. They think it's soul or Laosi-related. He's probably got follow-up questions about that night, and I'm not looking forward to it. But the sooner I answer, the sooner they can bring her back."

"Dang, bro," Devon says with a heavy heart. "That sounds tough... I'll let you handle that. I gotta get back to the missus. She sends her well wishes and told me to tell you that if you need *anything*, we got you. Just say the word, my dude."

Do you have to leave?

"Well," I say with a grin, "you can hook me up with some of those free portal passes."

Devon rolls his eyes. "Of course you'd pick the *one* thing I can't give you. It don't work like that, man. You gotta be immediate family."

"Man, I thought DNA was all about family! How many people in high school did we convince we were twins?" I laugh, and Devon joins in. "For real, though, tell Sabrina I said thanks. Real quick before you go, man—I know you've been using those free portals. What's the best place you've been to so far?"

"Eternity. No question." Devon's eyes light up as he reminisces. "The beaches are unreal. Some even have a no-technology policy. You know me—I love tech. But it was really nice to unplug and find other ways to recharge. We're not machines, ya know? It's healthy to maintain that distinction."

"I feel that. It's good to see you again, bro." I dap him up and pull him in for a hug. "And now that I know you can portal whenever and wherever, we gotta hang out soon. Maybe when Leia wakes up, we can double date or something."

"Say less! I know Sabrina will be down. Just let us know when and where. In the meantime, take care of yourself, take care of Leia, and watch out for shadowy dream women named Alexi. Let me know when Leia wakes up, okay? I'm outta here. Love you, bro."

Now he wants to get sentimental... just before he leaves me here alone.

"Later, dude," I say, walking him to the door. "Thanks again for checking on me. For real."

After closing the door, I walk back down the hallway, passing the bathroom on my left. I head straight to my bedroom, wincing when the lights brighten as I enter. Raising my hand to my head, I slowly lower it, signaling the lights to dim to about sixty percent.

Much better.

I glance around and roll my eyes at the clean laundry piled in the corner.

Why do I act like someone's gonna come fold my underwear for me?

The pile reminds me that I haven't been here much. I decide, responsibly, that I will *not* fold those clothes tonight—which probably means not for the rest of the week, either.

I grab my Solo and place it on the floor. Sitting on my unmade bed, I say, "Lil' A, pull up the hologram from Dr. Merit."

Blue beams of light shoot upward, outlining a man at a desk. The hologram fills in the image of a chubby older man, probably in his sixties, wearing a comfortable-looking gray cardigan. Behind him stands a wall packed with encyclopedias, textbooks, and dictionaries from floor to ceiling.

People still read paper books? I guess my industry isn't fading as fast as I thought.

The recording awaits my command to start playing. Dr. Merit sits motionless, his left hand preparing to swoop what remains of his thinning gray hair into something resembling a style across his balding spot. That doesn't give me much to look forward to as I think about what kind of old man I'm likely to be, but I accept this as a condition that aging men must endure.

His full, round face actually seems like it's missing a set of black, thick-rimmed glasses to give it a more scholarly appearance. After checking him out and disarming myself based on his unintimidating appearance, I say, "Play hologram."

Dr. Merit finishes styling his hair. He then folds his hands on the desk in front of him, clears his throat, looks straight forward at me, and begins.

"Hello, Aiden. My name is Dr. Merit. I'd like to ask you a few questions to discuss Leia's condition. I understand that the injury that caused Leia's coma is related to your LET. Don't worry. I'm not here to get you in trouble. But the more I understand about Leia's condition and what caused it, the more specifically I can tailor a type of treatment or therapy to make sure Leia wakes up as quickly as possible. So please reach out to me at your earliest convenience. I'll be up late tonight reviewing my notes and looking for any related cases to inform my treatment, so feel free to call me back when you get this. Thank you, and I look forward to speaking with you soon. End recording."

The hologram turns off, leaving a thick silence.

Okay... Let's get this over with.

"Lil' A, call Dr. Merit."

As the blue lights from my Solo scan my bedroom and everything in it, Lil' A responds, "Calling Dr. Merit. Rendering holographic images. Network connection stable. Reaching Dr. Merit's Solo. All right, you're good to go!"

Maybe I should have tidied up a bit more. The room looks like a clumsy palderon has been trying to learn how to run and fly in here. I should probably be making a better first impression.

"Aiden, thanks for responding so quickly."

He probably hasn't moved since he made the recording.

"No problem, sir. Um... Anything I can do to help, ya know?"

"Yes, well, we will just get right to it, then. I already spoke with Dr. Larson about the issue, and he explained to me what happened as best as he could from what you told him. Now, I don't want you to have to repeat yourself or relive what was obviously a very negative experience. But I do want to clarify a few details that you may not have known were important as you shared them with Dr. Larson."

As the lump in my throat grows, I say, "Okay... Um... What can I clarify for you?"

"I need to know exactly what it was that hit Leia. Obviously, it was your Laosi energy. But I need to know more about what form it took or how that energy was transmitted from you and how it impacted Leia."

I tilt my head a bit. "I don't... really... understand the question, sir."

"Okay... Let's try this way. Your Laosi energy seems to manifest as some type of force. From your retelling of the events on the night of the Achievement Week Festival, it seems that you push things apart. For instance, when you flew to the top of Sheridan Tower, my guess is that there was a physical force that expanded the distance between you and the ground by pushing you away from each other. And I would apply that same principle to explain the force field that protected you when you came down—your energy took the form of a force that kept everything away from you and you from everything. My question pertains to whether or not there was a force that pushed Leia back. When the energy, for lack of a better word, 'exploded' out of you, was it like a bubble that expanded from you and pushed everything else away from you?"

I stroke my chin and look up at one of the corners of his room. "No, it wasn't a bubble. It felt different from the force field. Instead of there being a tangible edge, it... I guess it felt more like wind. It felt like the wind was blowing in all directions from inside me."

"Okay, wind. Wind, yes. That's good to know."

I know he's recording the conversation, so why does he need to also write notes so feverishly? What else is he thinking?

"Now, when you say wind, was it a hot wind, a cool breeze, or a cold gust of air? And how intense was this wind? Was it strong enough to move a sofa or damage a wall?"

"Well, it wasn't actually wind in that sense. I guess it was just, like, raw energy. And I don't think it actually moved anything else but Leia... I never thought about that until just now, though. What do you think that means?"

"Yes, that is quite peculiar. And unfortunately, this case is very unique. I don't have answers just yet. When I have a plausible theory, though, I'll be sure to let you know. But I need a little bit more information. One last question, I think. What did you see when the energy was released? Anything that you saw, no matter how insignificant you may think it was, could be very helpful. For instance, what color was the energy that came from within you? What visual details can you share with me?"

"Well, when it happened, the sensation was so strong that I closed my eyes. Or, I thought I did. But... even with my eyes closed... It was really strange. It was like I could still see Leia standing there. Everything around us was black, so I thought my eyes were closed. But I could *see* her standing there. But then, when it happened, it was... I don't know. I thought I was dreaming or something. But it was like..."

I pause for a second to gather my thoughts. Dr. Merit leans in with an intensely concerned look on his face, anxiously anticipating each word that comes out of my mouth, making this process all the more difficult.

"It was like I saw Leia... With my eyes closed, I saw her. Then, I saw this greenish energy flow out from me in all directions. And when it reached the Leia I was seeing with my eyes closed, she started flowing back away from me with the energy. But then, when I opened my eyes, Leia was right there on the floor. I... I don't know... That probably doesn't make much sense, but I don't really know how else to explain it."

He mumbles to himself again, and the only thing I can make out from his monologue is "Quite peculiar." Abruptly, he puts his stylus down, and says, "Aiden, thank you for your cooperation. You have answered all the questions that I had. Have a good night."

"Wait! I mean... So, like... What's next? Do you have a diagnosis or a plan to treat her? You're kinda just leaving me hanging here."

"Ah, yes..." he says, clearing his throat. "Well, the plan is to revisit Ms. Hart tomorrow with a spectrometer specifically designed to measure the frequency and intensity of Laosi energy being generated by a human body. This may give us a glimpse of how your Laosi affected hers. I suspect that there has been an alteration to the permutation of her Laosi pattern. If we can find it, we can begin to develop a modified LIST treatment to help reintegrate her whole soul with her whole body. That should help her wake up."

"That's the best news I've heard in weeks. Thank you, Dr. Merit. So, I'll see you tomorrow with the specto-thingy? What time will you be there?"

"It depends on how long it takes ARL to prepare the spectrometer for me to use. But Aiden... The results won't come back for a few days, and even then, this type of LIST treatment can take a week or more before we start to see any results. Anyone can tell you care about Leia, but... you'll have to be patient here."

"Yep, that's fine. I'll see you tomorrow! Goodnight, doctor."

Dr. Merit recognizes there's nothing he can say to curb my enthusiasm at this point, so he just nods. "Goodnight, Aiden."

"Call ended," Lil' A reports.

So there's a plan! She's gonna wake up! Yes!!

I pick my Solo up off the floor, and my reflection off its glass screen shows me the big, goofy smile plastered across my face. I sigh, that smile frozen in place, and I put my Solo on its charger. My eyes wander around the room, and for the first time in weeks, I anticipate a return to relative normalcy.

Man, a full night of sleep... my own comfortable bed... pillows fluffed just right... ambient sleepy sounds playing at the perfect volume. I didn't realize how much I missed all this!

"Lil' A, play raindrop sounds and turn off my lights."

I crawl into bed, exhausted, and begin the ritual of tossing and turning to find that elusive, comfortable position. After 30 minutes of wrestling with my blankets, I'm still wide awake.

What if Alexi shows up in my dreams again tonight? The thought sends a chill through me. *Am I going to be lucid enough to face her without ending up in the kind of pain that makes my Solo tell my friends I'm dying?*

Or worse... What if she wasn't just a dream?

Devon's explanation made sense at the time, but doubt creeps in.

What if there's an actual psychopath out there plotting my demise?

I shake my head.

I'm just overthinking it. Get a grip, Aiden.

But still, I can't shake the unease. I need something external to validate that I'm safe.

"Lil' A, read my front door access log."

"You got it. Last access to the front door: Emergency Contact Devon Murray. Before that: Owner Aiden Lore. That's you!"

Thanks, Lil' A… Glad you're here to remind me what my name is. What would I ever do without you?

"Before that: Owner Aiden Lore. Before that: Owner Aiden Lore. Before that: Owner Aiden Lore. You need to get some friends, Chief."

"Lil' A, shut down for the night. I think you've got some updates to download or something."

At least I know no one else has been in my apartment. I must've been way too stressed. A good night's sleep is exactly what I need…

But as I try to drift off, the dryness in my throat keeps me conscious. I stumble out of bed, walking through the dark toward the kitchen. The faint light streaming in through the window is just enough for me to see without flipping a switch.

I grab a glass from the cabinet and fill it halfway with cold water. After a few gulps, I set the glass down on the counter, but it doesn't sit flat. It's leaning slightly.

Confused, I pick it up and realize it was resting on Leia's engagement ring.

When did that get there?

I stare at it for a moment, my thoughts hazy with exhaustion.

Did she take it off here before we went to the fireworks show? She did say her hand felt a little itchy. That's what I get for buying a cheap ring.

I decide to leave the ring in front of the picture of us on the counter, designating it as a mystery for another day. I head back to bed. Sliding under the covers, I pull them up to my neck and close my eyes for what I hope is the final time tonight.

*Tomorrow, I'm gonna put that ring back where it belongs—
on your finger, Leia. Or better yet, maybe on a necklace. I wonder
what you'll say when you wake up and see it!*

End Part 1

PART 2 - FROM HERE TO WHERE?

CHAPTER 6 – MOM

One Week Later

"Well, hello, Aiden!"

The subtle sarcasm in her voice and the familiar expression on her face remind me how long it's been since I've spoken with her.

Chuckling sheepishly, I reply, "Hey, Mom. How's it going?"

"Everything's going well on our end. How are *you* doing?"

"That's… a really good question, actually."

I glance around the holographic projection of my parents' bedroom. The gold curtains flutter gently in the breeze from the open window behind her. Watosi Lake glistens in their backyard as songbirds chirp cheerily to one another.

As long as it's been since I looked into my parents' room, it still looks exactly as I remember—with the exception of my Young Engineers' trophy on the mantle over their fireplace.

After all these years, she kept that trophy? And she moved it to the mantle in their bedroom?

"Well, it's good to see you and hear from you," she says, her tone bright. "But when are you going to let me *see* you see you? Not through this Solo thing. You're a little overdue for a visit. But, you know, it's okay."

"Yeah, it's been a while since I came over, huh? Sorry I missed last time," I offer, trying to soften the blow.

"I think you mean the last *three* times, sir. But, you know, it's okay. I know you have a lot on your plate." She smiles with saintly patience.

"I do, but… I'll be there as soon as I can. It's just… between work and going to see Leia, I barely have time to see myself."

Are you really making excuses for not spending time with the woman who gave birth to you? Get it together, Aiden.

"But... I'm going to put it on my calendar. Um... let's see. Actually, what are you doing tonight?" I ask.

"Maybe hanging out with my son?" she suggests.

"Haha! Great. Let's do that. Oh, is Dad gonna be home?"

"No, not tonight. He and Zoe are at a conference."

Typical, I guess.

"Are they in Sanctuary, or...?"

"Yeah, they're speaking at the Ethridge Civic Center," she explains.

"Oh, out in the Vestavia area? Oooh, ask him if he can bring home some imptahs from Uncle Maven's Diner! I haven't had one of those in years!" My stomach growls in anticipation.

She chuckles softly. "I didn't know you liked those so much. You used to say the breading was too chewy or something."

"No, the bread was my favorite part. It was the meat that gave your jaws a workout," I snicker. "But you're right— they weren't my favorite or anything. They just... taste like childhood."

"Well, if you want them so badly, I *suppose* I could ask your father to bring some imptahs home. Ya know, I was thinking about cooking some braised targon steak tonight. But if you'd rather have Uncle Maven's..."

"Whoa, whoa, whoa! Stop right there, Mom," I say. "I see what you're doing here."

"And what might that be?" she asks.

"You're going to cook my favorite meal as an insurance policy to make sure I actually come over."

Feigning shock, she places a hand on her chest, her mouth agape. "Why, Aiden, whatever do you mean? Do you think *I* would do something like that?"

"You know I'm powerless against your steak. That's why you won't share the recipe. That savory blend of herbs and spices... the way you keep the meat so tender... You won't tell me because you want to keep it in your back pocket for times like this!"

Still pretending to be offended, she says, "Of all the manipulative things I could do to the son I love..." She trails off, noticing I'm not buying it. Slowly, she adds, "But if I *were* to try something so appalling as that... would it work?"

"Yep. See you at 7:30!" I reply immediately, making her laugh.

But she didn't need to play her trump card. I was planning to come over anyway. It's my day off, and aside from this court-ordered therapy session, my schedule is wide open. Maybe I should tell her I love her enough to come over just to spend time with her.

But I haven't actually made the time to spend with her, so maybe I shouldn't say that.

"I'm looking forward to it," she says warmly. "I know we'll have more time to talk tonight, but... how are you, really? If I judged by the look of your room, I'd say not very well. Are you taking care of yourself?"

I sigh heavily. "No, not really. It's just... it's kinda hard to take care of yourself when you're the reason your fiancée is in a coma. Every day that I wake up, and Leia's still... sleeping, it's just hard."

"Yeah... I'm sorry. But, you know, it's okay. I'm sure she'll wake up soon," she says with a small, hopeful smile. "Maybe sooner than you think."

"Hopefully. But when she wakes up, she's going to tell her side of the story about that night. She might press charges or never want to talk to me again. I don't know what she's going to do or say or... It's just..." My voice trails off as I glance around her room, hoping for a distraction.

"I hear you. But, you know, it's okay. You two love each other. And she knows it was an accident. Plus, your dad will make sure you don't end up in prison or anything. I'm just believing it'll be okay."

"Mom..." I pause, feeling a lump form in my throat.

It's been a week, but the truth still doesn't feel real.

"I almost killed her. I injured her *soul*. That's not the kind of thing that just… goes away, ya know?"

Can you please let this shallow optimism go for a moment and live with me in reality?

"I hear you, son… But, you know, it's okay," she says, her calm demeanor unwavering.

I guess not.

"Because worrying about the outcome isn't going to help anything now, is it? Besides, I believe things will work out for good."

But what if they don't?

"Who knows? This might draw you two closer together."

Doubtful.

"Maybe you're right. I hope so…" I stop trying, realizing this conversation, like most I have with Mom about the heavy stuff, won't dig deep enough to be meaningful.

"Yeah… Keep hoping, Aiden. I know you're upset, and I wish there was something I could do," she says, her tone unusually tender. Then she adds, "But, you know, it's okay. All right, I'll see you this evening, son! I won't keep you from whatever else you have going on today, especially since we can talk more once you get here. Thanks for the call."

"No problem at all, Mom. You weren't holding me up from anything. I'm taking it easy today."

"What did you just say?" she asks, cupping her hand around her ear and leaning closer. "It sounded like you said, 'I'm cleaning my room today, Mom.' Did I hear that right?"

I smirk and reply, "Um, no ma'am. That is *not* what I said."

"Well, it *should* have been," she says with a frown. "Jeez, Aiden. Your room is a mess. I can only imagine what your kitchen looks like."

"Don't judge me, Mom! You don't know my life!" I protest.

"I actually *do* know your life, son. I gave it to you," she counters.

"You're pulling the mom card on me, huh? Okay, okay... I'll clean up a little before I come over," I concede with exaggerated reluctance.

"What a wonderful idea, son!" she replies with so much sarcasm it practically drips from her words. Her full-faced, *I'm-so-pleasantly-surprised* smile is impossible not to laugh at.

"Bye, Ma."

"See you later, son."

I wave at her as I tell Lil' A, "End call."

Laying back on the bed, I close my eyes, trying to mentally prepare myself for this therapy session I'm probably about to be late for.

I just don't know what to expect. On one hand, it could be an inconvenient formality. Dad already said there haven't been any major breakthroughs for treating people like me who still have powers after going through LIST. I'm probably just gonna waste time dredging up memories I'd rather forget—with nothing to show for it. Can't say I'm thrilled.

The sun peeks out from behind a cloud, infusing a soft brightness into my bedroom.

But what if this could be the start of something new? A breakthrough in the science? What if the therapist and I actually figure out the missing piece of the puzzle? I wouldn't mind being a guinea pig if it meant I could get freedom from these powers. Maybe this therapy helps pave the way for Leia and me to finally be together without the constant threat of out-of-control LETs hanging over us.

Leia... I'll do whatever it takes to make it safe for you to be with me.

"Lil' A, call a carrier for me."

"You got it, boss. Looks like I can get a carrier here in seven and a half minutes. You want to prepay with the usual account?" Lil' A asks.

"Yep."

Can't touch my savings.

"Wait—how much is the ride gonna cost?" I ask.

"22 credits."

"And how much is in the usual account?"

"24.5 credits."

Why am I always so broke?

"Go for it," I order.

Well, let's see what happens.

I sit up in bed, glancing around.

My room's not that junky. I'll take care of this tomorrow.

Standing up, I walk over to the mirror and give a half-hearted effort at styling my hair. I give myself a wink, trying to muster some positivity for what's ahead. Leaving my bedroom, I pass through the living room, and out the front door.

"Lil' A, lock up for me. And don't open up for anyone who's not me."

"Confirmed," Lil' A responds.

I walk to the carrier pickup spot at the end of the apartment building's hallway. The door slides open, and the mechanical voice of the bioscanner greets me.

"Your carrier has arrived, Mr. Lore. Where would you like to go?"

Stooping to get into the black, rectangular vehicle, I reply, "City Sector JF, Office Building 89, please."

The platform lowers the carrier to street level, and I begin the journey to the ARL Center for Psychological Wellness. I look out the window, nausea preventing the nap I intended to take en route.

Was it something I ate? Wait—did I even eat today?

I crack the window to see if the fresh air will help settle my stomach. The afternoon is pleasant, with a partly cloudy sky. Some of the pedestrians I pass look less thrilled with the warmth and humidity, their expressions betraying mild discomfort.

To pass the time, I start making up stories about the people I see.

He just got off from a looong day of work. She's on her way to see her boyfriend she's, like, totally in love with. That guy's gotta be military or something—he's scanning the crowd like he's expecting something to pop off. I'd want him on my team if things went south. That little girl is so cute, but I bet she drives her mom crazy. Manipulative little mastermind... you can never trust a seven-year-old with that much charm.

As we roll past a monorail station, I spot Marcus in his CLU Enforcer uniform.

What's he doing here? A patrol assignment this far from his precinct?

I lower the window further to get a better read on his emotions. I pick up on a trace of fear—not strong enough to freeze a person, but strong enough to keep them on edge.

I wonder what's up. If it's anything serious, I'm sure it'll hit the news.

The carrier continues on, and my thoughts drift toward the Center just a few blocks away.

Okay, Aide... What are we thinking? Breakthrough discovery or massive waste of time? Probably the latter... This is so stupid.

"Arriving at City Sector JF, Office Building 89: ARL Center for Psychological Wellness. Please remain seated until the carrier has come to a complete stop. Remember to take all your belongings, and enjoy the rest of your afternoon."

Stepping out of the carrier, I squint against the brightness of the sun reflecting off the whitestone building. I ascend the stairs to the entrance and place my hand on the check-in tablet outside the glass doors. When the screen flashes green, the doors open, and I step inside.

My eyes take a moment to adjust to the dimmer lighting inside the waiting room. I look around the gray-themed space and calculate which seat is farthest from everyone else.

Maybe I'm just a little antisocial today.

I spot a couch in the center of the room that faces the entrance. I make my there so I can keep an eye out for anyone who might come in unannounced and trigger an unwanted LET episode. As I cross the gray-tiled floor, my footsteps echo in the silence. That golden silence is evicted just before I sit down, however.

"Aiden?"

"Oh, what's up, Yousef?"

"Hey, man! Good to see you," he says, either unaware or unconcerned that this is the last place I want to bump into someone I know. He walks around the receptionist counter in the corner to come join me in the middle of the lobby.

"Likewise... It's been, what, ten years since Ms. Evans' class, right?"

He runs his hand through his short black hair, thinking back. "Yeah, I guess it has been. Time flies, huh?"

"It does. But I don't know why it caught me off guard to see you here. My dad told me he helped you land the internship."

His face lights up. "He did? He talked about me? What'd he say?"

"Uh, not much... Just that you were a good pick—and not just because we went to school together. And that makes sense, though. You were always into Laosi research. So how's the gig working out for you?"

He beams. "Honestly, I couldn't imagine it going better... except if they paid me. But it's amazing seeing how much our work helps people. And that's actually why I was surprised to see your name on the schedule today. What are *you* doing here?"

I raise my voice, "Whoa, Yousef!" drawing a few curious glances from others in the room. Lowering my tone, I suggest, "Maybe we save this for a less public setting? Client confidentiality and all?"

"Oh! Yeah, of course. Sorry, Aiden. It's just... it's not every day Richard Lore's son shows up for therapy at a center that his father practically built with his own hands."

Before my palm hits my face, I notice several clients

glancing at me with recognition in their eyes.

Why does my dad have a groupie?

Covering my face, I mutter, "So, is Dr. Cambridge available?"

"He is. Right this way, Mr. Lore."

The weird thing is that he still doesn't realize he did something wrong.

Maybe I should just be grateful that Yousef's reverence for my dad got me to the front of the line.

I follow him down a sterile gray hallway until we reach a door with "Dr. Ronald Cambridge" printed on the placard. Yousef knocks and cheerily announces, "Aiden Lore is here!"

The shadow of a man approaches the translucent glass. A moment later, an energetic man in his early 40s opens the door.

"Thank you, Yousef. Aiden, come in and make yourself comfortable. Can I get you some water or coffee?"

CHAPTER 7 – RON

"Ah, no thanks."

I walk into his office, taking a moment to observe the space. It's surprisingly open, colorful, and inviting. In the far-right corner, there's a cherry oak desk facing the door, holding a few holopics of Dr. Cambridge with his wife and kids. Following the back wall to the left, past a picture of a flower garden, there's a mini fridge with a coffee pot sitting on top.

It smells so warm and rich, but then it tastes like dirt. Why do people drink this stuff?

More important to me than observing the space is getting a read on this guy. A very comfortable-looking, 100% cotton royal blue polo shirt hugs his slim upper body and rests untucked from his khaki slacks. His office and attire present a casual impression that begs me to take him lightly. But three things about him demand my respect: his impressive mini library on the left wall, his connection to my dad, and, most importantly, the genuine compassion and enthusiasm I sense in him. The best actor couldn't fake this kind of energy.

That's positive. Maybe we'll actually make some progress.

Don't trust his words.

My face tightens.

What was that? That didn't even sound like me... Where did that come from?

"Most people are a little thrown off when they walk into my office. Bean bags and bar stools aren't your typical office furniture. I get that. I just want my clients to choose whatever makes them comfortable. What kind of mood are you in today, Aiden?"

I notice the seating options in the corner to my left—an assortment of wildly different chairs arranged in an oddly deliberate pattern. I grab a desk chair and roll it toward the middle of the room. As I sit down, Dr. Cambridge crosses the light-blue carpet to his desk, wheels his chair out, and joins me in the center.

"Well, Aiden," he begins with an optimistic smile, "I'm not exactly sure where to start, but I am excited about the journey we'll be taking. I hope you won't approach this as a court-ordered obligation but as something that will be helpful to you in your life."

"No, no. I see this as something I probably should have tried years ago. At least, Leia said as much," I say with an empty chuckle. "I'm just not sure what to really expect, I guess. Just to let you know where I'm starting, though, I don't really think anyone can fix me." My gaze shifts to the rug on the floor between us.

"Really? Why's that?"

"Well, I mean... I went through LIST already, and it didn't work... at all. They hooked me up to all these probes and high-tech machines—the same thing they do to help hundreds of others—and... nothing. It's hard to believe that sitting down and talking with you is going to make that big of a difference. No offense."

He smiles. "It's important to have realistic expectations when entering therapy. What kind of difference would make you consider this therapy successful?"

"I want to get rid of these powers," I say confidently.

"That's not going to happen here," he replies matter-of-factly.

"Okay..." I pause, thrown off by his directness. "So what should I expect, then?"

He leans forward. "Well, most clients come out of therapy understanding themselves better. Maybe that's a good expectation for us to start with. Understanding what makes Aiden tick. That could lead to us learning where his power comes from and how to control it. Maybe there's something deep within Aiden that made the LIST process ineffective.

There may be a part of Aiden that sees his LET as a gift he can control and use for his own benefit and the benefit of others."

Why does he keep referring to me in the third person?

"Control it?" I ask, skeptical. "I guess that could be okay if I could, like, really, *really* control it. But trust me, I do not see these powers as a gift."

"I hear you... But have you ever used your powers to get something that you wanted, that you would've otherwise been unable to get without them?"

"No!"

"Really, Aiden?" He leans back and jots a quick note onto his digital writing pad.

He's judging me. He's trying to make me think I like having powers. But I don't. That's the whole reason I'm here.

"You know, it's interesting that you could review the last 24 years of your life in less than three seconds," he says casually.

"Well, that's because I know I hate having these powers."

"But that wasn't the question I asked, was it?"

I blink at him. "With all due respect, what's your point? I mean, what are you trying to do here?"

He interlocks his fingers, resting his hands in his lap, maintaining a very direct eye contact. "The hardest part of therapy for the client," he says, "is the necessity to be honest with yourself. But change is impossible without it. I'll be the first to admit it—the formalized study of Laosi and LETs is still rather new, and there's a lot we're still learning. On top of that, there aren't many Users like you who want to get rid of their powers but find that they can't.

"But one commonality among those who retain their powers after LIST is an unwillingness to let the power go. That might be the result of an intellectual uncertainty, an emotional discomfort, or a subconscious conflict of desires. But many of my clients have come to realize that the goal they were trying to give their powers up for wasn't as important to them as the possibilities available to them if they kept their powers."

"Doc, if you're going to try to find something in my life that I want more than being with Leia, this is going to be a long nine weeks."

His calm, optimistic demeanor doesn't falter. "I'm not comparing the strength of any of your desires against each other. I'm asking you to be bold enough to explore all of them. Even if you don't desire your LETs, there might be a goal tied to them that creates this inner conflict. Our best bet for therapy to be effective is to see if you honestly hate these fantastic abilities—and their possibilities—as much as you *think* you do.

Giving a smile in return for my scoffing, he adds, "If —and admittedly, it's a big if—but *if* we can expose an attachment to your powers and we face it, then the data suggests you'll have a better chance of surrendering them to the ALPHA. *If* that's what you truly want at that time. But let's not get ahead of ourselves. I have a question for you: if we do find that you have even the smallest desire to maintain and use these powers for good, do you think it would be possible for you to not judge yourself for having it?"

He pauses, likely reading my body language to see if I'm buying into his methodology.

If I have to be here, I might as well go along for the ride.

"I'll try," I mutter.

"That's the spirit!" he says, smiling with kind eyes. "Now, I've reviewed the case information the courts sent me. The night of the incident that resulted in Leia's injury... you flew the two of you up to the rooftop of the ARL building to watch the fireworks, right? I bet the view was breathtaking. How was that experience for you?"

"The flying? It was... I mean, it was... It was, like..." His eyes soften, communicating to me that he's fine with waiting.

He'll let me squirm for the rest of the session if that's what it takes. No use delaying the inevitable.

"Okay, yeah, there was... I mean, I really can't put it into words. I've never experienced anything like it. It was probably the best night of my life."

"So your LET made it possible for you to experience the single greatest night of your life. That wasn't so hard to admit, was it?"

I chuckle and shake my head, avoiding eye contact for a while.

"Now we're getting somewhere," he says, partially in jest. "It may feel uncomfortable, even selfish, to say it, but you've used your power to get something you wanted. And I know that's not the whole story because putting your fiancée into a coma is *not* what you wanted. But it is the part of the story that has been covered up. Often, the best place to look for solutions we haven't found is the place we've been unwilling to look into. If we want LIST to work, I think you're going to have to admit that your powers aren't your biggest problem, even if you hate what they've caused."

"Can we just skip that and cut to the part where you recertify me for another three hours with the ALPHA and I come out powerless?"

"That does sound nice," he says, leaning back in his chair, "but we don't have that option. Especially because— wait, do you know what LIST actually does? How much do you know about your father's work?" he asks.

"All I know is it's supposed to give people with LETs the chance to live normal lives by suppressing or removing their abilities or something. How it does that? No clue."

"Okay…" He tilts his head. "And what do you know of Laosi?"

Feebly, I offer, "It's the energy of the soul?"

"You're not wrong," he says, smiling faintly. "Laosi *is* the energy of the soul. More specifically, it's the energy that allows the immaterial consciousness of a person to influence the material world. To simplify: your body is the link between your soul and the world around it. Laosi is the link between your soul and your body. It's the energy that allows your soul to control your body as it navigates and impacts the world. Stop me if you're not following."

"I think it makes sense... Okay, so it's like my soul is the AI piloting system, my body is the carrier, and Laosi is the anti-grav propulsion engine?"

He turns the analogy over in his head before nodding. "Yeah, something like that."

So did I hit Leia's pilot system or just damage the wiring between the AI and the engine? Why won't she wake up?

"There's a lot more nuance," he continues, "but you've got a firm enough grasp of the concept. About 30 years ago, Zoe and your dad developed sensors that could detect the energy of the personality that animates the body."

Huh?

"Without diving too deep into the science—which is a bit beyond my scope—they isolated at least three frequencies of energy that make up what we believe the soul to be. Think of light frequencies. White light can be broken into its component colors with a prism. Your dad's spectrometer functions much like a prism for Laosi energy. They isolated three distinct frequencies: one is intellectual, another emotional, and the third volitional. People often call these the mind, heart, and will—or thoughts, feelings, and desires. The human soul is a triad of these three energy streams. Still with me?"

I nod.

I never really thought about it, but my dad must be really smart.

"These streams of energy converge in the soul and empower the body to do incredible things. When they work together in harmony—when they're *integrated*—we see people achieving amazing feats like building skyscrapers, developing new technologies, and saving lives. Your dad and Zoe's work are prime examples of what happens when Laosi is fully in sync."

So my dad is perfectly in sync, and I'm completely out of

control. Why doesn't this surprise me?

"The LIST *procedure*—remember, it stands for Laosi Integration Soul Therapy—uses technology to help people reintegrate their soul streams. But LIST *as a whole* is about observing the contents of the mind, heart, and will and helping people resolve misalignment between the three. This session is a part of LIST. It's not just a one-time treatment for Users to remove their LETs. It's a framework for self-awareness that enables a more fulfilling life."

Noticing my glazed-over expression, he chuckles. "Sorry. I get passionate about my work. I didn't mean to lecture. But it was important to set the context about the components of Laosi. Because when it comes to LETs, what we believe is that there are people like you who have one stream of soul energy that is so potent that it supercharges the link between their soul and body, overflowing into the material world. In other words, your soul generates a surplus of power that is able to extend beyond the limits of your body and directly influence the world around you."

"Hang on, Dr. Cambridge—"

"Just call me Ron."

"Yeah, so, Ron... I have powers I can't control because my soul is... too strong?"

He leans forward. "How are you processing that idea?"

"It doesn't *feel* like strength, ya know? I mean, sure, I'm flying, making force fields, teleporting... so yeah, that *sounds* like strength. But it's weird to think that my soul controls my body, yet I'm too weak to control my soul—or my soul's energy, or whatever."

Ron lets me sit in the silence to try to grapple with these ideas.

Man, I should have paid more attention when Dad used to explain all this to me.

"I have a theory about why you're having so much difficulty controlling your powers and why that makes you feel 'weak.' It has to do with identifying the energy stream that is most dominant in your soul. I wanna get your opinion first, though. Of the three, which do you think is manifesting in these LETs?"

"That's a good question... Sorry, this is just a lot to take in!"

"I understand," he says. He pauses before re-engaging. "Think back to the last time you activated your powers. Were you thinking really hard, feeling an intense emotion, or was there something you really wanted? Take your time with this, because it's critical to our work. Was the last night of Sanctuary Achievement Week the last time you used an LET?"

I sense his enthusiasm... and maybe even hope.

"Yeah... Wait, no. The last time was at the hospital. Dr. Larson had just told me that Leia's coma wasn't caused by a physical injury. That I had damaged her soul."

No... Not now! Hold it together, Aiden.

"Aiden... Hey, stay with me. You're okay. You don't have to relive the moment. Just observe it. What were you thinking, feeling, or wanting then?"

I can feel Ron's fear creeping in, but his focus and calm resolve to help me through this keeps me centered.

He's really committed to his work.

"Okay, okay... ummm. I was thinking that I couldn't believe I actually damaged my fiancée's soul... And I just really wanted to, like, go hide. Get out of there. I didn't want anyone to see me."

"And then what happened?"

"Well, I... I teleported. I teleported to the swamp just over the Kerioth River."

"Hmmm," Ron says, a smirk creeping across his face. "I think we're onto something, Aiden. You wanted to hide. You wanted to be away from everyone. You didn't want anyone to see you... And you teleported to a place where no human has been in probably 40 years or more. You see where I'm going with this, right?"

"So... it's my will..."

Leia thought the same thing.

"That's what I suspect," Ron says, stroking his chin, his eyes twinkling with the spark of discovery. "And that makes even more sense as to why your power is so hard for you to control. The will is entirely subconscious and instinctive. It's impossible to control the contents of the will. We can only hope to manage its impulses."

He's saying I actually want these powers? That doesn't make sense... Why would I want something that has done so much damage? Or maybe... what could it be that I want that I can't get without these powers?

I did tell Leia I dreamt about using my powers to help people, but that was just a dream. I don't really care about that. As long as Leia and I are good, I'm good. So... is it something I want to use my powers for with her? She does like my powers. She said they're amazing... So I guess if I could control them, she'd think I'm amazing, too? Is that why I can't let them go? Because I want Leia to think I'm amazing?

I mean, I do want that, but that doesn't seem like the reason I can't let them go. LIST failed on me before I even met Leia. Doc said the will is unconscious... I guess this is going to take a while.

Recognizing how lost in thought I was, I say to Ron, "I guess that might also be why LIST didn't work on me. If it's my will that's too strong, and if I actually want to have these powers like you suggested, there's no way it could've worked. That makes sense. Wow... I guess... I actually want these powers."

Ron squints and asks, "How does it feel to say that out loud?"

"I don't know," I blurt out. "It's just weird because I don't want to want it, but apparently I do. And that kinda makes me not want to want *anything,* if that makes any sense. Because if I want something too bad, I might catch the building on fire or something."

I take a deep breath, close my eyes, and hold it long

enough to let my mind wander before releasing it. "So... what do we do now?"

Ron hangs his head for a second, then looks up and says, "Nothing. For now. Unfortunately, we're out of time for today. But one of the first things we need to do in our next sessions is identify the types of desires associated with the activation of your powers. I don't think it's a craving for ice cream or the desire for a good night's rest that's presenting a threat to anyone. So let's explore those strong-willed desires your soul manifests in the form of an LET."

"Yeah... Yeah, I can get behind that."

"Well, Aiden, I don't know about you, but I'm excited. I think we made a breakthrough rather quickly, and I look forward to building on this success. I spent too much time talking this session, but next time, I'll leave more space to explore your experiences."

He stands, and my body instinctively follows. "We're going to get you through this. Do you know why? Because you *want* this. And as we just discovered, your will is very strong. Strong enough to defy gravity and rip open a wormhole through space. You can do this."

"Don't forget—my will is also strong enough to damage Leia's soul."

Ron gives me a warm smile, his expression filled with compassion. "That might be what brought you here. But that doesn't have to define where you go from here."

You mean he's not even gonna let me wallow in my self-pity?! This guy's good.

"So, I believe the court ordered weekly meetings, right? I'll see you next week at the same time?"

"Yeah, that works."

We meet in the middle of his office, shaking hands. He clasps my hand with both of his and looks me in the eye. "I'm looking forward to it. Have a great day, Aiden!"

"You, too." I turn and walk out of his office.

That went better than I thought it would! I kinda wish the session had gone longer. Ron knows his stuff!

He's only half-right.

Okay, so now I'm legit hearing voices.

I almost want to question this random voice about why I shouldn't trust the only person who's started to help me understand my LETs, but validating it by asking a question would confirm that I'm actually losing my mind.

"So, Aiden, how'd it go, man?" Yousef asks as I reenter the lobby.

"It was pretty good."

"Yeah, Dr. Cambridge is the best, bro!"

I envy Yousef's constant enthusiasm. How is it possible to be this excited about everything all the time? Maybe I need to find a career I actually care about. Working at Clamp Em's clearly isn't my life's passion. But at least it pays the bills... kinda?

"I like him," I say. "I think we can make some progress."

"Great! So, listen. When's the next time you're gonna see your dad? I was wondering if you could have him sign my—"

"Yousef! For the umpteenth time—no, man!" I snap, trying not to make a scene.

His ever-bright demeanor dims for a moment, but before he sinks too deep, I add, "But... I'm going to my parents' tonight for dinner. When I see him, I'll ask him if he could make some time to stop by and check everything out over here."

"That. Would. Be. AWESOME!"

"Shhh!"

I can't help but marvel at how little Yousef cares that everyone else in the waiting room is now glaring at him.

He is completely untethered by public opinion. The world could use more people like Yousef... even if he is annoying.

Watching his freedom stirs something in me.

What kind of person would I be if I stopped caring about what people think? Would I dress differently? Dance more? Grow out a beard just to see if I liked it? Who would I even be? How much of who I am has been shaped by other people's expectations? And if

I stripped all that away, would there be anything left of me worth keeping?

"What time are you going over there?" Yousef asks, breaking my train of thought.

"Not that it's any of your business, but right now, actually. Speaking of which, let me call my mom. I'll holler at you later, okay, bro?"

"Oh, okay. You're not gonna forget about me, right?"

We dap each other up, and I walk out of the office.

"Lil' A, call Mom. Audio only."

"Calling Jackie Lore," Lil' A responds. "Connection made. The next voice you hear will be—"

"Hey, Aiden! You on your way over?" Mom asks, her voice bright and welcoming.

"H-h-hey, Mom. I was wondering... any chance you could give me a ride? I'm not far from you."

"Why don't you just catch a carrier? I've got the steak in the pressure cooker, and I want to keep an eye on it."

"Well, carriers can take a while to catch sometimes. I just wanted to get there quick so I could help you get dinner ready."

"You're broke, aren't you?"

How do moms always know?

"Well... Since you asked, I mean... yeah. I'm in a tight spot."

She laughs.

Should I be comforted or insulted by that?

"I'm on the way," she says, still chuckling. Then, after a pause, she adds, "By the way, did you clean your room?"

"Bye, Ma! See you soon!"

CHAPTER 8 – DAD

"Dan? Hey, what's up, sir?"

I step out of the Center for Psychological Wellness and see Daniel Emmaus at the bottom of the stairs. His black CLUE uniform with its red highlights stands out sharply against the streaks of orange and purple scattered across the sky as the sun sets. The uniform accentuates his muscular build.

"Aiden? Good to see you, brother! You doing all right?"

He glances at the sign displaying the name of the building I just walked out of.

Dan, you don't need to act like you forgot where you're posted.

"Yes, sir!" I say, trying to keep my voice casual, hiding the fact that I know he knows I'm seeing a therapist. "I'm good. Well, as good as can be, ya know? How are you?"

"Ah, you know how it is, man. Another day in paradise!" he says.

"Is it, though? Listen, not to pry or anything, but what's going on today?"

He furrows his brow and tilts his head. "What do you mean?"

"Hey, if it's top secret, I get it, ya know? But I saw Marcus a few blocks down at the TU station looking like he was ready for something to pop off. And now, here you are, way out here. Looks like y'all are setting up a perimeter or something, right? So, what's really good?" I ask, my words spilling out faster than I intended.

He gives a slight smirk before replying, "Like I said, another day in paradise."

"Okay, so I'm onto something, but you don't think you can tell me. Dan, listen, man—I'm making progress. I just had a session today where I learned about streams of Laosi. It's my will. That's why my LETs have been outta control. I think I can turn that all around if you—"

Firmly, he cuts me off. "Not the time nor the place. I'd be glad to put in a word with Tim if you're ready, but only when you're ready."

"I think I'm ready!" I exclaim.

He sighs and then asks the question I didn't want him to ask. "Okay, so what have you done *on purpose* with your powers?"

"Well... nothing yet, but that's why I'm asking you to—"

"Then you're not ready," he says. "You've got a lot of potential, young man. The sky's the limit for you—I've always felt that way. And there are plenty of people at the academy who are eager to process your application. I've seen your resume, and honestly, I can't figure out why you're settling. I know you want more for yourself. You can accomplish more than you even realize. But you gotta get this under control first. But until you do, please... don't go trying to prove yourself."

"I hear ya. Thanks. Well, hey, that's my ride coming, so I'll see you later. Be safe out here."

Dan watches as I walk to my parents' midnight blue carrier and get in. I can feel his gaze lingering on my back.

I'm tired of being such a disappointment to everybody.

"Aiden! Good to see you!"

"Hey, Mom."

I settle into the seat beside her, and she gives me a careful look. Her gaze makes me want to hide, but I resist the urge.

Don't teleport out of here, Aiden. You can do this. Let's address the tension head on.

"What's up?" I ask nonchalantly.

"Well, it's just been so long since I've seen you... And you look like you've got something on your mind. You wanna talk about it?"

"Nah, I'm good."

Totally not addressing the tension head on.

"Okay, 'Mr. Good,'" she replies knowingly. "But, you know, it's okay. Once you get this home-cooked meal in your stomach, I'm sure you'll feel better. Carrier, take us home, please."

"Acknowledged."

As the carrier glides through the streets toward my parents' house, she asks, "When's the last time you ate a home-cooked meal? You look like you've lost some weight. You taking care of yourself?"

"Whoa, Mom. Why so many questions?" I chuckle, but her expression doesn't change. "I'm good. Seriously! You don't have to worry about me like that all the time."

"I'm your mother—it's my job to worry," she says with a smirk.

The tenderness in her eyes... It's been a while since I've felt that kind of warmth from anyone.

"Yeah, but can you take some PTO or something?" I tease.

We share a laugh, but I can sense the restlessness she's felt since being laid off a few years back. I want to tell her I believe in her and that I love her, but... the timing seems off.

"Arriving at the Lore residence. Please stay seated until the carrier has come to a complete stop. Remember to grab all your belongings, and please enjoy your evening. Welcome home!"

I step out of the carrier and walk around to her side, opening the door for her. She gives me a brief hug.

"It's good to see you," she says.

"You, too... And this house." I glance around, taking in the familiar sights. "You know, Ma, I never thought about it much when I was growing up... But now, it kinda throws me off that you guys found a single-unit house on a lake so close to town. I mean, here in this neighborhood, I'm about as close to nature as I've ever been in Sanctuary."

I look out at the houses lining Watosi Lake, their

backyards forming the edge of the water. The crisp spring evening air holds my childhood memories, each breath bringing with it a story from a different phase of life.

Like the time I shoved Candace into that bush when she ate the last slice of my birthday cake. And the porch swing I broke showing off in front of Leia. The living room window Jack shattered with a ball only to push the blame onto me. Even the front door Devon would always open for my mom, determined to keep chivalry alive.

Good times.

We walk through the door, and the familiar aroma of my mom's braised targon steak hits me like a tidal wave. My body pulls me through the living room toward the kitchen.

"So, Mom... How long til dinner is ready?"

"Let's see. Solo, how much longer on the steak?" she asks, pulling her device from her handbag.

"Eight more minutes until steak reaches optimal internal temperature," her Solo responds.

"You call your Solo... 'Solo'?" I ask, genuinely baffled.

She looks at me, a bit defensive. "Yeah... Don't you?"

"Uh, no. Neither does anyone else I know."

With her hands on her hips, she rolls her neck and says, "Well, you know I don't just go along with what everyone else is doing. I'm my own woman."

"Be honest. You didn't even know you could name your Solo, did you?"

"Nope," she admits without hesitation. "What do you call yours?"

"Lil' A."

"What's up, boss?" Lil' A chirps in.

"Nothing, Lil' A," I say, rolling my eyes.

"That's kinda neat. Can you show me how to do that on mine?" Mom asks.

"Of course."

"I wanna call mine Jackie L. Could I just say 'Jackie L' and the Solo will do what I want?"

"You can call your avatar whatever name you choose," I explain. "You can even change her voice, how she looks, what she wears... all kinds of stuff. Depending on how much freedom you give your avatar in the settings, it can even try to, like, represent what it thinks you're like. It's kinda funny to think about what a computer thinks of me sometimes, ya know?"

"What a computer thinks about you... Hmm," Mom says. Her mood turns somber.

"What's wrong?" I ask.

"You... want to have a seat while we wait?" she asks.

We walk over to the dining room table and take our seats. The table is already set, and the golden chandelier overhead is as brilliant as ever. Mom interlaces her fingers and props her chin up with her thumbs, elbows resting on the table.

"Jackie L. I'm Jackie Lore, Aiden. The wife of one of the hardest working and most respected people in Sanctuary. He's out doing speaking engagements with Zoe Withers, pioneering science that most people will never even begin to understand, writing books, making a huge impact on not just Sanctuary but the whole world. Sometimes, it just feels like he's doing everything and I'm doing nothing... I don't know. You were talking about what a computer might think about who I am... But it got me thinking about how *I* don't really know who I am."

Mom...

"I don't know why I'm telling you this, really. I guess because you asked. But sometimes I feel like I'm not good enough for him."

Wow.

"Have you ever told him you feel like that?" I ask. She raises her eyebrows and nods. "What does he say?"

She leans back in the chair. "He says the things a good husband should say. 'You're enough for me.' 'I couldn't do what I do without your support.' 'We just gotta find your thing like I found mine.'" She pauses and shakes her head softly. "I wouldn't have married him if he wasn't the type of man to say these things to his wife, but that doesn't make them true. I guess I just feel like I'm holding him back sometimes."

"How so?" I ask.

"Your dad is a remarkable man," my mom says with conviction.

Would Leia ever say something like that about me?

"I have no idea how he does all that he does," she continues. "Sometimes I wonder if he would have been better off with somebody more... on his level."

"Mom... Do you ever think that he and Zoe are... There's no easy way to say it. You think they... you think they might be involved?" I ask timidly.

This is not how I expected our dinner date to go. But... then again, maybe it's for the best. I doubt she has anyone else to talk to about this stuff.

"Those rumors are out there. I don't believe them, though."

"Have you... ever asked him?"

She laughs suddenly. "No, I haven't asked. And I won't. I don't need to. Like I said—your father is a remarkable man. One of the things that drew me to him and why he is so respected at work is because of his integrity. The name Richard Lore is like the gold standard in Laosi science because he doesn't cut corners. He doesn't let bias or what he stands to gain personally affect how he goes about his work.

"You can't fake being a man of principle like that. It's just who he is, who he's always been as long as I've known him. So, if he ever did cross the line, he wouldn't be able to hide it. It would be written all over his face as soon as he walked through that door. And if he could actually hide it that well, then we've got even bigger problems. But no, I don't think he's had an affair."

I exhale slowly and look down at the prints my fingernails have carved into my palms.

If Mom trusts him, so will I.

"Okay, I've decided. I got my counseling sessions every week at this time, so I'll just plan on coming over here each week after that. Sounds like you got some real heavy stuff you might want to talk through. And if you don't have anything to talk through, I'm sure I will."

"Maybe we'll just take turns," Mom says, chuckling.

"Right!"

"But that presents a problem," she says with a shift in seriousness.

"What's that?"

"I can't cook targon every week. I ain't got that kinda money! And clearly, neither do you!"

"C'mon, Ma!" I say, laughing.

She laughs, and for the first time in a while, her smile reaches her eyes.

"Speaking of counseling, though, how did your first session go?" she asks, her curiosity cutting through the moment.

"It actually went better than I thought it would. And I'd love to tell you all about it, but I've been watching the clock, and it's time to get that steak out," I say, talking over the loud growl of my stomach.

"All you're thinking about is eating, huh?"

"I just want to make sure I can focus while we talk. That's all," I reply with a grin.

She gets up from the table and heads to the kitchen, throwing a glance over her shoulder. "Mmm hmm. I hear ya."

I follow her into the kitchen, grabbing the pot with the rice while she takes the veggies. We set them on the table before heading back to fetch the pressure cooker and serving utensils.

"Were we supposed to be saving some for Dad?" I ask.

"Not really. The conference hosts are feeding their guests. But what do you mean 'save some?' I cooked a lot!"

"Yeah, but... let's just say it's been a while since I've had a home-cooked meal," I say.

Mom shakes her head while smiling and says, "Enjoy yourself, son."

"Oh, don't worry. I plan to!"

I start with a bed of rice pilaf on my plate, but I pause when an impossibly complex moral dilemma presents itself. The choice forces itself upon me, paralyzing me with the realization that my decision will define—or completely redefine—everything I've believed to be true about myself.

How am I going to plate these vegetables?

The bright red belrums Mom sliced have a sharp but sweet, mouthwatering aroma, perfectly paired with the slight bitterness of roasted advent root slivers. The diced herbs sprinkled on them smell fresh, like she plucked them from the backyard.

Veggies on the rice… or beside it? Decisions, decisions.

Putting them on the side feels more proper, letting each flavor shine on its own. But piling it together makes it so much easier to devour fast. One bite containing that juicy, tender steak with the broth soaking all the flavors into the rice and veg—

Get it together, Aiden! Eat like a civilized person. Veggies on the side.

Finally, the main event—the targon steak. I can't get it out of the pot, onto my plate, and cut into a bite-sized piece fast enough. The fork is halfway to my mouth. My senses attune to what's right in front of me. The anticipation builds and—

"Aiden!"

I freeze and turn to find the source of the voice, my fork frozen in mid-air.

"Dad?"

He stands in the doorway between the kitchen and dining room, slightly out of breath. As he catches some of his breath, I sense a deep concern and urgency in him.

What's going on?

"Aiden, Leia woke up!"

CHAPTER 9 – LEIA

"How long ago did you get the call?" I ask my dad, trying to fill the awkward silence and distract myself from the elevator's sluggish climb to Leia's floor.

"Thirty minutes ago, at most. I was just getting up to speak when Dr. Simon tapped me on the shoulder and told me," he says.

"So, then... What about your speech?"

My dad shrugs, a faint smirk on his face. "What about it?"

"I mean... people came from all over to hear your presentation. You could've just called me and let me know–"

"You don't know your father that well, do you?" Mom cuts in gently.

"Yeah, a speech? Zoe can handle that. I told her what was happening, and she sent me off with her blessing. Even if she hadn't, I would've been here. You've been waiting for this a long time, son. We wanted you to know we're here with you."

Wow.

"Thanks," I mumble, unsure of how to respond. "I wonder why didn't they call me? I'm her emergency contact."

This elevator is moving way too slowly. Leia's awake. She's finally awake. I have to see her. C'mon, c'mon, C'MON!

"Well, Dr. Merit was calling to tell me he broke one of the devices. He got so startled when she woke up that he dropped it before the procedure started. He wanted me to know the prototype I developed will need to be rebuilt," Dad explains.

"He was probably wondering if he still had a job!" Mom chuckles. "I know those things are expensive!"

"Yeah, maybe," Dad says. "But he wasn't calling about Leia's status—he was calling about the device. That's why I dropped everything to come tell you."

I drum my fingers on the elevator wall, a nervous rhythm that matches every floor we pass.

Patience, Aiden. If you want this too badly, who knows what could happen? You're almost there. It's okay. One step at a time.

"So Dr. Merit was the first person she's seen in three weeks?" I ask.

Uneasily, Dad replies, "Seems that way."

I shake my head. "It should've been me... Who's in there now? Dr. Larson?"

"Most likely. He hasn't called you yet, has he?"

I pull out my Solo and say, "Lil' A, any missed calls?"

"That's a negative, sir," he says back.

"Don't forget - you still have to show me that," Mom says.

I crack a small smile. "I gotcha."

"That probably means Dr. Larson is still examining her," Dad says. "I know you're anxious to see her, but I want you to have the right expectation. They still have protocols to follow."

"Thirty-sixth floor," the elevator announces cheerily as the doors slide open.

Will she be excited to see me? Will she be mad I wasn't there when she woke up like I promised? Does she hate me? Does she love me? Will she hug me? Will she say, 'Let's forget the past and focus on the future'? Does she even remember the past?

I stop and hug Dad tightly.

"You didn't have to drop everything. Thanks for being here," I tell him.

"Of course, son."

I hug Mom next, look into both of their eyes for a moment, and then I walk down the hall.

Dad says something about checking with the nurses first. I walk right past the nurse's station and overhear a debate about which brand of shoes is best for long shifts.

No need to interrupt such an important conversation.

I see Dr. Larson coming around the corner, but I don't stop.

"Aiden, hold up a sec–"

Too late. My hand's already on the doorknob. I push it open.

And there Leia sits, upright in her bed. She turns her head and locks eyes with me. My body freezes except for a single tear that slips down my cheek. She holds her arms out to me.

She remembers me. And she still cares.

I walk over to her and melt into her arms while being as careful as possible to avoid the IV line attached to her arm.

Does she remember the accident? Does she know why she's here?

Calm down, Aide. Relax. She's hugging you. That's what matters.

"Hey, Pretty Lady," I whisper.

"Hey, old man."

Still holding me, Leia looks past me to Dr. Larson, who stands respectfully just inside the door. She nods at his unspoken question.

"It's okay, doctor. He can stay for a bit."

"Then I'll leave you two to catch up," he says, exiting as quietly as he entered.

"Thank you," Leia says softly.

I hear the door click shut, but I stay where I am, leaning into Leia's embrace, undisturbed by Dr. Larson's brief intrusion. Her arms slowly loosen around my neck, and I take the hint. I sit carefully on the bed beside her.

"I-I-is this okay?"

She nods gently. "Yeah, that's fine."

"Good," I say. "So... how are you feeling, Babe?"

Leia exhales deeply, her shoulders shifting with the release. "Physically, I guess I feel okay. It was just a little weird waking up to Dr. Merit and all those probes. Imagine waking up from a strange dream, only to find some middle-aged white guy you've never met hovering over you with wires everywhere."

I can't help but laugh, though I try to keep it light. "That sounds awful!"

She giggles softly. "It wasn't great." Then she pauses, her expression growing thoughtful. "How long was I in a coma?"

I glance at the clock and say, "Three weeks, two days, twenty-two hours, and thirty-nine minutes."

Her incredulous look dissolves into a teasing smile. "You're such a nerd. Of course, you'd know the exact time."

"You surprised?" I ask, grinning.

"I shouldn't be." She shakes her head and then turns to gaze out the window. The city lights reflect in her eyes as she tucks a strand of hair behind her ear.

Why does she feel so unfamiliar right now?

"Well, obviously I'd know," I say, hoping to break through whatever's holding her back. "I was here every single day. I remember the moment because it was the same moment my heart stopped. Leia, I am so sorry for what I did to you."

She reaches towards me and places her hand over mine as it rests on the bed, her touch gentle. "I know you are. And I know you were here every day, too."

How does she know that?

"Did... Dr. Larson tell you?"

She shakes her head. "He didn't have to."

"How did you know, then?"

"I don't know... It's like I felt you there. Or something."

My heart skips a beat.

I knew it! The emotions I felt in her actually were in response to the things I said while she slept! But... how...?

"You felt me here? Okay, so... this might be the wrong question for me to ask, but what's it like being in a coma? Was there, like, a bright light you had to avoid or something?"

Leia looks down, pressing a hand to her stomach as it growls loudly.

"Oh, are you hungry? Are they not feeding you in here?"

She chuckles. "I don't know. I just woke up."

"That's fair," I say, nodding. "Hey, I wonder how long it will be before they discharge you. My mom made targon steak! You could come over for dinner if they let you out tonight."

Her eyes light up. "Mrs. Jackie's targon steak? That sounds sooo good right now. But is there any left? I know how you get with that steak."

"Right?!" I laugh. "But no, there's plenty left. My dad walked in right as I was about to take my first bite and told us you woke up. The next thing I knew, I was yelling at the carrier AI."

Leia laughs, the sound warm and familiar. "So you even put down your mama's steak? There must've been something really important going on."

"Of course. My fiancée just woke up from the coma she was about to describe to me."

Leia's laughter fades. "Apparently, my coma wasn't like most comas," she begins. "For me, it was... scary. It felt like I was here, but kinda not. Like I could feel you coming in every day, but I couldn't hear what you were saying. I could feel vibrations from your voice, but it wasn't like... I don't know. It's like I could... feel what you... meant? That's probably not making any sense, is it?"

"Not really," I admit, leaning closer. "But I want to understand. Keep going."

She fidgets with the edge of her hospital gown. "I guess... Intentions! I think that's the best word for it. I could sense your intentions. Not just yours, really. Everybody's! The nurses, the doctors... even other patients and their families. And sometimes, it felt like I left the hospital entirely, like I was in some dream world. And then, I was talking to—well, not talking, like... *feeling* to this... I don't know. It was like... But I know it couldn't have all been a dream because I would recognize you, and when my mom came in and stuff. I knew certain people. I recognized your vibrations."

"So, like, no sensory information, right? You couldn't

hear, feel, or smell me? Just my intentions?" I ask, trying to put together the scraps she laid out.

"Y... yeah... mostly. I was conscious, but also kinda not. Really, it was like that the whole time. I was never really fully asleep I don't think. So... that gave me a ton of time to myself. And I did a lot of thinking."

The flow of affection from her suddenly dries out.

"I thought about where I was and why I was there. The last thing that happened to me right before falling into the coma kept replaying over and over. Not just in my mind—it was like I actually saw it. I was reliving it. The anger on your face, the way you yelled at me, the fear I felt when your energy went all crazy? I relived that moment a hundred times. It's the worst thing I've ever experienced."

I grab her hands, holding them tightly. "Leia, I am so, so sorry. I never meant to—"

"I'm not done," she says, calmly pulling her hands away.

A shiver runs down my spine as her gaze hardens. A fierce but controlled fire burns in her eyes.

"Like I said, I thought a lot about where I was. When I couldn't figure that out, I turned my thoughts to how I got there. And not just where I was mentally, but where I am in life, Aiden. I know it's going to hurt you to hear this... but Aide, I'm engaged to be married to a man who can't stop hurting me. I'm just... I'm tired of getting hurt. But, like I said, I was talking to... or, maybe just thinking to... I don't know, but the point is, I guess I just–I finally started to believe that I'm worth more than what I've been allowing to happen to me."

Now I'm starting to wish Alexi's daggers were real. Or that I would've stayed in that swamp in Reality.

"You're right," I say, swallowing hard. "You're absolutely right. You deserve more than what I've been giving you. That's why I started going to counseling. My first session was today, and it was—"

"See, that's part of my problem." Leia's voice cuts mine off decisively. "Why did I have to get knocked into a coma before you went to counseling? When you broke my leg, I begged you to go. I pleaded with you, Aiden. But you always had your reasons and excuses for why it wouldn't help. You had a better way. You were just so *stubborn*. Do you remember when your powers slammed me into the wall in my living room—"

"Hey, come on." I stand abruptly, the intensity of the moment pushing me out of my seat. My voice wavers as I add, "Can you not say it like that? You're saying it like I meant to do that stuff to you. Like I meant to hurt you. You know the real me, Leia. I'm not that kind of guy. It was the Laosi in me that—"

"The Laosi," she repeats bitterly. "Right. It's always 'the Laosi.' Aiden... I just feel like you've pushed the problem so far outside yourself that you don't even see it anymore. You get to remove yourself from it like it's something happening to you instead of something coming from inside of you. But it's not."

Tears fill her eyes as she continues. "It's not happening to you. It's happening *to me!* I don't know what's in you that needs to change or how to change it. I don't know how Laosi works. But what I do know is that when I look at how you've gone about trying to figure this out, it looks like I'm the only one *desperate* for it to stop."

I start pacing, dragging a hand through my hair to try and burn off the restless energy.

We shouldn't be arguing.

"You're right," I say finally, my voice quieter now. "I... I could've done more. I *should've* done more. And I'm sorry. I'm sorry for all the ways I've hurt you. That's why I'm going to therapy now. That's why I'm trying to learn how to control it."

Her emotions shift in the space between us, the heat of anger giving way to the heaviness of despair. As the tears begin to spill down her cheek, she asks, "But... how long am I supposed to wait, Aiden? And how many more times will I get hurt between now and then? How much more of *my* life will I lose waiting for you to figure *yours* out? How many excuses am I supposed to make for the bruises that the man I love gave me?"

She pauses, the weight of her words hanging in the air and pressing down on both of us. With a trembling voice, she adds, "I don't even know what I'm going to tell my mom or AJ about how I ended up in a coma. I haven't told anyone what's really been going on all this time because I was worried about what they'd think of you. Or... what they might do to you. But what about what this is doing to *me*? Who do I go to for help dealing with this? I've got no one, Aiden. No one but the man who put me in this position."

"You can tell them," I say, my voice deepening. "Tell your mom, AJ—tell them the truth. You don't have to protect me. If I go to jail, then I just go to jail, I guess."

Exasperated, she shakes her head. "That's not the point, Aiden. The point is that this ring..." Her trembling hand moves to the engagement ring. My chest tightens as I watch her twist and slide it off her finger. "Wearing this ring represents a promise. A promise to spend my life with someone because I trust them to take care of me. But I don't trust you anymore, Aiden. I wish I could, but... I just can't! And that means that... I can't keep this promise."

No. No, no, no! Please, Leia! No...

She sets the ring down on the nightstand. All I can do is stare at it. I can't move. I can barely breathe. Time stands still as the future my mind knew is erased. I can't look at Leia. I can't handle her tear-streaked face or the grief in her eyes.

Eventually, I turn to the window, gazing through the glass into a well of memories with Leia. The night we met at a mutual friend's party—I wasn't looking for love, but I couldn't look away once I saw her. The first time we told each other "I love you" on a late night Solo call. The honesty in her eyes when she told me she wanted to start a family with me. The promise we made to face my problem together. The fireworks. The ring.

She's throwing it all away?

"I need you to hear this, Aiden," she says softly. "I don't

hate you. I really don't. I love you with all my heart. I wish that could be enough to fix this. But... where does my love for you end and my love for myself begin? I can't keep loving you so much that I neglect my own physical and mental well-being."

I turn back to her, my voice low as I ask, "Mental?"

She pauses, her shoulders quivering from suppressed emotion. "Yes. I can't tell you how much fear I've lived with since the first time your powers hurt me. Did you know that Laosi has a sound? It's faint, like a high-pitched hum. I didn't put it together until the night of the festival. Remember when I asked you if you heard something up there on the roof? It was the sound of your Laosi activating. And now, every time I hear it—whether it's in a movie or from someone rushing past—I panic. Because so many times in the past when I've heard that sound, I ended up getting hurt. I can't live like that anymore."

"Leia..." My throat tightens, and I struggle to find the words. "I didn't know it was like that for you. I didn't know I'd made it so hard just to live. I don't even want to say I'm sorry because I know it doesn't fix anything, but I am. I'm so sorry."

The anger has drained from her face now, leaving only sadness. But she's still guarded.

"I know you are, Aiden. But I need to live my life. I want to be free to share my gifts, to explore my passions, to really live. To be happy. But I won't be able to do that if I'm always scared, sad, angry or hurting. I have so much I want to give, but I can't give it if I'm frozen by fear or laid up in a hospital bed."

She takes a shaky breath and says, "That's what I kept thinking right until I woke up. I want to live, I want to do more, I want to heal. But I think... I think I have to do that on my own."

I go sit beside her again, taking her hand in mine. "Leia, we can work this out. I *know* I'm on the verge of figuring it out this time with this counselor. This is the turning point."

She looks right back at me, her eyes firm. "I've made peace with the decision."

"So... I mean, what about all the good times we've had?"

I ask, my voice softer now.

"I'm so thankful for those! I really am," she says.

I drop my eyes. "But we just... we had so many plans together, ya know? The places we were gonna visit. We said we'd see the frozen waterfalls of Infinity together. And the community center we wanted to establish." I pause, searching her face for any sign of hesitation. "I'm still paying for your License in Social Engagement and Improvement. I've even been working overtime and saving up to cover your rent while you were in here."

"And I'm thankful for that, too," she says. "But those were choices you made because you love me, not to keep me indebted to you. Besides, I didn't ask you to do that. And if you hadn't done it, I would've figured it out another way. That's what I need to do now. I have to figure out how to live my life my way. And I think that would be good for you to do, too."

The silence following her words stretches on, interrupted only by the monotone announcement encouraging patients to order dinner before the hospital kitchen closes.

I'm not giving up on us!

I ask, "So what would it take? What would you need to see from me to feel safe? Like, if I went six months or even a year without my powers going out of control, would that be good enough for you to want to stay with me?"

Leia sighs, her eyes softening slightly. "I don't know... I mean, I can't know. We don't live in that world, ya know? So I can't really tell you how I'd feel if we did." She hesitates, then adds, "Have your powers activated without you trying since I was in a coma?"

Why is she asking me that? Is she testing me?

If I say no, then maybe she'll...

The image of Dr. Larson's panic-ridden expression when I teleported on top of him flashes into my mind.

"No," I say firmly. "Nah, I've been good. And I'm getting better."

She smiles. "That's good. And I hope you keep getting better and better at it. Honestly, I'm confident you'll learn to control them one day. There's no doubt in my mind that you'll get there. I don't want to not be your friend unless you don't want that, which I'd understand. And... I don't know. Maybe when you reach six months, we can talk. If things change, then I'm open to changing with them. But I can't make decisions today based on what might happen in six months. I have to live in the here and now."

I look away again, my heart beating hot in my chest. "Then... I guess you've made up your mind. I'm sorry, again... for everything. But hey, you gotta do what you gotta do to survive. I can't be mad at you for that."

Her lips press together—lips that once kissed me with a love we thought was eternal—and she nods in agreement.

I sit there for a moment, my mind searching for the perfect words that might change her heart. But there aren't any. With a lump in my throat, I say, "I'll just leave, then, I guess."

I let go of her hand and walk out the door. As I pull it closed, Leia's voice stops me.

"Hey, Aiden?"

"Yeah, Babe?"

"Can you tell Dr. Larson he can come in to finish his examination?"

"...Yeah, I can do that."

"Thank you," she says.

I close the stained-glass door behind me and lean my head back against the red and blue echrin bird etched into the glass.

I thought this bird was supposed to be a symbol of hope.

I bury my face in my hands and stay there, unmoving. My unwillingness to accept the fact that Leia just broke up with me holds me at the door.

If she looks left, she'll see me here. Maybe if she sees how sad I look... No, I can't look back at her. That would make it too obvious. Wait, should I project sadness? No, pity isn't what I want. I'd rather she think I'm strong. So... head high, chest out? But if I look too strong, she might think I don't care. I should... I should probably just do what she asked, or she'll think I'm not reliable.

I straighten myself, gathering my resolve, and walk toward the nurse's station.

"Hey, Avaya," I say flatly.

"Hey, Aiden!" Avaya responds brightly. "How's our girl?"

Another nurse elbows her gently, a silent encouragement to pay more attention.

"She said Dr. Larson can come in now," I say, unfazed by Avaya's slip.

I head toward the waiting room, and my parents meet me halfway. Their hopeful smiles are soon replaced by furrowed brows and soft, worried eyes. My mom places her hands over her heart. My dad shifts his weight awkwardly, his gaze dropping to the floor.

Might as well cut to the chase.

"Well, she wants to call off the wedding and break up with me."

"Oh, Aiden, I'm so sorry to hear that, son. How are you taking that?" my dad asks. My mom places her hand gently on my shoulder.

"I... don't really want to talk about it right now. Y'all understand, right?," I say, backing away from them slowly. My eyes dart around, trying to get away from their concerned expressions. "Thanks for the ride here. I'm gonna just walk back home or something. I think I just need to be alone, ya know? At this rate, I'll probably just teleport home with my LETs anyway, so... I'll, um, see you guys later, then."

I turn around and start to walk away.

"Aiden!"

"Yes, ma'am?" I respond without looking back.

"I'm sorry to hear what you're going through. Take as long as you need. I'll be here whenever you wanna talk, okay? I love you."

I let that last sentence bounce around the walls of my brain for a second, trying to let it find a home in my heart. For some reason, it doesn't quite connect like I know it should. The sentiment is appreciated at least.

Maybe I should say 'I love you' back?

"I know you do," is what comes out of my mouth instead.

I continue walking away, barely catching my mom asking my dad, "Wait, he can teleport?" before I'm out of earshot.

Back to the elevator, down the shaft, and out the front door. I walk aimlessly through the still-crowded streets of downtown Sanctuary. I don't even know where I'm going. I'm just walking. Take a left. Another left. Then a right.

Who cares where I go, really? I just want to get away from people and their feelings.

Another right. Then one more. The streets here are just as well-lit, but not nearly as crowded. Fewer restaurants and businesses. It's quieter. My feet seem to have a mind of their own, leading me to a place where I can hear myself think.

She's breaking up with me... She's calling it off. She... doesn't want to be with me anymore. And it's all because of these stupid LETs. It's all because nobody can help me with them, so I kept hurting her. Ugh, what is so wrong with me? Why can't I stop? Why'd I even have to have them to begin with?

Since my will is so strong, maybe I want to hurt Leia. Is that it? Maybe I wanted her to break up with me and find somebody better for her?

I guess she's doing herself a favor, really. My life is going nowhere. I was just holding her back. At least now she'll be free to move on, pursue her dreams, and find happiness. I feel like I wouldn't know happiness if it hit me in the face right now. My life is just... I mean, what am I even accomplishing? Why am I even here? What's the point?

There's much more to your life than the opinion of one person.

There's that voice again!

Who are you?! Where are you? Why don't you just leave me alone? It's not like you understand me. No one understands me. Why doesn't everyone just leave me alone?!

It activates. And this time, I don't even care.

Another shockwave of green Laosi explodes out from my body in every direction.

At least no one's around to get hurt this time.

After the shockwave subsides, I fall to my knees in the middle of the street, panting. Lifting my head slightly, I notice a pair of white stilettos standing about thirty feet away. They belong to a silhouetted figure in the dark doorway of an abandoned building.

I follow the shadowy outline up to her face as she speaks, her voice calm and deliberate. "I can leave you alone like you asked... Or... you can commit to me, and I can teach you how to use your powers to do good. Your choice."

She slips back through the pitch-black doorway and disappears.

CHAPTER 10 – TESSA

"Hey!"

What the heck? Who gives somebody a choice and then walks away before giving them a chance to respond?

"Hey, wait up!" I yell at apparently no one.

Who is she? I didn't notice her before I... Did she see that shockwave?? She can 'help' me? Use my powers for good... What does she want me to...? She seemed like she knew me.... Her voice...

My mind and my body both struggle clumsily to regain their bearings. Once on my feet, they carry me across the vacated street without asking for my permission. With the doorknob already turned in my hand, I pause for the first time and try to slow my racing thoughts enough to consider what I'm doing. I let go of the doorknob and take a step back to survey the building.

Aiden, slow down. You have no idea where you are, and you're just about to walk into an abandoned building following a strange lady in the middle of the night?! Are you crazy?!

My only clue about my whereabouts is the faded sign that looks so tired of hanging through all the years of neglect that it just hasn't had the motivation to take the 10-foot plunge to the sidewalk. I can barely make out "Otto's Autos." I sigh.

What do I have to lose?

I open the front door and walk in, finding myself in a dimly lit, narrow corridor with a low ceiling that spills out into what used to be a huge automobile showroom 30 feet ahead. Along each wall, there are two doors, behind which I imagine are spacious offices. Faded pictures of Otto at groundbreaking moments of his career hang in between the doors.

How has a building this old remained standing? I bet Otto

sold his last auto at least 70 years ago. I remember my granddad telling me about TU's anti-grav carriers replacing combustion engines when he was a boy.

The second door on the left opens, and a spirited young girl walks out, bopping along her way to the front door. I assume she can't be much older than 12 given her plaid, knee-length skirt and white button-down shirt that is mostly covered up by her unzipped brown fleece.

What's a middle schooler doing out this late?

Startled by my presence, she freezes, but then she relaxes her body again while taking a good look at me.

What's she looking for? Did she see what I did out there?

Out of nowhere, she gets so excited that her pigtails bounce as she jumps and extends her hand for a shake. "Hi! You're here! Oh my goodness! I'm so happy to see you!"

I reflexively shake her hand while responding, "Ummm... You know me?"

"Ye— ummm, well, kind of. It's... Well, Tessa will explain, I'm sure. She's right over there. I'm leaving now, Tessa! Goodnight! Bye, Aiden!" She giggles and walks out the door into the night.

She knows my name and she's happy to see me?

"She knows your name because she's seen you three times. In dreams."

Tessa, I presume, stands at the end of the hallway, a relatively slender lady wearing a seamless, flowing purple dress with short sleeves. Her white belt holds the dress around her waist and matches her white hair and her high heels. Her stance and demeanor are at once elegant and classy, yet comfortable and inviting. I acquiesce to her beckoning wave and slowly draw closer to her until I'm fully in the open showroom.

"She's... dreaming about me? Why is...? Who is she? And who are you?" I ask, trying not to come off aggressively while seriously needing answers.

"Hello, Aiden," she says, her voice soothing and soulful.

She smiles and says, "It's so nice to finally meet you in person. My name is Tessa. I'm really glad you accepted my invitation."

"What're the chances I could get you to let me know what I've been invited to?" I ask, noticing that rather than answering my questions, her words give me more questions to ask.

"Take a look around," she says.

Following her suggestion, I glance around the well-lit showroom, observing the high ceiling and the glass wall that stands opposite the entrance, overlooking a wooded area.

I walked all the way to the edge of town. How long was I walking?

There are about 15-20 other people scattered around the vast open area. A guy and a girl, in their late teens or early twenties, lean on a counter and laugh as they chitchat out of earshot. Elsewhere, a guy in his late twenties manifests electricity out of his palms to the applause and encouragement of three others standing near him and watching. In a corner, an older gentleman is concentrating really hard on causing the metal in front of him to change its shape and phase of matter.

"What do you see?" Tessa asks.

Unsure of what she's looking for, I offer, "I see some people using their LETs and just hanging out."

She smiles and then looks at me intently. "Yes. And what do you feel?"

"I feel the peace in all these people. I'm kind of an empath, so it's really easy for me to feel what other people are feeling, so... Yeah, peace. And different levels of joy. Freedom. And—what is that? Love? Yeah, it's like a family feel or something like that. Everybody here feels like they belong."

That's really cool.

She takes a few steps toward me. Her shoulder-length white hair shifts a bit as she walks, and I realize it's been flowing in an intangible breeze the entire time. Her face looks young, but the white hair, the soulfulness in her voice, and her overall presence suggest otherwise. She practically exudes wisdom, dignity, and warmth.

"Right," she says graciously, though clearly not satisfied. Pointing her finger at me, she asks, "But what do *you* feel?"

"I don't know. I'm not... Listen, you said you could help me with my powers. Can you—? How do we...?"

Shouldn't I be the one asking questions?

"Again, not trying to be rude or anything... but who are you? And how did you know I have a problem with my LETs? And why does your voice sound so familiar? Why was that little girl excited to see me?"

She chuckles. "You have many questions, as do most people when they come to me. I don't usually give the answers people want, though, but I do guide them to what they need. Let's take your questions one at a time, shall we?"

Finally, some answers!

"As mentioned, my name is Tessa. I'm the one who oversees this 'family.' I knew about your problem because my Talent, to state it without arrogance, is complete understanding of the human soul. When I look at a person, I don't see their outward appearance as you see them. No, I see the energy of their mind, their will, and their heart as they work, interact, and conflict with one another. When I look at you, I see your entire soul. If you think a thought, I hear it. If you experience an emotion, I feel it. And if you desire something, I understand why you want it. That's how I knew you were curious about Talia's familiarity with you."

Then, she adds with a smile, "As far as why my voice is familiar—that's easy."

Though I'm sure she isn't moving her mouth, I hear her voice inside my head say: *You've heard it before.*

"Okay... That's not creepy at all." Suddenly, I want to use my hands or something to block her penetrating view. "But did you answer why she seemed happy to see me?"

Did she also pick up on the fact that I enjoyed being wanted for once?

"I did," she says with a twinkle in her eye.

Did what? Answer about Talia's excitement or notice me feeling flattered?

After a brief smirk, Tessa continues, "She's excited because she's had multiple dreams about you. Talia has a Talent for seeing the future, but she can only use her Talent while she sleeps. When unconscious, the mind has free reign, and subconscious realities can be accessed should the unconscious mind choose to go there. She has no control over it, but it happens on occasion. Your arrival here was her third dream about you."

"Third? Well, what were her first and second dreams about?"

Her facial features harden as she says, "She saw what's to come and your role in it."

Following her statement, there's an awkward pause, as if my next question isn't the obvious one.

"So... what did she see about me? Are you gonna tell me what's to come?"

"I'm not gonna tell you, actually."

"Well, why not?"

"You're not ready to know it yet."

"Wow. Okay, I hope you don't take this the wrong way, but you're really embodying every stereotype of every old, sage character ever. Could you give a little more than these cryptic answers that don't actually answer anything?"

This conversation feels like a waste of my time. I turn around and look at the door, considering my options.

But I know my feet won't actually move. This encounter feels too weighty, like it was supposed to happen. I couldn't leave if I wanted to.

Can we just get to the point?

She laughs and counters with, "Maybe there's a reason these wise old characters act that way. Let's reason together for a little bit. What do you think would happen if a child tried learning to run before he or she could walk?"

Where is this going?

"I'm not a fan of being called a child, but I'll play along," I say defiantly. "The child would never learn how to do either."

"Correct. The motor skills, balance, and coordination that get developed through learning how to walk get built upon to make running possible. The reality is that if you knew the future that Talia has seen, you would end up so anxious to bring it about that you would end up getting in your own way. You're desperate to fix what's broken in your life, but there are no corners to cut. Trust me, and let time run its course so that you can learn all that you need to learn along your journey. I could convince you of this by planting the idea in your mind, by the way, but it would be more useful if you learn it for yourself."

"Useful...? What am I going to be used for?"

"You misunderstand. I didn't mean you would be useful for me. I meant that learning my lessons for yourself would be useful for you when the time comes. I'm not here to control you. You're gonna have some tough choices to make for yourself in the future. But the future is not what you need to learn right now. You can't control that. You don't need to understand *what* will happen. What you need to learn first is that there is a *why* behind every what. Every effect is the result of some cause. And understanding the why will help you to deal with the what, especially when you can't control the what itself. That said, I want you to tell me something. Why... are you here?"

I put my hands in my pockets and shift my body weight from foot to foot.

Can we just skip to the part where she stops asking me all these questions and starts helping me with my powers?

"Because Richard and Jackie Lore had sex?" I offer.

Disappointed but not discouraged, she says, "I'm not asking about your life. I'm asking about your purpose. Your intention. Why did you come here?"

"Because you started whispering in my head."

What do you want me to say, lady?!

"True, I did do that. But you'll never grow if you see your actions primarily as the effect of external causes... So why are you here?"

Why does she keep asking me this question?!

Trying to maintain my composure, I answer, "Ok... so, looking internally, I'm here because I don't know how to control my powers, and I keep hurting people or breaking stuff with them. So I need someone to teach me how to get them under control. You said you could help me, so here I am."

Thoughtfully, she says, "That makes sense. That's a very logical answer. But remember, we're working on seeing the why behind the what. The whole why. Logic is never the only source of motivation in decision-making. The whole soul is *always* involved. Yes, the thoughts, but also the emotions and the desires, whether you recognize this or not. So what did you feel? What emotions led you to answer my call?"

Is it just me, or did everyone stop talking and start staring at me?

"I just told you... I want to stop hurting people."

"Oh, Aiden... I've never met anyone who has repressed so much of their own soul. It's no wonder your powers are out of control..."

She feels such a deep sadness. What's going on? Why is she looking at me like that? I don't like how she's making me feel. I should go before this—

"You're completely unaware of how much pain you live in."

"Pain?" I scoff. "I'm fine! You're the one who just got sad all of a sudden. I just need somebody to help me to control my powers, and I'll be even better!"

Why am I yelling?

She tilts her head to the side and squints while saying, "It's fascinating that someone so empathetic towards the feelings of others is at the same time so oblivious to what's going on inside himself. If you can't feel for yourself, then feel yourself through me."

Oh, no... It's activating.

She places her hand on my chest and calmly says, "It's okay. You can go there. I'm here with you."

"GAH!"

A bright flash of golden light radiates from the place where she's touching me. Then, I see myself surrounded by nothing. Darkness as far as the eye can see. An infinite black abyss with only swirls of red and purple floating around.

Just like when I put Leia in a coma.

I feel a warm stream descending down my cheeks.

Am I... crying?

The tears flow without the possibility of restraint, and I find this to be so strange. There are no conscious thoughts, but I'm inundated by feelings of loneliness, fear, sadness, and anger. And while they seem to have come from nowhere, these feelings are distinctly familiar.

These are my feelings. My pain.

How long have I been feeling all of this? I don't even remember what it's like to not feel like this.

No words can describe the sensations raging through my body as I watch vague images of memories that I thought I had long forgotten play out in the nothingness all around me. My dad scolding me as I sit in the corner with my head between my knees. The time my parents took my brother and sister to the movies and left me with the babysitter. A moment when my LET activated in grade school and all the kids were looking at me, scared. And a thousand other memories fusing into one another. It's suffocating. Between my heavy sobs and desperate gasps for air, it feels like the whole world is shaking apart.

Over the sound of my own weeping, I hear Tessa asking, "What did you feel that brought you here?"

"I... All my life, I've felt out of place..." I struggle to squeeze out between sobs. "I've felt like I didn't belong. I was too different, too inconvenient, too... I was a burden to everybody, and I kept hurting them. I was so lonely! I just wanted someone to just care about how I felt! But then... But then you called out to me, and it seemed like you really just wanted me to be here. You weren't scared of me or angry at me or ashamed of me... And I thought that for once in my life, I could just... I might fit in somewhere... That there would be... someone who understood me, ya know? That I... wouldn't feel so lonely... or so useless. I've always felt like something was wrong with me, so I came here... so you could fix me. More than just my powers, I want to know if you can fix me!"

Between gasps, I hear Tessa say, "That was *so* honest. Thank you for sharing with me. I want to share something with you as well."

The line between hearing and feeling blurs, and all around me, I perceive her to be saying, "Aiden. I *hear* you. And I understand your fear, your loneliness, your sorrow and your shame. You are *not* a burden or an inconvenience. You are worthy. And wanted."

These words... different people have expressed that they held similar feelings towards me in the past. But the depth of Tessa's intention embeds itself into my soul in a way that I've never known before. As her words resonate in my heart, I feel... a shift. The sensations in my body, though just as intense as before, now feel invigorating and empowering. It's the same way I felt the night of the festival when we flew up to the roof, and it's how I felt right before Leia threw us over the edge.

The abyss and its images of my life dissipate. I see Tessa's figure with clearer and clearer vision, and then the rest of the room we're in comes back into view.

I look at Tessa's face as she smiles at me and says, "I wish you could see yourself the way I see you right now. What are you feeling?"

"I feel... h-happy. I feel like a huge weight that I forgot I was carrying just fell off my shoulders."

That's when I notice that I'm actually looking down at Tessa.

"Wha—"

I'm floating!? Is this my LET? I'm using my powers but not hurting anybody! I'm not even scared of hurting anyone. It's like in my dreams! This is... amazing!

Tessa just laughs with a deep, infectious joy.

I hear her talking, and what she's saying would probably make more sense if I were to think about it harder. But right now, I'm having too much fun flying around the showroom. I can't let her kill my high.

Some of the others in the room watch me as I fly by, vocalizing their support. They're cheering for me! In particular, the guy with the electricity from before looks up at me with an air of respect. On my second lap around the showroom, I swoop by and give him a high five before flying back to the outer edge.

Tessa watches me fly with a smile on my face. I feel how happy she is for me, and that makes me really happy, too, which causes me to fly even faster. I want to know how fast I can go, but the fear of flying faster than I can control and crashing through the wall slows me down.

Okay, ride's over. Fun while it lasted.

I land in front of Tessa. I can tell she has more to say, and I want to listen.

"I see you're enjoying the freedom of embracing your Talents. It's truly amazing what our people are capable of," she says with such pride in her heart. "All this time, you've put so much thought and effort into trying to turn off your powers. But your problem was never that you couldn't get rid of your powers—your problem was that you were always trying to. You said that you wanted me to fix you. You asked me to tell you what I'd invited you to. Rather than fixing you, I invite you to join The Broken."

CHAPTER 11 – BROKEN

"Yo, Aiden! Your dad's calling," Lil' A announces.

"Ummm... Just... Send vitals and coordinates and tell him I'll call him back later."

"Aye aye, captain!" he says.

"You could've answered the call, ya know?" Tessa says warmly.

"Yeah... but, I mean, I'll just talk to him later. I know your time must be valuable."

She leans her head to the side ever so slightly, taps her temple twice, and responds with, "You remember the part where I see everything you think, feel, and want, right?"

Kinda hard to forget...

"Yeah, but... I'm good," I say.

With an unsettling gravitas, she says, "We have a lot of work to do."

What did I say? Am I that messed up? Even if I am—

"Speaking of work... You said 'I invite you to join The Broken.' Is that your group's name?"

Kinda sounds like a rock band name to me.

"That's one of the names. It's probably my favorite. It is, at least, the most honest. Take a walk with me."

Tessa turns and walks toward a collection of six chairs forming a semi-circle in one of the far corners of the showroom. She walks with her arms folded behind her back, and each step seems carefully planned. Wondering if her intentionality displayed a pattern I should follow, I analyze her steps and discover she avoids stepping on the cracks in the checkered tile.

As whimsical and light-hearted as this shows her to be, each member of The Broken holds so much respect for her in their eyes as she walks by them.

They would all die for her if it came to that.

We make our way to the chairs and take our seats. Once settled, she leans over toward me. I suddenly feel like the guest of honor at a private banquet, getting a premier screening of a rare art collection before the public exhibition.

"This is my favorite seat in the building. I just love to watch. Look at them, Aiden! Do you see the potential, the connection, the peace? This is why I've done all that I've done and will continue to do it... Just to sit back and enjoy them as they explore who they really are and what they can do."

She lets out a contented sigh with deep, immovable joy manifesting in her smile. Her chest rises as she inhales the moment, taking it inside of her and feeling it with her whole being.

She then shakes her head as if snapping out of a daydream and says, "Anyway, you're wondering about the name. I can tell you don't understand how LETs work, so I'll tell you."

"No, I get it. The mind, the heart, and the will, right? When one of the three is exceptionally strong, then—"

"No, remember, I told you Cambridge was only half right," she interjects firmly, her eyes flashing at me sharply. "It's not the strongest soul stream that manifests in what we call Laosi Empowered Talents. It's the most neglected. You see, there is a near limitless amount of energy in each stream, yearning, desperate to be accepted and channeled. Think, for instance, about when the rationale of your mind tells you that it's a bad idea for you to eat another one of those fruity Smackers but the strength of your will drowns that out because the thing just tastes so good... what do you think happens to that energy from your mind?"

I cock an eyebrow. "I honestly have no idea," I say. "I've literally never thought about it. This whole 'soul stream' thing is pretty new to me. I mean, I feel like it usually just goes away... but I guess we wouldn't be talking about it if it were that simple."

She raises a finger and says, "First law of thermodynamics—energy cannot be created or destroyed. It can only be converted. That energy does not simply go away. It cannot. It has a right to exist in this world, and ignoring the impulse doesn't change that. Instead, the mind uses self-criticism to convert its rational impulse into an emotive one. Now, you feel so guilty about taking that additional piece that you won't go back for another."

"Interesting..." I say, nodding slowly. "What does that have to do with 'The Broken'?"

"Everything!" she says, energized. "What happens to the soul stream that is constantly rejected and denied, even after converting its energy to another form? Aiden, in trying your best to keep a level head, your mind has become so dominant in your soul that your heart has been disintegrated from the unit. It speaks, it cries out to be heard, but you never listen to it. So your heart converts its impulse into volitional energy, but even then you suppress it."

She pauses, and her tone lowers as she continues with, "Somewhere along the way, you were told that emotions were extraneous to your soul at best and a hindrance at worst... and you believed it. Your powers are the manifestation of the desperation of your heart to be heard."

All I can do is turn my head from her. My eyes are filled with burning hot tears, and there's too much to digest.

"I'm going to ask you a question, but I want you to know that I already know the answer," Tessa continues. "What are you feeling right now?"

"I feel... I don't know. I feel ashamed. I feel so stupid. Like... I just feel sad, ya know? Is this for real? Like, this is why I've had so many problems—because I don't accept my emotions? That feels... it just..."

She gently places her hand on my shoulder. "That's why they go by 'The Broken.'" Gesturing with her other hand, she adds, "These aren't squeaky clean superheroes. There's a mix, but few of my followers are what you would call the cream of the crop. Med school graduates and tertiary school dropouts. Law enforcement personnel and released convicts. Divorced, unemployed—you name it. But do you know what they all have in common?"

"They all have LETs and you're teaching them how to use them?"

"That would be the what, but what's the why?" she asks with conviction. "The why is that, like you, each one of them came to a place where they realized what they've been doing on their own isn't working. These are men and women who have abandoned all hope of maintaining the pretense that they have it all together. These are troubled souls, and desperation has forced them to accept the reality of their situations, leaving no alternative but to seek out healing and connection. And they're finding it—together."

Abruptly, I say, "Wait... Back up. So you're saying I'm strong because I'm weak? I have powers because I lack control? I... That doesn't make any sense."

She straightens her posture but leaves her hand on my shoulder. She takes a deep breath.

"It makes perfect sense. You're having a hard time accepting it because you hold the notion that you're going to be the hero of your story. In your worldview, it's supposed to be your strength or cunning that will save you. That's a foundational misunderstanding of how life works. You'll learn that lesson soon enough, though. But for now, if you don't believe me, let's test my theory. Go back to the night you took Leia to the top of Sheridan Tower. What were you thinking when you were hugging her just before takeoff?"

I turn back to Tessa, letting a tear fall. I chuckle a bit, relaxing long enough to remember that moment as she lets her hand gently fall from my shoulder.

"I was thinking that she smelled really nice. She's not too quick to wear perfume, but I guess she wanted it to be a special night like I did. And it smelled good."

She smiles tenderly and says, "Okay, so your mind says, 'She smells nice.' And what did you want?"

I wipe my nose on my sleeve.

This is why I hate crying! I can barely breathe out my nose now.

"I guess I just wanted her to enjoy herself. And me, too. I wanted us to have a good time," I say, enjoying the nearly-forgotten, pleasant memories.

"Your will wanted a good time for the two of you. And what did you feel?" She leans in, as if the fate of the Broken hinges on this answer.

"I felt... I don't... really—"

"Happy?"

"Yeah, I guess so," I say, chuckling with an awkward gleefulness that I wish I could have held back. "Yeah, I was happy. I was happy that I was in the arms of the woman of my dreams."

With soft eyes, Tessa says, "Aiden, that's so sweet. It pains me to have to bring that up in light of the events of this evening, but we have to go there. And speaking of this evening, I want to take you back to when you were flying around the showroom here. What were you thinking?"

Without thinking, I stand up.

That struck a nerve. We've been through so much since that flight up to the top of Sheridan Tower. And now, she doesn't wanna be with me anymore. Now, she thinks she's better off without me. Now, she—

What was that high-pitched–? Oh, no! It's happening!

Calmly, Tessa says, "Aiden, I'm right here with you. Stay with me. What are you feeling right now?"

I start pacing in front of the semi-circle. "Ummm, mad."

She stands up, walks over to me, and grabs both of my arms, looking into my soul.

"No, Tessa... Get away! I don't wann—"

"Can I share something with you that you won't believe? It's okay to be mad at Leia."

"What? No! I'm... She's hurting because of me!"

"I know."

"Then how can I be mad at her!?"

"Because you are."

The painfully simplistic, yet irrefutable statement echoes in my mind a million times over. I stand motionless, arrested by the sound of three words I didn't know I'd been wanting to hear for years.

It stopped. She stopped it!

"How did you do that? You can stop my LETs?!" True hope enters my mind for the first time in recent memory as I consider the possibilities of living a life where Tessa can stop my powers when they activate.

If I could finally be free of this problem—

"No. I didn't stop you," she says, as soulful as ever. "You did. The question is how did *you* do that?"

"I dunno, I just... I've never been able to stop it once it got that far. That was great!"

"Yeah, I get that a lot," she says with a smirk.

She looks back at our chairs and then to me. I nod. Following her lead, I take my seat.

"You did that by giving yourself permission to feel," she explains. "Emotions like anger, sadness, or hope—you have to come to understand that they are not good or bad. They just are. They're just a part of what you're experiencing, and for the first time in who knows how long, you accepted your feelings. That's why you were able to stop it. The more we work together, the more common that will be, by the way."

"That sounds great, actually... But wait. So does that mean if we keep working together, I won't be able to use my powers anymore? Because, like, the better I get at acknowledging what's going on in my heart or whatever, the soul stream won't be as backed up anymore... so the powers will go away, right?"

Stroking her chin quizzically, she asks, "How would you feel about that? If your powers went away?"

I chuckle and dodge her piercing gaze. "Come on..." I tap my finger on my temple twice and say, "You already know, right?"

"You're catching on," she says, highly amused. "But you need to hear you say it."

"Do you just enjoy other people's suffering, or...?" She smiles but continues to press me to answer with her eyes. "I mean, I just kinda feel like it might be a bit of a waste to get rid of these powers before really seeing what all they can do. I feel... special now. I've never really felt like it was okay for me to have these powers, but now here with you, it feels okay."

"Just okay, or...?"

"Give me a break, lady! Jeez!"

She bursts into laughter, and I can't help but laugh as well.

Catching her breath, she says, "This brings me back to my point, though. Just before you began flying around the room here, what were you thinking?"

"What? Oh, um... I don't know. Nothing really. It was weird. That doesn't usually happen to me."

"I've noticed," she says with a twinkle in her eye. "And what did you want?"

"I... I guess I wanted to be accepted."

"Yeah... And what did you feel?"

"That's your favorite question, isn't it?" I ask.

She shrugs one shoulder. "Depends on who I'm working with. For Arvind over there," she motions to the guy who was bending metal earlier and then continues, "it's always, 'What do you think?' It's a counterintuitive idiosyncrasy of the human race, but it's often the case that people most need what they most avoid. So stop avoiding the question. What were you feeling when you opened your eyes and saw that you were defying gravity?"

"I felt... happy. Is it bad that I had forgotten what it felt like to be happy?" I ask bashfully.

"It is pretty bad, actually. But part of our work will be to forget what you have forgotten and to learn what you'll want to remember," she says.

What does that even mean?

"Notice the common elements in both your experiences with flight," she continues. "The contents of your mind were different—the fragrance of perfume during Sanctuary Achievement Week vs. cognitive silence tonight. The contents of your will were also different—enjoying the evening in contrast with being accepted. But the heart was the same—happiness. Aiden, when you get happy, you can fly! That's the most fun discovery I've seen one of my followers make in a long time."

"When you put it that way, it does sound pretty cool," I say with that same goofy chuckle from before. "But it doesn't seem like you think that will go away, even as I get better at accepting my feelings."

"It won't anytime soon, at least. Soul streams don't just want to be acknowledged. They want to be accepted or even channeled. I heard your heart screaming, *'Let me just be mad at her!'* That was all your heart wanted. At its core, the anger you feel towards her doesn't want to hurt her or anyone else, so it didn't need to be channeled into any tangible form."

So what about the times when I did hurt Leia? Was that because my heart wanted to...? Or just because I wasn't letting it out?

"There will be times, however, when your feelings want to motivate an action. In fact, as you become more aware of your feelings and give them the respect that they deserve, you're likely to see your powers activating more often. You're opening the floodgates, so to speak. Your challenge, among other things, will be to learn effective ways of channeling the energy of your heart. It seems that for you, a different emotion manifests a different Talent. I wonder if there's a theme that connects the manifestations...?"

"So you can help me keep my powers and learn how to use them without hurting other people or breaking stuff?"

"That's what I'm offering," she says compassionately.

"Well, then, where do I sign? Like, how do I join?"

Please don't let this be a dream! Or at least don't let me wake up before I learn more about controlling my powers.

"I love your enthusiasm, but I don't want you to jump at what I offer without considering what I require. Speaking of, one moment, please." She peers off into space, and her eyes change color. They glow like orbs of dark blue stained glass. She blinks twice and they return to normal.

"Talia made it home safely. She wanted me to tell you good luck." She pauses as she looks at me, and then says, "I'm telling her you said thanks and that you're excited to see what she saw."

"Hold on. I guess you already know that's what I would have said, but… privacy? Like, I didn't ask you to read my mind or say anything to her for me. That feels kinda intrusive," I say, alarmed.

"I understand why you feel that way. But I'm not going to sugarcoat it for you, Aiden. My access to your soul at all times is a standard condition of membership in the Broken—one of six."

I feel the muscles of my forehead tightening as I stare at her, eyes wide open. "I don't know if I'm entirely comfortable with that."

She looks back at me, her face emotionless.

She doesn't find anything ridiculous about asking for the right to invade someone else's privacy whenever she so desires?

"Who do you think you are, that I should just let you into my thoughts, feelings, and desires to do who knows what with that information whenever you choose?"

Without missing a beat, she responds with, "It doesn't matter who I think I am. What matters is who you think I am, and who you think you are. Am I the person who can help you do better with your life than what you've done with it so far, or can you handle it from here without my help?"

I don't even know how much time passes in silence

before she continues with, "If you feel like I'm asking too much or you don't trust me, then no one's keeping you here. I can see your will, but I won't override it. You're free to leave. We can part ways and go on with our lives. But I can promise you that you will never find a more dependable friend or source of support than you will find in me—if you can accept my terms."

I look down to the floor, hands clasped together with fingers intertwined in my lap. "You said there were six terms... right?"

"That's right."

"What are they?"

"I began with philosophies to govern the work that we do as an organization. Over the years, the members noticed themes in my teaching and condensed my principles into these six concise rules," she says, pointing to a poster on a wall near us.

She watches my reaction as I read the Six Tenets of Tessa:

1. Yield to Tessa.
2. Accept your weakness.
3. Help when you can.
4. Wait for the light.
5. Embrace the brotherhood.
6. Hold your enemies blameless.

"Don't expect to learn them all at once," she says. "There's a lot to take in. It's going to be a process. Be patient with yourself. And that part about embracing the brotherhood includes the fact that other members of the Broken will share what they've learned with you to help you along the journey."

Her eyes do that dark blue glow again, after which she says, "I've got a young guy in mind who's willing to help you get started." She stands up in anticipation of the young guy's arrival, looking fondly at him as he approaches. I look over to the right and see the guy with the electrical LET making his way over to us.

"Tirrell, meet Aiden. Aiden, this is Tirrell. I'll let you two get acquainted. Tirrell, can you show Aiden around?"

As Tessa turns to walk off, I stand up to shake the guy's hand as a courtesy, but I make sure Tessa hears me say, "I didn't say I agreed to the terms."

She pauses, and then turns back to me. "What if this is your destiny?"

"What if I don't believe in destiny? What if I believe in choice? As in how you chose to reach out to me and bring me here because you wanted me to join you in whatever it is that you're doing. If you want to help me with my powers, then I'd really love that. But I want to be able to choose for myself how I live my life."

She leans her head to the left as I speak, opposed but not offended. With concern in her voice, she replies, "If the life you have lived so far is the result of your choices, then how well has your belief in choice served you? I see a life for you that is more fulfilling than what you even know how to dream of. And I can lead you into it, but only if you're willing to let go of your attempts to control your life. I get that you want to be free to make your own decisions. With me, you can become free to choose to surrender your freedom to choose."

Who in their right mind surrenders their freedom to choose?

"Tirrell is a good resource who knows a lot about what we do, as well as why and how we do it. He'll be more than happy to help you process it all and answer any questions you have. There are some other matters that require my attention at the moment. I've really enjoyed our time this evening, Aiden. Let's do it again soon."

And with that, she walks off. There are so many questions bubbling up, I don't even know which one to ask. I stand there, dumbfounded, watching her walk towards another group of people who usher her into an office room on the side of the building.

"So, I'm guessing you're not sold yet, huh?" Tirrell asks with a sympathetic smile.

"Nah, man. She whispers in my head, tells me she can help me manage my powers, and then drops a bomb on me that in order to get her help, I gotta give her my firstborn child or something. Like, seriously?"

Laughing, he says, "I don't think those were quite the terms… but I got you, man."

"Okay, that may have been a slight exaggeration… but come on, man! Are you really cool with her being able to just roam around in your soul whenever she feels like it?" I ask, seeking validation for my reluctance.

"Honestly, I know it may be weird to accept, but I am. I mean, I've seen Tessa and the other members bring a lot of people into the Broken. Some join the Brotherhood and stick around, and some don't, so I get why you're feeling iffy. But me on the other hand? That's a different story. My parents have been working with Tessa since before I was born, so I'm pretty much a lifer. I've been following The Six since I was in utero, so I'm used to it."

"Really?" I ask. "How old are you? If you don't mind me asking, that is."

"28. You?"

"24. I'm just trying to get a read on how old Tessa is. She doesn't look anywhere near old enough to have been working with your parents."

"Yeah, nobody really knows how old she is. Isn't that weird? But to answer your question, whatever she sees when she looks into you… she wouldn't share anything if it's negative. I mean, she wouldn't, like, try to use it against you or nothing like that. That ain't her game. I know that if she sees something in me that ain't good, she'll help me work on it. And she'll only share it with someone else if she thinks they can help. I mean, it takes some getting used to, but at the end of the day, it just really depends on if you want to grow or not. She does it out of love… For real, man."

"If you say so."

Tirrell shrugs his shoulders and says, "It really comes

down to trust. I know trust is usually earned, and earning that trust is normally the job of the person asking for it. But my guess is you've never really trusted before. Have you ever trusted anyone with everything? Like, nothing to hide, hate me or love me, here I am?"

A shiver runs down my spine at the thought of being so exposed. "What?! Of course not. That sounds crazy."

"I hear that," he says. "Some people don't deserve the trust they ask us for, and that's on them. But if we're not willing to give trust to people who are trustworthy, who actually care and want to help us, then that's on us. And we're only holding ourselves back by not receiving the help they want to give us."

"I'm gonna be real honest with you, Tirrell. I can't tell if that was profound insight or cult programming."

He laughs and says, "Hey, man, you got every right to be skeptical. I can promise you we're not a cult, but that's exactly what someone in a cult would say, isn't it?"

"Pretty much," I say, laughing at the dilemma.

"I get it," Tirrell sympathizes. "What questions can I answer for you to help ease your mind? I'll answer any question honestly and thoroughly, and I can show you the next steps if you decide you're in."

"I'm still not sure about that decision... about any of this, honestly. Before I walked through that door, I asked myself, 'What do I have to lose,' ya know? Anything has to be better than how it's been. But at the same time, she's asking a lot," I say, annoyed.

"It's definitely a commitment. And most people just walk right back out that door. The ones that stay, more times than not, are the ones who are out of options. The ones who have made too big of a mess or are scared they will make an even bigger mess. I'll be real with you, Aiden—that's the kind of vibe I'm getting off of you. Maybe you'll decide that the Broken isn't for you. But if you don't mind me asking, bro, what brought you here?"

Tirrell's genuineness and compassion are undeniable, but the sacrifice required for The Six is more influential at the moment.

Surrender my freedom to choose? About that...

"That's... a pretty long story, actually." I pull out my Solo and check the time. "It's getting pretty late. I gotta get back to my side of town before the carriers stop running."

Tirrell says, "We can give you a ride."

"Eh, no thanks. I'm just gonna head out. Good to meet you, though, bro."

I turn and walk towards the door. I hear Tirrell calling after me, "Likewise. Hey, I'll be here tomorrow, too. What time are you free?" I keep walking.

Don't hold your breath.

When I make it out the front door, I pause, listening to the sounds of nature all around me. I don't know how I didn't notice before, but just behind Otto's Autos is the boundary of the Yra Forest Zone. The wind whistles through the branches of the Sardonis trees, causing the crystals that grow on them to clink together and emit low, hypnotic reverberations. I take in the soft melodies and the scent of the woods for a moment while gathering my thoughts about everything I've been through today.

"Lil' A, call Dad, audio only."

"No prob, Bob. Calling Richard Lore."

"Hey, son. How are you?"

"Hey, Dad. I'm, um... I don't really know right now," I say.

"Okay. Would you like to talk? Are you still near the Yra Forest? I can come pick you up."

"You don't have to pick me up. I'll just catch a carrier. I was wondering, though. Since I'm in JM, do you think I could just crash with you and Mom tonight? That way I won't have to ride all the way back to RE."

"We'd love to have you, son! Your mom and I didn't know where you went after leaving the hospital. I'm glad you sent me your location, but what were you doing over in JM?"

"Yeah, I just went for a walk to try to clear my head. Then I ran into a... well, I guess you could say an acquaintance. At first, I thought they wanted to be there for me, but then it felt like they mainly just wanted something from me. I don't know. I don't really want to talk about it."

My dad pauses and then says, "No pressure."

"Thanks... And thanks for letting me stay with y'all. I just don't want to be alone tonight."

End Part 2

PART 3 – REDESTINED

CHAPTER 12 – QUESTIONS

Two Months Later

"You ready to get to it or what?" Tirrell asks, shifting into his fighter stance. I shift the weight of my bookbag on my shoulder.

"I don't know, man... I just ain't really feeling it today. I mean, I hate feeling like I'm letting you down, but... I'm just out of it. I'm sorry for bringing you all the way out here on a Saturday like this. I don't wanna waste your time."

Tirrell relaxes his posture, compassion softening his stance. "Nah, man. I'm just glad you came back, bro. Showing up is never a waste of time. You're fighting for your growth. I'm here to support you."

"Thanks."

"No problem, bro. Besides, I remember when I started. It was intense! I already knew most of the stuff you're learning now from my parents, but it was still a lot just physically. So I give props to anybody who keeps showing up during those first couple of weeks."

"Yeah," I interject, "but it's not just that. The training itself is a lot, but I'm cool with that. I need that, ya know? I'm ready for it. It's more so some of the personal stuff I got going on. Mainly with Leia. I've only talked to her twice since she woke up, and it never really played out how I thought it would."

"Tell me about it, bro. You wanna sit down?" He motions to the ivory counter in the middle of the room, which juts out from the dark wood pillar supporting the large Holo screen above. We walk over together and sit down beside each other. "How you feeling?" he asks, turning his body toward mine.

"That's the thing, man," I begin. "I feel kinda... numb.

Detached. When Leia and I were together... she was my everything. You know how some people have their careers, their kids, or maybe hobbies and passions that they pour themselves into? I feel like a balanced life would mean having a bunch of things you're really involved in. But my job is super boring, I don't have kids, and I'm still trying to find my place in the world. But being with her felt like home. She motivated me to keep striving, to do better for myself, to be a better person. Now, it just feels like I'm drifting, looking for a purpose in life." I squint at him, hoping he can relate.

Tirrell nods slowly. "That sounds tough, man. It sounds like what you two had was really special. If enjoying that connection with her was your everything like you said, then I can see why your life would feel out of balance, especially with her ending it like that."

His sympathetic approach emboldens me to delve deeper. "But here's the crazy part. It wasn't just the enjoyment that was motivating me. I've taken a step back, and I'm realizing the main thing driving me when we were together... was fear. I wanted her to like me as much as I liked her. To be as happy with me as I was with her. So every time I hurt her or made her mad, it pushed me to work twice as hard to be better, to make her happy. I think I was scared of her disapproval. And I'm not saying that fear was a good motivator, but now that she's cut things off... at least I had a motivator."

Tirrell sits quietly, giving me space to hear what I've just said. I drum my fingertips on the counter, filling the silence with rhythmic taps. Ta-ta-ta-tap, ta-ta-ta-tap!

Please say something...

"For someone who's Heart Disintegrated, that was very self-aware, my friend. And honest. Sounds like your first couple weeks of training have been really fruitful. How do you feel after saying that?"

I chuckle and glance around the big, empty space. "To be honest, I feel better getting it off my chest to someone who might actually understand. I mean, I talk to my therapist, but... he doesn't have LETs to deal with. I don't know if he really gets it, ya know?"

"Well, you're in good company here. You're exactly where you should be. For the record, I don't think Leia's done with you yet. But, either way, I hope you'll find purpose in what we're doing."

I nod. "I hope so, too. But, hey, enough about me. What about you? How's the whole 'soul reintegration' thing working out for you?"

He leans back in his chair, laughing as he reminisces. "Whoo! It's been a journey, for sure."

"Yeah? Tell me about it. You said you were practically born here. I didn't want to say anything earlier, but I was surprised you have LETs. I mean, if your parents are so tight with Tessa, I would've thought you'd be fully integrated from the start." I pause to read his body language. "I hope I'm not crossing any lines. People say the same thing about me, being the son of Richard Lore. I guess I just wanted to understand more."

Tirrell shrugs. "Nah, I'm an open book, bro. So, I told you my parents supported Tessa and her mission a long time ago. They were so on board, they started a satellite branch of the Broken in the Cestria side of town, where we're from. You can imagine starting something like this takes a lot of work—helping people with LETs, handling the admin side, all that. My parents saw leadership potential in me early at home with my younger siblings. So they started giving me more responsibilities while they got the place up and running."

I point to the colorful character on his black shirt. "Is that where Baby Za-Za comes in?"

He laughs. "Bro! That's all my younger sister wanted to watch as a toddler. She knows how much I hate that show, so she bought me this for my birthday, trying to be funny."

I shrug. "Hey, man, there's nothing wrong with being a grown man who's into Za-Za. She's a cute little praytor."

"I have *never* been *into* Za-Za," Tirrell says, laughing

harder. "If I was, I wouldn't have cut the sleeves off to use this as a workout shirt. Ugh! Now you got that annoying theme song stuck in my head!"

His demeanor shifts as he continues. "It's really just another example of how it never mattered what I was into."

I guess reintegration doesn't mean the pain goes away.

"My parents weren't big on asking me what I wanted to do, so after a while, I just stopped telling them. Give that scenario about six years of rinse and repeat, and bam! You get a Will Disintegrated Tirrell manifesting electrical energy with his Laosi."

He looks down at the floor for a second, his fun-loving composure completely gone. "You also get a burned-down house and years of shame. Because of the property damage, CLU started pushing me into the LIST process, saying I had to give up my powers or give up my freedom in Atheria. My parents reached out to Tessa about it, and somehow she convinced them I could work things out with her. That's when I met Tessa for the first time. I still help my parents out occasionally, but I spend most of my free time here, learning everything I can from her. She saved my life, man."

I nod slowly, even though I don't fully understand. "What do you mean she saved your life? Would it have been that bad to go through LIST? I actually did LIST. It just didn't work for me."

He leans an elbow on the counter and props his head on his palm. "I guess it wouldn't have been the end of the world. Most people go through life without LETs, so it can't be a bad thing. But to be one of the ones who can experience a life like this and have to pass that up? I didn't want to lose even more of myself, ya know?"

"Interesting..." I say, detached. "You talk about your LET like it's a gift. It's not like I don't want to see mine that way. But when I look at my powers, all I see is pain."

"So when you say 'pain'... are you talking about the pain your powers have caused, or the pain that caused your powers?" Tirrell asks.

"I'm not sure I understand the question."

"Well," he says confidently, "right now, you're just learning about Laosi and some basic self-mastery techniques. But once you start Dynamics classes, you'll dive deeper into the tough moments in your life that got your soul streams out of whack."

I shake my head. "That's the thing, though. My life was actually really good. I grew up in a stable home. My dad worked hard in a field he loves, providing for us while becoming a role model for the whole Sovereign State. Both my parents were always there for me. I didn't get bullied in school or anything like that. My life was as normal as they come. That's what makes me feel pathetic!"

Tirrell strokes his chin thoughtfully. "I'll bet there was a lot of pressure growing up as the son of Richard Lore. But what I really want to know is this: what made you stop believing it was okay to have feelings?"

"What?" I ask reflexively, though I know exactly what he means.

"I'm just saying..." He turns his head toward the massive windows at the back, gazing out at the forest behind the building. I follow his gaze, noticing how the wind stirs the trees, making their green and red crystals sway beneath the partly cloudy sky.

"If you turned your emotions off early on," Tirrell continues, "that might explain why you can't see the pain in your own life story. It's so easy for you to see the pain you've caused, Aiden, but you don't seem to have much compassion for yourself about the pain you've gone through. You need to learn something: hurt people hurt people. You wouldn't be here if it wasn't for pain in your life."

He turns back to me, blinking.

Were his eyes... blue?

"Dude... Did you just... Was Tessa, like, talking through you just now?"

"I hope so," Tirrell says.

"Bro, that is so weird to me! You're cool with that?"

"I am, actually. If there was someone wiser than you who could help you make good decisions in situations you've never faced before... wouldn't you want to ask for help whenever you needed it?"

"Well, yeah... it's just..." I glance across the showroom, listening to the faint chirping of birds outside as the breeze rustles their feathers. My thoughts drift to Tessa.

Where is she right now? What's she doing?

"I still don't really get her, so it's hard to trust her. Like, who demands full access to someone's soul at all times? And why is the number one rule of her community to yield to her? It just seems like a lot..."

"Yeah... I won't lie and say it ain't. But... this is kinda hard to put into words, but my life just makes more sense when I follow the Six," Tirrell says.

"That seems weird to me. Ignoring your will leads to uncontrolled electric powers, but the number one rule you live by is ignoring your will?"

"Well, there's a big difference between ignoring and yielding," he says. "And that difference? That's where freedom and control are. That's what makes the Six so powerful. It's about accepting what's going on in your mind, heart, or will for what it is and then channeling that into something good. 'Yield to Tessa' means I accept what I want, but I consciously choose to yield that desire into something better. Tessa helps me peel back the layers to figure out what I really want."

I want to pity him for needing someone else to help him figure out what he wants... but I'm no different when it comes to my own feelings. Maybe we're all a little broken in our own way. I guess I do belong here.

Tirrell continues, "And when it comes to 'accept your weakness,' that's a rule of the mind. It's about being aware of who you are and what's happening around you. You try to understand your small part in this big world. You think for yourself without judging yourself, and you learn to ignore other people's criticisms about what you can or can't do."

He's gesturing a lot. Who gets this hyped about rules?

"And then there's 'wait for the light.' That's about the Heart. You acknowledge the darkness or pain you're dealing with. Don't deny it. Own it. But while you sit with that pain, you also wait for the light. You believe in hope. You let yourself feel it, even while you're struggling, so the darkness doesn't consume you. Some things might be bad, but not everything is, ya know? At least, that's how I understand the first three of the Six."

He watches me, giving an opportunity to respond and show whether what he said has made any sense to me.

"I see... I still have a lot to learn. But one thing doesn't make sense—why are we doing martial arts training if we're supposed to 'hold our enemies blameless' and 'help when we can'? Why are we learning to fight?"

Tirrell doesn't miss a beat. "Two reasons, as far as I can tell. First, training in martial arts has always been used as a means of growing in discipline and self-restraint. And let's be real—most of us could use more of that, or we wouldn't be here, right?"

I chuckle. "Fair point."

"Second, it helps you get familiar with your body. That way, when you use your abilities, it feels natural—whether it's for defending yourself or helping someone else."

Does he realize he's dodging the actual question? He's definitely been spending time with Tessa.

"Okay, but how does that square with all the 'hold your enemies blameless,' pacifist talk? Feels like a contradiction if we're training to use LETs against people."

Tirrell leans forward. "I get what you're saying. Let me break that down. 'Hold your enemies blameless' doesn't mean you don't have enemies. It means you stop them from hurting you or anyone else without making it personal. You're not out for revenge. You trust the authorities to handle justice, but you forgive the person as an individual."

"Well… What if you don't have any enemies?"

His tone shifts, growing more serious. "You asked me that earlier this week. Remember?"

"Yeah, but my life's always felt pretty simple. I don't have some big cause worth fighting for or anyone opposing me."

"You might not, but as a member of the Broken, we do. Did Talia ever tell you what she saw about you?"

"Nah. I've been hoping to run into her again, but no luck since that first night."

Tirrell's face darkens. "She saw a war, Aiden. Apparently, it's been a cold war for a while, but it's starting to heat up."

"A war?!" I blurt out. "Isn't that what Tryon United is supposed to stop? Why are we training for a war? And who are we fighting?"

I knew it—they want me for something. Aiden's got powers. Let's recruit him for the cause! So much for just helping me out.

Tirrell raises his hands like he's trying to calm me down. "Maybe calling it a war was a little dramatic. It's not Sanctuary versus Modernity or anything like that. But you remember Sympathy's former president, right? What was his name again?"

"Di-Dionis?" I offer.

Tirrell snaps his fingers. "That's it—President Dionis. Remember how he was leading in the polls, and then out of nowhere, he dropped out a week before the election?"

"Yeah, he said it was to spend more time with his daughter or something, right?"

You said you wanted a purpose. Is this what you had in mind? A war?

"We've got a guy in Sympathy, a User like you named Allonz. He can sense the will the way you sense the heart. He's also a poli-sci nerd, so he went to the concession speech since it was such a big deal. The third president Sympathy has ever had choosing not to extend his term? Well, our friend Allonz got close enough to the president and his daughter to read them, and he said Abrina—the daughter—didn't want her dad to step down."

"Huh? Hold up. That doesn't make sense. I thought they said Mrs. Dionis passed away and Abrina was struggling. Being in a crowd like that, it's easy to misread an emotion or desire. Happens to me all the time. Please tell me the Broken isn't prepping for war over a possible misread."

Tirrell's jaw tightens. "If that was the only thing, I'd agree with you. But there's more. We did some digging and found out one of Dionis' security sentries was killed."

"I didn't hear about that."

"Exactly," Tirrell says. "Come on, man—one of the president's bodyguards turns up dead right after he suddenly steps down? And no one's talking about it?"

"Yeah, that's sketchy," I admit.

"Right. And Allonz said he felt Dionis wanted protection, not more time with his daughter. There have been a few other strange little incidents that are really hard to ignore if you put them together."

"I get that it's suspicious, but why not take it to Tryon United or CLU?" I ask.

"First off, there's no CLU in Sympathy. They're still restructuring politically as a Sovereign State. Tryon United's been trying to get more influence there, but it's been an uphill battle for them. And without CLU, Sympathy handles LETs differently."

"How so?"

"Well, you have to register as a User and specify your ability. And let's just say any unsanctioned use of powers is… frowned upon. If our people had told the government they found the sentry's body, they'd also have to explain how they found it. And that involves Talents."

"I see," I say, eyebrows raised. "I don't think I've ever been so glad to have been born in Sanctuary in my life."

"Right? But there's more. We didn't tell anyone because we believe there are plants within TU. We don't know who they are or how many, so Tessa wants to keep things quiet for now. We're preparing for the time when this conflict becomes unavoidable... which, honestly, could be any day now, especially since you showed up."

I sigh. "Bro... I still don't get why I'm so central to all this. It feels like my presence here is expected to change the world or something. That's why I really have been trying to talk to Talia to see what this 'fulfilling life of destiny' is supposed to be about."

Tirrell places a hand on my shoulder. "If it helps, I don't think it's about you specifically. It's just the timing, man. And with your ability to manipulate distance based on emotions? I'm glad you're on our side. How many Talents have we identified so far?"

He's... glad I'm here?

"Well, there's flight, which is tied to happiness. Teleportation, which I think comes from loneliness—or maybe something else? Still figuring that one out. Then there's that force field I made the other day when I got scared. Oh, and this weird attracting telekinesis thing, but I don't know how to control it—stuff just starts moving toward me sometimes. And, of course, the force blasts from anger."

"There are few people for whom the term 'Laosi Empowered Talent' fits so well. You're seriously talented, bro. I might even be jealous if my lightning powers weren't so amazing."

The dead-serious look on his face is hilarious. I burst out laughing, and so does he.

Tirrell's a good guy, and he's really helped me feel better today. I almost didn't notice how much lighter I feel compared to when I walked into Broken HQ this morning.

As we settle down, Tirrell adds, "But it seems like you have another Talent, too. You're an empath. So... two LETs?"

"Yeah, I guess so. Is that normal? Have you met anyone

else in the Broken like that? Or am I just that broken?"

He pauses. "I can say you're unique. But I don't know everything about LETs. Maybe ask Tessa next time you see her."

"Not a bad idea. But what about this war? Do we know who's on the other side or what they want?"

I joined the Broken to keep my powers away from people. Now they want me to use them? When did I sign up to be a soldier?

"Unfortunately, we don't know much. And the other side is doing a good job of keeping us in the dark. It could be anyone."

I lean back and cross my arms. "And Tessa wants us to fight them?"

"If it comes to that. Remember the third rule—help when you can. We have these abilities. We should use them for good when we can. Not everyone here is a fighter, but with powers like yours and mine, we can make a bad guy think twice before deciding to hurt somebody. I don't think of it as fighting. I think of it as protecting. But if that's not for you, no pressure. We can just keep training for self-control."

I could stay on the sidelines, but what if I could be part of something bigger? What if this is my destiny—if that's even a real thing? They're not forcing me. I could always quit if it gets out of hand.

"You're right. If we've got these powers, we should use them to protect people. I want to be part of that. Maybe even help train new recruits someday. That feels way more meaningful than anything else I've got going on."

Tirrell smiles. "I like your enthusiasm. I can see you leading others one day. I'm glad you came back, man."

"Me, too."

Maybe this is my choice. And my destiny.

"So? You feel up for training? We won't be any good at defending others if we can't defend ourselves, ya know?"

"True. Let's do it!"

"After you."

We walk to an open area of the room and take ready

stances. Tirrell says, "First thing to know is your enemy won't be as scrupulous as you. They'll have no problem hurting people. Our goal is never to kill, but if you go easy on them, you'll probably find yourself in trouble. I recommend starting powered up—maybe not your strongest attack, but something reliable that you can access quickly."

"That's the thing," I say, squaring up with him, shaking out my hands and bending my knees. "I've never really been able to access my abilities on command. I just... go with the flow."

"I get that, but we don't know who we're up against or what they're capable of. You need something strong and easy to tap into. For me, it's easier. I'm Will Disintegrated; all I have to do is want something bad enough, and sparks start flying. For you, it's trickier. What are you feeling right now?"

"Excited... nervous... confused?" I offer.

"Hmm. I don't think any of those are going to help you out. Let's dig deeper. Imagine I'm your enemy. I'm here to hurt your mom, dad, sister, or brother. Or—please forgive me for saying this—imagine Leia is—"

That's it.

I thrust my palms toward Tirrell, and a translucent purple force blasts out. The crackle of electricity buzzes in my ears, and just as quickly, Tirrell disappears.

Where'd he—

A hand grabs my arm. Before I can react, a surge of electricity shoots through me.

"Aaagh!" I yell, kicking at his midsection to break his grip. He dodges the blow, jumps back, and charges again, sparks flying from his hand. He rushes back with unavoidable speed, so I cross my arms and close my eyes, bracing for impact.

Instead of feeling pain, I hear a muffled thud. Opening my eyes, I see Tirrell on the other side of a pale green force field. He smirks as he circles the bubble, inspecting it. As he relaxes his stance, the force field disintegrates.

"Not bad. Not bad at all!" Tirrell says, smiling.

I roll my eyes. "I don't know. I feel like I chickened out. I closed my eyes and hid."

"You could look at it that way. But that fear you're complaining about is what would have what kept you alive if I was a real enemy. Your emotions aren't bad, Aiden. I guarantee you'll continue to struggle with your powers until you accept that they're here to help you."

"That's what Tessa keeps telling me," I groan.

"I can teach you fighting techniques," he continues, "but your real training has to focus on ending the internal fight between your mind and heart. When two parts of your soul fight for control, the whole loses. But when your soul streams work together, you win."

"I hear ya."

"Sounds like you're not sold yet, but that's fine. You'll get there. For now, ready for round two?"

"No, this will be round one. That was just the warm-up!"

"I love the enthusiasm!" Both of his hands spark with electricity, and my force field immediately rushes back out of me to protect me. Another stalemate. I close my eyes and take a deep breath.

I know you're trying to protect me, Fear, and I appreciate that. But trust me to figure this out. If it gets too close, I'll lean on you to keep me safe.

The force field dissipates.

"Well done, Aiden. I saw you recenter yourself. Good job. Let's continue."

We square up again. Tirrell says, "You won't come across many as fast as me, but some will be stronger. I won't use my speed this time, but I'll add a little charge to my punches. Don't worry—my love for training will be activating my LET rather than a desire to hurt you, so I won't be able to use enough Laosi to cause any real damage."

"That's comforting, I guess. But don't expect me to go easy on you."

"I wouldn't. That's why I'm sparking. We don't know what all you can do. Come at me when you're ready."

What do I start with? He'll expect a force blast. What else do I have? What else do I feel?

He mentioned Leia, and anger immediately activated my power. But anger wasn't the only emotion present. There was also this... emptiness. She was the best part of my life. If I'm honest, the only reason I'm here is to get these powers under control for her. But if she just doesn't want me anymore, what's the point? If I can't have her, then—

A tear rolls down my cheek.

"Aiden! Aiden, stop!" Tirrell cries out. He struggles to hold himself up on his hands and knees under a gray dome that spans a third of the showroom floor.

"What's going on here?"

A guy and a girl walk into the showroom from the entrance.

The dome vanishes. Tirrell stands slowly, breathing hard. "Did you know you could do that?" he asks.

I shake my head. "I don't even know what I did."

Still catching his breath, Tirrell looks toward the newcomers. "Hey, guys. This is Aiden."

The guy nods. "What's up, Aiden? Tirrell, we got a live one. It's about to go down. Tessa told us to find you here. Ready to do some good in the field?"

Tirrell straightens. "If Tessa thinks it's time, it's time. I guess I'm as ready as I'll ever be. Is this... where it begins? I didn't think I'd be in the thick of it from the beginning."

The girl speaks up. "Yeah, this is where it begins. Talia confirmed it."

Tirrell nods slowly. "Did she at least see who wins?"

The guy smirks. "She saw the outcome, but you know Tessa ain't gonna tell us."

"Of course not. Do you know if she saw Aiden coming with us? I think he should. If he's up for it."

The guy exchanges a glance with the girl, then

hesitates. "I don't know. He just got here—what, a week ago?"

"Bro, he's got a ton of talent," Tirrell says.

The guy retorts, "I ain't worried about what he *can* do. I need to know what he *will* do."

The girl cuts in. "We don't have time for this. Let's ask him. What do you say, friend? You in?"

All eyes are on me, waiting for an answer.

Am I in? In what?

CHAPTER 13 – ANSWERS

"Aiden, if you're coming, you gotta come now. And if you don't know if you want this, then just sit this one out. We ain't got time to waste. Tirrell, let's go!"

This guy is annoying.

"Guys, I'm down. I just need somebody to explain what's going on. Who are y'all, where are we going, and what's the mission?"

Tirrell says, "We'll explain on the way. Auriel, can you call a carrier?"

"Oh, we kept the one we rode in. Tessa's tab, of course," she replies, smirking.

"Let's move," the guy says.

As we run out, Tirrell asks, "What's the location?"

"Carrier station in Felicity," Auriel answers.

Leia's hometown.

"That's like 11 hours from here!" I recoil.

"Good thing we're portaling," Auriel says in a sing-song tone.

On the way out of HQ, I notice that the guy is barefoot under his white tank top and blue jeans.

Huh.

As we climb into the carrier, Tirrell says, "Carrier station."

"Acknowledged."

My first time portaling will be with a group of strangers on a mission to... fight bad guys? What am I doing?

As the carrier rises and glides down the street, Tirrell helps us all get acquainted. "Aiden, this is Auriel and Zane. Can y'all explain your powers and types to Aiden?"

Zane goes first. "Sup? I'm Zane. Will-Dominant, Heart-

Disintegrated. My LET is kinda hard to explain. Basically, I can harden anything I touch. We think I'm manipulating how dense—or undense?—the molecules are. I've run on water, made a metal door as soft as a pillow... stuff like that."

"Cool. Nice to meet you," I say.

Auriel speaks next, and her gentle, maternal voice brightens the tone of the conversation. "Hi, Aiden. I'm Auriel. I listen to my heart all the time, but my mind? Not so much. My LET makes me a human undo button."

My blank stare prompts her to add, "I can reverse things after they happen."

This I've got to see.

"Nice to meet you, too," I say. I rub my sweaty palms on my gym shorts and say, "I guess it's my turn. Okay, so I'm Aiden. How did you guys do it? Um, I'm Mind-Dominant, Heart-Disintegrated. And... I have two abilities."

Zane and Auriel raise their eyebrows, clearly interested.

"Yeah, so I'm an empath. I can literally feel everyone's emotions around me. Like, Auriel, I can feel how much hope you have right now. There's some happiness... and a bit of fear, too."

Slightly taken aback, Auriel responds, "Hold on. Don't be putting my business out there like that," rolling her neck dramatically.

Good thing I can sense she's not actually mad.

I grin at her, showing the others she's joking. She smiles back and says, "Lucky for you, I like being known. But we're talking about you right now. What's your other power?"

"Right. So my other LET lets me manipulate distances between me and other things. Different emotions trigger different reactions: repulsion, attraction, teleportation, flight... I'm still kinda learning the best ways to channel it, though."

Tirrell chimes in, "I think you two should share your reintegration stories with Aiden, too."

Zane balks. "What? I just met him."

"Bro, accept your weaknesses," Tirrell says firmly. He then reassures him, saying, "He's one of us. Trust me. Understanding each other's triggers will only help us work together."

Zane sighs and relents. "I hear you... All right - you want the sob story? Cool. I'm from Reality, right? The oldest of four kids. My parents were high when they met, and as often as they could be after that. Amazingly, my mom stayed clean while pregnant with the first three of us. My baby sister wasn't quite so lucky. She has a weak heart and cerebral palsy. But life didn't seem that bad because it was all I knew, ya know? Until one day - I'm 15 years old at the time, right? One day, my pops don't come home. All I knew was he went to see his dealer, but apparently he owed him some money.

"Well, it turned out that the dealer owed his supplier, too. Desperate people do desperate things, I guess. Anyway, he shot my pops. Word gets back to us that he's gone, and what does mom do? She uses the only way coping strategy she knows. So she's heavy into using, OD'ing a couple times, and leaving me to take care of the 5 of us. So it goes like that for a couple years until it gets to a point that I just can't take no more. I'm still a kid, but I been working so hard at school, work and home that I haven't had time to grieve losing my dad, ya know? I'm just grinding everyday.

Anyway, I'm on my way to the grocery store and I see the guy who we think shot my dad. The next thing I know, my hand is around his neck. I literally have no memory of what happened in between. What I do know is that the first time I used my powers, I was hardening Roberto Hall's windpipe.

"Fast forward, I get arrested and put on trial. My lawyer put together a strong case. Roberto didn't die - lucky for him, the effect wore off before any brain damage occurred. And since he had a gun on him, we argued self-defense. On top of that, I was a minor who didn't even know I had LETs. So I only did 2 years in the Atheria step-down facility and was released on my 19th birthday. The crazy part was that we don't know for sure that Roberto Hall was my dad's dealer. The ballistics for the gun he had on him didn't match for the bullet that killed my dad.

"That haunted me the whole time I was locked up, so when I got out, I knew I had to do something. I started looking for help, and that's when I learned about ARL. I came to Sanctuary looking for your dad, believe it or not, but I found Tessa. Or she found me. Either way, as far as how the reintegration is going, I can tell my story without phasing through this carrier right now, so that's something, right? And I'm in school studying civil engineering. So I'm gaining some control of my powers and my life. But you do not want to be nearby if I feel powerless."

A shiver runs down my spine as I sigh and drop my gaze to the carrier's floor. Fighting through the discomfort, I force myself to meet Zane's eyes again. "Zane, I'm so sorry, man."

He shrugs. "It is what it is. Can't change the past, right? But… thanks for caring, I guess."

"No, that's not what I mean," I reply quickly. "I mean, yeah, I'm sorry for what you've been through. But I'm apologizing because I know I've been just one of the many people who judged you as a guy with an attitude problem. I didn't make room for how your life shaped you. I can't imagine what it's been like to live your life, so who am I to look down on you for being in a tight mood? You reminded me that no one is unhappy because they want to be."

I don't want to stare, but I catch what looks like the glimmer of a tear in his eyes.

He shifts uncomfortably before answering, "I appreciate you sharing that, man. But I ain't doing nobody a favor by staying stuck in my past and treating the people around me now like they're the ones who put me there. Mood is a choice, and I chose to treat you like you were one of the villains from my past. So I owe you an apology, too."

"It's all good, bruh. Maybe we can start over?" I ask.

He extends his hand, and I dap him up.

Mood is a choice? Is that true?

"In a way," I say slowly, "I relate to you about being Heart-Disintegrated. But I won't compare what I've been through with your story, man. Honestly, I hate to admit it, but... I *am* the villain of the past for someone else. Someone I..."

My voice cracks, and I realize I have about half a second to decide if I'm going to share more at the risk of my powers activating or keep it in.

"Hey... save that," Tirrell says. "We're gonna need it soon. We're here. Let's move, guys."

One by one, we exit the carrier into the overcast afternoon air. As I slide out, Auriel grabs my arm and stops me, her brown eyes locking onto mine. "Aiden, I don't know what you and Tessa have uncovered, but this—what you feel right now—this is shame. And I bet you never get a break from it. Do you know what power your shame manifests as?"

I shake my head. "No... I didn't even know it was shame, honestly."

Her lips curve into a soft and nurturing smile. "Whatever it is, I hope we don't need it. I hope you can let go of that shame with us."

"Thanks. But, um... we should go catch up with the others," I say back.

She nods. "Right."

Am I blushing?

As we make our way up the stairs and into the station, the sliding glass doors open, releasing a wall of noise. The hum of chatter and laughter make it hard to think. People are everywhere—rushing to catch rides, loitering with friends, and filling the space with chaotic energy.

I focus on the emotions of my teammates, trying not to get overwhelmed. Apprehension. Excitement. It's hard to tell which belongs to who—or how much of it is mine—as we weave our way toward the portal platform.

It's getting real.

"Hey, so what exactly are we walking into?" I ask.

Zane answers, "We've picked up on some chatter that someone's about to make a move on the carrier station in Felicity. Honestly, we don't know exactly what kind of move. We'll need to split up and look out for anything that doesn't seem right."

"Anything... like what?" I press, just as confused as before.

Tirrell speaks up, keeping his voice low as we inch forward in line. "From our best leads, it's a fledgling terrorist group with an anti-globalization agenda. If the intel checks out, lives are at stake—including yours. We're getting close to the front of the line. If you need certainty, we don't have it. I believe you'll be an asset, but you've gotta consider the risks and decide for yourself."

I'm way too amped to back down now.

"Are you kidding me? Use my powers to do good in the world? I've been waiting my whole life for this moment. I'm probably too anxious for it."

Auriel places a comforting hand on my shoulder. Zane nods with approval, and Tirrell grins.

"I like that enthusiasm!" Tirrell says. He then turns his attention to the guy in his late 40's wearing the crimson Tryon United uniform shirt with black trousers standing at the terminal on our right.

"Where to?" the man asks.

"Felicity. All four of us," Tirrell replies.

The attendant looks us over and asks, "What's your business in Felicity? You haven't checked any luggage."

"Oh, we're just going for an event. We don't plan to stay long," Tirrell answers.

"Okay. 250 credits a person brings you to 1,000 total. Your Solo, please?"

Tirrell pulls out his Solo and hands it to the attendant. "Use the third account, please."

"Payment received. You're all set. Hope you enjoy your

event in Felicity. Wait—have you all portaled before?"

Tirrell glances back at me.

"I haven't, sir," I confess.

"Ah, well, there ain't that much to it to be honest. The main thing is to just keep your muscles relaxed. You're gonna feel a lot of pressure on every part of your body for a quick second, but if you tense up, you'll feel more pressure, and it will last even after you've arrived at your destination. I'll have the four of you step onto the platform now," he says, waving us to the appropriate area.

We pass through the bioscanners and walk up the stairs to the raised portal platform. Behind us, the TU employee calls out, "Okay, destination platform is clear. Have fun, folks. Three, two, one..."

"...One... two... and three..."

A soothing female voice greets us on the other side. "Deep breaths as you release any tension in your body. Take a moment to orient yourselves in the new space you now occupy. Are any of you experiencing a headache, heart palpitations, or dizziness?"

We all shake our heads no.

"Good. Welcome to Felicity! Please exit the platform via the stairs on your right." She waves us toward the exit line with a smile.

As we descend, Zane glances over. "So, how was your first time teleporting?"

"Well, actually, that wasn't my first time."

Zane raises an eyebrow. "You just told the guy you've never portaled before."

"That's true—I've never used a TU portal. But I've teleported twice. Honestly, it felt pretty much the same as when it happened spontaneously. The guy was right about that pressure, though! I tried keeping my eyes open this time to see what it looked like, but I guess the pressure got to me again."

Tirrell chimes in. "That, and it happens so fast there's probably nothing to see. But we've got plenty to look at here.

Let's sync our Solos and switch to Neural Link mode."

We all pull out our Solos. I triple-tap the area behind my right ear, activating the Neural Link implant.

"Neural Link activated. Can you hear me, Sarge?"

"Loud and clear, Lil' A," I mutter under my breath.

"Scanning for other linkers... Zane Arroyo, Auriel Yamada, and Tirrell Givens detected. Would you like to establish a connection with these profiles?"

"Yes," we all say in unison.

"You need a refresher on how it works?"

"No thanks, Lil' A. Just hold my finger on the node, and they can see what I see and hear what I think. No updates or anything, right?"

"Nope. You got it, Captain! Just remember your range is 50 meters, and this is a serious battery drain." He yawns and adds, "I'm getting sleepy already." I look at the Solo and see that I still have 47% battery life.

An AI yawning? Lil' A is so dramatic.

Auriel's gaze lingers on me, probably mistaking my frustration with my AI for trepidation about the mission. "Hey... The stakes are high, but I've got your back. Trust me— we've got this."

I nod in response.

Tirrell takes charge. "Okay, everybody. We'll be splitting up from here. Everyone takes a floor—I'll take one, Zane two, Auriel three, Aiden four. Scan your floor for anything suspicious, then move up four. Stick near the stairs, blend in, and act natural. No one gets a pass—not CLU, TU staff, or even a childhood friend. Suspect everybody, but don't make a move unless you're made.

"Keep communication to a minimum, but if something's off, report it. Wait for backup. Embrace the brotherhood; we're behind enemy lines, and we're all we've got. Three's the magic number—don't engage unless three of us are there. Before we split, Aiden, are you picking up anything?"

I clear my throat, trying to sound confident. "Not yet. There are too many people. Emotions are everywhere. I can't really distinguish anything specifically off. But as soon as I catch something, you'll be the first to know."

He'll be the first to know? How, when I'm Linked with 3 people? Get it together, Aide.

"Right. Assume we're being watched right now. I'm heading to the bathroom—someone hit the gift shop or grab food. Be a tourist. See y'all in a bit. I really do have to pee."

The three of us chuckle as Tirrell walks off. Zane, Auriel, and I express our support with our eyes and silently split up.

Taking a deep breath, I shake off the jitters and head for the stairs. As I climb, I notice the station's layout mirrors Sanctuary's but on a larger scale. Six raised portal platforms line the north wall, two rows of three. Open stairwells flank the east and west ends, with a central stairwell wrapping around the elevator shaft. The 29 floors above don't fully extend to the north and south walls, leaving a gap where a person could lean over and see the portal platforms below or the entrance on the south side.

As familiar as the architecture is, the color scheme here stands out. In contrast to the vintage feel of Sanctuary's carrier station, Felicity's station feels alive with bold colors and floral arrangements brightening every corner. I take the moment in and find the mood to be distractingly invigorating.

If only I could soak this in longer.

I step out of the stairwell on the fourth floor and take a look around.

With so many people around, this is the perfect target for a terrorist attack. I never would have dreamed of fighting terrorists. Is this what Tessa and Tirrell meant about finding purpose? Is this the purpose of the Broken? Is it... my purpose?

Hoping to subdue some of my unease, I casually observe the crowd. A family of four tourists radiates genuine happiness. Their excitement feels pure, like the joy of fulfilling a wish made long ago.

Okay, they're not the enemy.

Nearby, three skater kids wearing hoodies and ripped jeans scroll through their Solos. I doubt they're even aware of each other based on how deeply they've immersed themselves into their devices.

Couldn't they do that at home?

What does a terrorist even look like?

I head toward the gift shop, passing a husband and wife holding hands and sharing ice cream. The man's white hair suggests they're in their sixties, enjoying their own kind of adventure. Two men lean against the wall outside the shop, talking to each other. The guy with a sleeve of tattoos glances at me, and I quickly look away. Further down, a man in a brown suit swipes a badge to enter the security office, his white briefcase tucked under his arm.

Tirrell probably gave me the floor with security on purpose. Not that I'm complaining.

To my right, a middle-aged woman paces back and forth, visibly upset as she argues into her Solo. Beyond her, more families and travelers mill about, blending into the busyness of the station.

It would really help if I knew what I was looking for.

I pass the two men by the shop and give them a small nod. "What's up, brother?" one replies. Inside the gift shop, I wander through aisles filled with overpriced trinkets and souvenirs.

If I wasn't broke already, I would be after leaving here. Wish I could afford to grab something for my mom, something to show her I've finally left Sanctuary on my own. And... maybe something for Leia, too—

"Hey, everybody. If you're able to, close your eyes," Tirrell's voice plays in my head through the Neural Link. "I'm sending a visual of Owen Hopkins. If anyone doesn't know, he's a TU exec."

I step out of the shop and head toward the railing, peering down at the first floor where Tirrell stands. A man near him looks familiar, though I can't say why.

"Yeah, but isn't he usually based in Serenity? What's he doing here?" Zane asks.

"Probably the same thing we are," Tirrell replies.

Auriel adds, "If he's here, maybe we won't have to get involved."

I close my eyes to stream Tirrell's vision of a man wearing a brown suit carrying a briefcase walking toward the elevator.

"Or maybe he's working with them. Tessa said—"

"Tirrell," I cut in, touching the node behind my ear. "This is gonna sound crazy, but I just saw that guy—the one with the briefcase. He went into the security office 30 seconds ago."

"You sure, rookie? We can't be—" Zane starts.

"I'm 100% sure. It was him, or his identical twin with the same suit and briefcase."

"Auriel, Zane—get to Aiden!"

"Got it," Zane confirms.

"Coming, Aiden!" Auriel says.

My heart pounds as I head toward the central stairwell.

This doesn't make sense. There's no way he got downstairs that fast. What's going on?

"Aiden," Tirrell says, "when he comes out, don't make a move on him no matter what. Just see if you can get a read on him."

"Okay, I can do that. But what about you? You're all alone with one of them."

"True, but you know how fast I am. Besides, my Owen came from the portal. Cloning a key card is one thing, but I doubt anybody could fake such a high-profile TU ID and make it through the bioscanner. If I had to bet, I'd say your guy is an impostor."

The door to the security office opens, and Hopkins emerges, walking briskly toward the eastern stairwell.

"My guy is heading out," I inform the group.

"What are you reading?"

"...Nothing," I reply, surprised.

"Okay, so we still don't know—" Auriel begins.

"No, it's him," I insist.

"But you didn't get a reading. How do you know?" Tirrell asks.

"Because there's *nothing*. People are always feeling something, even if it's just barely there. I've never focused on someone and felt nothing, but with this guy..."

"Auriel, Zane—how close are you?" Tirrell asks.

"I got a lot of people on my row," Zane replies. "Give me 30 seconds."

"A little longer for me," Auriel adds.

I spot Hopkins heading toward me. He looks me straight in the eye while casually closing the distance between us.

"Aiden Lore?"

He knows my name?

"Um, I don't think we've met," I say.

Standing face to face with me, he lowers his tone and says, "Aiden... I'm going to ask you a very simple question. What are you doing here?"

"M-m-me?" I stammer, scrambling for a response. "Well, I'm... Wait, who are you again? I don't remember meeting you before."

'Owen' mutters, "Of all the people they could have sent..." He exhales heavily before locking eyes with me. "Listen to me—you're on the wrong side of this. You need to make the right choice and leave. Now."

Leave? No, it's too late for that. This is my chance to do something meaningful with my life!

"But I want to stay. In fact... I think you should stay, too. Maybe you can tell me where we know each other from. Plus, I'd like you to meet Owen Hopkins." I grab his briefcase to stall him.

Bystanders turn their attention to us, and the impostor notices. He knows that any minute now, the real Hopkins will appear. He's out of time. His jaw tightens.

"Aiden, stand down," Tirrell's voice commands in my ear.

The impostor leans in closer. "So you've committed to them? I wanted you on my side, but that doesn't mean you're not disposable. Let go and leave—this is your last chance."

"You wanted me...?"

By now, a crowd of onlookers has surrounded us. A few are recording the confrontation with their Solos.

Why did he want me?

Through the crowd, I catch sight of Zane stepping out of the eastern stairwell. Turning back to the impostor, I say, "Who are yo—"

"You had your chance."

I barely notice his left hand transforming—black scales ripple across his skin, and razor-sharp talons extend from his fingers. He strikes like lightning at my chest. I don't have time to think. Instinctively, I dodge left, releasing the briefcase as I fall to the floor.

I look up and see Zane running on the air to get above the crowd. As the impostor lunges towards me to strike at my core, Zane dives at him and delivers a powerful left cross to "Owen's" cheek, knocking him back a few feet before he falls.

Zane turns to me, extending his hand with a smirk. "I guess it's showtime, huh?"

Taking his hand, I get back to my feet, adrenaline pumping through my veins. The impostor rises, and says, "I don't have time for this!" Black scales spread across his frame as his entire body transforms. Wings erupt from his back, and he drops to a quadrupedal stance, his face elongating into the snout of a Mukozi dragon. The twelve-foot-long beast snarls at us, its glowing yellow eyes scanning the terrified crowd.

Screams erupt as people scatter in every direction. Others freeze, paralyzed by fear and disbelief.

"This ain't good. Tirrell, get here, *now!*" Zane yells in our minds.

The dragon's mouth opens, and a torrent of fire surges toward us. Without thinking, my force field activates, shielding us from the flames.

That was close! Thank you, fear.

The fire rages against the translucent barrier, deflecting around us. As I scan around for Tirrell, a heart-stopping scream pierces through the roar of the flame and penetrates the walls of my force field. I whip my head to the right and see the little girl from the family of four, caught in the downdraft of the reflected flames. Her body is ablaze, and the sound of her cries sinks deep into my heart.

No! What do I do? Do I let her die so Zane and I can live? Whose life is more important?

CHAPTER 14 – INTERRUPTION

"You think you can let me out? We gotta—man, we can't just sit here. We gotta help!" Zane paces inside the force field, his fists clenching and unclenching.

I feel lightheaded.

This is more than I signed up for.

"I... I don't know. I don't want to go out against that!" I cry out.

Zane glares at me, his desperation bubbling over. "Do you see what's happening to her?! Open a hole in the back or something. Let me out, man! Let's go!"

His nervous energy only amplifies my own, but I take a deep breath, nodding shakily. "Okay, I'll try. Hey, man... save her if you can."

Zane gives me a brief, determined nod and gets light on his feet as I focus internally.

The threat is in front of us, not behind.

The force field opens in the back, and Zane bolts out, circling around to the girl. He leaps into the air, turning a front somersault above the burning child. As he lands, he slams his fist into the floor. A shockwave of icy air explodes outward, racing back to the dragon and extinguishing its flames.

Zane sprints at the dragon and jumps over the frozen shards that the dragon swatted back at him with its wings. Before the beast can fully react, Zane's fist crashes into the top of its head, slamming it into the floor with enough force to crack the concrete.

"RRAAARRGHHH!!" the dragon bellows, shaking the station.

The force of Zane's punch bounced him upward on impact. He rolls over midair and spins into a corkscrew to drive his knee into the softer scales under the dragon's neck. The dragon counters, whipping its tail toward Zane's midsection. At the last second, Zane dodges, the tail swiping just above him. As Zane falls, the dragon launches a claw swipe at him, but a lightning bolt strikes the beast, paralyzing him momentarily.

"Good hit, Tirrell!" I shout as my force field drops.

Auriel sprints up the central stairwell and finds the girl in her mother's arms. The mother's wails pierce through the chaos as she clutches her child's severely burned body.

"Jasmine! Jasmine, honey, keep breathing! Somebody go get help! I turned my eyes—it was only a secon... Somebody, help us!!"

Heartbreak and resolve merge in Auriel's eyes. "Ma'am... you're Jasmine's mom? Can I help?" She extends her arms gently to receive the child.

The mother hesitates, a storm of distrust and hope twisting across her face. On the verge of despair, she gives a tearful nod, handing Jasmine over.

Auriel cradles the girl tenderly, her voice soft but firm. "This was senseless, wasn't it? There was no reason for this to happen to such a precious child. Let's undo it."

She lays Jasmine gently on the floor, glancing at me for confirmation. "Aiden, where was she before her mom picked her up?"

I point shakily. "There. She was laying like this."

Auriel moves around Jasmine, positioning her exactly as I indicated. She takes three steps back, then drops to her knees, her hands raised over the child.

Auriel's body becomes rigid, her eyes glowing bright white. Flames materialize around Jasmine, shooting back toward the dragon with each wave of Auriel's hand. And with each wave, Jasmine's burned flesh becomes healthy again. Finally, the girl's eyes snap open. She gasps and then bursts into tears.

The mother rushes forward, scooping her daughter into her arms. "Jasmine! Jasmine! Oh, honey! Thank you! You saved my baby! Thank you!"

"No problem! Take her and go. It's not safe. Go, now!" Auriel urges.

The family flees. Auriel stands, her chest rising and falling as she collects herself.

"That was incredible!" I exclaim.

Auriel smiles. "Now you know why they bring me on missions. Damage control."

The sounds of battle roar from farther down the hallway. I look at the shattered walls and collapsed ceiling around us. "Can you help with all this?"

She shakes her head. "No. It's the stuff that defies my logic that I can reverse. But all this collateral damage... I hate it, and I don't agree with it at all. But I can understand it. Greed, political agendas, selfishness in the human heart... That's kinda what I expect at this point. But I've never understood why innocent children have to suffer. That never makes sense."

"It actually makes sense to me, though," I say while walking toward the long-forgotten briefcase.

As I pick up the object of our conflict, the dragon growls, "Give that back!" Fire builds in his throat.

His words only fuel my anger. As the flames erupt toward me, I extend my free hand. A deep purple force explodes outward, slamming the dragon onto its back and engulfing it in its own fire.

"About time someone showed up!" Zane calls with a grin.

"That won't keep him down long," Tirrell replies. "Mukozi scales are practically impenetrable. We could fight like this all day and not leave a scratch on him."

"He's right," the dragon says, recovering quickly. "This is pointless. All of it. If Aiden had just done what he was told, none of this would've happened."

The dragon takes a step toward me, its glowing yellow eyes fixed on mine. My teammates move into defensive stances.

"Give me the briefcase, and let's call it a tie... for now."

He's right. If I hadn't provoked him, Jasmine wouldn't have been hurt. Who knows how many others were injured because of me? Why was I so stubborn? I should have known better! I should have just done what I was told!

"Aiden, you good?" Tirrell's voice barely registers.

The dragon opens its mouth, flames glowing deep in its throat. Zane steps forward, readying an air shield. Tirrell pulls Auriel and me closer. I hear the hum of Laosi. The roar of the fire. And then—

Birds chirping.

"We're outside?" Zane turns to me, one eyebrow raised. "This you?"

I stare at him, equally surprised.

Yeah, this has Aiden special written all over it.

I nod.

"Impressive," Zane says. "Did you know you could teleport multiple people?"

I sigh. "No, I didn't."

"Okay... So where did you bring us?"

"I'm not sure."

"Cool, cool... Well, how far can you travel? Maybe we can —"

"I don't know that either," I admit, my chin sinking deeper into my chest.

Zane throws his hands up. "Bruh, so, what *do* you know about your teleportation ability?"

"Nothing, man. This is only the third time I've done it." I glance at Auriel before adding, "Well... there's one thing I know now. This—what I feel right now—this is shame."

I hand Tirrell the briefcase, muttering, "I hope this was worth all that damage. If not, I'll probably end up in Infinity— assuming we're not there now." Turning away, I start walking down the unfamiliar road I brought us to.

"Where are you going, bro?" Tirrell asks, concern in his voice.

"I just... I gotta clear my head, man. Sort through some stuff. Plus... teleporting takes it out of me."

Auriel steps forward, pleading softly, "Sticking together is the best thing for us to do right now. We can figure out where we are and how to get back home as a team."

I glance back at her. "I won't be far. Besides, we're still Linked. Just... let me know what you find out. You'll probably have more success without me."

Her eyes lock onto mine, rooting me in place. "You're blocking us out, Aiden. But you don't have to. We're in this together. We can figure it out—*together*. That's what embracing the brotherhood is all about. But... I understand you need time to work that out for yourself."

I nod in silent gratitude and make my way to the nearest street that runs through this abandoned neighborhood.

The scenery is unlike anything in Sanctuary. To my left, the road I stand on runs straight for a few miles, ending at a beach with white sand and crystal-clear water that sparkles on the horizon. I turn away from the beach and walk parallel to a short mountain range off in the distance to my left.

Eternity, maybe? Devon told me about the beaches there. But Felicity has beaches, too.

As I move east, the boarded-up doors and windows of houses lining the road validate my shame. The eerie silence haunts me, but I welcome the solitude.

I guess my teleportation prefers to take me to empty places.

Scanning the horizon, I spot a cluster of skyscrapers far to the southwest. Helijets fly in a swarm toward the area.

The station... they're going to the carrier station we destroyed. At least I know we're still in Felicity.

I keep walking. Away from the station. Away from my team. Away from—

Anger. Intense anger. At me? Who's mad at me now? Wait.

Don't tell me.

"Fancy running into you here of all places."

My body stiffens. I don't turn. I don't move. A bead of sweat glides down my cheek.

That voice... She's... I thought she was just a dream. A manifestation of my guilt. A nightmare I forgot about two months ago. But I'm wide awake now. I know everything I've been through today was real. Which means... she is, too!

Last time, she caught me off guard in a closed-in space. But all bets are off out here.

I try to conjure up images from the past to fuel some anger, but those thoughts disappear as quickly as they arise, washed away by the flood of today's trials. I'm drained, which means I'm powerless.

This has to be the first time I ever wanted to use my powers and couldn't.

Slowly, I turn around to face her, and we stare at each other, projecting our disdain for each other silently.

"Who *are* you?"

Alexi smirks. "You haven't forgotten my name already, have you, sweetie? Didn't I leave a strong enough impression last time?"

I snap, "I'm not asking your name. I'm asking who you *are* and what your issue is with me."

"You've got some nerve being mad at me, mister. But you've always been good at blame-shifting. And lying. And hurting people. Now that I think about it, it's no wonder the Collective wants you," she says with infuriating sarcasm.

"The Collective? Who's that?" I ask, noting how much more coherent she seems compared to our first meeting.

"The bad guys you were just fighting," she says nonchalantly.

"Okay... And why are they trying to recruit me?"

She circles me slowly as she answers, "Isn't it obvious?" From behind me, she leans in close, and concludes with a venomous whisper, "Because you're a bad guy."

"You're insane." I step away, glaring. "I don't have time for this! If you came to fight, let's get this over with."

As she finishes her lap around me, I feel my Laosi rising, and I drop into a ready stance.

"Oh, please, Aiden." She stands before me, unphased. "You and I both know you wouldn't stand a chance against me. You think you can just summon up some anger and then use it to your advantage against me? You think channeling fear in the moment will be enough to stop me? No, baby. I *live* in anger, and fear flows through my veins thanks to you."

There she goes blaming me again. What do you think I did to you, lady?

"And seeing how you barely survived your battle at the station, I wouldn't even break a sweat turning your world upside down."

"You... saw that?"

"Sweetie, by now a third of Tryon has seen it. Congratulations—you're viral!"

Not exactly the kind of publicity I would have wanted.

"So what are you here for, then? To finish what you started two months ago? Are you here to kill me? What do you want?"

"Well, what would be the fun of killing you, dear?" she asks.

"Then, Alexi, what *are* you here for?"

She just stands there and smiles at me.

It's like she's here just to get on my nerves. No, it's more like she's trying to waste my time.

I press the Link node behind my ear and think, "Hey guys, what's your status?"

Silence.

"I ran into a hostile over here, but it was just a diversion. How are y'all doing?"

More silence.

I pull out my Solo and tap to awaken it.

Dead.

"That Neural Link is a serious battery drain, huh, Aiden?"

"Ughhh!" I groan, and I take off running back west.

Out of nowhere, a bolt of lightning shoots upward into the clear sky. As it dissipates, I see a body falling from at least 80 feet up.

"Zane, you have to get a hold of yourself! What are you doing?" Tirrell shouts before striking himself to the top of a nearby three-story house.

Zane jumps, climbs, and flips his way to the top of a nearby house and then runs from rooftop to rooftop (and on the air in-between) in Tirrell's direction. I sprint toward my teammates.

Did the impostor follow us?

Tirrell throws a lightning bolt, but Zane twists and dodges midair, using his agility to maintain momentum. Tirrell throws another, and Zane somersaults to avoid it.

But Tirrell's third bolt isn't just lightning. He rematerializes at the front of the strike, delivering a sharp knee to Zane's gut.

Zane doubles over, gasping. Tirrell charges his hand with electricity and chops Zane at the back of his neck.

"Mmmph!" Zane grunts as his limp body crashes onto a rooftop, sliding down the shingles until he falls out of sight.

Turning a corner, I find Auriel sitting in what used to be someone's front yard, her knees pulled to her chest as she sobs uncontrollably.

"Auriel? Hey, what's wrong?"

She looks up, scrambles to her feet quickly, and then throws herself into my arms, crying into my shoulder.

Startled, I awkwardly hug her back. "It's okay. We'll be okay. Just... tell me what's going on."

Auriel pulls back enough for me to see her tear-streaked face. "Aiden! It's just... I'm so sad! And Zane... and Tirrell... they're fighting each other, and it... it makes me so sad!" She buries her face against me again, her cries growing louder.

I rest my hand on her head, hoping it will comfort her, but her tears don't stop. I pull back and gently hold her shoulders. "Why are they fighting?"

She gasps for air between sobs. "I don't know! Tirrell made a joke—something about Zane not pulling his weight. We all laughed, but then Zane... he just looked at Tirrell like he wanted to kill him! They started fighting, and I couldn't stop them. I couldn't do anything! I just feel so useless!"

"Auriel, listen to me. Try to breathe, okay? You're hyperventilating. Just take a couple of deep breaths, and I'll go check on them."

She nods, sniffling, and collapses back onto the overgrown lawn.

She wasn't kidding about being Heart-Dominant. Poor thing is a mess! I hope I never get that integrated with my emotions.

I turn and run toward where I last saw Zane and Tirrell.

"I'm so sorry, bro!" I hear Zane say as I approach. "I don't even know why I was so mad. I was just... mad!"

"Are we good now?" Tirrell replies. "Because if you come at me again for no reason, I'm not pulling my punches."

"I take it this wasn't a sparring match?" I ask, stepping closer.

Zane hangs his head. "I don't know what that was. I haven't felt that angry in a while! I was just... overwhelmed. My bad, man. I—"

My force field suddenly activates, trapping me inside. My heart races, my skin damp with cold sweat, my breath shallow and rapid.

My force field? So... fear? But what am I so afraid of?

I look around frantically, trying to find the threat. Tirrell looks at me puzzled, but then, with determination, he gives orders to the rest of the team. Through the force field, all I can make out is "...briefcase!" before seeing Tirrell and Zane running off in the same direction.

I try to follow, but I'm so afraid that each step only

makes my force field grow larger and my steps more awkward. Auriel runs up to the edge of my force field and then stops. She extends her palms and her eyes glow white. Then, with effort, she cuffs her hands and squeezes her palms together, causing my force field to shrink and my body to walk backwards.

That... felt weird.

As the force field retreats all the way back into my body, the fear also dissipates.

"Thanks! I don't know what happened."

"Me neither. But we need to catch up with the guys."

"Right!"

We run to Tirrell and Zane, finding them facing off with a young woman holding the briefcase I took from the impostor.

Tirrell's fists crackle with lightning, ready to strike, but the woman holds the briefcase in front of her.

"What if I told you there was a bomb in here?" she taunts. "Would you still attack me with electricity?"

"She's bluffing!" Zane snaps. "If it were a bomb, they would've blown it at the station!"

Tirrell hesitates, then charges.

Before he reaches her, she looks directly at me. "Sadness," she whispers, and her body releases a black aura.

Tears stream down my face as I collapse to my knees. I wipe my tears feverishly, straining to look up and persevere against the overwhelming weight of the stranger's emotional manipulation. But through my blurred vision, I see my teammates buckling under the gravity dome my sadness generated.

The woman raises her free hand, and the dragon swoops in, grabbing her by the arm and lifting her into the air.

"It's not too late to join us, Aiden!" she shouts as they fly off.

As she vanishes, the gravity dome weakens, allowing my teammates to stand. As they regain their bearings, they all look at me.

Panting, Zane is the first to speak. "What did she mean by... 'It's not too late to join us'?"

"I think she was saying that the Collective still wants me to join them."

"The Collective?" Auriel asks.

"Yeah, that's the name of their group," I say, pointing toward the duo flying off in the distance.

"How do you know their name?" Tirrell asks.

After a heavy sigh, I say, "When I was walking by myself, I ran into this... somebody I knew—or thought I knew. She attacked me before I joined the Broken. She's, like, a stalker or something. She keeps talking like I did her wrong, but I don't even know who she is."

"Aiden, focus," Tirrell cuts in. "What did you learn about the Collective?"

"Oh, yeah. Sorry. Um... all she really said was they're bad guys, and they want me because I'm a bad guy or some garbage like that." I shake my head. "I feel like she was just stalling me, to be honest."

"So... she works for them?" Zane asks.

"I don't think so. But somehow, she knows about them," I answer.

"Well, next time you see her, make sure you get some meaningful intel," Tirrell says, his voice cold. "At least that way, you'd be doing something that was *actually* useful."

Zane breathes in between his teeth. "Dang, Tee! That was kinda harsh, wasn't it?"

"No, it wasn't," Tirrell fires back. "It was the truth. I tell him to stand down—does he? No. Instead, he went and engaged with a shapeshifter who turned into a dragon and destroyed the carrier station. And did he help us fight the guy he provoked? Not really. One little blast that almost got me and Zane caught in the flames. Then he warps us to the middle of nowhere and disappears while we're dealing with a User who can manipulate emotions. And let's not forget—his powers stopped us in our tracks so the bad guys could escape. So tell me, what did he do that was useful?"

Auriel walks to Tirrell and slaps him across the cheek. "That's enough! We've all had a rough day, but you don't get to tear Aiden down like that. *You're* the one who told him to come because you believed in him!"

"Clearly, I was wrong," Tirrell says.

"Tee, c'mon, man! Cut him some slack!" Zane says, stepping in.

"No... no, he's right," I say quietly. "I thought I was special, but all I really did was screw everything up. I didn't help at all. I thought everything would go great just because I was here and I have all this potential, ya know? I've got at least 6 different Talents, but what did I do? Waste my potential and make stuff worse."

I drop my gaze to the street and turn to walk away.

"Oh, nah. Don't walk away now," Tirrell says, grabbing my shoulder and spinning me back around. "Look me in the eyes and own up to how you screwed up."

Zane steps up, putting a hand on Tirrell's shoulder to push him back, but Tirrell resists. Auriel gently places a hand on my back.

I meet Tirrell's hard stare. "You're right... I... I screwed up. I should've just stayed home. I never should've come—"

The air reverberates with the hum of Laosi, and a strong pressure hits my midsection. My eyes wide open, I see the air around us splitting apart. Tirrell's body glows with electric current. And just as suddenly, all is calm again.

"—here...?"

"Yep, we're here!" Tirrell shouts, his face lighting up with triumph.

I blink and realize we're back in the showroom of Otto's Autos.

"Whaaaaat? That worked? Whoo!" Zane shouts as he gives Tirrell a high five.

What's going on? I brought us back to Sanctuary?

"Good work, you two!" Auriel exclaims, clapping.

"Guys! Anybody wanna tell me what's going on?" I demand.

Tirrell continues celebrating. "It worked!"

"What worked?" I demand.

"Aiden, man, I'm so sorry," Tirrell says, his tone softening. "But I had to do it. When you told us shame triggers your teleportation, I came up with a plan for getting us back home. I figured if I channeled my electricity into your Talent, I could boost it and guide us back. It was a gamble, and I feel really bad about coming at you like that, bro... But it worked!"

Auriel chimes in, "I've never seen people combine Talents before! I didn't even know that was possible!"

Zane jumps between us, grinning. "Whatever you do, sis, do *not* rewind this!"

We all laugh nervously at the thought of being sent back to Felicity.

Auriel smirks. "I won't, I won't. I'm just saying—you two must've gotten pretty tight real quick to pull that off."

"Yeah, something like that," Tirrell says, throwing an arm around my shoulder.

I playfully punch him in the gut. "You didn't have to go *that* hard, though, bro! Here I am, taking a walk to try to clear my head, completely unaware that you were over there scheming on me. But I guess it's a good thing my Solo died. We'd probably still be in Felicity if I'd Linked in and heard the plan. By the way, let me charge this up while I'm thinking about it."

I walk over to the counter and place my Solo in the charging field. As the white cylinder of light surrounds it, I lose myself in thought.

Tirrell and I were here just a few short hours ago talking about The Six. I was... a guy trying to figure out how to control his powers. Now, I'm part of a team battling an anti-globalism terrorist group called the Collective. I guess I don't need to ask Talia what she saw anymore. But if she had told me, would it have happened? Was this my destiny? Or did I choose this? Or... both?

I make my way back to the group, still contemplative. Auriel leans toward Tirrell with a smirk. "We had to keep you in the dark for the plan to work. But Tirrell didn't have to be so critical! I told him I'd slap him if he went too far." She winks at me.

"I probably deserved that slap," Tirrell says, his tone softer. Turning to me, he says, "But I honestly didn't mean a word of it. You did *great* out there. If the shapeshifter had a bomb, you stopped it. You teleported us to an abandoned area, saving all of us from the flames and ending the fight. And you learned the name of our enemy. That was clutch because our team can cross-reference 'The Collective' when they monitor the chatter on the Disconnect pages to narrow in our searches. To be honest, bro, I'd be glad to have you on another mission."

"Yeah, man. All I did was punch a dragon," Zane laughs.

Auriel just speaks with her eyes, confirming everything Tirrell said with her smile and subtle nod.

As I feel my feet lifting off the ground, I grin down at the team. "What can I say? It was showtime, right, Zane?"

CHAPTER 15 – MISCOMMUNICATION

"Sit yo big head down somewhere," Zane jokes, grabbing my ankle and pulling me back to Tryon.

When my feet hit the floor, I shrug and say, "Haters gonna hate, I guess."

Zane pushes me playfully. "Yeah, whatever. But, seriously, though, you did some good work out there."

"Thanks, man. But you put on a show yourself. I almost felt bad for the shapeshifter... until I remembered he was trying to kill a bunch of innocent people. But remind me not to get on your bad side, bro."

Zane laughs, but his mood becomes somber. "Yeah, man. Sorry for snapping on you when we were in the force field. I just... I saw Jasmine—I think that was her name, right? When I saw Jasmine lying on the floor, all I could think about was Celine, my baby sister. I just remembered how powerless I've felt watching her struggle so much just to grow up, ya know? So, yeah, I kinda lost it."

"Hey, no worries. Really, it was you pushing me that helped me learn how to manipulate my force field. I didn't even know I could open it like that! We're good," I say, smiling.

"Awww, this little love fest is so precious!" Auriel gushes, her heart practically bursting with joy.

"Aaaand you just ruined it," Zane says, throwing up his hands and walking away.

"She just wanted to feel included," I tease Auriel. Then, with more sincerity, I add, "Thank you so much for saving Jasmine, though. Like Zane said, I felt powerless, just watching her get burned like that. I froze. She would've died because of me if you hadn't been there, and I wouldn't have been able to live with myself if that happened. Thank you."

Auriel blushes subtly. I feel it in her emotions more than I see it on her face. "All in a day's work," she says. "But what about our fearless leader over here?"

Zane jumps in with, "Yeah, Tirrell was the man with the plan! Who knows what would've happened if we didn't have Coach keeping all of us together?"

I cup my hands around my mouth and start chanting, "Speech, speech, speech," until Tirrell has no choice but to say a few words.

"First of all, y'all are crazy," he starts. "More importantly, I'm just happy to see the team coming together like this. I didn't know exactly how our strengths would complement each other, but I knew they could. That's why I wanted y'all to accept Aiden for the mission, even though you didn't even know him a couple hours ago. And it worked out way better than I imagined. Our success today was a team effort, and I'm just happy to be a part of this team. I can't wait to—" Noticing my bashfully raised hand, he says, "Yes, Aiden?"

"I know we're kinda having a moment, and I hate to be a mood killer. Because, I mean, I feel like we'll only get better from here. But it feels a bit early to call today a success. Feels more like a delayed loss. We might have minimized the casualties for today, but who knows when and where they'll pop up again?"

Tirrell smiles and says, "We will."

After waiting for the explanation that he's oddly determined to make me ask for, I say, "I'm sorry—say what?"

"We will know where they are, and we'll know when they try to pop up next."

"I'm sorry—say what?"

"Oh yeah, you were gone at the time. When you handed me the briefcase, I tried to open it," Tirrell explains. "Obviously, it was biometrically locked, and trying to force my way in was a terrible idea. But I scanned it with my Solo to see if it could detect any kind of electric current or radiation that would indicate a bomb."

Solos can do that?

"In the time we had before our new friend started messing with our emotions, I wasn't able to run enough searches to know exactly what was inside. But knowing they'd be doing whatever they could to find it, I put a tracking algorithm inside the biometric lock code. In other words, as soon as they open it, I'll get a notification on my Solo, and we're on our way."

Nodding slowly, I say, "I am impressed." Then, looking at Zane and Auriel, I demand, "What are you two just standing around for? We need to pour up some drinks and get the celebration started!"

They laugh, and Tirrell says, "On that note, though, we do need to check in with Tessa and let her—"

"Hey, boss... You got a video call coming in from Leia Hart. You wanna take it now?" Lil' A says in my Neural Link.

"Hey, guys, sorry to interrupt. Is there a private room here that I can use?" I point to my ear and say, "Important call coming in."

Pointing to the hallway at the front entrance and the office rooms that branch off from it, Auriel says, "Those doors are only locked if someone's using them. You can take your call in there."

"Okay, thanks!"

I grab my Solo from the charger and bemoan the fact that the battery only gained a 7% charge. I jog to the first office room I come to, hoping Leia doesn't hang up before I get to answer. Luckily, there's another charging field on the conference table in the center. I put the Solo there and say, "Answer the call."

Pale blue laser beams scan all around the office room, bouncing off the walls and the digital display boards hanging on them. I consider sitting in one of the 12 cushioned chairs tucked neatly underneath the oval table, but before I come to a decision, the laser beams converge in the middle of the ceiling. As they spread out from there, they transform the office into Leia's living room.

"Receiving call from Leia Hart. Rendering holographic images. Network connection stable. All right, you're good to go!"

I see her on her couch, on the edge of her seat.

That couch...

Trying to hide how much I miss her, I say, "Hey, Leia."

"Hey, you okay? Where are you right now? Are you in Sanctuary or—"

"Yeah, I'm good. Slow down. Why do you seem so nervous?"

She sighs and recenters her energy. "Okay, good. I'm glad you're okay. I was nervous because I saw you—wait, was that you? That was you in Felicity, wasn't it? On the news?"

So Alexi was telling the truth. I am viral.

"What exactly did you see?"

"Was it you or not? At the carrier station? And where are you now?"

"Hey, Leia. Too many questions at once. Yes, I was there. But as you can see, I'm okay now. Would it be better if I come over so we can talk about it face to face?"

"Y... yeah, that's fine."

"Okay, cool. I'm gonna catch a carrier, and then I'll head your way. I'll see you in a sec," I say.

"Okay. Bye. End call."

I step out of the office and find that my comrades are now sitting at the counter. I walk over to them and say, "Hey, guys. Something came up and I have to roll out."

The group seems puzzled, and Tirrell speaks up. "Embrace the brotherhood, man. What's going on?"

Zane tags in and says, "Yeah, man. I told you my deal. With powers like yours, I know you got a juicy story. I need all the details. I'll go ahead and grab some tissues now."

I laugh it off, saying, "Some other time, guys. This is

urgent. But, um… I'm kinda broke. Any chance Tessa can cover a carrier for me? How does that work?"

"I got you covered, bro. One should be here by the time you get to the door," Zane says, tapping and swiping on his Solo. "But now you owe me your story. Let's get *intimate*," he jokes.

"Yeah, I'm… really looking forward to it," I reply with exaggerated sarcasm. "I'll catch y'all next time."

I turn and make my way to the front door of Broken HQ.

So the fight was caught on video and leaked to the news. That can't be good. I wonder what the world has seen and what they're saying about it.

I pull out my Solo and double-tap the top left quadrant for the latest news. It doesn't take long before breaking news holograms rise out of the device with headlines demanding their articles be opened: *LETs Out of Control! Felicity Carrier Station Under Siege! Death Toll at Four So Far as Crews Work to Remove Rubble! Users to Blame for Felicity Deva-station!*

I can't help but roll my eyes at that last headline.

Leave it to the media to slap a terrible pun on a tragedy.

I hesitate for a moment, nervous about watching the videos.

This is definitely not the kind of publicity the Broken needs. They're just gonna blast Users as villains. We've complied with the registry, endured the stricter laws, and avoided major incidents for decades. But the Protectors Against Laosi are gonna have a field day with this. We just gave them everything they need to justify their hatred.

I walk out the front door and step into the waiting carrier. "City Sector RL, Apartment Building Q9, Floor 14," I say.

"Acknowledged. Enjoy the ride," the carrier replies as it glides off silently.

I tap on the thumbnail of the longest video in the list. Judging by the angle, it's probably from one of the skater kids I saw at the station. There I am, locked in a standoff with "Owen Hopkins," both of us gripping his briefcase. Then the male newscaster's voice cuts in, smooth but grave: "What started as a simple misunderstanding ended with four deaths and 15 injuries."

Okay... so far, so good. My face isn't visible. I really hope it stays that way. Wait—four deaths?

When I fall to the ground, half my face comes into view. The video pauses and zooms in on it. The shot is blurry due to motion and bystanders, which is just as good as it is bad. The man's dragon-clawed hand is out of frame, so it looks like I'm just picking on an older man.

"Authorities are running facial recognition to identify this man, who appears to be the main agitator," the voice says.

There's Zane. Man, what a solid punch! He saved my life.

"Suspect 0 then gets aided by an accomplice who jumps in and assaults the victim."

The victim? Aw, come on!

"That's when a third User shows up, taking on the form of a dragon, and the three go on to cause massive damage."

The cameraman shifts for a better angle just as the impostor transforms into a dragon, making it impossible to tell the two are the same person.

"This appears to be a concerted effort, a planned attack resulting in lives lost, structural damage, and delayed transportation. Authorities estimate the repairs will cost upwards of two hundred seventy-six thousand taxpayer credits."

The dragon comes into full view and breathes fire. My force field activates just before the camera shakes as the cameraman flees. The footage freezes on a frame of my pale green bubble.

"Eyewitnesses say this Laosi deflected the dragon's fire in multiple directions, resulting in structural damage and third-degree burns to a six-year-old girl named Jasmine. Jasmine was on her way to the beach for the first time with her family before their dream vacation turned into a nightmare."

My fists start glowing purple.

Hello, anger. I understand why you're here, but I'm going to ask you to be patient. Everything that you want to do, I promise you we will do to the Collective.

I watch a few more videos, but they all tell the same story. Amazingly, Skater Kid's video got the clearest shot of my face, and I let out a grateful sigh because there are no clearer images.

Leia heard a story, but at least she's giving me the benefit of the doubt because she knows me. What happens if the rest of the world isn't so forgiving?

The carrier enters the loading zone and rises to the 14th floor. The door opens, and I step into the building, making my way to unit 14135. I knock on the door, and Leia opens it. A mix of emotions gently flows through my consciousness as I stand in front of her, face-to-face for the first time since she called off the wedding.

She looks... comfortable.

Her hair reveals that she hasn't dressed it for the day, but even still, it's not messy. Her gray wool pajama pants and baggy white t-shirt let me know what kind of Saturday she's been having today. Her face alone holds tension.

"Come in," she says.

I walk in and sit on the couch. She gives a half-disappointed smirk, and then walks over to the love seat.

"Can I charge this?" I ask.

"Of course," she says, pointing to the base on the coffee table in the center of the room.

Is she mad at me? Or disappointed...? Afraid? I'm having a hard time reading her. The energy seems...

"So... you wanna tell me what you were doing in Felicity, 'Suspect 0'?"

I sigh. "I can't imagine what it must have felt like seeing me in your hometown carrier station... Seeing my powers activate and hearing that people died in the fight. But I promise you there's more to the story."

"I felt a lot of things. But the main thing was I wanted

to know you were okay. I mean, I know you, Aide. You've never been the type to pick a fight like the news is saying about you. So I want to hear your side."

She seems very open to this conversation. So where is this fear coming from? Her neighbors having a fight or something?

"For starters, let's just say that when I woke up this morning, I had absolutely no intentions of going to Felicity. It was the farthest thing from my mind. It just kinda happened because... Well, I mean, I don't even know how much I'm supposed to say." I dodge her gaze by looking down at my white tennis shoes and the dust that's accumulated on them throughout today's activities.

"Aiden, it's me. I know things are a little difficult between us right now, but you've always been able to tell me anything. I don't think I want to lose that just because we're figuring out some things between us, ya know? You can talk."

Even though her words are exactly what I want to hear from her, I still glance around nervously and say, "Yeah, but... I mean, is someone else here? I keep feeling this—"

"When did you get so paranoid?" she laughs.

"It's just been a crazy day, I guess. As you saw. But you're right. Let me chill out for a second. Okay, so the night you broke up with me—I'm not bitter about that, by the way—I just went walking and met this group of people who are just like me. There's this lady named Tessa who helps people learn how to control their powers, and she was in my head talking to me about how it's my feelings and not acknowledging them that makes my LETs activate. Now that I mention feelings, I am a little bitter about the breakup... Just a little."

"Aiden, focus," she says.

"Right. So the group is called the Broken, and—I'm not gonna lie—they're kinda weird. Like, their philosophies and stuff are kinda... Anyway, I'm training and learning how to use my powers with a guy named Tirrell all week. All of a sud—"

"Wait. I thought you were going to counseling to get your powers under control? With Dr. Cambridge? Did you stop that?"

Anger. But it's not Leia's anger... is it?

I slide to the edge of my seat, trying to shake the discomfort by repositioning. "No, I'm still seeing him. But it's not really helping anything. It's more of a formality, honestly, because I have to go since I... ya know..." I let my voice trail off rather than relive that moment.

"Formality? So you trust Tessa and the Broken more than a trained professional?" she asks.

"Well, the thing is, Dr. Cambridge doesn't really understand how these powers work. Nobody at ARL does. Not even my dad. They're wrong about where they come from, what triggers them, and what to do about it. And I can't tell him because I don't know who's on which side."

She sighs. "I'm glad these people you've met are helping you with your powers. We used to talk a lot about how different things might be if you had a mentor, and it sounds like this Tessa person might be filling that role for you."

I lean my head to the side. "Then... why do you sound so sad?"

"I don't know. It just... When we talked about someone who could help you, I..." She pauses, sighing again. "I thought we had in mind someone who would help you use your powers less—not someone who would have you in even more dangerous situations."

"I hear you," I say sincerely. Scratching the back of my head, I add, "But to be fair, Tessa didn't send us there to fight or whatever. That actually happened because I got a little carried away."

"That may not have been her intent, but it was the effect, right?" she asks.

"Yeah, but—"

"It just sounds like yet another situation where I thought we were on the same page on how to move forward, but then you go off to figure it out on your own."

The muscles in my forehead tighten. "You broke up with

me, so it's weird to hear you talking about us being on the same page."

She leans back. "You're right. I did. You just asked me why I was sad, and I was trying to explain. I'm sad because you chose a path that puts you in danger rather than a safer, research-based path."

Aiden, what's wrong with you? Why are you getting so defensive?

Okay, this feels too familiar. I feel threatened. I just fought and defended myself against a dragon—why am I scared of Leia? I know I don't like her to be mad at me, but... Let's just diffuse this situation.

"You're right," I say, exhaling. "I'm sorry. I didn't come here to argue."

Her body is still tense, but I can see her trying to relax. "It's all good," she says. "I just... I just want you to get the help you need. And what I saw on the news—that didn't look like help."

"That's because they didn't tell you the full story, which is what I'm trying to do. I actually did some good with my powers this time, Leia."

"Okay. Okay. So... you were with this group this morning. With Tirrell. Then what happened?"

It worked. She's calm again. Is she starting to trust me again? I hope so.

"Right! So I was beating him up with my powers, right? Like, I'm holding back with one eye closed and my left hand in my pocket, and he's just like child's play to me. Like, 'You're supposed to be training me?' All of a sudden, a new dude and a girl walk in saying, 'Yo, something bad is about to go down, and Tessa wants us to stop it. Aiden, you look like a cool dude— we need you to help us beat the bad guys.' I was like, 'Yeah, let's do it!'"

Leia laughs at my animated retelling. Between giggles, she says, "Okay, wait. Be serious. What really happened?"

"Well, it got dicey once we got to Felicity. See, when

I first met Tessa, there was this girl who dreams about the future, and she saw me before I even showed up! And Tirrell was saying there's a war coming, but we don't know who the real enemy is. He was like, 'You can't even trust yo mama!'"

"Ohhhhh, so is that why you didn't want to tell me anything?" Leia asks.

"I mean... maybe?"

"Okay. I hear you. So you're making new Talented friends who happen to be in a war... Hmm... That doesn't sound sketch at all," she says. "But they're fighting... over what exactly?"

"Well... We don't really know, exactly. What we're going on so far is that they're an antiglobalism terrorist group."

Leia leans back into her seat. "Okay... That's... a lot. Because, like, if you don't really know who you're fighting or over what, then how do you know you're on the right team?"

"Well, Mr. Briefcase? The 'victim' I assaulted? He actually told me I was on the wrong side seconds before he tried to kill me. His—or her...? Actually, we don't know that person's gender because their talent is shapeshifting. He or she was impersonating a TU exec to get clearance into the security office at the station. We know it has something to do with that briefcase. That's why I grabbed it. Next thing we know, the impostor turned into the dragon! And if you saw how mercilessly the dragon was burning poor Jasmine... And then Auriel—the girl who came when Tirrell and I were training—came up and healed her by reversing time. That was more than enough for me to know which side has the good guys on it. Plus, the rules these guys live by—"

Leia stares at the floor and takes a deep, shaky breath. Slowly, timidly, but with deep desire, she says, "Aiden... I... think... you should stop... hanging out with the Broken."

"What?" I ask. "I'm finally helping and doing good with my powers, and you want me to stop?"

"I'm just... I'm just not comfortable with you putting yourself in danger without even knowing why," she says, looking down and to the side before returning her gaze to me.

I stroke my chin and say, "I follow... But what if I'm not putting myself in danger? What if danger is already coming and these are the guys standing up to it? And I can help so many people like this! I don't know, I guess I finally feel like I'm on track to do something meaningful with my life. I thought you'd be happy or supportive."

Leia folds her arms, looking at me with a mix of frustration and sadness. "So you want to go out and save the whole world while the woman you love is at home scared for her safety and yours? You're not a fighter, Aiden. I know you can be great at whatever you want to be great at, but, I mean, terrorists? Antiglobalism? I don't think this is your fight."

"I think it is."

"And I think you never listen to me!"

There's gotta be somebody else here... I can feel the anger moving down the hallway.

I look over my shoulder, and my heart drops into my stomach. My eyes widen, the hairs on my neck stand on end, and my whole body tenses as I see her standing there. Dark blue jeans. Black hoodie. Disdainful eyes glaring down at me. I'll never forget them as long as I live.

What is she doing here?

"YOU!" I jump to my feet, ready to engage.

Leia flinches back so hard that she moves the whole loveseat a foot. "Aiden!" she screams, terror written in every curve of her face. She looks up at me desperately, her voice trembling as she begs, "Please don't hurt me again!"

Alexi smirks, her purple aura flaring around her. "You know this is why you're single now, right?" she taunts, nodding toward my hands, which are glowing a dark purple with streaks of red Laosi swirling around them.

Leia must've heard the hum of my Laosi. That's why she's so scared right now.

"Stand down," Alexi continues. My fists clench tighter, the aura around them intensifying. "You mad?"

I am mad, but now is not the time to engage her. Anger, you have the right to be here, but I can't let you take control right now. If I let loose, Leia gets hurt. As long as Alexi isn't throwing daggers, ignoring her might be the best play for now.

I release the tension in my fists, letting the Laosi fade. I take a step toward Leia to comfort her, but Alexi warns, "If you so much as think about hurting one hair on this beautiful head, I will end you."

Is she defending Leia or just looking for an excuse to hurt me?

"I don't want to fight," I tell Alexi firmly. Turning to Leia, I add, "See? I turned it off. I'm learning. That's progress, right?"

"It is, but... I'm still scared," Leia admits, her body still rigid.

"I'm just waiting for the next time it gets out of control," Alexi sneers. "Do you think turning it off this one time makes up for all the damage you've done?" She glares at me, holding a small psionic dagger—not as large as the ones she's hit me with before, but still threatening.

"I know it doesn't make up for everything I've done," I say, keeping my voice steady. "But I'm working on that, too. I'm moving forward. All you see is whatever I've done to you in the past, as if that justifies you attacking me!"

Leia places her hand over her heart, her face bewildered. "I just told you I'm scared... Why are you yelling at me? I'm not trying to attack you or hold your past against you. I've just been through a lot, and I'm scared of you."

"What? No. Leia, I—"

"You act so high and mighty, like everything's supposed to be forgiven because *Aiden, the saint,* is trying," Alexi interjects coldly. "I can't stand you. You ruined my life. And you want to talk about me attacking *you*?"

I glare at Alexi. "Can you tell me exactly why you hate me? You act like I'm the worst person to ever walk on Tryon! Like you haven't hurt me or done anything wrong to anyone else. Why all this self-righteous hatred toward me?"

"I'd rather you not compare us," Leia says. "I just want you to care about how I feel because of the things you've done to me. Is that asking too much?"

Does she not see Alexi standing here? It's like Leia hasn't heard a word Alexi's said this whole time. Is Alexi just in my head, like Devon was—

Alexi's dagger flies into my leg. The pain isn't as intense as before, but it's enough to make me collapse into the chair.

Nope... She's real! This pain is real!

I open my mouth to tell her how uncalled for that was, but she cuts me off.

"I would say, 'Answer the question,' but we know the answer, don't we?" Alexi asks. "That is too much to ask, isn't it? Because you don't care about anyone but yourself. Rather than owning the responsibility of the pain you caused... Rather than honoring the request of the woman who is still trying to love you... You just want to stand here, talk about how you're gonna keep doing what you want to do, and deflect the conversation to how *widdle Aiden* has been hurt, too. You call yourself a man?"

"So because I'm a man, the hurt you caused me doesn't matter?" I fire back. "Apparently I've done some really awful things to you, and I'm sorry for that. Okay? But no matter what I did, you can't just keep coming at me like this."

"Aiden... you're the one who asked to come here," Leia replies. "I called to check on you to see how you're doing, but... it doesn't seem like anything has changed. I'm still just as scared as I used to be around you. I knew it was a bad idea for you to come over, but I just... got weak, I guess. I wanted to believe things could be different. But this cycle isn't healthy."

"Get out!" Alexi yells.

I stand there... speechless.

My experiences with these two women couldn't be more different, but they are undeniably connected by a shared truth— the truth that my powers cause pain when they get out of control.

As mysterious as their connection is, that truth itself keeps me from whatever joy I thought I could have.

I let myself believe that joining the Broken and making progress meant I could pretend none of the bad things I did ever happened. That Leia and everyone else would just join me in this fantasy world where I'm the hero again. But seeing the fear in Leia's eyes... I realize how wrong I was to think trust could be rebuilt so easily. She'll never look at me the same way again.

Then, I hear that high-pitched hum.

Surges of Laosi flow from my hands and feet into my chest. My blood feels like ice but my skin is on fire. It feels exactly the way it felt that night two months ago—the last time I was here in Leia's apartment.

I'm no better equipped to stop it now than I was then. I see the same fear in Leia's eyes that I feel in my own heart. We've been here before. We both know what happens next.

"Hey, bossman, you're getting a call from Tirrell Givens," Lil' A chimes in, oblivious to the tension in the room.

"Answer it!" I say.

The connection clicks in. "Hello?!" I yell out.

"What's up, Aiden? I hope I'm not interrupting anything. You left like something urgent was going on, but I felt like this couldn't wait."

"... Wh-what's going on?" I stammer, trying to steady myself.

"Yeah, so the Collective tried to open the briefcase! We've got their location! They're still in Felicity. Tessa gave us the okay to check it out, but we have no idea what we're walking into. It could be their base. We'd love to have you with us if you're up for it."

I glance at Leia and Alexi, their fear mirroring the chaos inside me. There's nothing left for me here.

"I'm on my way," I say firmly.

"Aiden!" Leia protests.

"Cool! We're still at Otto's. What's your ETA?"

"Are y'all ready to go now?"

"We're waiting on you. But I want to be upfront this time. We don't actually have a way to get back to Felicity with the carrier station down. I hate to ask you to channel your shame, bro, but—"

I cut him off. "Don't worry about that. The way I'm feeling right now—" I grip my Solo, manually ending the call. I close my eyes. When I reopen them, I'm standing face to face with Tirrell.

"— I can take us anywhere we need to be."

CHAPTER 16 – REPEAT

"Yo, I'm all for people making progress in managing their Talents... but if you're gonna just pop up at random like this, we might end up fighting," Zane says, standing with his muscles tight and fists balled.

Tirrell shoots Zane a look that says everything I would've told him about how out of place that comment is. But Zane keeps going. "What? I'm just saying, dude needs to announce himself or something. I was about to swing on him."

As Zane walks off, muttering to himself, Tirrell shifts his attention back to me. He's just as startled as Zane, but his concern softens his face. "Anyway... it was that bad, huh? I'm sorry to hear that. Do you want to talk about it, bro?"

I shake my head and say, "Nah, not really. Besides, I think we need me to feel this way, at least until we finish the mission, right?"

Reluctantly, Tirrell concedes. "I wish it wasn't the case, but it seems that way."

I glance at Auriel and shrug. "Guess we needed it after all."

"Yeah," she says, her voice heavy. "But, embrace the brotherhood. We're here for you no matter what. And don't forget to wait for the light. I don't know where you just went or what happened there, but it *will* get better. Just keep hoping. Keep believing in hope."

"Right," I reply halfheartedly. "But anyway, what's the situation? Where are they?"

"They're still in Felicity," Tirrell answers. "At the Solo Center."

"Ugh," I groan, rolling my eyes. "I guess they're taking advantage of the crowd. They know we don't need another PR nightmare. Wait—have y'all seen the news?"

Intrigued, Auriel asks, "No, what's going on?"

I pull out my Solo, cue up the video I was watching earlier, and toss it to her. "See for yourself."

Tirrell and Zane crowd around Auriel to watch. As the report plays, Auriel places a hand over her chest, trying to contain her dismay. Zane's fists ball and release, over and over, as the newscaster's commentary continues. Tirrell processes the news with squinted eyes and clenched jaws.

When the video ends, Zane starts pacing, his emotions boiling over. "So we just protected who knows how many people from a threat they didn't even know existed, yet they're spinning it like we had nothing better to do than go destroy a carrier station?"

"Yeah," I say, adding fuel to his fire. "And they're all saying that."

"Wait," Tirrell interjects. "Let's think about this. *All* the news outlets are saying the same thing?"

"Yeah, I watched like four or five videos. It's like they're reading the same script and showing the same footage."

Tirrell folds his arms, staring at the ceiling as he takes in this information. "There were so many people recording what went down. There's no way someone didn't get a better shot of what was actually happening. If the only story out there is that we're on the same side as the Collective... that dragon is connected to some *very* powerful people." His voice lowers as he asks, almost to himself, "Who is my real enemy? How do I hold them blameless?"

"I don't know," Zane says, "but I do know that whoever it is, they plan to finish what they started unless we stop them. Y'all ready?"

"Hang on," Auriel says. "Tirrell and Aiden are right. Whoever runs the Collective also controls the news. They're controlling the narrative. We were lucky they didn't get a clean shot of our faces without exposing their own. If we give them another chance, that might be all they need to put us all away. I can't take care of Brice from behind bars."

"I agree," I say, "but we also can't just let them do whatever they're planning. Otherwise, we'll never get the chance to prove we were the good guys."

"Exactly," Zane says emphatically.

"Okay," Tirrell says, his tone pensive. "We can't risk another high-visibility battle, but they've picked a location where avoiding that is nearly impossible. If we all go in at once, it'll provoke them. In that scenario, even if we win, we lose. But we also can't let them finish whatever they came to do and disappear without a trace.

"We got lucky in discovering *their* name this time. If we're not careful here, we won't get anything to help us clear *our* names. I know we all understand what's at stake, but I hope you see that we've only got one option. We send one of us in while the rest hang back for support in case it goes sideways. I'll go in and see what I can—"

"No. It'll be me. It's gotta be me," I say, my voice quiet.

"You sure, Aiden?" Auriel asks.

Tirrell shakes his head. "No, bro. I'll handle it."

"Look. For some reason, they want me. The impostor knew my name. They told me they wanted me on their side. I want to know why."

"Yeah, but are you in the right state of mind?" Tirrell challenges. "This isn't just about satisfying our curiosity."

"I get that," I reply. "But I can use the fact that they want me to our advantage. I can act like I'm interested in joining their side, get them to trust me, and get some more information out of them before shutting down whatever they're planning."

"No, man. I'm going to do this!" Tirrell's hands crackle with electricity.

"Um, Tirrell?" Auriel's voice wavers as she tries to get through to him.

I don't care what his hands are charged with. He's not stopping me. He continues trying, though, saying, "You're clearly emotional about this, as we all are. But out of all of us, being upset makes *you* the most dangerous person to send in alone—no offense."

I double down and say, "But being upset also makes me the best person to send in alone because I'll have the firepower to defend myself alone if the Collective wants to take it there."

Tirrell starts to protest, but Zane steps in, placing a hand on his shoulder. "Yo, Tee, chill. New Guy has a point."

"I said I'll handle it! I'm the leader so I'm..." Tirrell exhales sharply and looks at the group. "You know what? Fine. It's fine." He takes a deep breath, grounding himself. "All right, Aiden. You'll go in. We'll hang back and make sure you're good. If it gets hairy, teleport whoever you find back to where we regrouped after the station. I'll get the rest of us there, and we'll have your back. Sound like a plan?"

"I just want to say for the record that I don't like this," Auriel says. "We've already been through so much today. Maybe we've done all we can. I think we should just wait—"

"No," I cut her off. "It's too late. We have to finish this now, or I'm going to be in Atheria in two weeks. Y'all don't know my whole story."

"Maybe not," Zane says, "but I'm right there with you. Tirrell, you ready?"

Tirrell nods, shakily. "Yeah. I think so."

"No offense, but I don't know where we'll end up if you're not ready," I warn.

"You're right. You're right. Okay. Help me, Tessa. All right... I'm ready when you are, Aiden."

I nod at him and close my eyes. My mind's eye recreates the image of Leia sitting on her loveseat fearfully while Alexi's psionic daggers point straight at my chest. The hum of Laosi rises in my ears, fire and ice coursing through my body. Pressure intensifies in my chest and abdomen. Tirrell's lightning crackles. And in an instant, it all ends. As the pressure dissipates, I feel a cool evening breeze flow around me.

I open my eyes to see the sun setting beautifully over the western horizon. Rays of fuchsia stretch across the sky, breaking through the clouds and glinting off the buildings of downtown Felicity. The Solo Center is just a few blocks to the east. One look at my teammates confirms we're all on the same page. Without a word, we start walking toward the battle we hope we won't have to fight.

"You can teleport with your LETs?" a scruffy, mid-40s pedestrian asks.

"Yeah," I reply, too overwhelmed by the moment to offer more.

"Rad, man!" he exclaims.

"Something like that," I mumble under my breath as we cross the street.

Turning to the group, I voice a concern. "Hey, guys... I'm not sure if I'll be able to get us back home. Teleporting really takes it out of me. Before today, I'd only done it twice. In the last few hours, I've done it four times. If it goes sideways with the Collective, we might need to crash at a hotel or something."

"I'm sure we can get Tessa to pay for that," Zane says with a chuckle.

"Aiden? You okay?" Auriel asks, her compassion palpable.

"Yeah... I'm good. Just a little lightheaded. Nervous, I guess."

"I hate that we've had to put so much on your shoulders," she says. "You're the newest member, and you're doing the hardest work. When this is all over, I wanna hear how you're dealing with everything. I still haven't shared my reintegration story with you yet, and I'd love to hear yours."

Normally, that would've made me smile, but nothing about today has been normal.

"Here we are," Tirrell says. He pulls out his Solo and taps and swipes on it for a moment. "I can't pinpoint exactly where they are, but they're most likely still inside. Aiden, you're going in solo on the—"

I can't help but chuckle.

Tirrell blinks. "What's funny?"

"I'm going in solo... into the *Solo Center*... get it?" I look around at their blank faces. *"Nobody* else thought that was funny?"

The chorus of sighs and eye rolls make it clear they didn't.

Tirrell shakes his head. "You're going in *alone*, but we'll be here for you. We're still Linked, so broadcast anything you need us to see. The shapeshifter probably isn't posing as Owen Hopkins anymore, so focus on the briefcase. We've got the door —trust your instincts and go as deep as you need to."

"Sounds good." I glance up at the five-story structure that is mostly glass, supported by evenly spaced rows and pillars of white brick. Unsure of how to prepare for what's to come, I sigh. "In the interest of time, I'll check the first floor quickly, then head up. If you guys can keep watch down here, that'd be great."

"We got you," Zane says firmly.

"All right. I'm going in. Wish me luck."

I step through the sliding glass doors, scanning the space. The first thing that catches my eye is a ticker-style banner running where the walls and ceiling meet. Messages about the latest security updates, tech innovations, and product launches scroll across it. Apparently, TU is doubling down on assurances that the government-issued Solos are secure, quelling ongoing debates about whether they're tools of benevolence or surveillance.

The rest of the space mirrors the Solo Centers in Sanctuary—open, with minimal walls and glass partitions doubling as product displays or interactive screens. The nostalgia of late-night video game tournaments tugs at me briefly, but I quickly remind myself of the mission I'm here to accomplish.

"Hello, and welcome to the Sonic Hologram Center! What brings you in today?" asks a young woman at a glass podium near the entrance. Her navy-blue polo has "Stacie" etched into it just below the collar on the left side.

"Oh, I'm just here to meet a friend."

"No problem! There's a lounge on the third floor with refreshments if you'd like to hang out there."

"Uh... Thanks. I'm not from here, but am I right that Computer Connections is on the second floor and Chargers and Wearables are on the fourth?"

"You certainly are! All Solo Centers follow the same layout, so if you've been to one, you'll feel right at home here!" she says brightly.

"Cool."

"Have a great day!"

What kind of coffee has Stacie been drinking?

I turn aside from Stacie and scan the first floor, deciding to walk the periphery for a better look. Before I've taken two steps, Stacie says, "It's not too late to join us." I sense no emotion in her tone or her presence.

I freeze. Whipping around, I snap, "What did you just say?"

Her perkiness restored, she replies, "Ummm... for the *N Force 2* premiere! There are still three seats available, so you and your friend can join us if you want to!"

I scan the room cautiously, my instincts on high alert.

Everything seems normal.

"Oh," I say. "No... no, thanks." I turn away from her, walking along the wall to my right.

"Hey, man. What was that about?" Tirrell's voice buzzes in my Neural Link. "It looked like it got pretty tense with the host girl. Did you get a read on her or something?"

Touching the node behind my ear, I think back, "Oh, no... I... No, she was fine. She just reminded me of something, and I guess I got triggered. Have you guys seen anything from out there?"

"No, but we're looking. Yeah, I was thinking it wouldn't make sense for the impostor to impersonate the host, but then again, they probably picked a crowded space so they can hide in plain sight. Stay sharp."

"Will do. You, too."

Halfway around the building, I stop at a counter where a salesman demonstrates a Solo-programmable ball. He tells the parents gathered around him all about how the toy can help babies learn to walk, potty-train them, help with sleeping through the night, and provide hours of entertainment. All I've seen it do is flash colorful lights and make cheerful sounds.

Yeah, right. The only thing that kept Jack entertained for hours as a baby was tearing up the living room and pulling Candace's hair. Wait... Is he the reason I don't like kids?

"Aiden, check the stairs," Auriel thinks to me. "I can't get a clear view, but I see a guy in a red t-shirt coming down with a briefcase."

"On it!" I reply, breaking into a brisk walk toward the central stairwell.

I see the guy Auriel was talking about, and, sure enough, he's holding "Owen's" briefcase. I fake a loud sneeze that stops him in his tracks. He looks directly at me and quickens his pace. I subtly lean my head toward the Hands-On Demo section, which is currently empty. His confirming nod sets me in motion.

As I head toward the section, Tirrell and the others start firing overlapping warnings about not provoking the guy. *Not helpful right now,* I think to myself. I can't even tap the Neural Link node to mute them without tipping the guy off. I take a seat at one of the tables, hoping I look more relaxed than I feel.

A few seconds later, the shapeshifter sits down across from me, setting the briefcase on the table. "Why don't we just cut to the chase?" he says, his voice low and steady.

Why can't I get a read on this guy's emotions? What's going on?

"I gave you a chance to join us, and you declined," he continues. "You barely escaped last time, so what—are you here for a rematch?"

"No," I say slowly. "I want to join up. The girl you flew away with said it wasn't too late, right?"

"She did," he says, leaning back with his arms crossed. "But it seems to me like you've already chosen a side. Why change your mind?"

"Because I chose the wrong side," I say, meeting his eyes. "Your side obviously has power. I know a losing battle when I see one."

His posture shifts, his interest piqued. "So it's self-preservation, then?"

"Would you blame me if it was?"

"No. But I don't believe you, either."

Quick! Think of something convincing to say!

"Look," I begin, "as soon as I met them, they started talking about a war. I didn't understand it, but they told me I had a huge part to play. They made themselves out to be the good guys and made me feel special for the first time in my life, so I went along with them. Then I met you and saw a group with real power and purpose. So I reconsidered."

He raises an eyebrow. "But you have no idea what our purpose is."

"That's the thing, though," I say. "At least you have one. I don't. My life is going nowhere—or that's what I thought until today. Then someone powerful shows up who knows my name and tells me they want me on their side. So, no, this isn't about survival. I don't want to just stay alive—I want to live with a purpose."

The shapeshifter studies me for a long moment before speaking. "Okay, Aiden. That's compelling enough. I've always wondered why you were settling for such a mediocre life. You've got such potential."

How does he know me? How long has he known me?

"I'm usually a bit of a human lie detector," he adds, "but, fortunately for you, I can't read you one way or the other."

"Why not? Do you know what makes me so special? My guess is you do since you want me on your side, right?"

He smirks. "I know some things, and I'd love to learn the rest. But I'm still not sure I can trust you. You'll need to prove yourself."

I hope he doesn't see the sweat seeping through my skin. I'm doing everything I can just to keep saying words!

"How do I do that?"

"You do know that joining us means you'll probably end up fighting the people you're working with now, right?"

"I thought about that, but I think we can avoid it. Keep me on the inside with the Broken, and I can feed them bad information about you."

"'The Broken?'" he asks, tilting his head.

"Yeah, that's the name of the group. Or one of them."

Why did I just tell him that?!

"Noted," he says, his tone unchanging. "Your plan is clever, but it wouldn't work. The Broken already has a reliable source of information on us. They'd see through your little charade and probably expel you. If you don't want to fight them, fine. After that impressive display of power I saw today, I had hoped we could use your strength. It seems like you're getting better at controlling it, too. What a shame. But your power for your knowledge is a trade I'll have to settle for. Give us the information you have on them, and we'll take care of the rest. How did they know I'd be at the station today?"

I swallow hard. "Honestly, I have no idea."

He shakes his head playfully. "Tsk, tsk, Aiden. You'll have to do better than that."

There's still no emotion I can sense, but his tone is relaxed now. He's in complete control and he knows it. I don't like this.

"I really don't know," I say, trying to steady my voice. "I just started hanging out with them a couple weeks ago. Two of them showed up out of nowhere, talking about chatter they picked up on some antiglobalist terrorist group."

"Antiglobalist, huh? Interesting."

Shut up, Aiden. You're saying too much!

"I still need more," he says. "What are their names?

Where do you meet?"

"I... don't feel great about giving you their names when I don't even know yours."

"Oh ho ho!" He laughs, leaning back. "I respect a healthy negotiation. Everyone wants to feel like they've got some agency in their choices, don't they? I can't give you my name just yet, but I'll tell you who you're speaking with."

Convinced I misheard him, I ask slowly, "What does that even mean?"

"The shapeshifter's name is Elon Goings. He's unconscious right now, but I need to get him home soon— he works overnights. He'll wake up in a few hours with no memory of this."

"You're controlling him? Like... telepathy?"

"Again, Aiden," he says, patronizing me, "I'd be happy to explain more if I knew you were committed to my cause."

I have to give him something, but on my terms this time. I've been reckless.

Trying to sound casual, I say, "Okay, how's this? You want information, right? The three people with me today— Tommy Arroyo, Amy Givens, and Zeke Yamada."

"That's a start," he replies, his expression unreadable.

"So now it's your turn. What's in the briefcase? What's the end goal?"

"Very ambitious, aren't we? Not surprising for Richard Lore's son. But this," he says, standing, "is where we part ways for now."

I haven't gotten any useful information out of him. I can't let him leave!

"What? Why?"

"I've shared as much as I'm willing to share. I need to verify what you've told me, and I doubt you'll offer up more now that you know I'm done talking. But trust me when I say I know how to find you. Once I track down Tommy, Amy, and Zeke, we'll talk again."

I stand as well. "What are you going to do to them?" I

ask, my voice rising. Heads turn in our direction.

"Not your concern," he says calmly.

"What about me?" I demand, stepping forward. "What do you know about me? Why did you want to recruit me?"

"I guess I should expect such impatience from a 24-year-old, but you're pushing the limits. Go home. We're closer than you think."

He's just gonna walk away? He hasn't told me anything! No. No, I'm not letting him leave.

I lunge forward, grabbing the briefcase. "I'm not leaving until I get answers!"

Nonchalantly, he lets go of the case. "You still want it? Take it. I've already gotten what I needed."

"What? So... we were too late?"

He smiles. "I almost believed you, Aiden. But the face rec I ran didn't find any matches for the names you gave me. Still, I admire your creativity in this verbal sparring match of ours. Let's try it again soon. Next time we meet, though, it'll be for keeps. Now, if you'll excuse me, I need to return Elon to his home."

"Tirrell!" I tap the node behind my ear and think into the Neural Link. "Go to the spot. Now!"

"Stay safe!" Tirrell responds. "We'll see you there!"

Elon turns to leave again, adding, "Go home and lick your wounds. Spend some time with Leia. She woke up two months ago, right?"

How dare he say her name to me? It's the information he's withholding that made her wanna break up with me!

Grabbing Elon by the shirt, I close my eyes, channeling everything into teleportation. A moment later, I feel the cool air of the condemned neighborhood on my skin. I shove Elon back as Tirrell, Zane, and Auriel rush to my side.

"Ah, backup. Smart," Elon says, brushing off his shirt. "But unnecessary. My business is done."

"Done? I don't think so," I snap.

"What's the word, Aiden?" Tirrell asks as he and Zane

take their fighter stances. "You hurt?"

"Guys, this is Elon Goings. He's one of their puppets. I don't fully understand it, but whoever is running the Collective is able to control its members remotely. I've been talking with the leader or whoever, and he thought I was just going to let him get away. But he hasn't given me the information we came here to get."

"Well, then, let's hear it. Explain yourself!" Zane yells.

"And why would I do that?" Elon asks.

That's a really good question.

"Um... Because we need answers!" I respond clumsily.

"Not my problem. So what are you going to do? Kidnap Elon and torture him until he gives you answers that he doesn't have? I'd prefer we just part ways so that I can take Elon back to bed. Since he was nice enough to loan me his LET, I'd like to at least let him get a couple hours of rest."

Tirrell uses the Neural Link to say, "I hate to admit it, but he's right. We don't really have a play here. We have no leverage over him. Maybe a diplomatic approach?"

Auriel jumps in and asks, "What are you doing that's so important that you're willing to hurt innocent people?"

Feigning dismay at the accusation, he answers, "I wasn't trying to hurt anyone. You provoked me by trying to take something that belonged to me. I only defended myself."

"What about President Dionis' bodyguard? Did he 'provoke' you, too?" I fire back.

"Ah, so the Broken is international as well? That's good to know," he says.

His nonchalance is really pissing me off!

Tirrell steps forward, his voice sharp. "Explain yourself. What were you doing at the station? What was in the briefcase?"

Elon sighs, as if bored. "Ask Aiden. He's the one holding it. Now, if you will excuse me, I'm returning Mr. Elon to his house."

"No! Stop right there! I said STOP!" I yell, my Laosi surging instinctively. I thrust my hands forward, releasing a force blast that sends Elon flying ten feet back.

"Aiden, that's enough!" Tirrell shouts, but I'm already running.

Anger, I promised to give you your moment. It's all yours— do whatever you want to do! Make them pay!

I reach Elon's position and kick him in the stomach with everything I have. Then, I do it again. And a third time.

"Aiden, stop!" Auriel cries.

Elon coughs and looks up at me. "I never knew you had all this anger. But what good is this doing you?"

"SHUT UP!" I yell, dropping to my knees and punching him in the face.

Before I can hit him again, Zane tackles me, pinning me to the ground with his knee on my chest.

"Get off me, Zane."

"You ain't thinking straight, bro. You need to calm down."

To the side, Tirrell asks, "Is your partner here? The girl who messed with our emotions? You'd better tell her to stand down because he's only going to get worse!"

"Get off!" I shout, my voice raw as I release another force blast, this time directly at Zane. He reacts quickly, crossing his arms in front of his face and chest to absorb the impact. The blast sends him flying off me, his body twisting midair before he lands solidly on his feet, skidding a few inches before regaining his balance.

Elon coughs weakly and says, "No. Eboni has been enjoying an evening with her grandmother since I got the briefcase from her. This is all Aiden!"

I push myself to my feet, anger coursing through every fiber of my being.

"You need to hold your enemies blameless, man," Zane says. "I know that ain't easy, but what's fighting him gonna solve? We already lost. It's time to let this go."

His eyes lock on mine, searching for a sign that I might stand down. That's not an option for me.

Without a word, I lunge toward Elon. Zane steps between us and shoves me back. My fists clench, and I swing at him. Zane ducks the punch effortlessly and counters with a sharp roundhouse kick that connects squarely with my jaw. My force field bursts outward at the moment of impact, throwing him slightly off balance. I stagger back, shaking off the daze, and retract the field.

The anger surges again. I charge at him, tackling him to the ground.

Standing over him, I pant and say, "I'm not mad at y—"

Electricity courses through my body, cutting my words short. My muscles seize, and I collapse to the ground, my head hitting the pavement with a dull thud.

I look up to see Tirrell standing over me, sparks of electricity still flickering from his hand. "Sorry, Aiden," he says, his voice low. "You didn't really give me a choice, man."

Auriel approaches cautiously, her face a mix of sadness and fear. "What a mess we've made," she whispers.

"Yeah..." Tirrell exhales. "Aiden, can you stand?"

My body feels like lead, every movement a struggle. My eyelids flutter as I force them to stay open. Tirrell leans down, grabbing my arm and wrapping it around his neck. He hoists me up, my weight sagging against him as we walk back toward town. Zane and Auriel follow silently.

As we pass Elon, my eyes fall on the blood trickling down his face. My voice barely above a whisper, I say, "I... I'm sorry."

Auriel shakes her head, her tone quiet but resolute. "We never should've come here. I knew this wasn't the right call." She moves toward Elon, kneels beside him, and activates her LET.

The scene is almost surreal—watching my force blast reverse in time, returning to the spot where I unleashed it. Elon's body rises from the ground as gravity itself rewinds.

Auriel then says, "With this, maybe we can call it even? All the damage we caused to you is undone."

"Thank you," Elon's controller says. "He's really a sweet man. I'm glad he won't have to explain any mysterious injuries to his wife. Though, as a shapeshifter, I could've made him heal himself. But I'll take this as a token of good faith."

His detachment sends a shiver down my spine.

How can someone be so callous about the lives they manipulate?

"This has been informative," Elon's controller continues. "Aiden, next time, I'll expect a different answer—or at least a more prepared one. Either way, I'll get what I want. Auriel, Zane, Tirrell—until we meet again."

With that, Elon transforms into a bird and disappears into the night sky.

The four of us stand silently, transfixed by the revelation we don't want to accept. The fear from each of my comrades casts an oppressive aura so strong that I wonder if it will cause my force field to activate.

Auriel breaks the silence. "He knows our names?"

Zane whirls on me, suspicion flaring in his eyes. "I didn't tell him!" I exclaim, desperation in my voice. "I swear! I gave him fake names to throw him off! I promise, man!"

Tirrell places a hand on Zane's shoulder, calming him. "I believe you, Aiden. The Collective clearly has resources. But if they could find our identities out this easily, why didn't they expose us on the news?"

"They're toying with us," Auriel says. "But... strangely, that gives me some comfort."

"How?" I ask, incredulous.

"Because they could've turned us over to CLU. We know what happens if CLU identifies us. Whoever's running the Collective is powerful enough to destroy us, but they didn't. That has to mean something. They aren't heartless killers or terrorists like we thought."

"That's a good point, Auriel," Zane adds. "It wasn't a bomb in the briefcase. If you can turn into a dragon, you don't need a bomb. Plus, they could have blown it up anywhere, but they took it to a Solo Center? They must've been after information. That ain't really giving off 'murderous villain, world domination' vibes."

"They want something from us. Maybe Aiden isn't the only one they're recruiting," Auriel continues.

"Either way, it seems like the immediate threat has passed," Tirrell concludes.

I lower my gaze, shame weighing heavily on me. "I wonder... if there would've been any threat at all if I hadn't provoked it."

No one responds. The compassion I sense in their hearts is real, but their silence only deepens my guilt.

After a moment, I pull away from Tirrell, determined to stand on my own. My eyes follow the bird disappearing into the darkness.

I wish you well, Elon. I'm sorry you got dragged into this.

Turning to my friends, I say, "Guys... I'm sorry. Zane, man, I—" My voice falters. "This would've gone so much better if I'd had more self-control. I'm sorry, y'all."

Zane looks at me, his expression unreadable, before turning his gaze forward. "How are we getting back home?"

"I... I think I've got one more left in me." My voice cracks as I fight back tears. "You ready, Tirrell?"

End Part 3

PART 4 – ACCEPTING THE THINGS I CANNOT CHANGE

CHAPTER 17 – CRAWLING

Two Days Later

"I knew it was coming. All day yesterday, I just kept thinking, 'When I see her, she's going to ask me that question.' I'd been dreading it, but you know what? I came up an with answer. The thing that I felt most was powerlessness."

The gentle smirk on Tessa's face tells me that she's amused but intrigued even more so. The look in her eyes invites me to share more, an invitation that transcends an obligation to listen as the overseer of the Broken. She hangs on every word I say because she's interested in me as a person.

I accept her invitation.

"It's weird. I'm teleporting across Tryon and throwing force blasts everywhere, demonstrating more control over my powers than ever. But at the same time... It felt like I wasn't actually accomplishing anything. I felt as powerless as I did the day that I knocked Leia into a coma and couldn't get her to wake up."

"Powerlessness turned into rage, and rage led you to assault a man who was being telepathically controlled and had no intention of fighting you back." She pauses. "But you wanted him to fight you back, didn't you?"

My shoulders drop, and I let out a heavy sigh. "Yeah. I guess I did."

"Tell me why," she says firmly. "Why was it so hard to hold your enemy blameless?"

I rub the back of my neck, avoiding her gaze. "Hmmm. I think... I think I wanted to face an opponent and win. It felt like we'd been losing all day."

"Really?" Tessa asks, raising her eyebrows. "The rest of your teammates relayed Saturday's events as a series of breakthroughs. Why did you take it as a loss?"

"Well..." I glance at the photo on the mantle—a picture of Leia and me from my birthday two years ago. We're laughing, arms wrapped around each other like nothing could touch us. It's almost painful to look at now. "My experience was a little bit different from theirs."

"Weren't you all together the whole time?" she asks.

"No... I actually separated from the group a couple of times."

Tessa taps her temple the way she always does. "I know that, Aiden. So why do you think I'm asking? What was it about those separations that made you feel like you'd lost when your teammates saw success? Well, until that last tragedy, anyway."

I sigh and shrug, trying to ignore how exposed I feel.

I'm still not used to having a conversation with a telepath.

Suddenly, I sit up straighter and say, "Actually, you're probably the best person to ask about this. Can you read my mind and look for this girl with a black hoodie? She keeps popping up, wrecking my life, and saying everything she's doing to hurt me is my fault. Do I know her from somewhere, or...?"

Tessa's eyes glow blue for a few seconds before returning to normal. "I could tell you who she is. But what matters right now is what she said and how you felt about it."

Finally, an answer! Or... maybe not?

"She said all kinds of crazy stuff. She called me a bad guy. She said that's why the Collective wanted me. Then she showed up at Leia's apartment and started bullying me. The weird part is that Leia acted like she couldn't see or hear her. Every time I said something to Alexi, Leia took it like I was talking to her. After a while, *I* couldn't even keep track of who I was talking to."

Tessa tilts her head. "Are you a bad guy?" she asks directly.

Shocked she'd even ask, I shake my head sharply and

say, "No."

But Leia's fear and Alexi's disgust hit me all at once.

Would a good person make people feel like that? Especially someone they cared about?

"Maybe? I don't know! Sometimes, I feel like I *am* a bad person. Like you said—if I'm not the hero in my own story, then I must be the villain in someone else's."

Tessa arches an eyebrow. "Is that what I said? What I *know* I said is that there's a lot more to life than one person's opinion. That was my first lesson to you, but you still haven't learned it."

"What do you mean?" I ask as I change my position on my couch, squaring my shoulders with hers. I look in her eyes and wonder what she sees when she looks at me.

What does my Laosi look like?

"Your teammates saw Saturday as a win, even though you saw it as a loss. The only difference between their experience and yours was the opinion of one person."

"Well, actually, two."

A gentle smirk flickers across Tessa's face. "We'll come back to that. The point is that you still care too much about what other people think. You can't even form your own opinion of yourself without thinking about other people. I want you to understand that who you are is not the sum total of what other people think about you. When you finally grasp that and learn to live in *your* truth... When you see yourself the way I do—the raw, objective, unfiltered reality of who you are—and *accept* yourself? You know that green energy explosion thing you do?"

Captivated by her words, I nod, not wanting to break her flow.

"You will never do that again once you learn this crucial lesson."

Her gaze holds steady, studying me as I take it in. "Wait... You're saying that if I saw myself as I am, I wouldn't have knocked Leia into a coma? But the only connection I've noticed between those radius blasts is that they happened after she rejected me."

Tessa folds her hands in her lap, her expression unwavering. "Which brings us back to considering the why behind the what. Internal versus external motivators. Remember that conversation?"

"I do, but... I don't see how that's relevant here."

As usual.

"If you really accepted yourself internally, how much do you think external rejection could really do to you?"

As uncomfortable as it is, she lets me sit in the silence of the thoughts that rise to answer that question. I say, "Touché," to keep the conversation going.

Tessa leans in and continues, "Because you were so dependent on Leia for the acceptance that you never felt like you could give yourself, you gave her your power. And when she didn't give you what you needed, you took that power back and used it against her. That's how these things go sometimes."

Her voice dips lower, more pointed. "And while we're on the topic, you also need to understand this, though it won't be an easy pill to swallow... Aiden, Leia wasn't rejecting you as much as you thought she was. You're just sensitive to being rejected, so you never really heard her for what she was trying to say. You never heard what it was that she really wanted. And what happens when the Will gets denied over and over and over again?"

"LETs?" I ask, trying to keep up. She nods and stops as if that was supposed to clarify something for me. It didn't. "Hang on... Slow down. I don't understand what you're trying to say... Leia doesn't have any powers."

"Alexi does," she says matter-of-factly.

"Okay..." I blink, trying to follow. "And who is Alexi, exactly?"

"Who does Alexi remind you of?"

I'm kinda over the psychological gymnastics I have to do

with her.

"Nobody."

"That's not true. There's someone. You know that anger. You've felt it before. You know the frequency of that pain. You haven't felt it as strongly as you do with Alexi, but you know exactly what I'm talking about. I don't expect you to understand all the details yet, but I want you to be honest when I ask you again, or the details won't make sense. Who does she remind you of?"

What is she even talking about? Someone whose anger I've felt many times? My dad? Candace? What does this even have to do with anything?

"You're going to have to take her off that pedestal, Aiden. She's only human—just like you."

"Who? You mean Leia?" I blurt out.

Tessa lets out one of her contented sighs and looks out my living room window, observing the rainy view of downtown Sanctuary City. When she speaks, her voice sounds like an invitation to share an enjoyable dream that she has lost herself in. "Love is the most amazing thing in the world. It's so powerful, so intrinsic to the human soul. I love love. Everyone does, really."

She turns back to me, her face emanating an otherworldly joy and peace. "Humans are so driven by the desire to love and to be loved that most people just go for the attraction, the romance, and the passion. You want so badly to be the object of someone's desire and to feel it as intensely as possible. All of that is good. But it's shallow. It's incomplete. The attraction, romance, and passion have their place, but without acceptance and commitment, they're like a monorail without the command center. Strong and driven, but ultimately aimless and destined to crash."

I stare at her, frustrated at how lost I am. At the same time, I can't deny the resonance between the words of her mouth and the truth in my heart.

"You've felt attraction, romance, and passion with Leia.

That much is written on almost every fiber of your Laosi. I see it like a neon light shining out against the night sky. Everyone in Sanctuary knows how Aiden feels about Leia."

With a quieter, sharper tone, she says, "But you haven't accepted her."

Could this woman be any more confusing? Would that be possible?

"What do you mean? I've never rejected her. She rejected me," I snap back.

"Sure, you've never told her you don't want to be in a relationship with her anymore. But you've never fully accepted her either. Not *as she is*. You hold this picture in your mind of who she is—or rather, who you want her to be. How you think she should think, feel, and act. And you reject, rather than understand and accept, anything about her that doesn't fit into your boxes."

I scrunch up my face. "What? No, I—"

Her gaze sharpens, cutting straight through my protest. "You haven't accepted her rage, her fear, or the way she deals with those feelings by trying to control your life so that she can feel safe. You'll *admit* she's not perfect, but you've rejected her specific imperfections. You try to act like they don't exist rather than accepting the reality that this is just who she is. You never truly committed yourself to her *as she is*. That's why you're so confused. Your love for her is intense, beautiful, and sincere—even enviable. But it's also shallow."

"Okay, so… what you're saying is…" I take a deep breath, trying to make sense of it all. "Because I love Leia with an incomplete love, I don't let myself see her flaws…? And if I did, Alexi would remind me of Leia?"

Stop waiting for a straight answer. She's not going to give you one. You already know what her next question is going to be.

"That feels… man, that's like… I don't know." I exhale slowly, letting the realization settle. "I guess you're right, though. I never really thought about it, but yeah, I see what you're saying. It's like I want her to be perfect in how she responds to me. But she just wants to be Leia, and I don't really give her the space to just... be herself."

"Yeah. Good. I'm glad you're taking this in," Tessa says gently, her voice softening, sparking a quiet gratitude in my chest.

"You have to think about this. She's been traumatized, Aiden. Remove yourself from the picture for a moment and try to see it from her perspective. The love of her life has caused her more pain than anyone else ever has. She feels more fear in the presence of the man she wanted to marry than in the presence of a complete stranger. Try to imagine how confusing that must be."

Ouch, Tessa.

"I never excuse anyone's actions, and Leia is no exception," Tessa continues. "But you have to accept her anger as a part of who she is."

I nod slowly. "Yeah... that makes sense. And, I mean, you're right. Now that you mention it, it does feel like the same anger and hurt I've sensed in Leia so many times. There's this... It's hard to explain, and I know this sounds weird, but there's this almost beautiful, heartbreaking sadness beneath her anger. And the fear—it adds this silvery..."

I trail off, searching for the right words. "It's like watching the sun set behind puffy clouds. A couple of rays try to break through—a few rays of hope, but..." I shake my head, embarrassed. "I'm sorry. That probably didn't make any sense."

"To the average person, probably not," Tessa says with a laugh. "But you're not talking to the average person."

"Thanks," I reply. "But I never noticed people's emotions having a similar... composition before. But now that you mention it, Leia's and Alexi's feelings are identical. Alexi's are just louder. But... how is that even possible?"

"It's funny that you mention the sunset," Tessa says, straightening her posture. "That's actually one of the most common analogies I use to explain your next lesson."

I raise an eyebrow, intrigued.

"Like most people, you're more active during the day, while the night finds a quieter, more dormant version of Aiden. It's a bit awkward, I know, but try to imagine the duality of night and day as two realms where the same Aiden exists. Each realm sees a different version of you, but those versions are inseparable, interconnected, and constantly influencing each other.

"What you do in the daylight realm determines how tired you are at night, and how well you rest in the nighttime realm dictates how much you can get done during the day."

I got a lot of sleep last night, but I still haven't gotten much done today.

"The analogy isn't perfect because these two physical realms follow one another in succession. But... the human soul exists in two realms at the same time. Your conscious awareness interacts with this one—the material realm.

"But there's another realm where your soul also exists: the Gaius realm. This is the nighttime version, if you like that phrasing, of the material realm. And there's a Gaius version of every single human being on the planet."

I squint at her, trying to absorb everything she's saying. Her presence projects a warm, calming aura. But even with the connection we share in this moment, her words leave my mind spinning.

What does that even mean? How am I supposed to make sense of that? The Gaius realm? Wha...?

"The Gaius realm version of a person is the human soul in isolation. In that realm, people's souls don't interact with each other, so the Gaius side doesn't care about rules or empathy—it simply wants what it wants and doesn't care about hurting others to get it. That realm is the source of every selfish and harmful impulse in a person's Laosi. It's a place of pure, primal instinct: rage, pride, greed, lust—all uninhibited. It's the dark side of the soul, Aiden. But when I strip it all down, do you know what I find at the core of it all?"

I shake my head, still staring blankly.

"Fear," she says softly. "Fear that in the loneliness of isolation, the person won't get what they want, need, or think they need. Think of a baby who hasn't learned to trust that his parents will provide all the nourishment he needs. Until he sees that bottle in his mother's or father's hands, he screams in anger and sadness over his powerlessness to meet his own needs. He has no concern for the disruption that his cries might present to his parent's business meeting, shopping excursion, or sleep. It offends some people to hear this, but babies are entirely selfish."

"It doesn't offend me at all," I say, laughing. "That was my favorite word for describing my brother Jack until... well, honestly, it still is."

Tessa smiles at my joke. "A person's Gaius never grows out of that self-absorption. The needs of the human soul are embedded in its Gaius. The need to be safe, understood, recognized, accepted, valued and more are all in the subconscious side of the soul. And there's a beauty in the design of the isolation in that these desires can flourish in the freedom of existence without pressure to conform to the opinions or needs of others. These needs deserve the same dignity you've only recently begun to give to your emotions, and in the Gaius realm, they have it. But these are not needs that can be met through self-reliance in isolation."

"If I'm following you, then you're saying people act selfishly because their Gaius has a need and feels like it has to do whatever to get it met? The baby cries without caring about who he offends because that's the only way he knows to get his needs met. Something like that, right?"

With conviction, Tessa says, "A starving, caged herbivore backed into a corner will kill you faster than an apex predator with a full stomach." Her tone softens. "You're a very bright young man. I'm pleased with how quickly you're putting the pieces together."

"Thanks... but it's really how you explain things." I pause, smirking. "Speaking of, how come most of your analogies have to do with kids?"

Her smile deepens. "Because adults have far more in common with children than they like to admit. The main difference is that children haven't learned to hide or sugarcoat who they really are."

"That's a fair point... Man, the Gaius realm, huh? I guess I should probably just get used to the fact that my questions just breed more questions. If I didn't see where you were going with this, it would be really hard to believe."

"Thanks for being a good sport," she says, her voice warm with sympathy. "But it shouldn't be that hard to believe. Every time you take an action that you disagree with, that seems inconsistent with who you are, you're proving the existence of the dual realms. Almost all of your regrets come from the interplay between you and the other you."

"This is a lot to take in... especially since, if I'm following, you're saying Alexi is Leia's Gaius. But how is that possible? I thought you said a person's Gaius doesn't interact with other people."

Make it make sense, Tessa.

"Typically, it doesn't. At least, not so directly. But there are exceptions—like your experience," she says.

"You mean... my experience with Alexi?"

Tessa's smile holds an edge that almost feels patronizing. "You still have a lot to learn. And if you stay on this path, you'll uncover some very uncomfortable truths. I told you I won't give you the answers you want, but I will lead you to the answers you need."

"Surprisingly, I have no idea what that means," I reply, chuckling lightly along with her. "But if Alexi is Leia's Gaius, how did it—or she—attack me in the real world?"

"You'll be surprised by how powerful you and Leia could become together. If and when you two get healthy enough to use your powers in harmony, the world will be better off because of it. We could do a lot of good together."

"So... wait. Be straight with me for a second. You're

telling me Leia has LETs? I can't ev—"

"More than I'm telling you anything about Leia, Aiden, I'm telling you that you need to accept her for who she is and apologize for not doing so thus far. Work on understanding her experience the way she understands it. That's your next right step. If you don't, Alexi is going to keep opposing you every step of the way."

"Apologize?" My voice rises. "The last time we talked about Leia, you told me I had the right to be mad at her."

"And I stand by that," she says.

"But now you're telling me to apologize?"

"Yes. You find that confusing?"

"You tell me her dark side or whatever almost killed me, got in the way of our mission, belittles and threatens me, and will keep doing it… and you want *me* to apologize *her*? Yes, I do find that very confusing. Plus…" I pause, lowering my gaze and volume. "I just thought you were on *my* side."

"I am," she says earnestly.

It doesn't feel like it.

Tessa folds her arms. "I have no intention of pacifying you. That's not what I offered when I found you on your hands and knees in the middle of the road two months ago. If that's what you want, I'm sure you can find it somewhere else. What I offered was to help you grow. And if that's still what you want, then do what I said: own up to what *you* did, go confess that to her, and apologize for not accepting her."

"Okay, okay," I grumble, crossing my arms. "But what if Alexi shows up and attacks me again?"

"She won't… unless you provoke her. Remember what I said—Alexi, like all Gaius, is fueled by the fear of going without. Give Leia's heart what it needs, and Alexi will have no reason to go on the offensive."

"Yeah, but what if she starts arguing with me, and then I 'provoke' her accidentally? That's what usually happens. That's why we don't talk that often as it is."

"I'll give you a free tip," she says, leaning in as she

makes her point. "The most effective weapon you have in an argument is your silence. When you're silent, either the other person will hear their own foolishness and stop, you will hear the futility in reasoning with them and stop, or you'll hear validity in their experience. Either way, you're not adding fuel to the fire. If the conversation turns into a lose-lose, use your silence."

"That's hard when someone's accusing you or yelling at you," I say, trying not to become defensive.

"Harder than the frustration, the remorse, and the distance you feel after engaging in a fruitless argument?" she counters.

"Well, when you put it that way... All right. If I'm going to do this, I should do it now," I say, tapping my Solo to check the time. I sigh, glancing back at Tessa. "I want you to know I'm *not* looking forward to this. But I will yield. I really am committed to the Broken. And... thanks. Thanks for having lunch with me. I didn't know you made house calls," I add, smiling.

"It's been my pleasure," Tessa replies. "It means a lot that you used some PTO to spend time with me. Lunch was delicious, by the way. Pass on my appreciation to your mom for teaching you how to cook," she says as we rise to our feet. "And it wouldn't hurt for you to tell her you love her every once in a while."

I chuckle softly, looking down. "I might just do that. I probably should. We just... never really had that kind of relationship, ya know? Anyway, I'll let you get back to... whatever it is you do during the day," I say, laughing. "I won't hold you."

She looks me in the eyes with an air of disbelief and says, "Hold me? Do you think there's anything I'd rather be doing than spending time with my people?"

Before I can find a response, she steps closer and pulls me into a hug. During the brief embrace, she says, "You're traveling a hard road, but you're making progress. I'm proud of you."

"Thanks, Tessa," I reply, my voice catching as I blink quickly, trying to play off the tears welling up in my eyes. "That means a lot."

"No problem," she says, releasing the hug and stepping back. "Go talk to Leia. And when you're done, bring her to HQ. I've been looking forward to meeting her in person."

CHAPTER 18 – WALKING

"Lil' A, start a video call with Leia Hart," I say as the door closes behind Tessa.

"I'll think about it," Lil' A replies.

"What?" I ask, already annoyed.

"I'm just saying, you've been real bossy lately. Why don't you try being nice to me?"

That last software update clearly did not help.

"You get on my NERVES!" I yell at Lil' A.

"If you called me just to yell at me," Leia says, her voice suddenly filling the room, "then you can hang right back up!"

"What? No, no, no… Leia, no! I was yelling at my AI!"

See what you made me do!

"You're still yelling," she observes dryly.

"That's because I—!" I stop, take a deep breath, and say, "Can we just start over?"

Leia laughs. "I think we should."

Switching to a falsetto, I say, "Hey, Leia, you're getting a video call from Aiden Lore."

"That's not how Precious talks," Leia says, though I can tell she's amused.

Still in my falsetto, but adding a touch of sassiness, I reply, "If I were you, girl, I'd hurry up and answer this call. I'm gonna do you a favor and patch him through right now!"

She giggles. "Hey, Aiden. What's up?"

"Hey, Leia. You busy right now?"

"Not at the moment. What's going on?"

"Well… I was wondering if I could come over real quick. You know, our last conversation kinda got cut off," I say, trying to gauge her mood. She chose audio-only, so I can't read her body language.

"It did," she says. "I was like, 'Where did he go?' Did you know you could teleport? Where did you go, actually?"

She doesn't sound too mad. That's good.

"I... Wait, can I come over? I'll explain everything. Plus... I want to give you something," I say.

"Give me something? Like what?"

"Something like... something."

"You're being weird," she says with a chuckle. "What are you trying to give me?"

"It's something I should've given you a long time ago," I explain.

"Aiden, I hope you didn't spend any money on me. Because I don't know if—"

"No, no... It's nothing like that," I say quickly. "It's... Can I come over or not?"

Did that sound like I'm annoyed? Maybe I should laugh.

"Yeah... yeah, that's fine," she says hesitantly. "You coming over now?"

"If that's cool with you."

"Well, I guess I mean, like, are you gonna teleport or fly or something? Or just, like, take a carrier?" she asks. "I'm just trying to figure out your ETA."

"You know what? That's a fair question, all things considered. I'll take a carrier, so 20 minutes?"

"Okay," she says with a sigh. "Let me get dressed for company, then."

"I mean, you don't *have* to get dressed if you don't want —"

"Don't push your luck, buddy," she cuts in, playfully but firmly.

"Okay, okay," I say, laughing in surrender. "Get dressed. I'll see you soon. Lil' A, end call."

"Call ended, big dog!" Lil' A replies enthusiastically. "I already called a carrier for you. It's waiting in the pickup zone," my AI companion says.

Not bad, Lil' A. Trying to redeem yourself, I see.

I grab my purple and green rain jacket before heading out the door just in case we decide to go for a walk. At the loading zone, I hop into the carrier and call out Leia's coordinates to the nav system.

"Lil' A, call Auriel Yamada. Audio only," I say as the carrier pulls out.

"On it!"

Wait... Why am I calling her?

"Aiden, hi! How are you?" Auriel answers, her voice warm with surprise.

"I'm okay. How about you?"

"Now, Aiden, you've been with the Broken long enough to know that 'okay' doesn't cut it."

"Ha! Yeah, reintegration work kinda ruins one-word answers, huh?"

"Exactly," she laughs. "So? How are you *really?*"

"I'm good. For real. A little sore—my back especially—but nothing major. I was pretty much out cold all day yesterday, so I took today off to recover. Who knew saving Tryon was so physically demanding?"

"Right?" she laughs again. "I'm glad you took the time to rest. Saturday was a lot for all of us, but Tirrell and I agreed you had the hardest job. I'm sorry we put so much on you. And on your first assignment, too! If you want to talk about it, I'm here."

"Thanks. Actually, Tessa came over for lunch, so she helped me kinda process through what went down."

"Ooh, how nice! I love hanging out with her," Auriel says. "How'd it go?"

"It was... okay."

"Aiden."

I sigh and say, "Right. No, it was... I mean, I feel like it's always good, right? She's so insightful and stuff... But why can't she ever give simple answers?"

"Hmm... probably because life isn't simple," Auriel replies thoughtfully.

"Yeah, it definitely is not... Especially with her introducing me to this whole... what did she...? Um, the... Gaius Realm? Has she talked to you about that?" I ask.

"Ohhh, you had *that* conversation today? Your brain must feel like scrambled eggs right now," she laughs.

"At some point, you just keep nodding and smiling while you try your best to make sense of what she just said."

"Except she *knows* what you're thinking," Auriel points out.

"See? There's no winning with that lady!" I say, and we both laugh. "But anyway, how about you? I just wanted to check in and see how things have been for you since we were all together."

So why I haven't checked in with Zane or Tirrell?

"That's so sweet of you. Thank you," she says gently. "Well, by the time I got home from HQ, Brice was already asleep. I didn't get to tuck him into bed like I usually do, but my sister did a good enough job."

Sister? Not Brice's dad?

"I was so tired I just crashed when I got there anyway," she continues. "Sunday was pretty uneventful, though. So, all in all, I'm good... I think I'm good," she says, but her voice falters.

"Are you, though?" I ask.

"I just..." Her pace slows, like she's piecing her thoughts together as she talks. "Do you think we made the right call out there? I mean... I believe in my heart that we did good work, but I guess I'm scared about what's going to happen from here. Ever since the name 'The Broken' got leaked to the press, I keep second-guessing everything. Maybe we shouldn't have gotten involved at all. Maybe we should've just let CLU handle it.

"I just think about people like Talia in our group, people who aren't in this to make headlines. I feel like the Broken will never be the same after this weekend... Sorry for dumping all my worries on you," she finishes with a sigh.

"You're good," I say, trying to reassure her. "I wouldn't

have asked if I didn't want to know."

I take a moment to collect my thoughts before continuing. "For me, I try to think about whether I'd make the same decisions if I were in that situation again. And yeah, I'd probably do some things differently. But if we got a call today that the Collective was targeting someone else, I'd absolutely engage. I mean... they can control people's minds? Who knows how many Elon's, Eboni's, or Stacie's are out there? And honestly, I don't like the idea of trusting CLU at this point. If the Collective runs the news, who's to say they don't control CLU as well? I feel like I can only trust the people Tessa trusts, since she can see people's Laosi."

"Hey, Aiden, I've been having trouble hearing you. I think I caught most of that, but it sounds like rain or something. Are you outside in this downpour?" Auriel asks.

"Yeah—well, I'm in a carrier. Sorry about that. What did you miss?"

"I think I caught enough to put it together," she says. "I'm just surprised you're going anywhere in this weather, though. This is 'stay inside and snuggle up' weather if you ask me."

I laugh. "That does sound nice."

"So, where are you headed that's worth braving this nastiness? If you don't mind me asking," she adds.

"Oh, I'm headed to... Do you remember that— um, on Saturday... I had that friend call me and I had to leave all of a sudden, and then I ended up teleporting back? We, uh... We didn't really finish that conversation, I guess."

Friend?

"Oh, okay. That makes sense," Auriel says, but then she starts chuckling.

"What?" I ask, feeling extremely self-conscious.

"No, I was just thinking... It's ironic because word is spreading around the Broken that people can't hide their emotions around you. But now that we know which of your Talents are triggered by which emotions, you can't hide yours either," she says with a laugh.

"You think you've got me figured out, huh?" I challenge while smirking.

"Like it or not, you're the most open book I've ever met," she fires back, laughing. "Seriously, though. That last conversation obviously left you feeling a lot of shame. If you're walking back into a tense situation, just remember we've got your back. Lawrence is throwing a little social tonight. If you need to offload some heavy feelings, that might be a good space for you. Had you heard about it?"

"I had not. You going?" I ask.

"Yeah. I'm bringing Brice, too. He's such a crowd-pleaser with our people," she laughs. "The most extroverted 2-year-old you'll ever meet!"

What kind of social do you bring a 2-year-old to? The Broken is weird.

Intrigued despite myself, I say, "Okay... send me the time and address. Could be a good chance for me to get to know some more of the brotherhood."

"Yeah, that's exactly why he planned it. There'll be people from our other branches there, too. But with everything that's happened, I think the vibe might be a little different. I'm sure most people will be talking about the 'Felicity Devastation,' as it's being called. But if you need to decompress or anything, I'm sure we can find a quiet corner to chat. We still haven't shared our stories, by the way."

That doesn't sound too—

"City Sector RL, Apartment Building Q9, Floor 14. We have arrived!" the carrier's AI announces. "Please stay seated until the carrier has come to a complete stop."

"Sounds like you're there. I hope it goes well, and maybe I'll see you tonight," Auriel says cheerfully.

"You just might. We'll see. Glad you're doing okay, Auriel. Have a good one!"

"You, too! End call."

Right after the beeps signal the disconnection, Lil' A

chimes in, "Did she just hang up on us?"

"Shut up, Lil' A."

"Aye, aye, Captain!" my Solo avatar replies.

I step out of the carrier into the hallway of Leia's apartment building. For some reason, it feels unfamiliar, even though I've walked this path so many times before. The cozy aesthetic given off by the incandescent light fixtures suddenly feels less inviting... almost cold.

I glance down at the blue and gray patchwork carpet.

This used to feel like it was a symbol of Leia and me—like we were the missing pieces of each other's lives, completing an exciting picture. But now, standing here feels more like the start of a puzzle, having no idea which pieces fit together—or if they even do.

I walk to her unit, press the doorbell, and wait as the red lasers of the bioscanner read me. Through the door, I sense a calm presence approaching.

That's reassuring.

The door opens, and Leia appears, standing there in blue jeans and a loose-knit top that looks comfortable but stylish. "Hey," she says.

"Hey, Leia."

We just stand there awkwardly for a moment until I gesture toward the interior of her apartment. "So... can I come in?"

"Yeah, sorry," she says. "I was just—"

"Looking at my empty hands and wondering what I came here to give you?"

She cocks her head to the side, one eyebrow raised. "You can read minds, too?"

I laugh. "Not that I'm aware."

As she opens the door wider and steps aside to let me in, she asks, "Okay, so what all can you do? I need to know." She sounds curious, more interested than demanding.

I walk over to the sofa and sit down, immediately reminded of how comfortable this seat is. The light, mildly sweet scent of incense fills the air. The rain patters softly against the window, adding to the cozy atmosphere. For a second, I think about how perfect it would be to take a nap right now.

To my surprise, Leia sits down on the sofa with me. Closer than I expected. Though not quite as close as I'd like.

Emboldened by her nearness, I say, "Apparently, I can do a lot. I can teleport, as you saw. I can make force fields, fly, repel things from my hands, attract things to myself... I can manipulate the distance between things in all kinds of ways. That's the theme of it all."

Leia's eyes widen, and I catch a flicker of both awe and sadness. "Aiden... this is the first time in my life I've heard you talk about your abilities without sounding like you hated them. I don't know how I knew, but I always knew you'd get there. I knew you'd come to respect your powers."

The way she looks at me reminds me a lot of the look she had at the top of Sheridan Tower. There's just too much honesty in her eyes. As I look away, I say, "Thanks... You always did believe in me."

In this moment, it becomes clear to me that the affection between us never died. And the look in her eye suggests to me that some part of her doesn't want it to.

What can I say to make this moment last?

"No one's ever believed in me like you do. That's why you're so special to me. Well, that's not the only reason. There are a lot of reasons, actually."

Each word I say seems to be softening her heart towards me, little by little, so I keep going.

"It's also because you're ambitious. But it's not the 'Look at me and what I can do' ambition that most people have. You're driven to help people. It's crazy to me how big your heart is and how much you care about others. I love seeing the way you're wired, the things you value... You're just so special, Leia."

She smiles slightly and looks at the floor, gently

brushing a tuft of hair behind her ear. "Aiden? What are you doing?"

"I'm just telling you how I feel about you. How I've always felt about you," I say back, wondering if it would be too bold to hold her hand.

"I know, but... why are you doing that? You're not following the rules, mister," she says, wagging her finger at me.

"Maybe not... but you didn't seem to mind," I say.

She sighs and says, "I didn't... But, I mean, what girl doesn't want to hear why they're special? I kinda feel like that wasn't fair."

"What do you mean?" I say, trying to sound innocent to diffuse the tension I feel growing in her.

"I mean, you know I'm still trying to figure out everything between us. And it's not because I don't love you or don't want to be with you. I just... I'm trying to learn how to listen to myself and take care of myself," she says passionately. "So then, you come over saying you have something to give me, but instead, you start saying all this nice stuff that makes me feel good, and... I don't know. I'm vulnerable right now, Aiden. And this is what I don't need."

"I understand," I begin.

"Do you, though?" she asks, her voice sharp. "Because if I'm honest... this feels manipulative."

I freeze. The hairs on the back of my neck stand up. I can't even hear the rest of what she's saying. Every one of my senses has been hijacked by the emergence of something painfully familiar happening behind me. The anger, the sadness, the hurt, the fear—all converging into one presence. Alexi is here.

This is the exact opposite of what I wanted.

"Can you just give me the space to be where I am for a while?" Leia says. "I don't hate you... but I can't trust you either. So, I don't need to be emotionally invested in you until I figure that out. I know that's not what you want to hear... but is that okay? Because that's where I am right now. Can you accept that

that's where I am?"

Tessa's words charge into my mind: "You haven't accepted her rage, her fear, or the way she deals with those feelings by trying to control your life so that she can feel safe."

I take a deep breath, choosing silence. I wait. I listen. And for the first time, I hear her talk about the wounds she endured while weathering the storm of confusion, self-blame, and hopelessness caused by my actions. The rage of Alexi's presence breathes down my neck, but I keep waiting. I stay focused on Leia.

When she finishes expressing herself, I say, "Leia, that's actually why I came. What I need to give you is an apology. I'm sorry, Leia. Not just for losing control of my powers and hurting you physically. I'm sorry for trying to control how you felt about being hurt by my powers."

Alexi's fury weakens, and Leia's face softens. Leia takes a deep breath as she processes what I've just said. Alexi walks to the loveseat and sits down, her trademark psychic dagger hovering in front of her, as usual.

Is that really necessary? I mean, really?

"Took you long enough," Alexi says, scoffing. "But don't think one apology is going to fix everything that's happened over the last two years."

"Leia, I know one apology doesn't fix anything," I say, looking into her eyes. "If I could go back and change the past, I would. We actually have someone in The Broken who can rewind time a little, but I've only seen her go back a few minutes. I doubt she could undo two years of history…"

You're rambling, Aide.

I take a breath and refocus. "But that's not the point. The point is you've had every right to be angry with me. You've had every right not to trust me because I haven't proven myself trustworthy. My powers still get the best of me sometimes, even now. I'm learning and growing with Tessa and the Broken, but I'm not there yet. So I get why you felt like you had to take matters into your own hands to protect yourself.

"You pushed me to do what I needed to do to control my powers. And when that didn't work, you distanced yourself from me altogether. That makes sense."

I pause and look at Alexi. "I'm not mad at you anymore, Leia. And I'm sorry for not accepting the fact that you've been doing the best you can despite everything you've gone through... despite everything I've put you through."

Alexi opens her mouth to speak, but Leia says, "It's not just about what *you* put me through, Aiden," she says. "I told you before that I had another boyfriend who couldn't control his LETs either. But I didn't tell you that he burned down a house while I was still inside it."

Her words prick my heart, and every protective instinct within me engages.

"He was trying to impress me or something with his fire powers. But when I told him I'd seen enough, he just..."

Alexi's energy intensifies, her powers now fully unleashed. Seven blades of purple and crimson Laosi hover in the air—all pointed at me. I don't flinch. I just keep listening to Leia.

"He ends up losing control and sets the whole house on fire," she says, her breathing uneven. "Smoke is filling my lungs, I'm getting dizzy, and I'm freaking out. I don't even remember how I made it out alive. And to this day, he walks free. He should be locked away, but he's not. Because I didn't press charges."

"Why didn't you?" I ask gently, aware that she could be asked the same question about me.

"Because..." she says, sniffling. "When I told one of my friends at the time what happened, all she did was ask me why I went to that abandoned house with him in the first place. 'You should've known better,' she said. And she was right. I did know better. So it was my fault I almost died. Why press charges?"

"No, Leia... no, no, no," I say, leaning forward and reaching out to wipe the tear rolling down her cheek. "That wasn't your fault at all. I can't imagine how scary that was for you. I'm so sorry, Baby."

"Yeah... I mean, I know that now," she says softly. "But it doesn't change how I felt. I just... I felt so powerless."

I just called her "Baby," and she didn't even flinch!

"He almost killed me, and there was nothing I could do to stop it. I was voiceless. He wouldn't hear me." She pauses, so I grab her hand to reassure her.

This is still going well!

"So, when you came along, I knew it was a risk because you had out-of-control LETs, too," Leia continues. "But at least it wasn't fire, right? And even though all you did the first time was propel a Solo toward my head—which wasn't actually going to hit me—it triggered all those memories I thought I'd recovered from but clearly hadn't.

"Ever since then, I've been thinking, 'Here I am, being stupid again. He's gonna kill me, and it's my fault!' That's when I started getting so pushy. I was... it sounds kinda crazy, but I guess I was trying to protect the younger me. And... on some level, that's not fair to you. It probably activated more Laosi than it protected me from. But on another level, I can't help how triggering LETs are for me."

I sigh heavily and just look at her. Alexi's blades have disappeared completely. She sits on the loveseat with her face in her hands, her body twitching restlessly.

"Leia, I... Let me just say how sorry I am to hear that you went through all of that. That sounds terrifying and invalidating at the same time. I get why my LETs scared you so much now. LETs almost cost you your life because some jerk thought it was okay to completely ignore how you felt or what you wanted."

I pause to see how that lands. I sense relief in her, so I continue. "Also, thank you for telling me all that. I see how hard it was for you to go back through all those thoughts and feelings. And it helps me understand how things went down between us. I'm sorry... for reminding you over and over again of a time when you thought you were going to die."

She sniffles and says, "That's the part I keep saying isn't really your fault. You're a great guy, Aiden. I see so much greatness in you. That's why I never wanted to give up on us. But with what I've been through, I just don't know if I'm the kind of woman who can be with you, even as great as I see you to be."

"Wow," I say softly. "That was unexpected. You didn't have to say that. I came here just to give you a long-overdue apology."

She looks back at me with passion in her eyes and says, "There are so many compliments you deserve that I just never gave you. I didn't feel like you really heard me when I talked about the pain in my heart, so it was hard to get past that and talk about the good I see in yours. But today, you heard me."

Then, glancing toward Alexi, she says, "And there were a lot of hurtful things I said and did to you. So many times, I was controlling, uncaring, and just mean to you. I know I hurt you more than I ever intended. But it's almost like it wasn't me or something. It's hard to explain."

"Oh, trust me... I completely get it."

Can she actually see Alexi this time?

"Either way, I want you to know I'm not excusing the things I said or did to you. It was just my way of trying to protect myself, I guess. And I'm sorry."

"It's... it's okay. I'm not mad at you."

"Thank you."

"Let me ask you something. This isn't a 'let's get back together' question—though I'm obviously not opposed to that." I check for her reaction. She doesn't budge, so I continue. "What would it take for you to feel protected without needing to protect yourself in those more aggressive ways?"

"Um... that's a really good question," she says. "Honestly, I think I'd need more of this. These kinds of conversations. If I could trust that you actually want to hear me and protect me, I don't think I'd feel like I have to protect myself."

"That makes sense," I reply thoughtfully. "Are you willing to try trusting that?"

"That sounds terrifying," she says with a nervous laugh.

"I bet it does," I say, smiling gently. "That's why I'm not asking you to be perfect at it. I'm just asking if you're willing to try."

"If you would keep acting like you are now… then yes. I think I would be."

"Great!" I say, relief washing over me.

"Hey… can I…?" Leia starts.

Suddenly, Alexi's entire body begins to glow—not the chaotic purple and red Laosi she usually emits, but a controlled, purposeful, white radiance. She and Leia stand abruptly, moving in perfect sync with each other.

"I want to give you something, too," Leia says, stepping closer to me.

I stand reflexively. Leia stops directly in front of me, and out of the corner of my eye, I see Alexi moving in the same direction. I try to keep an eye on Alexi, but Leia leans in and hugs me, perfectly obscuring my view of her Gaius realm self. Alexi's hostility has evaporated, though, so I close my eyes and embrace the moment.

Just as I lose myself in her arms, Leia's skin glows white and feels warm. Or maybe it's my body that feels warm where we're connected. The spot where her hand rests on my back feels especially warm, almost hot.

Am I imagining this?

I decide not to overthink it and just stay present in the hug. But then, other words from Tessa echo in my mind: "You'll be surprised by how powerful you and Leia could become together. If and when you two get healthy enough to use your powers in harmony, the world will be better off because of it."

What did she mean by that?

Leia ends the hug and takes a couple steps back. "What was that?" she asks, inspecting her hands.

"What was what?" I reply, distracted by the sudden realization that I can't see or sense Alexi at all.

"How's your back?" she asks, her voice rising. "It was hurting, right? How does it feel now?"

"What?"

How did she know my back was—

I twist my lower back, testing for pain, but there's nothing. My back feels fine. Completely fine.

"Leia, what did you do? Did you just…?" I look at her, eyes wide. "It doesn't hurt at all anymore!"

CHAPTER 19 – RUNNING

"I healed you," Leia says, her tone and body language calm, almost emotionless. But as the words register, she tilts her head and squints, searching my face for answers. When she doesn't find any, she looks around the living room.

"Yeah... I healed you," she repeats, her voice softer, less certain.

"Leia... you have an LET? How long have you had an LET?"

"*I* have an LET? But... what? How is that even possible?" Her breathing quickens.

She's freaking out.

"Hey, it's cool," I say gently. "You've got a power that can help people."

She takes a step back, pacing around the living room. "No... no, it doesn't make sense," she mutters. "I can't... I've been afraid of people with LETs for the last five years of my life. And now I'm one of them? I don't..."

I step into her path, taking her hand in mine. "Come on," I say softly, guiding her back to the sofa. We sit down beside each other, and she takes deep breaths.

Wow! She's got an LET! Now she'll understand me better, and we can probably—

"You did this to me," she says suddenly, her voice low and dejected. "You made me a User."

I sigh. "Yeah... I guess I did."

What did I disintegrate within her?

"Did you know you could do that, too?"

"No... I had no idea. Well... I guess, technically, I did. I mean, anyone can, really."

"What's that supposed to mean?"

"It's..." I pause, searching for the right words. "It's hard to explain. And honestly, there's probably nothing I can say that will make any sense right now. I just... I remember the first time my abilities activated after going through LIST, after being so sure I didn't have powers. I was scared, I was angry, confused... I was a mess. Do any of those feelings resonate with you? What are you feeling right now?"

I sound just like Tessa.

"Don't be using your empathy on me," she says. She's too overwhelmed to crack a smile at her own playfulness. I fight to hold back a grin.

"But, yeah, I feel everything you just said," she continues. "I'm scared, I'm angry, I'm confused... I just... I never thought I'd be like you all. But now I'm a User. I'm disappointed and anxious, too."

Okay, she's more emotionally self-aware than I am even now. So she's not Heart-Disintegrated. Mind maybe?

"Leia... being a User doesn't make you a bad person," I say carefully. "You used to tell me all the time that you thought I could do a lot of good with my powers, right?" She hesitates, but then nods. "Having powers doesn't change who you are. Besides, your ability seems to be the power to heal people. Having your power isn't a bad thing. I'm... just... more concerned about *why* you have powers."

"What do you mean?"

"Well, the reason people have LETs is... Ah. Okay, now I see why Tessa wanted to meet with you herself. She can explain it a lot better than I can. There's a lot that I still don't understand. But she can help you make sense of it. I mean, if you'd like to meet her."

"You're talking about that lady with... What's your group called? The Damaged?"

"The Broken," I laugh.

"I was close," she jokes, and I can sense her starting to calm down. "If she can help, then I guess it might be worth it. Wait a minute. Is the Broken a cult or something? You said they had weird rules."

"No! No, of course not!" I laugh again. "You really think I'd just go off and join a cult and then invite you into it?"

Now, I feel as awkward as Tirrell must have when I asked him the same question.

"I don't know what I think right now..."

"That actually makes sense. I think you're *Mind-Disintegrated.* What were you thinking about when you healed me?"

"You think my *mind did what?*" she asks.

"Sorry," I say quickly. "That's... nevermind. But no, we're definitely not a cult. We're just... people. Trying to figure out the best way to live our lives with these LETs. You want to come? Actually, there's a little get-together tonight that could be a chill way to meet some people."

"I... don't know about any social events," she says. "That's moving way too fast for me. I just found out I'm a User two minutes ago, and you want me to go to a User party?"

"I get that, and I'll slow down," I say, backing off. "I just know what I needed—and didn't have—when my powers came online. But everyone's process is different, so I won't try to push anything on you. Just trying to give the help I wish I had."

She sighs. "And that's really sweet and thoughtful of you. It's just... a lot. I don't know what I need right now, you know? I feel like I was just born... again. Like a baby that doesn't know what it needs in this scary, new world that's so different from the warm, comfortable womb it was used to. So now it just cries and pees on everybody," she says, laughing. "But... what do you think? Do you think I should meet Tessa?"

"I'll just say this: if I had met Tessa 10 years ago, you'd never have ended up in a coma."

"Which also means I probably wouldn't have LETs and wouldn't need to meet her," Leia says, half-joking.

"You might have a point there," I concede with a smile. "I'm just saying that if you want help processing everything you're thinking and feeling right now, there's no one better on all of Tryon to talk to than Tessa."

"Okay. But why did you say she wanted to meet me?"

"Ohhh, right. I forgot to mention—she's a telepath. She reads my mind all the time. She probably even knows what you smell like by now."

"Thaaaat's weird."

"That was too much, wasn't it? My bad," I say. "It's just… you're on my mind a lot, so I'm sure she's very familiar with you."

"O… kay," she says cautiously. "What's she like?"

"She's not like anyone I've ever met before. Honestly, I don't even know how to describe her."

"Oh? You got a crush on her?"

"You jealous?" I counter.

"No, not really," she says, brushing it off.

Are you, though?

"I'm just asking if I should dress up or something. What should I expect?" Leia clarifies.

"Nah, don't worry about dressing up. She's really wise and profound, but also super chill. She's the kind of person who meets you exactly where you are. And putting on a show won't do any good—she can literally see your soul."

Leia hides her body behind her hands and arms. "That sounds like I'd feel exposed."

"That's exactly how you're gonna feel," I chuckle. "But you'll get used to it. Besides, it's not like you ever really pretend to be something that you're not."

"That's true," she says with a sigh. "Okay, so when do I meet her? Should I call and make an appointment or something? How does it work?"

"How do you feel about going right now?" I ask.

"I don't want to intrude or anything. I'm sure she's—"

"She'll make time for you," I interrupt. "After all, you'll be coming with Aiden Lore. Everyone else will just have to wait their turn."

"Oh, so you're the big man on campus, huh?"

"I don't like to brag, but... ya know," I say with a shrug and a smirk.

"You're so full of it," she says, laughing and jabbing me in the arm. "I can't stand you."

"I know, I know," I reply sarcastically. "So, are you ready to go?"

"Well... I guess so. If you think I should. Do you want me to call a carrier?" she asks, rising to her feet.

"Oh, don't worry about that," I assure her, standing up beside her.

"Well, you already caught a ride over here. I don't mind paying for one."

"Once again, you're coming with Aiden Lore. Let me show you how I travel."

Without giving her a chance to respond, I put my arm around her waist.

As I prepare to teleport, I think about this new dimension of chaos that's just been added to Leia's life. I recall the anger on Alexi's face the last time I was in this apartment. And Leia's words—how it's my fault she even needs to meet Tessa—bounce around wherever they want to go in my mind.

I hear the familiar high-pitched hum, feel the pressure building in my core, and notice the goosebumps running down my spine.

In a split second, we're standing in the rain across the street from Otto's Autos.

I came here for the first time just a couple of months ago. My life is so different now, but I've brought Leia into this unusual, broken life. Why did I have to have these LETs?

"Ah!!" Leia shrieks. "Aiden!"

"Sorry!" I call out, realizing she didn't grab a rain jacket like I did. Without wasting time trying to take mine off for her, I grab her hand and dash across the street for shelter under the awning hanging over HQ's front door.

Safe from the rain, I turn to Leia. She smiles at me, which makes me smile, too, even though I don't know why. I just like that she's happy when she looks at me.

"What are you thi—?"

Before I can finish, she throws herself into my arms, wrapping hers around me. The answer to my question feels unimportant as I hug her back.

She pulls away just enough to look me in the eyes and says, "You did that on command! You can control your powers now?"

I grin. "Something like that."

"I'm proud of you. You're really making progress," she says, her eyes sparkling. Then she glances back at the slightly flooded street and adds, "You could've given me a warning, though! I'm still working on my response to the sound of Laosi. Plus, do you have any idea what this rain is going to do to my hair? I just got it done yesterday!"

"Yeah, that's my bad."

She glares, shaking her head slowly.

Shrugging, I change the subject. "Shall we?"

"I guess so... but I'm nervous. What have you been telling these people about me?" she asks.

"That you're the most beautiful and amazing person they'll ever meet," I say with a dramatic flair.

"Uh-huh," she replies, unconvinced.

I open the front door, and we walk through the corridor into the open showroom.

"There are usually more people here," I comment. "But it's Monday afternoon, so I guess people are at work."

"Good," she laughs. "You know I'm antisocial."

"Don't be like that," I laugh. "It should be pretty easy to get some time with Tessa. She's probably in a meeting right now. Let me show you around while we wait."

We wander through the showroom as I point out different areas. Gesturing toward a semicircle of chairs, I say, "That's where they have Dynamics class. It's a space to talk about living with LETs and share experiences. They even give homework to help with reintegration."

"Reintegration?"

"Yeah… I'll let Tessa explain that. Oh, over there," I say, pointing to the open martial arts area, "is where I learned I have this weird heavy-gravity dome thing I can use when I get sad. But my favorite spot is right there."

She follows my finger to the glass door leading to the patio overlooking the Yra Forest.

"Oh, wow…" Leia says, her voice filled with wonder.

"Yeah. I'd never seen Sardonis trees in person until I came here either," I say.

"Oh, I've seen them before," she says, staring out. "But they're still beautiful."

"Well, excuse me!" I reply sarcastically. "How do you always experience the things I try to surprise you with *before* I do?"

"Because I… live my life?" she teases.

Deflated, I continue, "I caught my first glimpse of them when I flew around this showroom. Did I tell you that when I fly, it's because I'm happy?" Leia shakes her head. "Yeah, all my powers are tied to my emotions. That's why Dr. Cambridge and everyone else can't fully figure me out. See, I don't let myself feel feelings really, so they just kinda come out in other ways because there's a lot of energy stored up in my heart's soul stream."

I notice her familiar glazed-over look—the one she gives me whenever I start nerding out on a topic she doesn't understand. I stop talking and let her enjoy the view.

"Now, Aiden, if you explain everything, what will I have left to say?" a voice calls out from behind us.

We turn, and I respond, "My bad, Tessa."

After a brief pause, I add, "So… should I introduce Leia to you? Do you even do introductions? I mean, you pretty much know people as soon as you see them, right?"

"Hi, Tessa. I'm Leia," Leia says pointedly, bypassing my awkwardness.

"Leia, it's so good to meet you finally! I've heard so many

nice things about you," Tessa replies warmly.

As they shake hands, I look at Leia and say, "Told ya."

"It might feel impossible right now, but I'd like to help put you at ease. I'd love to hear your questions out loud and let you process how you feel about everything," Tessa offers.

"That sounds nice... but I thought you could already hear my questions. Aiden said you're a telepath?" Leia asks, puzzled.

"Aiden... says many things he doesn't fully understand," Tessa replies firmly.

"Hey, guys... I'm right here," I say, waving at the two of them.

"Oh, I know. I wanted you to hear that," Tessa asserts. "I will tell you what I told Aiden: I won't always give you the answers you want, but I will give you the answers you need."

As much as that line annoyed me, Leia actually seems relieved by it.

"You're very humble, Leia. You know there's a lot you don't know, and that will serve you well in the work we have to do," Tessa says. "But you'll also need to learn to give yourself more credit."

"I've been told that once or twice," Leia replies, blushing as she glances my way.

Tessa smirks at me. "I guess he's not wrong about *everything*," she says as she winks at Leia.

The gentle, knowing tone Tessa uses with Leia gradually chips away at the apprehension she felt when we walked in. I can feel Leia growing more comfortable in Tessa's presence, even if part of that comfort comes from them picking on me.

Tessa continues, "I see a very robust, vibrant, and resilient Laosi in you. Even with everything you've been through, there's still a harmony at the core of your soul streams."

"If she's in harmony, why does she have an LET?" I ask.

"You misunderstand," Tessa explains patiently. "All of

the streams flow from and back into the core, which—put simply—is the essence of one's personality. Leia's flow has been disrupted, but her core remains the same as it has always been. There's baggage and debris in the way, but it won't be as hard as you might think to liberate the real you into the world again.

"Some people are fundamentally changed by the difficulties they experience. You have been affected, Leia, but not changed. And that's a good thing."

Then she leans in toward Leia with sincerity flowing out of her eyes and adds, "It may be of little solace to you now, but as painful as all of this has been for you, it's all happened exactly the way that it needed to."

I find myself blurting out, "Have I changed?"

"Aiden, you brought Leia all this way so she could gain clarity about what's going on with her. Let's make sure she has the space to get what *she* needs. You and I will talk more later."

Turning back to Leia, Tessa says, "Why don't we step into my office and have a chat?"

"Just you and her?" I blurt out again.

"You've already made other plans, right? Check your Solo," Tessa replies smoothly. "Shall we?"

I watch as two of the three most important women in my life walk toward Tessa's office, leaving me behind to imagine what they might discuss. Sighing, I pull out my Solo and tap the opposing quadrants to wake it up.

An unread message from Auriel pops up, detailing the logistics for Lawrence's soiree. Before I can close it, a message from Tessa arrives:

"There's a carrier outside for you. I know you don't have a lot of money. You'll find more freedom when you learn to lean on the Broken rather than letting your shame carry you."

Thanks, Tessa... As usual, you're right.

I know.

CHAPTER 20 – FLYING

"Yo! It's Aiden Lore! Whoa! You're so cool, man! Fighting dragons and stuff. Can I give you my autograph? Wait... did I...?" a young guy who looks like he just hit the legal drinking age blurts out after opening the door to let me into the ballroom Lawrence rented out.

"Uh, no thanks... I'm good on that," I say, trying not to sound as awkward as I feel and deciding not to help myself to whatever is in his cup.

I slide past him, leaving him to stumble back over to his friends as I take a few steps toward the center of the room.

So, this is why no one was at HQ. They were all getting ready for this.

At first glance, there are at least 200 people here—more than I've ever seen at Otto's. I take a moment to absorb the scene.

Three massive crystal chandeliers with intricate golden latticework (probably actual gold) hang from the vaulted ceiling, and their thousand or more small bulbs cast a soft glow across the room. The velvet upholstery on nearly every piece of furniture soaks up the light, giving the scene a plush and luxuriant feel.

Guests sit at darkwood round tables throughout the room and on the couches lining the outer walls. In the center, a gold- and silver-trimmed buffet is attended by servers dressed in black and white.

To the left, a portable dance floor has been set up on the mauve, textured carpet, which feels too soft under my feet. Massive speakers in the far-left corners blast familiar party songs, accompanied by holographic music videos projected onto the walls. There's even a hologram insertion booth currently in use by a young man replacing the musical artists in the videos with his own singing and dancing.

Lawrence has some money. I need to embrace the brotherhood more often.

After taking in the lavish setup, I realize I'm awkwardly standing in the middle of nowhere.

"Lil' A, are any of my friends here?" I ask out loud.

"Scanning a 50-yard radius for Solos belonging to Leia Hart, Devon Murray, Tirrell Givens, Auriel Yamada, and Zane Arroyo. Those are your only friends, right?"

"Lil' A! Just complete the scan before I factory reset your settings!"

"Don't get mad at me, Champ. I'm just an AI doing what an AI does," Lil' A quips.

"What? What does that even mean?"

"It means—"

"Just finish the scan," I cut in, exasperated.

"Done. Auriel's here, but no one else. Want me to send her a message?" Lil' A asks.

"Sure. Say, 'Meet me at the food!'" I chuckle.

"Message sent, annnnnd received!" Lil' A confirms.

I head over to the buffet, perusing the options. Some of it looks delicious, and some of it looks... strange.

Rich people eat some weird stuff.

An attendant hands me a plate, and I start down the line, searching for entrees that actually look edible.

"Is that braised targon?" I ask, almost offended by the counterfeit in front of me. The aromatic herbs and seasonings on the steak fill my nostrils with a tantalizing, citrusy spice, but there's no way the texture will be as tender as Mom's.

"It is. Would you like some?" another attendant offers.

"I'll try it. It won't be as good as my mom's, though," I say with a smile.

The attendant shrugs before taking my plate and adding the meat.

"No cooking's better than mama's cooking," Auriel

chimes in as she walks into earshot.

"You got that right," I reply, glancing over my shoulder to see her approaching. "Do you have a specialty dish? Something Brice loves when you cook it?"

I add some grains and veggies to complement the inevitably inferior protein on my plate.

"That kid loves everything I cook—or anything anyone cooks, for that matter. It doesn't even have to be cooked. It really doesn't even have to be food," she says with a laugh. "That boy just wants to eat. End of story. Want me to grab a drink for you? What would you like?"

"Oh, I'm good, but thanks," I say, grabbing a glass of water at the end of the buffet.

"Where do you want to sit?" she asks.

"Well, where's Brice? I can head over to wherever you guys were."

She points toward a couch where a guy and girl are sitting, watching a young boy try his best to dance on beat.

"Is that your little man? He's got some pretty good moves."

"Ha! Don't tell him that or he'll never stop dancing," Auriel says as we start walking toward the couch.

When we arrive, I grab a chair from a nearby table and pull it over to the couch.

"Brice, this is Mr. Aiden!" Auriel says cheerfully as she sits down.

Brice looks up at me, closes his eyes, and sticks out his tongue. The guy and girl on the couch laugh, glancing at me to see how I'll respond.

"I'm sorry, Aiden... It's a phase he's in right now," Auriel says. "Brice, can you wave and say, 'Hello?'"

Brice looks at me and sticks his tongue out again.

"Hey, you!" I say, sticking my tongue out at him. He bursts into giggles.

I had expected to spend the evening fielding questions about the Devastation event. But this is nice.

Auriel smiles at me playing with Brice, then turns to the others. "Oh yeah. Aiden, this is Nadia and Elrond. Nadia and Elrond—Aiden."

"What's up, guys? Nice to meet you," I say.

"Good to meet you, bro. Call me El," Elrond replies, his voice gruff—surprisingly so despite his slender frame.

El sits on the arm of the couch, his feet propped on one of the dining chairs. He reaches out for a handshake, his right hand extending from the sleeve of an unbuttoned, black shirt over a white tee paired with khaki-colored work pants.

He seems comfortable.

"El. Got it," I say as I shake his hand and then start eating my food.

"These two started Dynamics the same week I did. It's been really cool getting to know them, and they've helped me out a lot over the years. Nadia is as sweet as a tira," Auriel comments, causing Nadia to feign a blush and give her a hug.

"Yeah? Tira's are my favorite fruit," I say, laughing as I shake Nadia's hand.

Was that awkward?

"El is a little bit crazy, but at least he knows it," Auriel continues. "But when he says he's got your back, he means he will hop out of bed at 1:30 in the morning with one sock on and come help if you need him. You remember that one time?"

"I do," El says, chuckling. "I was too sleepy to remember how to turn the light on. At some point you just forget about the other sock."

After shaking her head, Nadia says, "I know you've only just met her, but I'm sure you've already seen how thoughtful and kindhearted Auriel is."

Nadia's the only one here with makeup on and a salon-fresh hairdo. There's not a single wrinkle on her sky blue frilly jumpsuit. These 3 are so different yet so close.

"Oh, but of course," I confirm. "I would have lost my mind a few times while we were out there if it hadn't been for her."

"Speaking of," El says, "what was it like out there? On a mission like that? I got Auriel's perspective, but it sounded like most of the action really revolved around you."

Okay, I guess I am fielding questions.

"Have you never been on a mission before?" I ask, trying to figure out how much perspective needs to be shared.

"Yeah, I've been on several. But not one where I was fighting other people, and definitely not one against the Collective," he says, leaning in with interest.

"I hear you. Wait, so what kinds of missions has the Broken been involved with before now? This stuff with the Collective just started when I got here, right? Three months ago, I had never heard of you."

Auriel chuckles and says, "Yeah, you have. Do you remember that helijet crash not that long ago where everyone miraculously survived?"

"That was you guy— uh, that was us?" I ask, my eyes wide open as I look at Auriel and my two new friends in disbelief.

"Yeah," El says nonchalantly. "See, me? I'm a Mind-Disintegrated phaser. If I can map out a plan to accomplish something, not even the laws of physics can stop me... In most situations, at least," he says, pointing to his left pinky, drawing my attention to the fact that half of it is missing.

Don't overreact. Don't overreact!

"Thanks for sharing that, bro," is all I can think to say.

"And I've got a Will-Disintegrated telekinesis thing going on," Nadia chimes in. "Yeah, we worked together and saved everybody! Most exhilarating day of my life, let me tell you!"

"That's so crazy!" I blurt out, my mouth half full of food. I pause long enough to swallow and say, "I remember the pilot saying he felt like he fell through the jet and that his seatbelt was stuck. I just figured everything was happening so fast he couldn't think straight. Because how can you get out of a crashing jet with your seatbelt still attached? But you're saying it was us?"

Auriel and Nadia look up at Elrond and he starts chuckling mischievously. Auriel explains, "So Nadia here was doing her best to keep the plane up in the sky long enough for everyone to jump out—"

"But that thing was heeeeeavy!" Nadia adds. "My nose started bleeding, and I apparently almost had a stroke."

"Right," Auriel resumes. "So obviously, she's reached her limit, and that's when I'm thinking it's about to be time for me to step in, right? I mean, I don't understand why the engine died all of a sudden, so it should be pretty easy for me to rewind. But this fool," she says, pointing at El, "runs right to the impact point where the plane is about to land, dives *through* the jet, grabs the pilot—whose seat belt is in fact still attached—and phases them both through the other side of the jet."

"Yeah, and then I blew the rest of the fire and debris away from them, and then I passed out," Nadia adds gleefully.

"You guys are insane!" I say as a swell of contradictory pride fills my chest.

"Insane!" Brice mimics.

"Exactly!" Auriel and I say to him simultaneously. I smirk at her and then hold my hand up to Brice for a high five, which he joyously gives.

"Okay, so two questions: how did you know where the plane was going to land and get there fast enough to save all those people?" I ask.

"Talia dreamed it up and told Tessa about it. We asked Tessa what we could do and she sent us out," Auriel says.

"I'm starting to think Talia might really be the brains of this operation. That girl knows way too much sometimes," Nadia says, looking around suspiciously, as if Talia might be listening to us now.

"Wouldn't surprise me," I say. "Have you guys seen her lately? I haven't seen her since the first night I walked through the door of Otto's. I almost feel like she's avoiding me or something."

"I wouldn't take it personally," Auriel says. "She's 12, so, ya know... Puberty, body changes, self-esteem, hormones—she's got all that stuff going on."

"Oh, okay," I say, somewhat relieved.

"She has seemed sadder than usual lately, but that might be why," Nadia says to Auriel.

"It's just that Tessa told me she had three dreams about me before I ever showed up. I just want to know what she saw."

"Tessa didn't tell you?" El asks. I shake my head, so he says, "Then it's best you don't know."

"That's what everyone keeps telling me," I mutter.

"He's still new," Nadia says to El. "He'll figure it out."

"Hey, so what was your second question?" Auriel asks.

"Oh! So if the Broken has been saving lives and helping people for who knows how long, why stay underground about it?" I ask.

"I wonder the same thing sometimes," El says. "Knowing Tessa, I'm sure there's a good reason."

"My guess is so that people don't get the wrong ideas," Auriel says.

"What do you mean?" Nadia asks.

"Yeah," I say. "Users have been getting 'Mostly Favorable' for as long as I can remember in the polls."

"True," Auriel responds. "Tessa's probably trying to keep it that way. Think about it—people don't have a problem with us because there are things like LIST, Atheria, CLU Enforcers, etc. On top of all that, Users are normally pretty spaced out. A lot of people go their whole lives without ever meeting a User."

She pauses in thought, so I motion with my hand for her to finish making the point.

"Sorry... Sometimes I think faster than I talk and then get lost," she explains. "I was thinking that people might just feel comfortable with Users because Users are 'under control.' But if you tell the public that Users are gathering together and learning how to use their powers more and more, it might not be long before they think we're a threat. And, with how things played out this weekend, they wouldn't be wrong to feel that way. The Collective might have thrown us straight into what Tessa has been trying to protect us from."

"I think I see where you're going with this," I say. "And as much as I hate to admit it, I can appreciate the strategy behind it. The Collective is the real threat, but they're turning the media's attention to us. They'll do whatever it is they're planning and then feed us to the public as their scapegoat."

"The bad part is that we have an idea of what they're planning," Auriel says. "The briefcase you got from them had a jump drive in it. Our tech team had to dig deep, but they managed to recover the data Elon erased. They downloaded the entire Tryon United database—employee names and addresses, building schematics for current and future projects, unredacted incident reports, security protocols, Solo manufacturing details... everything."

"So they're planning to attack TU or at least someone in it and then blame us for it," I surmise. "And all we'll be able to say is, 'It wasn't us!'"

"But with Tessa keeping everything under wraps, how did they find out about the Broken to begin with?" Elrond asks, his tone tinged with agitation.

Auriel raises an eyebrow and looks directly at me. I try to mask my helplessness as I glance back at her and then divert my eyes.

Do I embrace the brotherhood and tell them the truth? "Hey, guys! The Collective has a target on each of your backs because the new guy couldn't keep his mouth shut! Enjoy the party!"

Would they still embrace me? I'm still in the brotherhood... right?

The silence stretches long enough for me to notice the change in the song playing in the background. I'm not the only one who notices.

"Sing?" Brice asks.

"Is this your favorite song?" Nadia asks him.

"Fave it," Brice says with a grin.

"He can barely string two words together, but he knows every single version of 'Bye Bye Now' by heart," Auriel says, covering her face with her hand.

"Sing?" Brice asks again, tugging on Auriel's leg and pointing toward the hologram insertion booth.

"Mommy's a bit tired right now. Maybe later."

"Sing? Sing! SIIIIING!" Brice whines, pulling harder with each repetition.

"Little man's not gonna take no for an answer. I'll take him," Elrond offers.

"No, he'll be fi—"

"Nah, it's cool. Let's go sing, Brice!" Elrond says, taking his hand.

"Siiiiiing!" Brice cheers as Elrond leads him toward the hologram insertion booth.

Auriel glances at Nadia for support.

"I'll go with them," Nadia says. "You know they need a chaperone."

"You just never know with those two," Auriel laughs. As Nadia hurries after El and Brice, Auriel shrugs and looks at me. "Well, that escalated quickly! I didn't think they'd run off so fast."

I chuckle. "Yeah... I'm kinda glad we're alone, though."

Auriel blushes, looking down. "Yeah?" she asks bashfully.

"Oh... yeah. Um, because, like, you know... they were asking questions and stuff about the Collective," I stammer.

"Yeah, right. Mm hmm," she says.

"And... I didn't want to tell them that I'm the one who let the name slip. I don't know how they'd take it."

"Well, how did Tirrell, Zane, and I take it?" she counters.

"Yeah, but that was different. You guys were there, in the heat of the moment. I'd have to explain so much to everyone else, only for them to realize I... kinda betrayed them."

She taps a finger thoughtfully against her chin. "I think I'm starting to understand your shame complex," she says after a pause. "It's like you've already decided you're not good enough. So then you have to prove yourself or maintain a certain image because you don't want people to judge you the way you judge yourself."

I let out a deep sigh, rolling my eyes. "You sound like Tessa."

"What a high compliment!" she giggles.

"So, you've known me for two days, and you think you've got me all figured out?" I say, trying to hide how vulnerable I feel.

"I told you—you're an open book," she replies, smiling gently. I quickly glance away.

Her voice warmed with compassion, she adds, "It sounds like a prison, Aiden. I wonder why you feel like you can't just be yourself. I can't imagine how critical that will be for you in your reintegration work. How freeing it will be."

"Oh, I know exactly why I don't know how to 'be myself.' It's because I've never known who 'myself' really is. In case you haven't put it together yet, my dad is Richard Lore."

Her eyes widen in surprise. "Really? Oh... Oh, so... I don't want to make you uncomfortable by asking this, but—"

"It's fine," I interrupt. "I've heard it and asked it myself enough times to not freak out when someone else does. 'How can the son of the man who invented the Laosi Integration Soul Therapy procedure have active, uncontrolled LETs?' Something like that, right?"

Auriel scratches her forehead thoughtfully. "Now that I hear it out loud, that question alone is loaded with shame."

"It is," I agree. "And I've heard a million versions of that question my entire life. How could the son of the man who helped build ARL into a multinational powerhouse have such a meaningless job? How could someone from such a well-off family have such bad fashion sense? Why did Richard Lore's son go to that school, pick that major, live in that part of town, eat that for breakfast? It goes on and on like that to the point that I don't know who I am. How could I? I've spent my whole life trying not to fail at being who everyone else thinks I should be."

I assume she's noticed my misty eyes when she asks, "Here I go being Heart-Dominant and everything, but... is it okay if I give you a hug right now?"

All I can do is nod.

Her embrace is so comforting. The tears fall without my consent.

Not where she can see them, of course.

When she pulls back, my heart feels lighter, but her words are heavy. "I think you really need to wrestle with the name of our group, Aiden. We're the Broken. It's okay to be broken. We're human. None of us fully lives up to our potential."

"Have you met my dad, though?" I ask with a dry laugh. "He's the epitome of rags-to-riches in Sanctuary. He grows up poor with an abusive father and becomes a family man, philanthropist, speaker, author, and head researcher."

"What your dad accomplished is nothing short of amazing, and I'm not trying to take anything away from him. But if he didn't teach you how to accept and love yourself unconditionally, then he could've done better. A great man? Absolutely. But not perfect. Just like you. And that's *okay*."

I let out a heavy sigh. "It's not that I disagree... It's just that my imperfections seem to cost more—especially for the people I care about."

Auriel gazes at me intently, hanging onto each word. So I continue.

"The whole out-of-control powers thing—and the physical damage it's caused—is a huge problem on its own. But there's been this ripple effect in my life. Like, failing to live up to my potential in this instance means I have to settle for less at another point. After LIST, I was so devastated that my LETs were still active that I pulled away from my friends and dropped my extracurriculars. That kept me out of the high-end universities, which crushed my dream of going into medicine... which left me feeling like my life had no purpose because I couldn't help the people I was supposed to help. Sorry... Here I go, dumping on you again."

"No worries," Auriel says. "But I want to go back to what you said earlier about your imperfections being more costly. I get that your LETs have cost you a lot—which, by the way, is just like everyone else here. But if I can be so bold, I want to ask you... Is it possible that you wouldn't have had LETs to *begin* with, if not for your *parents'* imperfections in not teaching you to accept yourself and your feelings?"

I cut a sharp glance at her unintentionally but don't say anything, so she continues carefully.

"I'm not blaming them," she clarifies. "And now, you've got these incredible talents you can use to help people as you learn to control them. I'm just saying—maybe it's time to focus on playing the hand you've been—Aiden, what's going on?"

"What?"

"Your hands," she says softly. "Who are you mad at? Is it me? Did I say something wrong?"

She's starting to feel panicky. Why's she getting so worked up? What did she mean by my hands?

I look down and see the red aura emanating from my clenched fists.

Anger? What's going on? I'm mad? What am I—?

Auriel slides away from me on the couch, her eyes locked on my hands. "Talk to me," she says cautiously. The fear radiating from her is stronger than the anger simmering inside me.

Okay, Aiden. Deep breaths. Anger, what brought you here?

I exhale slowly, and the fiery aura around my hands begins to fade as I say, "I'm not mad at you, Auriel. You didn't say anything wrong—you said everything right! I think I just... I wasn't ready to process that question yet."

"I understand that," Auriel says. "I'm sorry for moving

too fast."

"Not at all," I assure her. "I don't think I'd ever be ready for that question. I've been mad at myself for so long for having these powers. I've always thought my life would be so much better if I wasn't a User, and I hated myself for the life I didn't get to live. There's such a big gap between that life and my daily experience, ya know? So hearing that maybe someone else—my parents, of all people—might have played a bigger role in how my life turned out? It just…"

"It's a lot to process," she says softly, sliding back into her original spot. "I'm sorry. I should've left that for you to unpack in Dynamics. There's a whole section on family of origin stuff."

"It's cool. You didn't do anything wrong."

"Can I ask you something?"

"Go ahead."

"I can't rewind time to when your powers first activated," she begins, "but let's say I could. Knowing everything you've seen and experienced—meeting Tessa and the Broken, fighting the Collective, even this moment right now—if you could choose whether your powers would activate or not, what choice would you make?"

I raise my eyebrows and inhale deeply. I release the breath slowly. "I thought this was supposed to be a lighthearted social, not some soul-searching retreat," I say with a laugh.

She squints at me, waiting for me to answer.

"That's a really deep question," I begin. "On one hand, I really like being part of the Broken. I wouldn't have met you, Tirrell, or anyone else if I hadn't been a User, right? And I've found a sense of purpose and connection I've never felt before. But at the same time… who's to say I wouldn't have found that somewhere else in a life where I wasn't constantly afraid of blowing up every building I walked into? Who knows what I could've done—what I could've *been*—if I hadn't lost so much because of these powers?"

I pause, hoping the open-ended response will satisfy her. It doesn't. She keeps looking at me, her face hardening a bit with concern.

"If I had to choose, I'd say... Man, this is tough. But honestly, I think I'd go wi—"

"Hey, big dog! You got an urgent Holo call coming in from your dad!" Lil' A interrupts cheerfully.

Auriel chuckles. "Your avatar calls you 'big dog?'"

"That's beside the point."

I pull out my Solo as Lil' A asks, "Want me to answer it?"

I glance at Auriel. "Sorry—my dad never calls urgent. I gotta take this."

"I understand. I hope everything's okay. Take care of your business. I need to go find my son anyway," she says with a reassuring smile.

"Thank you."

Standing up, I walk toward the door. "Okay, Lil' A, answer mini Holo."

"Establishing secure network connection. Rendering holographic images. All right. You're good to go!"

I step out into the empty foyer and find a chair as my dad's holographic image materializes above my Solo. He smiles at me.

"Hey, Dad."

"Hey, son!" he says brightly. "Have you eaten dinner yet?"

"Just finished. What's going on, though? You called urgent?"

"You're right. I did. I want to tell you something that I've wanted to be able to tell you for a *long* time. I'd rather do it in person. I know you're grown and have your own life to live, but if you can drop what you're doing right now, I'll send a carrier to your location immediately. It's that important."

"The suspense is killing me, Dad," I reply. "But yeah, I'm free. Send it to my coordinates."

"Will do. See you soon, son!" he says.

"See ya," I say with a wave. "End call."

I tap the bottom-right quadrant of my Solo, pulling up Auriel's contact. I type out a quick message:

So sorry, but I gotta split. My dad still didn't say what it was but that I needed to drop everything. It doesn't seem like anything bad, though. This was really fun. Thanks for the invite, even though I never actually met Lawrence, haha!

After hitting send, I glance outside to see the carrier pulling up. I step out of the building into the evening air and plop down into the carrier.

'Drop what you're doing?' What's going on?

CHAPTER 21 – PATHS

"Hey! So glad you could make it! Come in, come in!"

I step through the front door of my parents' house and give my mom a hug.

"Hey, Mom! Where's Dad?" I ask.

"Oh, he's in the dining room." She seems more giddy than usual, which only adds to the suspense. She's smiling, though, which means it can't be bad news. "Why don't you go in there and grab yourself some dinner?"

As I make my way through the kitchen toward the dining room, she closes the door behind me and follows.

"Aw, not this time," I say, rubbing my belly, still full from the high-class spread at the social. But as I move closer, the savory aroma of my mom's cooking wafts through the air, teasing my senses. My thoughts stray to the empty fridge waiting for me back home. "But I guess it wouldn't be a bad idea to let CounterAid wrap up a to-go plate for me! It smells amazing in here! What's the occasion?"

She waves me on with a hand, her smile widening. "Go see for yourself. Your dad is so excited… I haven't seen him like this in a while!"

"Okay… so I'm assuming that's a good thing?" I ask, raising an eyebrow, fishing for more details.

"Very good!"

"Okay, cool. He called me all urgent and told me to drop everything and come over immediately. You know that's not like him. Do you know what's going on?"

"I do, but it's best to let them explain. You know I don't understand all that science stuff."

Them?

Convinced I'm not getting anything else out of her, I

round the kitchen corner and step into the dining room.

"Ms. Withers?" I blurt out, startled to see my dad's boss sitting at the table.

"Aiden, after all this time, I've told you that you can just call me Zoe," she says, rising and extending a hand.

She's taller than I remember.

We shake hands, and I manage an awkward, "Hi, Zoe. Sorry. I... just didn't expect to see you here."

She sits back down and smiles kindly. "Not to worry. Your father speaks so much about you, Jack and Candace that sometimes I forget I'm not part of the family," she laughs. "I can understand your surprise to see me here, though."

Still confused, I glance at my dad, then back to her. "Right... And why are—?"

"Aiden, my son," my dad cuts in, walking over and pulling me into a firm hug. He steps back, holding my shoulders and looking me directly in the eyes.

"This has been a long time coming—well past overdue. Zoe and I have been working tirelessly to perfect the science, and we've finally done it! We've developed a new version of LIST that will truly suppress your powers! It's been tested on eight other patients for whom the original procedure was ineffective, and it has a 100% success rate."

He pauses, still holding my shoulders. There's more affection in his eyes than I've felt from my dad in recent years... Maybe ever.

"This is it, son," he continues, his voice thick with emotion. "We can finally rid you of those LETs." He pats me on the arm and returns to his seat without taking his eyes off me. The broad smile on his face doesn't fade.

The happiest moment of my dad's life is when he gets the chance to tell me that he can fix me and my powers. How much shame have I put him through by continuing to have these LETs?

"Well, don't just stand there... Say something!" Mom chimes in from the entrance to the dining room, leaning against the doorframe.

"Oh… I'm sorry. It's just…" I hesitate as I sit down in the chair next to Zoe. The table is set with steaming pots and dishes, all resting on a beige tablecloth with golden embroidery along the edges. Mom moves to sit next to Dad, smiling just as brightly as him.

"It's just so sudden," I manage, trying to gather my thoughts. "I mean, that's great! Congratulations to you and the team. I just… wow! I guess I don't know what to say. I didn't know what to expect coming here, but I wasn't expecting that." I glance at Zoe and add, "And then, with Ms. Withers being here and all… I just—"

Zoe cuts in. "I want to apologize for the intrusion. It's just that your dad has been working so hard for so long to have this moment, and I wanted to be able to celebrate his success with him—and with you! I knew how much this would mean to him and to you, so I wanted, rather selfishly, to be part of it."

Her voice is smooth, and for some reason, it makes me think of flowers with red, yellow, and violet petals.

"No, I completely understand," I say, offering her a polite smile.

She probably feels out of place in the middle of this father-son moment, considering she doesn't have kids of her own—though I've heard she wanted them.

"It actually means a lot to me that you wanted to share this moment with us. It's no intrusion at all. Thank you for believing in my dad and giving him so much support."

Zoe smiles graciously. "No need to thank me. Richard's success is his own. Besides, being able to support this work and see its impact is its own reward. We're excited to roll out this second iteration to help as many people as possible." She pauses, her voice dipping slightly as she adds, "The likelihood of this might be pretty low, but if by some chance you have some friends who have struggled with their LETs as you have… Forgive me if this is a selfish plug, but I'd be honored if you spread the word and let them know that… it's not too late to join us."

Wait… what? 'It's not too late to join us'?

I freeze, her words ringing in my ears.

Eboni said the exact same thing when she flew off with Elon. And Stacie at the Solo Center… Same phrase, same cadence. Could they all be—?

No. No, it's probably just a coincidence. Right?

I blink twice, staring at Zoe. Her smile sends chills down my spine, and my heart pounds in my chest. I can feel the hum of my Laosi activating.

Oh, great. This is exactly what I don't need righ—

"I'll tell you who I think really needs help," Mom says from across the table.

Okay, fear. Let's not overreact. Stay calm. Focus. That's… a common phrase. Besides, I still sense emotion in her, unlike the other two. We'll stay alert, but let's try to stay calm as well.

"That Broken group," Mom says, her voice decisive. "Obviously, I have no problem with Users, but I just can't believe people would be so bold as to use their powers to cause such senseless destruction! But, you know, it's okay. I'm believing that they will get what they deserve when the time comes."

What?! But that wasn't us, Mom! It was—

"It's just weird to think there's an entire organization of people learning how to use their powers better," she continues. "That doesn't sound safe. What are they planning to do?"

Is this what everyone thinks about us?

"Yeah, no kidding," Dad says, nodding. "My friends at CLU say they're working around the clock to track them down. They're probably searching right now as we speak."

Of course, CLU's involved.

"Are they making any progress?" Mom asks.

Please say no. Please say no.

"Hard to say," Dad replies, and I let out a breath of relief, careful not to make it too obvious.

"What are they saying will happen if or when they do find the people involved?" I ask.

Dad sighs. "I'm trying to keep the death penalty off the table, but four people were killed. It's going to be an uphill battle."

The death penalty?!

"But didn't you say that if those involved were willing to go through the LIST 2.0 procedure, it might help them reconsider?" Zoe asks.

"Yeah, that's the argument we're presenting, but..."

As Dad's voice trails off, Mom chimes back in. "Not that I support the death penalty, but I hope they find them soon. People keep sending me videos saying that Suspect 0 looks like you, Aiden!"

"Really?" I say. "That's crazy... Unless I have a twin somewhere y'all haven't told me about?" I chuckle nervously.

"Believe it or not, I've seen my face on one of those videos," Dad scoffs.

"Good thing the news outlets stopped receiving video submissions," Zoe says. "Hopefully, that discourages people from sending in doctored footage to get someone they know in trouble. The original angle they released is the only one they've verified as unaltered."

"So people are, what, framing the coworkers they don't like as Suspect 0?" Mom asks, surprise furrowing her brow. "That's a thing?"

"Oh yeah," Dad replies. "It's trending."

Mom's jaw drops. "*You* know something that's trending?"

"That's a horrible trend," I say.

But at least it buys Tirrell, Zane, Auriel and me some time. Unless... Auriel was right and this is something the Collective is doing to keep the heat off us for now. That means they bought themselves some time. But what do they need time for?

"Anyway," Dad redirects, rolling his eyes. "Sorry, Aiden. That doesn't have anything to do with you. I imagine you've got a lot on your mind right now. Any questions we can answer?"

You have NO idea.

"Yeah, Dad... Can you help me understand the science a little bit? I know it's probably super technical and everything. I guess what I'm trying to ask is, why didn't it work on me before?"

"That's a great question, son," Dad says, leaning back in his chair. "We were stumped for a long time because we never considered that our success might actually be the root of our failure. You know how every person has their own unique genetic code, right? Your DNA is a combination of genetic information from both of your parents."

"Right. That's why I have Mom's nose and your forehead," I say, getting a laugh from around the table.

Is this why my friends at the Broken don't think I'm funny? Because my jokes only work on old people?

"Exactly," Dad continues. "But it turns out the same principle applies to Laosi. Everyone has their own unique Laosi frequency, but it's largely a combination of the frequencies from their parents. That's why we look like our parents and sometimes think, feel, and even desire the same way they do."

"That's... interesting," I say, starting to piece it together. "So having LETs is genetic? Like, I inherited my tendency to suppress my emotions from one of you guys?"

"First of all, Aiden, wow!" Zoe exclaims. "That is highly advanced! After decades of research, we only recently discovered that the primary assumption in the scientific community was wrong. We thought LETs were triggered by overexerting the soul stream someone used most often. How did you know it was actually the most suppressed stream?"

I can't very well say, "The Broken taught me," can I?

Looking down at the half-eaten plates around the table, I mumble, "Oh, I've just been, you know... trying to notice when my powers got activated and stuff."

With a look of pride in her eyes, Zoe looks at Dad before turning back to me. "Well, that's a very astute observation, young man. I'm impressed. A lot of people are perfectly content with their powers, so it hasn't always been easy for us to test some of our hypotheses. But if you've deduced that on your own, then you've probably gained more control over your LETs as well, haven't you?"

"Something like that..." I say, still avoiding eye contact.

"I thought so. You looked more confident the other day," Zoe says with a knowing smile that makes me freeze.

"The other day? What are you talking about?" Dad asks, glancing between us.

"Oh, I didn't tell you," Zoe laughs. "I ran into Aiden at the Solo Center not too long ago. Right, Aiden?"

Time feels frozen. My pulse races. Sweat beads on my forehead. My chest tightens.

This can't be happening. This CAN NOT BE HAPPENING!

"Hey, are you okay?" Mom asks, concerned.

"Oh, yeah," I say, trying to play it cool. "I just remembered why I was there. I broke my Solo and had to get a replacement. Such a hassle, you know? Zoe's comment just took me back to a very stressful day."

Mom and Dad relax back into their seats.

24 years old, and I'm still lying to my parents. When will I grow up?

"Oh, is that why you were there? I thought you were meeting some friends for the *N Force 2* premiere. That's what Stacie said, right?" Zoe asks, leaning towards me with her eyebrows raised.

"Stacie? From accounting?" Dad asks.

"No, no, a different Stacie. A mutual acquaintance between Aiden and me," Zoe says, sipping the bluish-green juice in her glass.

She's ENJOYING this!

"I didn't know you had any mutual acquaintances with Zoe," Mom says.

"Well, with Solos, carriers, and teleportation stations," Zoe says, her eyes sparkling as she emphasizes the last phrase, "Tryon's a much smaller world than we think."

"Mom, can I get a glass of water?" I ask, my throat dry and palms sweaty.

"Sure thing," Mom says, rising.

"Anyway," Zoe continues, "It's funny that I didn't mention it to you, Richard. I remember wanting to tell Aiden that we were closer than he thought. I guess I was so focused on work that I just didn't tell you."

What is her angle?

Is my dad part of the Collective, too?

"Right," Dad says. "We were very close for a while, but I didn't want to tell you before we were sure. It sounds like Zoe's enthusiasm almost got the best of her. I'm guessing that was around the time that we found the breakthrough?"

Mom returns with the glass of water, setting it in front of me. I gulp it down, nearly choking in my rush.

"'We'? Your husband is so humble. How does he do it?" Zoe says, flashing a smile at Mom.

"He's just a great man," Mom says proudly. "And, of course, he doesn't want any credit. I'm sure he'd say he was just doing what any father would do to help his son."

"I'm just trying to help Aiden understand what we've discovered," Dad interjects, smiling to mask the frustration I sense in him. "But you two keep interrupting. Maybe we should step outside?"

"Okay, okay, we'll be quiet. Zoe, shhh!" Mom teases. Zoe pretends to zip her lips.

Dad focuses back on me, his tone serious now. "The LIST procedure places a limiter on the soul stream that tends to manifest powers. The discovery that we made, which was really in front of our faces the whole time, was that the imprint that the LIST procedure makes on a patient's Laosi frequency becomes a part of the DNA, if you would, of their soul. When passed on to the next generation, it can lead to resistance to the old LIST.

"It certainly is not a pleasant analogy, but think of a virus that has been exposed to our immunizations so often that it evolves into a form that can resist the medication. It's much more technical, but that's the gist of it."

Like a magician adding the final "ta-da!" to her performance, Zoe concludes, "And now that we understand and can account for the generationally transmitted LIST imprint, we can once and for all remove LETs for anyone like you who wants to be rid of their powers." She pauses, glancing at my dad. "Sorry... Did I steal your thunder?"

Dad chuckles, rolling his eyes. "Does that answer your question, son?"

"I think I get it, but I'm not sure what this has to do with me. Unless you're saying..."

As my voice trails off, Mom leans forward and says, "We never told you who your dad's first patient was, the one who made all his success possible, did we?"

I shake my head.

She hesitates for second, and I see a glimmer of regret in her eyes. "It was me," she says. "After I had Candace, your father and Zoe successfully completed the first-ever LIST procedure and got rid of my powers for good. That was before I got pregnant with you."

Are you serious right now?

I stare at her, stunned. "You used to have an active LET? What was it?"

Go easy on her.

No! After all these years of watching me struggle, she never once mentioned this? Why should I go easy?

She looks up, searching for memories. "My LET empowered me to do whatever I was doing better. I could run faster, jump higher, see farther, sing clearer. Back then, we thought it was linked to my Will. We thought it was some kind of competitive drive, like if I really wanted to win, ya know? But now, knowing it's tied to the suppressed soul stream, I'm thinking..." She turns to Dad. "What do you think, Richard? Heart?"

"That'd be my guess," Dad replies.

I grip the edge of the table. "Different emotions trigger different powers for me. What emotion do you think triggered yours?"

She hesitates. "Oh, I don't know... It's been so long. Maybe if I wanted to be noticed? Wait, no, that's still the Will, isn't it?"

Her fumbling irritates me. "Neglect. It was neglect, wasn't it? If you felt neglected, your powers activated."

She nods slowly. "Yeah, that's probably a good word for it. I haven't really felt those feelings in a long time, though, so..."

A deafening silence fills the room, gnawing at my sanity.

"So all this time, you knew what it was like to struggle with unwanted LETs, and you never told me? You saw my pain, my confusion, my frustration... And you didn't think to say, 'Hey, Aiden, I've been there' or 'Let me tell you what it was like for me'? I felt like I was the only person in the world who hated having their powers! And when Dad's procedure didn't work for me, do you know how much worse that made it? How isolated I felt? Do you know how neglected I feel right now?"

"But, see, Aiden, I didn't really want to get ri—"

"No, Mom!" I snap, cutting her off. "It's too late for that now. I don't want to hear it!" I say enraged, folding my arms and looking away from the table.

I can't trust anyone in this room!

"I understand you're upset," Dad says firmly. "But you need to be really careful with that tone when you're talking to your mother."

If it doesn't come out in my tone, Dad, it's gonna come out through my hands.

Okay, Aiden. Let's think this through. Anger, your presence is welcomed. I just found out that I was betrayed by my mom, my dad, and my dad's boss. They withheld secrets and support that could have led to a completely different life for me, and they were dead wrong for that. But attacking them is not going to help anything. *I appreciate you for wanting to make sure I don't get taken advantage of, but for now, we need to look for another solution to the trouble they've caused me.*

I exhale slowly. "You're right... I'm sorry, Mom. I..." My mind flashes to Tessa telling me to thank her for teaching me how to cook and to tell her I love her, but the betrayal still feels too real.

"I just... This is a lot for me right now," I finally say.

Is this what you wanted, Zoe? Are you trying to force me to use my powers? What are you even trying to do?

I need a solution here. There's gotta be a way out.

Tessa, I don't know if you can hear me. But if you can, I could really use your help. I don't know what to do. My dad just told me they found a way to help me get rid of my powers, which is what I've wanted for, like, the last eight years. But I couldn't get rid of them because they came from my mom because she went through the old LIST. They never even told me she had an LET. But now they're saying that if CLU finds the people who were involved in Felicity, they're gonna kill us unless we take the new LIST. But now I know that Zoe Withers works for the Collective. She probably runs it! And my dad works for her! And I'm sitting at the dining room table with both of them right now! Tessa, what should I do? I feel like I'm out of options.

"I understand," my dad says calmly. "And the good news out of all of this is that now we can do the same thing for you that we did for your mom. I know how bad you've wanted this. I know the shame you've carried around for having this struggle. And, you know, everything that happened with you and Leia. That's why I've been working so hard to figure this out, and we've done it. I promise, it won't hurt a bit. You'll lay down and take a nap, and when you wake up, this will all be behind you, and you can live your life without this struggle. Let us help you with this. Please."

Is that the solution? "If you can't beat 'em, join 'em?" What other choice do I have?

Zoe adds in, "We don't have a waitlist right now, Aiden.

If you sign up today, it will take three weeks for preliminary screenings—well, probably less for you since we've already got most of your information on file... But by this time, in two weeks, your LETs will be in complete remission. Oh, and don't worry about cost," she says, winking at me.

This is just too much. Maybe Leia was right... Maybe this isn't my war after all. I can get rid of these powers and walk away from all of this. I won't have to worry about CLU trying to kill me. Leia and I might be able to get back together again. I can live a normal life!

But I'd be letting down Tessa and the Broken. But then again... Do they expect me to give up my relationship with Leia by risking my life fighting a war that I don't even understand? What's the point? Once CLU tracks us down, it's LIST or die anyway. Why not just go through it now?

I look at Zoe and say, "That's very generous of you..."

Tessa, Tirrell, Zane, Auriel... I know you guys believed that helping you win this war was my destiny. And it sounded so cool on paper. I wanted that destiny... I've dreamed of having an exciting and fulfilling purpose for so long. I've had so many fantasies about how to make my life count and do something meaningful with it. But this choice isn't a fantasy. This is real life!

I'm not a soldier! I'm just a guy. And if the head of the ARL is running the Collective, I'm way out of my league. Who knows how many Users she has mind control over? I never chose these powers! And I didn't join the Broken because I wanted to save the world fighting in some shadow war about anti-globalism! Auriel asked me what my choice would be... I know this is so messed up, and I hope you all can forgive me for this, but—

"Yeah, let's go ahead and set that appointment."

A normal, Talentless life—that's the destiny I choose.

End Part 4

PART FIVE – LIFE AND DEATH

CHAPTER 22 – CHOICES

Twelve Days Later

"Well, Aiden, I feel I need to make a shift in this conversation. We're approaching the end of your court-ordered therapy sessions with me. Of course, I'm more than happy to keep working together if you'd like. I'm sure we can figure out a way to have ARL cover the cost," Dr. Cambridge says with a smirk. "Otherwise, we'll need to discuss some considerations for termination to ensure the transition is smooth for you."

I snicker. "That would be nice of the lab, but I don't think I'll be... Oh, wait. I don't think I told you, but I signed up for the new LIST procedure. My appointment is right after this. So yeah, this will be our last session."

Ron shifts slightly, his expression turning thoughtful. "When I heard about the breakthrough, you were the first person I thought of. But no, you hadn't told me. I try not to assume anything about my clients. I only know what you're willing to share—that's where the real work gets done."

"Honestly," I say, leaning back in my chair, "I feel like I've done my shift and then some. I'm ready to clock out." I chuckle.

"We certainly have done a lot of hard work, and if I may say so, I'm proud of the progress that I've seen in you," he says brightly. "Learning to own your responsibility and sympathize with Leia was a huge step for you. Whatever the relationship between you two becomes, it will undoubtedly be better by you taking these kinds of steps.

"You also carry yourself with more confidence now, like you know you belong in the world for the first time. That's incredible. And you've even been honest about how you truly feel about your powers. Again, there's been a lot of good work.

But with that said, I can't help but to conclude that there's still some work to do."

"Why do you think that?" I ask. "I mean, as far as the courts are concerned, if I go through this procedure, they'll be satisfied that I'm no longer a threat. And that was what I said I wanted in our first session, so... "

Where are you going with this, doc?

"It was," Ron says, nodding. "But, you see, the answer to your question was in your response. You have an appointment scheduled already to guarantee the removal of your powers once and for all, which is what you *said* you've wanted all along. But just now, your words were '*if* I go through,' rather than *when...* I don't think you are fully settled in your decision."

He sits up straighter, studying me. I shift in my seat, hyperaware of my body language under his watchful eye.

You don't know half of what's riding on this decision, Ron. Let's just wrap this up, okay?

He continues, "You've gained more control over your powers recently, and you've used them to accomplish some positive things. And remember in our first session, I told you I didn't think you hated your powers—and I still believe that's true. So if you do decide to go through this procedure, you may actually have to grieve the loss of your LETs, just as people grieve when they suddenly become paralyzed or lose a loved one."

"Yeah, but those losses aren't voluntary. The people you're talking about didn't choose to lose anything," I counter.

"That's exactly right," he says, nodding slowly. "And that's what I'm curious about. Are *you* freely choosing this? There's pressure on you to make this decision, and I think you need to be honest about that. The courts will get off your back rather than reviewing my case notes for possible further sentencing. You have a better shot at being with the woman you proposed to since she won't fear being harmed by your LETs again... Is it even possible to freely choose with those kinds of consequences looming over your head? Talk to me about how you're processing all of that."

I wonder if Ron went through LIST at some point. It would make sense to have a counselor as a part of the Collective. It would be very easy to get information out of people if you had mind control over their therapist. I gotta be careful not to say too much!

I take a deep sigh and say, "You're right. It is a lot to process. More than I can even explain, really. But this seems to be the simplest way. There are a lot of powerful forces that are bigger than me, ya know? Things that are beyond my control, and I just have to accept that. We're talking life and death, ya know? Like, somebody could actually die if I keep going this way."

Most likely, me.

"My powers are pretty strong, and my control is getting better, but life is just… I feel like I have to. Like, it's the right thing to do. Some battles might not be mine to fight, ya know?"

"I understand," Ron says, "and I'm not here to persuade you not to do something that you want to do. I'm just here to help you process your thoughts and feelings about the things that you do and the things that happen to you."

After a moment of silence—the kind that I hated when we first met but have surprisingly gotten used to—he adds, "What are you thinking?"

I stare at the blank wall, imagining I could use it as a canvas onto which I project and observe the inner world of my thoughts. After considering what hues and brush strokes I might use to illustrate how I feel right now, I answer, "I'm wondering if anyone is completely free to choose." I look up to notice Dr. Cambridge looking at me with disappointment in his eyes for the first time ever. "What? What'd I do?" I ask.

With a quiet urgency, he says, "You tried to sit there and tell me that our work is done, and a few moments later, your feet are two inches away from the edge of an existential precipice. The way that you understand this thing called free will and your ability to choose will impact you for the rest of your life."

He pauses to gauge my reaction to the gravity of that statement. I divert my gaze and nod my head slowly, trying not to get lost in that precipice of his.

My decision about this procedure is going to impact the rest of my life. As if I don't have enough to think about, you want me to try to figure out free will right now?

"Until the point that you are linked up with the ALPHA, you have the power to choose. And whatever you choose, I want you to know that I'm available to walk with you through it."

I smirk and say, "At the end of our last session, you're running an ad for me to renew my subscription, huh, Ron?"

Still using sarcasm to deflect from difficult thoughts, huh, Aide?

"Oh, you think I'm offering this for the money? Aiden, I'm salaried. Whether I see ten clients in a day or just one, I get the same amount of credits deposited. I'd gladly get paid to sit right here in my office and watch gladeball highlights all day," he says, laughing.

"Oh, you're into glade? Who's your team?" I ask.

"The Konquerors. Who else?" he responds instantly.

"Did you see Umar make that catch off the wall last night?"

"I did! It was legendary!"

"Yeah, it wasn't bad. You know who I like?"

"Aiden?"

"What?"

"You're changing the subject," Dr. Cambridge says dryly, shifting the entire atmosphere in the room. "Admittedly, I brought up the topic, but you haven't responded this vigorously to anything else all session. We've talked about this before—your habit of dodging the tough stuff. It won't be easy, but you're going to have to face this head-on."

He glances at the holographic clock hovering over his desk, then sighs and smiles at me. He stands and offers his hand, just like he does at the end of every session. "And when it gets hard, that's what I'll be here for."

I rise, shake his hand, and say, "Except this time, since I won't have any powers, I won't need therapy."

He adds his left hand to our shake, his smile softening. "Therapy isn't just for powers, Aiden. The homework I've given you and the tools you've practiced using were never about the powers, were they? Speaking of, my last homework assignment will be for you to journal about your experiences in therapy. What insights have you gained, what new behaviors have been implemented, and what changes have you seen in your life since you started coming to therapy? You'll want to hold onto the wins."

I crack a faint smile. "Write about everything that's changed since I started coming to therapy? I'll have to list you on the acknowledgements page of the novel. Are any of your phrases copyrighted, or can I use them royalty-free?"

I'm bad at goodbyes.

Dr. Cambridge chuckles. "The only payment I'll ever take from you is knowing you'll use what you've gained to help someone else, however that looks for you. I've enjoyed our time together, Aiden. Take care of yourself."

I nod at Dr. Cambridge and take a look around his office. Then, I step out into the hallway, making my way back to the lobby, wondering if I will ever see this place again.

I walk out the glass doors feeling free on one hand and the weight of the world on the other. I flag down a carrier, climb in, and give the AI my destination. I try to unwind by pulling out my Solo and scrolling to Leia's Connect page. No new posts.

"Yo, you got a video call from Zane. I already accepted since you're not doing anything important," Lil' A interrupts, his smugness somehow audible.

"What makes you think I—"

"Connection stable! Holographic images rendered!"

Zane's grinning face materializes.

"What's up, Zane?" I say, unamused.

"And Tirrell!" Tirrell chimes in.

"Oh, what's up, Tirrell?"

"Nah, what's up with you? How you feeling, bro? It's *showtime!*" Zane says, practically vibrating with energy.

"You're hyped about me heading to Zoe and the ALPHA?" I ask, confused.

"When is Zane *not* hyped?" Tirrell quips.

"Good point."

"I feel like you two are judging me, and I don't like it."

"Deal with it," Tirrell replies. "Aiden, we just wanted to check in on you and see how you're doing. Are you nervous?"

"Of course!"

"Ah, don't be. You know we got your back, no matter what," Tirrell says.

"Yeah, I know. It's just... This is a *big move* to make, man. It all comes down to this. I just don't want anybody to get hurt, you know?"

"I want you to know that I believe in you, Aiden," a familiar voice says before the image of the speaker comes into view.

"Oh, hey, Talia! That means a *lot*, coming from you."

She giggles. "No duh! Of course it does!"

"Have you seen how this all plays out? Like, does this work and we all live happily ever after and stuff?"

She zips her lips. "You know I can't tell anybody what I've seen. Tessa's orders."

Feigning desperation, I say, " I mean, but can't you break the rule *this* time?"

"No! Yield, Aiden," she says, wagging her finger at me. "But... I did have another dream about you."

Oh, yeah? Do tell!

My excitement is curbed by the deflation in her mood when she says, "That's... actually why I haven't been around as much. But Tessa told me not to be mad at you anymore. So, I forgive you!"

"For... give me? For what?"

"I just told you I can't tell you, mister! Plus, I don't want you to be distracted!" she says, her cheerfulness returning.

"Too late."

"Sorry... bye!"

"Bye, Talia." After she fades back out of view, I ask Tirrell and Zane, "Do y'all know what that was about?"

"Not at all," Tirrell replies.

"Okay... Well, I'm pulling up to the building. Thanks for checking in, guys. I guess I'll see you on the other side. Oh, wait —is Leia still there with Tessa, or did she...?"

"Of course she is, bro! Where else would she be?" Zane asks, jeering at me.

"Yeah, she's in with Tessa right now. Those two have really gotten close lately!" Tirrell comments.

"Do you guys know if she...?"

"She's behind you, too, bro. 100%," Zane affirms.

"Okay... Cool. Thanks. Well, off I go. Stay tuned!"

"See you soon, bro!" they say, somehow in perfect unison.

I step out of the carrier onto the sidewalk in the shadow of Sheridan Tower. I follow the dark gray siding and huge glass windows all the way up to the sky.

How can anyone build something that tall and straight?

I walk through the center set of five pairs of sliding glass doors. The bioscanner greets me: "Aiden Lore, welcome!" A few steps in, I reach the security checkpoint, where the guard motions for me to step through the barrier. As I approach, a sign catches my eye:

"For our collective privacy and security, ARL systems emit a signal that scrambles all incoming and outgoing Solo frequencies. Entering through this barrier serves as your express consent to have your Solo signal scrambled. Entering the barrier also serves as consent to have your image and actions captured via video recording. These will not be released without your written consent, and we will gladly furnish you with our privacy practices in place."

I keep walking, lost in thought until I arrive at the desk near the first set of six elevators.

Am I really about to enter the Collective? The guys think I'm just here to gather information, but... I'm pretty sure that getting more info is only going to convince me further to side with Zoe.

Ugh, am I really about to do this? To betray them? Will I be able to live with myself after making that kind of choice? But then again... will I be allowed to live if I don't?

"Good afternoon," I say to the older lady behind the desk. "I have a 4:00 appointment to see Ms. Wi—"

"Ms. Withers, Aiden Lore is here to see you," she interrupts, speaking into the intercom. Her knowing smile is the only thing keeping me from being upset with her curtness.

Instantly, Zoe's enthusiastic voice comes through the speaker: "Delightful! Send him right up!"

It's almost like she was waiting for me...

My eyes wander to the desk's monitors, showing video feeds of every inch of the building, the grounds outside, and sections of the stairwells. One screen even shows my face.

Do these feed up to her office? Maybe she was waiting for me.

There's the ALPHA. That's where my life changes.

Even Zoe's office is on camera? Should I wave at her? No, that'd be weird.

"Thank you," I say, as I make my way to the elevators.

Why is this lady watching me like that?

"Aiden, are you just going to walk past me like you don't recognize me?" she says with exaggerated disappointment.

My eyes dart wildly around her frame—her graying bob-styled hair, her piercing green eyes, her softly wrinkled hands—for a clue to her identity. I glance desperately at her name tag. "Mrs. Gloria? Wow! Hey, how have you been?"

"I've been good," she replies with a bit of that older-lady sass. "I just thought the man whose dad promoted me from babysitter to day shift security manager would have recognized me. That's all I'm saying," she says and turns her head.

"Ohhhh," I stammer. "I'm so sorry. It's just, you know... the last time I saw you, I was, like—what—six? I didn't recognize you in uniform."

"Mmm hmmm."

"Plus, you've lost some weight, haven't you? And your eyes—have they always been that deep, vivid green?" I ask, trying to soften the blow.

"Every day of my life since I put these contacts in, honey —and don't you forget it!" she says, making us both laugh. "It's good to see you, though. How's Jackie doing?"

"She's good, she's good. Yeah, we're all doing fi—"

"Mrs. Gloria," Zoe interrupts. "Why hasn't our guest made it to the elevator yet?"

She's DEFINITELY watching me on camera.

"He's on his way, Ms. Withers!" Mrs. Gloria says into the intercom. Then, lowering her voice, she adds, "Your father got me the job, and now you gone get me fired! Get on up to them elevators!"

"My bad. Good to see you again, though!" I say, hurrying to the elevator. I press the button, and the door opens instantly.

I step inside and tap 30 on the touchscreen. As the elevator lifts off, I remember being amazed at how smooth these elevators are the first time I rode one with my dad.

This antigravity technology made me want to go to college to become an engineer. Then, that dream evolved into biomedical engineering, but... life happened. But, once my powers are gone, maybe I'll try going back to college! I'll finally get to make my life what I want it to be!

"Floor 30. You have arrived!" the elevator voice announces.

The doors slide open, and I step out into a hallway lined with granite walls holding gold-framed pictures. My footsteps echo loudly against the ivory tiles.

At the end of the hallway, I turn left, then take the first right.

I walk down the path to its end and stop in front of the double doors, waiting for them to slide open.

"Welcome, Aiden Lore," the AI's soothing voice greets me through the speaker as the doors grant me entry.

Stepping inside, I pause just beyond the threshold of the 15-by-25 feet room, surprised that it looks almost identical to the way it looked the first time I met the ALPHA 15 years ago. To my left, a crash cart stocked with emergency medical supplies sits tucked in the corner. A computer terminal rests in the center of the sterile, white wall on my right. The far wall holds a large Holovision screen that hangs just below the ceiling, displaying Zoe's face. And in the center of the room stands the ALPHA.

Images flash into my mind, memories of nine-year-old Aiden, bursting with hope that my dad's machine would make my powers go away for good. I can't help but think about how much has changed since the last time they slid that hovering table, with me on it, into those large black rings.

Last time, I thought I would be keeping my loved ones safe by going through with this. This time, it feels like I'm putting my friends—and maybe even the whole world—in danger. This is so messed up!

"Aiden, welcome. How are you feeling?" Zoe asks from the screen.

"A little nervous, if I'm honest."

"About what?" Zoe asks, her tone laced with curiosity. "You've been through this before. You know the process doesn't hurt. You'll just drift off to sleep, and when you wake up, you won't have any access to your LETs anymore. You'll finally be able to live the regular life you've always wanted."

"Right," I say slowly. "And my dad reminded me of all of that, too, but I just... Hey, is he in his office? I thought he'd at least come and peek his head in for this."

"Oh, didn't he tell you? He's at a speaking engagement in

Infinity."

Biggest day of my life, and he's not here?

"I knew I was omitting something," she says. "I neglected to tell him I was able to find an open slot for you to come in today instead of Monday. He wanted to be here for your procedure, but… the date changed, and it seems he wasn't informed."

That's probably for the best.

"Well, in that case, we can probably just cut straight to the chase, then, huh?" I ask, trying to sound braver than I feel.

"Have I told you that I've always appreciated that eagerness you show?" she says. "Why don't you lie down on the table and make yourself comfortable? I'm excited to see what life has in store for you."

CHAPTER 23 – CONSEQUENCES

"That's not quite what I meant. At the Solo Center, you said you needed to see that I was committed to your cause before giving me any more information. I'll be honest—I had no intention of buying in last time, so I totally get why you might not trust me now. But hopefully, the fact that I'm here, seconds away from going through the procedure, gives you some perspective on where my allegiance lies."

"'Allegiance?'" Zoe repeats. "I'm not sure what you're trying to imply here."

Wait. Now that I think about it, I didn't see a single person on this entire floor. She cleared it out on purpose. Maybe we can have a candid conversation.

"Ms. Wi... Zoe, I'll be straight with you, and I'll ask you to be the same with me. Ultimately, I'm not loyal to either side of this conflict. I'm here for me."

"I'm sorry. Could you be clearer with your wording?" Zoe asks, her tone shifting from enthusiasm to annoyance. "My best guess is that you're saying you have cold feet. Have you not fully committed to the procedure? Well, that's understandable. You came to me looking for an escape from your powers. If you don't want that anymore, you're free to leave. ARL will continue its mission either way."

"That's not what I'm saying," I reply, trying to diffuse the tension. "I'm just acknowledging that my reason for being here is that I'd prefer not to be caught up in the conflict at all. I'm sure that shapeshifter didn't know he'd get caught up in it, yet he was. And without even knowing why, he could've been killed.

"I don't know exactly what you do that lets you take over people's minds or bodies, but I'm assuming it has something to do with this table. Am I right?"

"I think I understand what's going on here," she says, her confidence returning. Clearing her throat, her expression sharpens, her eyebrows lowering as her eyes blaze with intensity.

"This table allows the ALPHA to connect with your Laosi and place a limiter on the most powerful soul stream, as we've discussed before. As you indicated in your waiver, we continue to collect data post-procedure—at both scheduled and spontaneous intervals—to ensure the procedure's continued effectiveness."

'Collect data?' That's what she's calling mind reading, huh?

"But if your plan was to make a pretense of sincere intentions in order to uncover some conspiracy theory about the organization that your father and I built, then I would like to redirect you to our Disconnect page. These matters have been brought up and debunked time and again, *ad nauseam*."

She's really doubling down on not giving anything away. Probably because she knows everything is recorded. I'll have to play her game.

"Zoe, I'm not trying to stir up any hostilities here. Look, maybe I *have* spent too much time on the ARL Disconnect page. But can you blame me? After what went down at the carrier station, people want to know the truth. You and I both know we aren't getting the whole story from the news outlets."

She folds her arms. "You have no proof to substantiate any claim that the ARL was involved in that in any way."

"You only need proof when you're accusing somebody," I counter. "That's not what I'm doing right now. With this ongoing data collection you mentioned, I'm pretty much going to be tied to Alma Research Labs for the rest of my life. I'm practically forfeiting my soul over to you. I just have a request before I sign on the dotted line. Is that fair?"

Zoe's posture shifts, and she leans back in her chair.

"Completing this procedure can have a profound impact on your life. If what I'm hearing you say is that you would like to consider the pros and cons of going through with the procedure, then I don't mind answering questions. After all, I want you to feel confident and informed about which decision will be *best* for you and your loved ones."

"Okay. Thank you," I say. "I don't fully understand the 'profound impact' of the procedure or how it all works or whatever. But I think you'd agree you're likely to gain some very valuable data from me going through this, right? And I'm willingly waiving those rights to privacy. You choose to use the data from my soul streams however you want, but I'm just asking that you don't collect or use any *physical* data from me."

Zoe stares at me through the Holovision screen, her expression blank. She blinks twice, then squints and raises an eyebrow.

Nervously, I clear my throat and try again.

"Our friend Elon told me that one of those spontaneous physical data examinations kept him out late one night. I want to avoid those altogether. You can have the Laosi data, but can I keep my *physical* data?"

Still squinting, Zoe presses her lips into a subtle frown.
Come on! She had to catch what I meant that time!

After a beat, she exhales heavily, smirks, and says, "It's a shame. All of that data could have been so useful for the cause. But I will respect your—"

"What exactly is 'the cause?'" I interrupt, seizing the opportunity. "Do I have the right to know what I will be used—I mean, what my data will be used for?"

"Yes."

"So… are you going to tell me?"

"You have the right but not the need," she replies, her tone calm but evasive. "To protect our trade secrets from competitors, we've made it a practice only to reveal the results of our aggregate data once we've reached certain stages in developing the project it's being used for." With a wink, she adds, "You'll know when it's done, though."

Her defenses are airtight. Mind control aside, she still has all the power here. I came here hoping I could find an advantage, some loophole, a weakness... something to make me think that if I stay with the Broken, we have a chance at fighting her and winning. But... I just don't see it.

Because CLUE will find us. It's not a matter of if, but when. The only reason they haven't found us yet is because she's been holding them back. But when she turns us over to them, my best-case scenario plays out with me being forced to go through LIST anyway if my dad has any luck. And the worst case scenario is death!

I just need to accept it. Zoe's gonna have control either way. The best thing I can do is try to negotiate while I still can.

"If you can agree to respect the privacy of our R&D departments, then I'll have no qualms respecting your personal privacy."

"Can I get your Imprint on that?" I ask, reaching for my Solo to set up the sync.

"That won't be necessary," she replies quickly. "First, Solos are scrambled here. Second, it's been so long since I linked Solos for an Imprint that I'm not sure I even remember how," she says, feigning embarrassment.

"What I'm trying to say," she continues, "is that my business partners and colleagues helped me build ARL into what it is today because they all know I will *always* keep my promises. Everything we do here at ARL is born from a promise. I'm not about to start breaking promises now. You have my word."

"Then... you have my thanks."

At least I know I won't end up like Elon. Zane and Tirrell were holding back on me that night. If the two of them go all out against me in a Broken vs. Collective battle, there's no way I don't end up in a hospital! I can't just shapeshift my wounds away. Leia could heal me if she... Leia!

I can't let her get caught up in all of this! Think, Aiden, think!

"You said at dinner that if I had other friends with LETs, I could tell them it isn't too late for them to join in!" I blurt out, hoping my desperation sounds more like conviction. "Does that still stand? Because I know an organization that also tries to help people with powers. Can they work together with the ARL to accomplish the cause?"

"The offer still stands, but I sincerely doubt we could work together," she says.

"Why not?"

"Because I think I've seen your group in action, and from what I've observed, there are certain... philosophical differences between our organizations. Plus, I doubt the group you're referring to would be willing to make the sacrifices necessary for real progress," she says.

"Sacrifices?" I exclaim.

"You don't think I've gotten to where I am without some sacrifice along the way, do you?" she scoffs.

No, you got to where you are because of my dad's discoveries!

The faint hum of Laosi vibrations reminds me to keep my hands hidden behind my back.

Dad... Is he...? Please tell me he's not a part of this.

"Is my dad... willingly making... those same kinds of sacrifices?" I ask timidly. I can hear my heart pounding.

She takes a deep breath, holds it for a moment, then exhales slowly as she lowers her head.

Ughhh! Just spit it out!

Finally, she looks back up and says, "That's the most important question you've asked. The answer is no. Your father's a good man doing great work. But there's a reason he's usually in the labs, and I'm usually in my office. There are certain applications of his work that he's not interested in. I don't bother him with those details."

"Thank you," I say sincerely.

"You didn't have the right to know that... but you

needed to." Her eyes burn with passion as she adds, "Family is everything."

Family... That's why she's doing all of this.

"Zoe... who did you make your promise to?"

"That is something you have neither the need nor the right to know," she says, folding her arms again. "Hopefully, I've answered all your questions to your satisfaction. To be respectful of the clients I'm scheduled to meet with after you, we should begin prepping you for the procedure. Lie down on the table, please, and I'll have one of our technicians come in to assist you further."

So... that's it, then, I guess. At least I know my dad isn't working for the Collective. And I won't be caught up in the fighting. But giving Zoe access to the Broken? What's she gonna do to them? What will she do to the world with the Broken out of the way?

You know what? That's not my problem! Not my battle to fight. That's why CLUE and TU Defenders exist. Besides, how could I help in a fight if I'm dead? Nah, no thanks. I'll pass on the hero complex.

Slowly, I step forward to the hovering table. Behind me, the double doors slide open.

"What's up, Aiden?"

I turn around to match the voice with its source. A young guy walks in with spiky brown hair wearing black and gray scrubs.

I stare blankly for a moment. "I'm sorry... You look familiar, but..."

"Aaron Voss! From Ms. Brine's class," he says, grinning.

"Oh! What's up, dude?" I say, giving him a fist pound.

Zoe clears her throat and says, "You two know each other? I'm sorry, Aiden. This may be out of line with our client confidentiality protocols."

"Well, it's not like the son of Richard Lore going through the new version of LIST wouldn't have become common knowledge for the department soon enough anyway," I say.

"I suppose that's true enough," Zoe says thoughtfully.

"But if you don't feel comfortable having a classmate involved in the procedure while you're asleep—if that feels too vulnerable to you in any way—you can let me know, and I'll gladly request another technician."

I just don't understand her! I know she means every word about making sure I'm comfortable, but I also know she'd put my life on the line in a heartbeat if it meant winning a battle against my friends.

"Nah, it's cool," I say, brushing it off. Turning to Aaron, I ask, "So, man, what have you been up to? How's life? Looks like a lot's changed since we played tag on the playground at recess."

Aaron strokes his chin with a smirk. "That it has. It feels like just yesterday I was writing my essay for the Sheridan Grant. Honestly, I was just throwing up a prayer, but all these years later, here I am—working at ARL with a wife and two kids."

"Wife? Bruh, don't tell me... Raina?"

Aaron smiles proudly and says, "Raina and I have been happily married for four years now."

"No kidding... Tertiary school sweethearts, huh? I'm happy for you, man! And the Sheridan Grant? They only take the best and brightest."

Before Aaron can respond, Zoe cuts in. "He's quite adept at doing his job, as he's about to demonstrate. The collar, please."

"Right," Aaron says, grabbing a black plastic device from the side of the terminal. "See you on the other side, man!"

He hands me the device and then returns to the terminal to activate the computer programs. I examine the "collar" in my hands. When stretched out, it's slender and just a little longer than the span of my hand from thumb to pinky. The middle is extendable, and each end features what looks like a two-inch speaker covered in silver mesh.

This is new.

"Thank you, Aaron," Zoe says. Turning to me, she adds,

"Aiden, please put that around the front of your neck. The two ends should rest just above your collarbone. It's a new type of Laosi suppressant, developed by none other than your father!" Her tone is celebratory. "Perfect, just like that."

I lay down on the table, the collar settling with me as I reluctantly comply.

I know you think I'm the oppressor, Aiden, but I'm not. I'm the liberator!

I glance over at the Holovision, surprised by Zoe's sudden shift in candor. But her mouth isn't moving.

How come I can hear Zoe's voice in my head!?

Given the fact that I control people to serve my purpose, I imagine that sounds contradictory. But I really would rather not involve you or anyone else.

Is it this collar? It must be the collar. Zoe, can you hear me?

If I could do this myself, I would! But my LET is not as intimidating or destructive as yours. We can only play the cards we were dealt.

You have an LET? You've been helping people get rid of their powers, but you've been using yours all this time?

I've spent my life defending freedom. Unfortunately, there are a handful of people whose abilities or positions are useful for my mission. Even though these select few aren't choosing to join my cause, experiencing a brief moment of having decisions made for you to gain a lifetime of freedom is a worthwhile exchange. I'm defending people's freedom to choose.

That doesn't make any sense! Who are you liberating by taking their freedom to choose?

I also know you're concerned about the sacrifices I mentioned along the way.

She can't hear me.

But just so you know, I don't aim for violence. Otherwise, I could have killed you quickly and discreetly in Felicity. It's not my purpose to kill, but I will kill for my purpose.

She says she wants people to have a lifetime of freedom, but she's controlling people's minds and using them to kill others. What is her deal?

However, if the Broken stands down, I will finish my work in 3 months at the most without any needless bloodshed. Only two more individuals need to die.

She's already picked her targets?

But, Aiden, everybody dies. You know that, don't you? If not by the hands of the Collective, they'd die in a carrier crash, get murdered, or die from an unknown disease. Death always wins. But don't you see that it's the certainty of death that gives life so much beauty? Knowing that you don't have forever—that you don't even know how long you have—that's what makes each moment count.

Everything about what she's saying feels so wrong... So why can I not refute her logic?

Death is not the enemy. The only thing about life you can count on is the fact that it will end someday. The real enemy is anyone who prevents you from being able to live while you're alive. I have to destroy the world's enemy. It's the only way I can make things right. And once I've done that, I'll never use the ALPHA to control anyone again.

The technician gives Zoe a thumbs-up, and she replies, "You may begin."

How was she talking in my head? It's a lot like Tessa, but Zoe's is more aggressive. And she can't hear back. And she did it with technology?

While I'm lost in thought about the similarities and differences between Zoe and Tessa, the table glides into the middle of the three large rings: one at my head, one at my stomach, and one just above my ankles. Panels on the inside of the rings light up, pulsating in shifting shades of green and red. I'm almost certain I can see the soul-altering waves radiating out from each of them.

I'm really doing this.

"I imagine your life should get much easier from this point on," Zoe says.

I'm instantly reminded of my conversation with Leia

this morning as I dropped her off at Otto's Autos. I can still hear her quoting her dad: *"The path of least resistance never leads to the most happiness."*

And then her words to me: *"If you do what's easy, I'll understand. But if you do what's right, the world will be better off for it."*

The ALPHA whirs as it comes online.

This is really it! This is the moment that will define the rest of my life. Zoe is gonna win... But... she's wrong.

Do I wanna be complicit in this? Take the easy way out while Zoe takes over the world? What kind of world will my loved ones live in? My dad...

And then there's the Broken... Tessa was the first one to see the real me and accept me. Unlike Zoe, who just wants to use me. Can I betray Tessa like this?

Tessa... Tessa, what should I do?

You already know what you should do.

I... Yeah... Yeah, I guess you're right. I do. Will you help me?

Of course, I will. Are you ready?

I think so.

"I'll adjust your Laosi frequencies when your soul is at rest and has let its guard down. As before, just let the sonar pulses lull you to sleep," Zoe says, her voice calm and controlled.

I close my eyes. A chill runs down my spine, and nausea sinks deep into my stomach. My heart races. My closed eyes begin to well up and my skin feels exposed, as though I'm lying here completely naked.

I thought they said you weren't supposed to feel anything! Did she already start messing with my Laosi?

No.

Tessa's voice in my mind is calming and stabilizing.

Then what is this terrible feeling?

Open the eyes of your heart and see for yourself.

As I try to understand and apply these cryptic instructions, an image forms in my consciousness. I'm at

Broken HQ, standing in the middle of the showroom. All the people I know within the Broken are there and a few that I don't. But something's off. The mood is dry and somber. The atmosphere feels like grief.

I notice people glancing in my direction, so I try to walk over... but my feet won't move. They're fused to the cement floor.

"Hey!" I call out to my friends. "What's going on? Why is everyone so sad? Can you help me with my feet?"

I reach out to them, but they walk past me, their expressions distant. The people I thought were looking *at* me were actually looking *through* me. As if I'm not even there—as if no one *wants* me there.

What is this?

"Your heart rate seems a little elevated," Zoe's voice breaks through. "Try to calm down, okay? I'm not going to start the procedure until you're soundly asleep."

This is what you think it will be like if you go through with this and join Zoe.

Is this the future?

No. Just your expectation of it.

Why am I seeing this so vividly right now?

You asked for my help.

You're showing me this?

Not really. I'm helping you see what you feel.

How is this helping, exactly?

"That's better... Yeah, take some slow, deep breaths. Good... good."

You know my next question by now, don't you?

I feel ashamed! You want me to be ashamed of myself?

Remember all that you've learned so far. Shame is uncomfortable, but it's just an emotion like any other. Emotions just teach you what you think and what you want, so stay with it for a while and think. What do you think you can do with this shame?

I can learn that I'll never feel like I belong with the Broken if I go through with this... even though you're the first group I ever felt I truly belonged with.

I can learn that I won't forgive myself for this decision. That I'll never be happy if I give Zoe my freedom. Being a pawn of the Collective is not a destiny I'm willing to choose.

This vision you've shown me—the shame I feel in it—has made me see the truth. The only way I have a chance at peace is if I fight Zoe. Because that shame, that loneliness... they'll never go away if I stay on this path.

But I can use that shame. I can let it push me, fuel me, and encourage me to fight back.

Well... I was thinking you could use it to teleport, but that's good, too.

Oh... right.

The effect of the sonar pulses grows stronger. My consciousness starts slipping away, no matter how hard I fight it.

Oh no! Is it too late?! I have to get out of here—now!

"All right," Zoe says, her voice calm and final. "When you wake up, your out-of-control LETs will be a thing of the past."

It's literally now or never, Aiden!

Groggily, I barely manage to mumble, "They already are..."

"I'm sorry—what did you say?" Zoe asks.

Regaining some strength, I lift my head and speak louder. "My out-of-control LETs..." I force my eyes open, locking onto the monitor, and I boldly proclaim, "They're *already* a thing of the past!"

The high-pitched hum reverberates through me, the fiery cold energy surging from my chest to the tips of my fingers and toes. My midsection tightens under the pressure, making me cringe for just a moment. And I smile.

As spacetime bends, opening and closing all around me, I nod at Zane, standing before me now.

A mischievous grin creeps across his face. "Is it showtime, bro?" he asks.

"I apologize for not announcing myself before entering," I say. But as I let his infectious energy overtake me, I grin back at him and say, "But it's showtime! Let's do this!"

CHAPTER 24 – FREEDOM

"Bet! So... what's the plan?" Zane asks, he rubs his hands together, ready for action.

"I don't know, but we gotta move fast. You guys ready?" I ask.

"Hold on, Aiden," Leia interjects. "We need to think this through, at least a little. You're the only one of us who's ever stepped foot in that building. The rest of us would be running in blind."

"Yeah, but by the time I explain everything and we come up with a plan, Zoe will have activated her security, and we'll lose our chance!" I reply.

"Who's to say she hasn't done that already?" Tirrell asks. "And that's all the more reason why we need to understand the lay of the land. What are the targets we need to hit?"

I shake my head quickly, trying to push away the nervous energy. "You're right. Okay... well, I know she's using the ALPHA to control people. That's on the 30th floor. But she's in—or at least was in—her office on the 45th floor, right next to my dad's."

"Okay, so we need two teams, then," Elrond says, stepping in. "One to take out the ALPHA, and one to take out Zoe."

"Take out Zoe?!" Auriel exclaims, her voice rising in disbelief. "You want to just walk into ARL, kill the world's most renowned authority on Laosi, and then just walk out like nothing happened? Guys, let's be—"

"Who knows how much more damage she'll do if we don't finish it now?" Zane cuts in, his voice hard and unyielding.

"Yeah, but... what about holding our enemies

blameless?" Leia counters, her voice trembling slightly. "I mean, killing...? Is that what we signed up for?"

No, it is not.

I look around and notice everyone's eyes glowing blue.

I didn't know she could think to multiple people at once. This woman never ceases to amaze me.

Are my eyes blue, too?

You can't just walk in there looking for a fight. You'll be guilty of trespassing and unlawful use of Laosi, even if you don't kill anyone. At this rate, you'll all be taken to Atheria for the rest of your lives.

"As usual, Tessa's right," Tirrell concedes, scratching his head thoughtfully. "Zoe already got us blasted on the news in Felicity. But on her home turf?"

"Cameras!" I blurt out. "There are cameras all over the building. Can we use those to our advantage this time somehow?"

"Now you're thinking," Tirrell says, his tone brightening. "If we can show we were provoked into fighting, we might stand a chance of maintaining our innocence. Do the cameras record audio?"

"They have to—for liability purposes. My dad told me that once," I reply.

"Even better!" Tirrell exclaims. "That means your conversation with her was recorded, right? Did she say anything incriminating? Anything we could use to put her in jail?"

"Um, maybe? I don't know..." I stammer.

"What do you mean you don't know?" Zane snaps. "Isn't that the whole reason you went there?"

"Well, it was just... I don't know because... she was being dodgy, and she—"

Do I tell them I was actually thinking about joining her? I guess I should be honest. Accept your weakness, Aiden... Embrace the brotherhood.

I let out a sigh, but before I can say anything, Tirrell cuts in. "So maybe it's not airtight, but it's better than what we've got now. We'll just try to get her to slip up and say something when we go back."

"Any chance your dad told you where the videos are archived?" Nadia asks.

"Um… yeah. The Records Department," I say hesitantly. "But it's down in the basement. I don't know how we can get there. If you don't have the right credentials, the elevator won't even move."

Leia smirks and nudges me with her elbow. "Good thing we know somebody who can teleport," she says with a wink.

"Yeah, but I can only *direct* my teleportation to places I've actually seen before. I have no idea where I'll end up if I try to jump blind," I lament. "My dad couldn't take me there because even his badge doesn't have clearance."

"It's all good," El says casually. "Just get me and whoever's going with me close to the elevator, and I'll phase us through."

"And then do what?" Auriel interjects. "Ask the security officers to kindly make a copy of all the video footage from the last 24 hours for you? That plan doesn't make any sense."

Suddenly, Auriel freezes mid-motion. She waves her hand in front of El's face.

"Urth su zafe ll'I," El says, and then he glares at her. "Very funny," he adds dryly as I try stifle my laughter.

Most people just ignore what you say when they disagree… But Auriel makes you unsay it? That's hilarious!

"Everybody try to focus because I'm hearing problems, not solutions," Arvind says, chiming in for the first time. "Aiden's right. Now's the moment to get things done. How can we get that footage?"

Tirrell snaps his fingers. "I got it! The jump drive we got from the shapeshifter! The data drain file they used to grab all that information on TU is still on it. We can use that to access the video footage! I'll go with Elrond to the basement. Anybody else wanna come?"

"Count me in," Nadia says without hesitation. "Just in case we need to move some things—or people—around in a hurry. And... I'll help you stay focused, El," she adds, placing a hand on his shoulder.

"Thank you," El responds, his voice soft.

Are they a couple or something?

Arvind claps his hands twice. "See that? That's what I'm talking about. Now, what are we gonna do about Zoe?"

"Wait... maybe Leia should go to the basement, too," Auriel suggests.

I raise an eyebrow, exchanging a look with Auriel.

"What? No, I'm going with Ai—" Leia starts.

"I was just thinking," Auriel interrupts. "You and I will basically be doing the same thing, right? Damage control? So maybe we should split up so both teams have a healer. Zoe's definitely going to double down on security around her, and since you're still learning to use your LET, maybe you should go where there's probably going to be less action."

"No! I'm—"

"You make a good point, Auriel," Tirrell says, cutting Leia off. "But security is probably gonna be pretty lax down there since access is already restricted. The three of us should be able to handle it. You should both go up to the ALPHA."

"That makes sense," Auriel concedes, shrugging.

"Ooookay," I say, trying to break the awkward tension hanging over the room. "So we're actually gonna need two more groups. The ALPHA is on floor 30, and it obviously needs to be destroyed. But as long as Zoe stays at her computer, she might be able to keep sending the Collective at us."

I hesitate for a moment before continuing. "She was talking to me in my head—kind of like Tessa does—just before I was... umm... I think she uses computers to do her mind control, is what I'm trying to say. And the building is probably crawling with her sleeper agents."

"Arvind, I think your metal manipulation is best suited for taking out the ALPHA," Zane says decisively. "Auriel, you cover his back. Me, Aiden, and Leia will go and shut Zoe down... in the most Tessa-approved way possible, of course."

"I'm not sure if that's where I'll be most needed," Auriel replies, her tone hesitant.

"I think I actually agree with you..." Arvind says, nodding thoughtfully. "But our mission will take the least amount of time. I just gotta bend a big ol' piece of metal outta shape, and then we can go join Zane, Aiden, and Leia."

"Okaaay," Auriel replies.

Auriel seems off for some reason...

The sharp click of high heels behind me causes my teammates—my brothers and sisters—to glance in the same direction with unmistakable respect in their eyes. It's no surprise when the next voice I hear is both familiar and commanding.

"It sounds like you've worked out a solid plan," Tessa says confidently.

"That's really encouraging coming from you," Tirrell responds, his tone reverent.

"Are you here to give us a rousing speech to motivate us to victory?" I ask, half-joking.

"There's no time," she says bluntly, though her voice carries a calm assurance. "But I do have a question for you."

"Uh oh... should I be nervous?" I ask, feeling a faint knot forming in my chest.

"Have I ever told you what you should feel?" she counters, one eyebrow raised.

"So you're going to ask me what I feel?"

"Good guess," she replies with a smirk, "but not quite. Aiden, you're about to lead a team on a mission to tear down an organization that your father helped build from the ground up."

The tension in my chest twists into a pit that slides deep into my stomach.

"Your dad's cutting-edge research took ARL from an experimental lab on the brink of losing its grant funding to a multibillion-credit corporation with global impact. My question is, how do you think he will feel when he learns that his son destroyed the organization built on his life's work?"

As chills run up and down my spine and radiate across my body, I quickly yell, "Okay, gather round!" to my teammates. The last thing I see before my eyes close is Tessa winking at me.

When I open my eyes again, we're in one of the stairwells at ARL.

Thanks, Tessa, I think to her dryly. *Did you have to dig that deep, though?*

Maybe, maybe not. But honestly, it upsets me that that question instantly produced so much shame in you. You really should have an honest conversation with your parents. It will be crucial to your reintegration to speak vulnerably with them. Ask your dad what he truly feels about you without assuming you already know. And tell your mom how much you love her without assuming she knows.

I'll keep that in mind, but I've got some pretty pressing issues to attend to right now.

Then, I'll leave you to them.

No, wait!

"Aiden?" Leia's voice trembles. "Where are we?"

"We're on the 30th floor of Sheridan Tower," I inform the group quickly. "Tirrell, your team should head down one flight and exit the stairwell. There'll be an elevator on your left —it's the only one that goes to the basement. Go down to the lobby floor, and I guess El can phase you through from there. Right, El?"

"I'm all over it," El replies confidently.

As they start descending the stairs, I call after them, "El and Nadia might be okay, but Tirrell, *do NOT look up!* Zoe's got your face logged into her facial recognition. If she gets a hit, this whole operation is blown."

I watch as Elrond walks past the door they should've exited through. Panic flares, and I shout, "Wait, guys! Wait!! I said *one* flight!"

"What difference does it ma—" an earsplitting alarm siren cuts off El's nonchalant reply.

"This building has cameras on *every other* flight of stairs!" I growl through clenched teeth. "Now the elevators are in lockdown."

"So what should we do? Should we abort?" Leia asks.

I turn to Auriel expectantly.

"Oh, sorry, Aiden," she says mournfully. "Unfortunately, I can't reverse what I expect. And I expect El to act without thinking."

"In that case," Zane says, "it looks like we're locked in! The mission hasn't changed. We just gotta be faster about it!"

"Remember!" Tirrell says, his voice firm as they regroup. "If at all possible, make sure it's obvious you're *not* the aggressor! Let's go, guys."

They place their hands on El's shoulders and phase through the stairs, disappearing from sight.

Turning to Arvind and Auriel, I say, "This is your floor. Go straight down the hallway to the end and hang a left. Then take the first right. There'll be two sets of double doors directly ahead. The big machine in the middle of the room and the terminal on your right are your targets. Arvind, if you can, destroy the camera before it catches you, then dismantle the ALPHA."

"On it!" Arvind declares, racing through the door with Auriel right behind him.

"Look at you—the man with the plan!" Zane teases, grinning.

"Not the time, Zane... not the time at all," I mutter, shaking my head.

"Okay, so... what are we gonna do?" Leia asks, her panic barely contained.

"Umm..." I hesitate, then turn to Zane. "Can you harden your own body?"

"It's risky," he explains. "If I harden a blood vessel, I could end up having a heart attack, and my aim ain't very precise. What are you thinking?"

"Okay, so the elevators are locked down, and running up 15 flights of stairs would take too long... We're gonna have to go out the window," I say, bracing myself against the weight of what I just suggested.

"I'm sorry—what did you just say?" Zane asks, staring at me.

"I can fly," I explain, trying to sound calm. "And when I'm flying, anything I carry is weightless, just like me. So I can carry you both up... but we gotta break the glass first," I add pensively. "Maybe you could harden your shoes?"

"Okay, I can do that!" Zane replies, suddenly enthusiastic. I glance down and notice the soft fabric of his shoes now looks as solid and unyielding as stone.

"Are they... still comfortable?" Leia asks, raising an eyebrow.

"Not at all," Zane replies. "So let's do this!"

"Okay," I say, taking a deep breath to steady myself. "Leia, I need you to give me a hug."

"O-okay," she says, her voice hesitant but trusting. She squares up to me, takes a few steps closer, and wraps her arms around my neck.

I breathe deeply, feeling the warmth of her body pressed against mine. Her gentle fingers stroke the back of my head, and a familiar fragrance surrounds me—the same one she wore the first time I flew.

The last time I smelled this fragrance...

"Speaking of not the time," Zane mutters.

But my mind wanders anyway, trailing down the path of every happy moment we've shared like this. *The time in the park when we decided to make our relationship exclusive... the garden party when I proposed... her graduation party... that moment when—*

"Ow!" Leia exclaims after her head thuds softly against the underside of the stairs above us.

"Okay, let's go!"

Zane flings open the door and holds up his hands. I maneuver my body horizontally, flying through the doorway to grab his hands. Leia lies on my back, clutching my shoulders, while Zane positions himself like a kid on a swing, his knees tucked to his chest.

I aim straight for the nearest window.

I always wanted my life to have a purpose. And I always wanted Leia to be part of that purpose. This is what I've always wanted.

With a burst of speed, we race toward the window. At the moment of impact, Zane extends his legs, shattering the glass into a million sparkling fragments. For a split second, I appreciate how the sunlight glimmers off each shard—until I remember we're 300 feet above the ground.

My flight path arcs as I propel us upward toward the 45th floor. But my mood dips the closer we get, weighed down by the enormity of what we're here to do. Realizing I don't have time to pinpoint Zoe's exact office, I head for the nearest window. Zane kicks it in, and we crash land into an unlit room.

We hit the floor hard, rolling several times before coming to a stop in the middle of the 12-by-20-feet room. Staggering to our feet, I take a moment to survey the damage from our not-so-graceful entrance. Facing the window, I let out a slow breath as I assess the scene.

Could've been worse. At least we didn't land on the oak desk tucked into the corner on the right. The tan and gray wool carpet, though? It's gonna be a nightmare to get the glass shards out—assuming this building even remains standing after we expose Zoe.

I sigh heavily.

A lot of innocent people are about to lose their jobs, including whoever's office this is.

My gaze falls on a tablet lying on the desk, its screen projecting a still image of me just above its surface. I wait for it to transition to another photo—maybe one with Candace or Jack, or even Mom—but the sequence only includes pictures of me or me with Dad.

"Aiden, is this your dad's—?" Leia starts. She doesn't need to finish the question. And before I can answer, the door in the far corner across from the window creaks open.

Three ARL employees step into the room. Two of them —a man and a woman—are wearing Hunter green security uniforms, and their eyes immediately lock onto us.

Yeah, I'd probably have Users as my security guards, too.

The third is wearing hospital scrubs.

Aw, come on, Zoe - Aaron? I gotta fight him now?

The three of them spread out in front of the wall separating my dad's office from Zoe's.

"I'm not reading anything off of them," I say cautiously as we regroup against the opposite wall. "Zoe's got 'em. We don't know what they can do. Know your soul and communicate with each other. We'll get through this. We'll end this."

Zoe's voice crackles through my dad's intercom speaker, "I'm very disappointed, Aiden."

"Why?" I fire back. "Because I chose not to go along with your psychotic plot?"

"Psychotic pl—? No. No, no, no..." she responds, almost laughing. "Like I told you, I want people to make their own choices, which is what you have done. That's not what bothers me.

"Do you think I've made ARL into the global enterprise by trusting that everyone will do what they say they will do? Of course not. I'm disappointed that you underestimated me so badly. You really thought that you and your five friends could, what, shut down Alma Research Labs?"

Good. She hasn't seen all of us. She's the one underestimating us!

"Zoe," I begin, trying to sound calm. "Like I said before, I don't want to fight. I'd rather you let us talk you out of whatever you have planned."

"Breaking and entering, unlawful use of Laosi, destruction of property, and trespassing," Zoe rattles off. "Of course you know CLUE has been notified. But yes, let's talk. Would you all like some water or maybe a soft drink while we wait for the authorities to come and arrest you?"

"Yeah, no thanks," Zane replies, rolling his eyes. "But why don't you let your guard dogs down? You know, give them their bodies back?"

"Hmmm..." Zoe muses. "Aiden and I were talking, but then he went and got backup. Clearly, you came back to do more than talk, so I thought I should get backup of my own."

This is getting us nowhere. I have to force her hand.

"I did get backup," I say, stepping over to Zane and placing a hand on his shoulder. "I brought a friend who can phase through matter." Zane grins and waves cheerily at the three in front of us. "He can walk right through the thickest walls when he puts his mind to it. I needed someone who could get to your mind-control device and shut it down."

Turning to Zane, I ask, "Shall we?"

"We shall," he replies, playing along.

"So, what do you think, Zoe?" I continue. "Should we use the door or the wall?"

"You're not getting anywhere close to my computer," she snaps.

The girl Zoe controls steps forward, clapping her hands together in front of her midsection. A spark of blue Laosi ignites between her palms. Slowly, she spreads them apart, the energy expanding into a glowing translucent blue cylinder about six feet long and two inches in diameter. She grips it like a bo staff and begins her offensive.

I fall back immediately, leaving Zane to handle someone who can materialize a blunt weapon out of thin air. She swings the bo at his head with incredible speed and power, but Zane ducks under it effortlessly. She quickly repositions and jabs at his stomach. Zane easily sidesteps, and in one fluid motion, he lands a leg sweep kick that plants her flat on her back.

Looks like Zane's got this under control. She's shown her cards, but what about the other two?

I walk over to Leia, watching the guards closely for a hint, careful to show no signs of fear. They stare back at me with lifeless eyes from 10 feet away. Keeping Leia somewhat behind me, I begin walking towards the door, my body tense and guarded, waiting for my opponents to reveal their powers.

The male security guard reaches an open palm towards me, and the instincts developed during my bouts with Alexi cause me to cross my arms in front of me to cover the vital organs. But rather than a frontal impact, I feel a hand grab my shirt just behind my neck and pull me backwards.

Why did Leia pull me back?

I look back at Leia to try to gauge what she was trying to help me dodge, but from five feet behind me, her face shows the same confusion I feel.

Before I can piece it together, the guard repositions and launches a standing side kick. As his leg extends, part of it... disappears?

"Hrmph!" I grunt as his foot crashes into my stomach. The blow doubles me over. I force myself upright just in time to see him throw a right jab—but it connects as an uppercut under my chin, knocking me flat on my back. Dazed, I pull myself up, and watch him carefully to assess the situation.

He's sending his limbs through portals? How do you even fight somebody like that? I can't tell where his attacks are—

"Ugh!!" I blurt out after getting punched in the side. I stagger backwards, watching his attacks for a pattern while trying—in vain—to defend my whole body at once. After a kick to the back and punch to the face, I find myself picking Aiden up off the floor again.

I can't track his movements.

Every time I think I see a pattern, another kick or punch lands somewhere else—my back, my face—knocking me down again.

Out of the corner of my eye, I see Zane struggling against the girl, faring no better than me. Her energy staff has morphed into a chain-like whip, which she flings at him, wrapping it tightly around his neck.

Zane grapples with her, straining against the whip, but she yanks it down hard, forcing his head to meet her rising knee.

He recovers faster than she expects, launching a powerful open-palm strike to her abdomen that sends her staggering backward. As soon as the blow connects, Zane jumps into the air and spins, using the momentum to unravel the chain whip from his neck as his opponent stumbles further away. He lands on one knee, coughing and gasping for air.

The girl reforms the chain into a gleaming katana, and my stomach knots as I consider what might happen to Zane if he isn't quite fast enough.

This doesn't look good! Leia's not a fighter, and we don't even know what this other guy can do. We're not gonna win this!

The guy throws another punch from five yards away. I tense up, instinctively closing my eyes.

And then... nothing. Nothing but a soft thud and a muffled yell. I open my eyes to see the faint green glow of my force field. Through one of the pale hexagonal plates of the barrier, I see the guard who was fighting me clutching his arm —or rather where his arm should have been.

I glance down and see the other half of his arm, lying still and bleeding at my feet.

This is... HIS arm? My force field just cut his arm off?! What the—

The guard screams in pain. And I feel a fear and confusion radiating from him that are triple the intensity of my own. My force field disappears instantly.

"What happened to my arm?!" he cries, staggering back against the wall. "Where am I? How did I get—what's going on?!" His wide eyes dart around the room, taking in the broken glass and the desk that Zane's fight somehow shattered.

"Leia! Can you heal him?" I shout.

"You mean the guy who's trying to kill us?" she calls back.

"No, the g—well, technically, yes, I guess. But he's not anymore! He's back! I think the pain broke the ALPHA's control. Leia, please, help him! If you can," I plead.

"Hold him blameless, Leia!" Zane adds between midair somersaults, narrowly dodging the girl's relentless sword strikes.

"That's impossible!" Zoe's voice erupts over the intercom. "The ALPHA's control has *never* been broken before!"

"Do you need his other arm, or can you just...?" I ask Leia, my voice shaky as I gesture toward the injured man.

Leia gags. "No, I think I can just do it," she says. "I can help him grow a new one."

As she starts walking toward him, Aaron's eyes flicker with yellow, then red Laosi. He takes a step toward Leia, his movements stiff but purposeful. Their eyes lock.

"Stay."

Leia freezes in place. Aaron walks toward her, his fist glowing as it pulses the same ominous colors.

"STAY AWAY FROM HER!!" I yell. My body reacts on its own, both hands thrusting forward instinctively. A blast of energy surges from me with so much force that it sends Aaron hurtling backward. He crashes through the wall, across the hallway, and into the office on the other side, debris scattering everywhere.

The room falls still, and all eyes turn to me. They all stare as I struggle to control my raspy breathing.

The more I let my anger take over, the stronger these blasts get! I thought it'd be the opposite!

Leia is the first to move. She breaks the stunned silence and resumes her walk toward the scared, injured man.

Meanwhile, Zane's fight takes a sharp turn. The girl lashes out with her sword, aiming for his face. Zane dodges with a quick backflip, grabbing a wooden chair from under him midair. He lands on his feet and uses the chair to block her strikes. Each swing of her sword cuts through the chair like paper, whittling it down until Zane is left holding only two of the legs.

She launches a powerful overhead slash. Zane crosses the two chair legs over his head and activates his talent. The hardening glaze races from his hands to the edge of the legs he holds, meeting in the middle *just* as the sword makes impact. The unexpected deflection catches her off balance, and before she can recover, Zane drives a kick into her stomach, sending her stumbling back.

Seizing the opening, he follows up with a roundhouse kick to her jaw, the impact echoing through the room.

Meanwhile, Leia makes her way to the guard who tenses up and pulls away from her.

"It's okay," she says softly. "What's your name?"

"M-M-Mark," he stammers, his whole body trembling.

"Hey, Mark. I'm Leia," she says, her voice soothing and calm. "I'd like to help you, if that's okay."

He stares at her distrustfully, his gaze darting around the room. "What's happening? I would think this was a dream, but it hurts too much."

"Mark," I interject gently, "did you go through LIST to get rid of your LETs?"

"Yes?" he replies, uncertainty still written across his face.

"And did your LETs give you the ability to send your arms or legs through space?"

"H-how did you know that? I haven't used that ability in 11 years. Only my parents ever saw it!"

"Mark..." I begin carefully. "Zoe Withers has been using the ALPHA to rewrite people's Laosi frequencies."

"O-of course she has," he says, confusion still growing in his heart. "Everyone knows that."

"Right... but what they didn't know is that she's learned to rewrite those frequencies in a way that gives her access to all of your Laosi—your thoughts, your feelings, even your desires. She can control you, Mark. That's how you got here," I explain.

"What? No, that's—" he starts, his voice shaking.

"I can't imagine how much this is for you to take in or how hard it must be to trust us. But you've lost your arm without knowing how, and the strangers in front of you are telling you things only your family would know," I say gently.

Mark's breathing grows more ragged as I continue. "I think losing your arm overloaded your nervous system somehow and allowed you to wake up, but I'm not sure. You've got more questions than I have answers, but my friends and I will help you make sense of this once it's safe. For now, let Leia heal you, and then get as far away from here as possible."

"Okay," he says shakily. "If you can heal me, please do it."

"I want this to end," Leia says softly. "I want all this pain to end."

She places her hand just above his elbow and closes her eyes. A brilliant, pure white light radiates from her touch, filling the entire room. Even Zane and the sword girl stop fighting, shielding their eyes against the blinding glow.

When our vision returns, Mark stretches out his restored arm, bending his fingers, rotating his wrist, and flexing his elbow. Tears stream down his face as he tightly hugs Leia.

"Thank you so much! I thought it was gone forever, and I didn't even know how I lost it! Thank you!"

"Okay, okay," I say, stepping forward. "Take it easy. Let's get some daylight between the two of you."

Leia giggles as the hug ends. "Jealous?" she teases.

"You know I am," I reply with a smirk.

"Thank you again, Ms. Leia, and...?"

"Aiden. And don't mention it. You were a victim in all of this," I assure him. "Now get out of here. If you want help making sense of this, we'll find you."

"I'd like that very much," Mark says, then takes off running.

We all watch after him, but then Zane swings his hardened chair leg at the girl's head and knocks her out.

Leia and I look at him with questions in our eyes.

"What?" he asks. "Just because *he* was free from Zoe doesn't mean everyone is."

"Oh, I assure you," Zoe's smug voice chimes in, "he is the only exception. This was a cute trial run, by the way. That was the first time I'd ever used any of their powers before. Why don't we play double-or-nothing with someone we're both more familiar with?"

I turn as a shadowy figure enters my dad's office through the hole I made when I blasted Aaron through the wall. My legs lose all their strength, and I drop to my knees as I recognize the person Zoe is making us fight next.

"Mom!?"

CHAPTER 25 – CAPTIVE

"This is your mom? Zoe has control of your mom?! That's foul, bro! Make sure you tell her I'm sorry when she wakes up! Hope Leia can heal her," Zane says, charging toward my mom without hesitation.

This isn't real... This can't be real.

I glance around my dad's office—or what's left of it. It all feels like a nightmare I can't wake up from. As Zane rushes toward Mom, I feel trapped, like my soul is locked behind the glass windows of my eyes. I watch, but my body won't move.

Zane lunges at my mom with a powerful punch, but she dodges to the left, catching him in the midsection with her right knee. While he's still bent over, she lands a lightning-fast left cross on his cheek, sending him to down to one knee.

Before Zane can recover, my mom kicks him across the office. He flips backward midair, landing on his feet right where he started with nothing gained for his effort—except, maybe, a bruised rib or two.

A little dazed but recovering, he looks down at me and asks, "What's her LET?"

"I-I-I'm not sure... I didn't even know she had any until two weeks ago!" I stammer.

Mom charges at Zane, launching a tornado kick aimed at his face. He barely manages to block it with his forearms, but the force of her leg sends him crashing back into the wall.

Still spinning from the momentum of her kick, she grabs one of the hardened chair legs Zane dropped earlier and hurls it—straight at Leia.

The fear Leia feels in that moment is so overwhelming that I can almost hear it, almost *see* it. Her terror floods my senses, making time seem to slow as I watch the jagged edge of the unbreakable cylinder soar toward her.

Leia... Please, please, please be okay.

My eyes track the object's deadly path, bracing for the worst.

Chink.

The sound of the leg bouncing harmlessly off the force field around Leia barely registers at first. But the echo of her muffled sobs grounds me in the fact that she survived the attack. And as the atmosphere of her fear finally starts to lift, I recognize the pale green bubble around her. But at the same time, I don't recognize it.

It's translucent from the inside, but more opaque from the outside... Wha—how am I outside it?! Did I just trans—

"Ugh!!" I yell as a sharp pain in my side interrupts my thought. My body is propelled sideways, airborne, parallel to the ground. Mom rushes toward me while I'm still midair, grabs my shirt, spins around, and hoists me over her head before slamming me down on my back.

"Kkhaargh!" I gasp as the wind is knocked out of me.

I roll onto my side, trying to figure out if the noise I'm hearing is ringing in my ears or the siren of approaching CLUE carriers. But before I can process anything, my mom kicks me in the stomach. Once. Then again. Then a third time.

"This feels familiar... but different, huh, Aiden? It's different when I actually fight back, isn't it?" Zoe taunts, her voice dripping with malice as it spills out of my mother's mouth.

The image of Elon flashes through my mind—him lying in the street as I kicked him mercilessly. The rage I felt then rises again now.

Mom swings her leg back and drives it forward for another kick, but this time, her foot meets a force blast from my palm. The momentum sends her leg flying backward, throwing her off-balance and onto one knee.

Seizing the moment, I curl my knees to my chest and kick her shoulder, pushing myself away to create some space.

She rolls over, and we both scramble to our feet.

Surprisingly, I'm the first to stand. With my fists surrounded by an aura of Laosi, I analyze her movements, looking for the point I could hit to do the most damage. But when I meet her gaze, I freeze.

All I can see is the face of the woman who never stops messaging and calling me, no matter how often I let myself get too busy for her. I see the ears of the woman who listened patiently as I vented about every difficulty in my relationship with Leia. I see the nose of the mom who doesn't even like the texture of targon steak but perfected the recipe just for me.

I look into her eyes—those same eyes I've always known. The nearly emotionless ones that stared back at me every time I scraped my knee, got picked on at school, or faced my dad's punishments. The same eyes I looked into when my eyes were full of tears—just as they are now—and I needed someone to nurture me but only got shallow optimism and instruction to keep moving forward because, "ya know, it's okay."

Mom... you were Heart-Disintegrated. You trusted Dad, and he led you to give your heart to Zoe. You couldn't connect with me emotionally when I needed you most, and I blamed you for how bad I am at dealing with my feelings now. I became apathetic toward you because I thought you were apathetic toward me. I always wondered why I couldn't feel much emotion from you—but it was Zoe. Zoe ruined my life. It's not your fault, Mom. I forgive you.

"Mom, I lo—" is all I can get out before her fist speeds into my throat.

I clutch at my neck, staggering backward, gasping, trying and failing to pry my windpipe back open. She grabs the other hardened chair leg and advances toward me.

"Aiden!" Leia shrieks.

Just as my mom prepares to attack, Zane crashes into her with a shoulder charge, knocking her off balance. He focuses his follow-up attacks on her legs, trying to bring her down.

"She ain't your mom no more, bro!" Zane yells as he dodges her counterattacks. "Not until we take out Zoe! Leia can heal her, but we gotta fight right now!"

Mom's legs move with precision, always one step ahead of Zane, effortlessly evading his takedown attempts. Both of them realize at the same moment that the advantage Zane's surprise attack gave him is gone.

She pivots sharply, sending her elbow crashing into his jaw. Zane stumbles, struggling to shake off the dizziness. Before he can refocus, the most heart-stopping sound I've ever heard fills the room, silencing everything.

Zane looks down at the hardened chair leg my mom just plunged into his chest. The sickening sound of the weapon piercing and breaking through his ribcage makes my blood run cold.

He staggers backward and collapses to the floor, his eyes locking on mine, filled with desperation and pain. His breaths come in shallow, hoarse gasps.

"Zane!" Leia screams, running instinctively toward him.

Mom moves faster than I can follow, intercepting Leia with a vicious left punch to her temple that knocks Leia down. Before her body hits the floor, Mom's foot drives into her, launching her eight or nine feet backward.

"No..." The word barely escapes my throat, weak and broken.

"This is why we can't work together," Zoe taunts through my mom's voice. "You had the opportunity to end this fight, but you didn't take it. Your purpose was to stop me, but unlike me, you don't have the drive to do whatever it takes."

I did this. This is all my fault. All this destruction, all this pain, because I thought I was so special. 'I can save the world,' I thought. But because of me, Zane is...

"And because you hesitated, you lost," Zoe continues, her tone brimming with smug passion. "So let's end this. CLU Enforcers are probably already in the building. The mission of

ARL will continue. I will *not* be stopped. I *will* complete my mission!"

Zane's chest stops heaving. He lies still—eerily, completely still.

He's... gone? He died protecting me... And we still failed. He died... for nothing!

"NOOOOOOO!!" I cry out as I collapse under the weight of my grief. Tears flood my eyes until all I see—all I feel—is darkness.

The sadness consumes me, and I lose control. My Laosi creates a gravity well so strong that the floor beneath Zane and my mom collapses. They fall into the evacuated office on the 44th floor.

No... this isn't my fault. This is all Zoe! She did this! And it will only get worse if I don't stop her!

In less than a second, my sorrow turns into a resolute rage. Any desire in my will to hold back has been burned away by the wrath in my heart, which now consumes every thought, feeling, and desire in my soul.

Only one thought remains.

Kill her.

My mind drifts to the time Tirrell first explained the Six Tenets of Tessa to me. I remember the way he laughed at my cluelessness at "Hold your enemies blameless."

"What if I don't have any enemies? I do a pretty good job getting along with everybody," I'd protested.

"Maybe," he said. "But let me ask you something. What gets you out of bed in the morning?"

"These bills I have to pay," I replied cynically.

"Survival is a strong motivator!" he laughed. "Staying alive is important. But what do you *live* for?"

I had no answer.

He continued, "When you find something you value and that you're passionate about—a cause that's bigger than yourself, something worth actually living for—you'll find someone who's just as passionate about doing the opposite.

"When that happens—when someone tries to tear down what you've built or attack what you find worth protecting—and that could be anything, bro. Philosophical or physical. People can attack with neglect just as much as they can attack with aggression. Either way, when that happens, the way of the Broken is to hold that person blameless. Their life is no less valuable, and they're no less worthy of dignity just because they disagree."

But when I think about what Zoe has done, I disagree.

What kind of person controls the mind of their most loyal supporter's wife, and sends her to kill his son's friend and beat up his ex-fiancée? What kind of human would do that?

No... she's not human.

She's a monster.

And I'm going to kill her.

Atheria is too good for her.

I start walking toward the wall separating my dad's office from Zoe's. The black and red Laosi swirling around my hands crawl up my arms, reaching my shoulders.

My whole life, I've fought to keep the full extent of what I'm capable of locked away. I played by the rules. Tried to be the Aiden everyone else wanted. I fit into their molds, did what made them happy, and followed the rules of what's "right."

But I don't care anymore. This time, I'm doing what I want.

Leia's voice flickers in my head: "I mean, killing? Is that what we signed up for?"

My resolve falters at the sound of her words, and I stop midstep. I glance at her as she struggles to stand now that the gravity has returned to normal. There's sadness in her eyes, but for the first time since I met her, I can't feel what she's feeling. There's too much hatred in my own heart to be able to perceive what's in hers.

Then, behind me, I hear the sound of feet landing on the floor.

The sense of a foreign grief slices through my anger, sharp and distinct, like a shooting star streaking across the night sky. It's a mix of sorrow, remorse, and... and warmth. It cuts through everything, forcing me to turn around and discover that Mom has jumped back up through the hole in the floor.

"Aiden?" she says.

My heart breaks all over again by my understanding of why I've never felt this grief before: the ALPHA never allowed it.

Who knows how much love and affection my mom may have wanted to express to me over my lifetime that she was never free to release? Who knows how much true joy and emotional intimacy she hasn't been able to experience with my dad, my brother and sister, her friends, or any other important people in her life? How much more passion could she have lived with, rather than just surviving?

But just that quickly, I feel her heart close off again. Her eyes go cold, and her expressionless face poorly masks the animosity in the heart of the one controlling her. As her body language shifts to a runner's stance, I say just loud enough for Leia to hear, "As soon as she's clear, go see if you can help Zane."

Leia hesitates but answers, "I'll do my best. But what about you? Can you fight her?"

"I know what I have to do."

The flatness of my voice makes Leia shudder, so I nod at her, hoping it's enough to assure her that everything will be okay.

Mom takes off, and so does Leia. I brace myself, but her fist still lands squarely on my cheek. She spins around with her other fist swinging, and I barely duck in time.

I see an opening and go for an open palm strike to her midsection, but she swats my arm aside, leaving my guard wide open. Her left cross follows, hard and fast, slamming my head into the wall behind me. I bounce off the wall right into her waiting right fist. Predicting the follow-up from her left, I duck, letting her fist smash into the wall. Using the moment, I push her back with everything I have.

"Mom, I need to tell you something."

She charges again, relentless. But I've seen Zoe's fighting style enough to analyze it.

She's a brawler—heavy on offense, always trying to overwhelm her opponent and dictate the pace of the fight. If she can't overpower you, she becomes reactionary, going for whatever opening presents itself. It makes her moves more predictable. My mom's LET gives her insane strength and speed, but if I can think a step ahead of her, I might survive long enough.

I'm pinned against the wall, and she'll want to keep me here. That means she's likely to focus on punches, channeling the strength of her legs into her upper body. If I can keep her moving and force her to stay light on her feet, it might slow her down.

I fake a move to the right, leaning just enough to bait her. She bites on it, throwing a heavy left jab. I pull my head back just in time for her fist to slam into the wall again. I immediately kick at her left leg. She moves it out of the way, but the dodge leaves her off balance. Before she can recover, I shove her back as hard as I can, creating enough space to get off the wall.

I had hoped for a force blast to add some power to the shove, but nothing came. I can't muster any anger toward her —not now, not with everything I've realized. I don't feel anger, sadness, shame, or fear—none of the things that would be useful in a fight.

All I feel is *love*.

"Mom," I say, stepping back as she charges again, "I'm grateful for every ounce of effort you put into being the best mom you could be."

She throws a punch too fast to dodge or block, so I angle my head, reducing the direct impact. The moment her fist connects, I grab her arm and pull her down with me to the floor.

I hit the carpet on my back as she lands face-first. Wrapping my legs around the arm, I'm still holding, I roll us over into a belly-down armbar.

As she struggles to push herself up with her free arm, I hold on tight and say, "You've been hard on yourself, but no one's perfect. Zoe and Dad's work made it impossible to be the mom you wanted to be, but you never stopped trying."

With one powerful roll, she shifts to her side, lifting me over her body and slamming me onto my back. The impact forces me to release her arm. She doesn't waste a second to jump on top of me, pinning me to the floor.

I didn't account for this!

Mom rains down punch after punch on me—some I dodge, most I don't.

I'm not gonna win this fight... But I don't have to. I just have to tell her.

"But regardless of the mis—hunh!—the mistakes and the successes... Mom, I—mmph! Argh!"

Too many punches. I can't dodge anymore.

"Shut up, Aiden! Don't you see it's futile?" she snaps. She rises to her feet, standing over me. She grabs my shirt with one hand, dragging my limp body toward the open window Zane and I broke earlier.

The closer we get, the louder the sound of the wind, the city, and the sirens below.

"Mom," I rasp, forcing the words past the tightness in my throat. "I haven't said this nearly enough to you... More than what you did or didn't do for me..."

Tears fill my eyes as she leans back, preparing to throw me out from 45 stories up. With everything I have left, I shout, "Mom, I just care about *you*! I love you, Mom!"

She freezes.

Her grip on my shirt loosens, and she looks down at me. For the first time in my life, I see a tear slide down my mom's cheek. She releases my shirt, and I prop myself up on my hands.

Then she drops to her knees and throws her arms around my neck, sobbing uncontrollably.

"Aiden, I'm so sorry! I'm so, so sorry, son! I couldn't stop it! I was trying, but I couldn't! I fought her, but she was winning, and you were losing. I never wanted to hurt you, Aiden! I love you, too!"

"I know, Mom," I whisper. "I know. That's why we came. To stop her."

Everything on my body hurts, but I try to reposition to get a bit more comfortable. I hold my mom close and say, "We can talk later, but we have to finish this now. Will... will you help me?"

She cries a bit more. The love that she feels for me, the regret, the fear and the fury—the ALPHA's hold over my mom is *completely* broken.

I didn't know my mom even could feel all these things. I've never felt these frequencies of passion before.

She reigns those feelings in, channeling them into two words: "Of course."

She helps me to my feet as my legs stabilize under me.

"Here, let me—" she says, reaching for a piece of her shirt to wipe the blood trickling toward my eye.

"I got it, Mom," I reply, pretending to be annoyed as I chuckle softly. Deep down, I'm glad for the moment of her care.

Together, we walk to the wall separating us from Zoe's office. Before I focus on the task ahead, I call down into the hole in the floor.

"Leia? How is he?"

Her voice comes back, thick with sadness. "I'm sorry, Aiden. I really, really tried! I... He was already gone before I got down here to him. I'm so sorry!"

I sigh, the weight in my chest heavier than ever. "I understand. Stay there. This will be over soon."

Placing my hands on the wall, I let the energy flow. A second later, Mom and I step over the rubble into Zoe's office.

The room tastefully blends sleek technology and luxury, like a fortress disguised as a penthouse. In the far corner, Zoe sits at a desk almost completely surrounded by hologram screens and computer equipment.

Between her and us lies the living space of a high-end apartment suite, furnished with abstract art, earth-tone furniture trimmed in gold, and the largest hologram screen I've ever seen.

Beneath the glass floor of the living room, a massive aquarium nurtures vibrant marine life—glowfish and other exotic creatures swimming in the tranquil waters. The aquarium flows into a fountain that separates the living area from Zoe's workspace. Playing in the ripples caused by the fountain's gentle flow are twenty or so sirensongs.

I've only ever read about these white-and-silver fish, each about four inches long. Seeing them with my own eyes, I realize the reports don't do them justice. As they leap from the fountain, the water trickling off their scales creates beautiful music, and their coordinated harmonies ripple through the room.

If I were here for pleasure instead of business, I'd probably stand here for half an hour, trying to understand the patterns in their synchronized performance. But I'm not here for pleasure.

A wave of gratitude rises within me—gratitude for the chance to disrupt Zoe's oasis, the place from which she has wreaked havoc in people's lives.

Just because I can, and because I know Zoe can't stop me, I shoot a force blast at the massive hologram screen in her living room. It explodes into countless pieces that rain down onto the floor.

"You know you're going to pay for that, don't you?" Zoe asks with disappointment in her voice.

"I don't think so," I reply, scoffing as Mom and I stride toward her desk. "It's too late for threats, Zoe. It's just you and us now. You already told me your power isn't anything destructive."

"No, I mean, you're *literally* going to pay for it," Zoe replies, her irritation breaking through. "You're going to jail. They'll seize your assets to cover the damages you've caused, and you'll spend the rest of your life in Atheria under Laosi inhibitors."

"You can drop the confident victor act," I retort. "Your plan to take over the world—or whatever you've been doing—has failed. It's over. You lost!"

"Is that so?" she replies, defiance gleaming in her eyes. "And how exactly do you think this ends? Are you going to kill me? Of course not. You don't have it in you. And other than my life itself, there's nothing here you've destroyed that can't be rebuilt. Once you and all your Broken friends are behind bars, my plan will be, at most, slightly delayed."

I feel my Laosi rising. But before I can respond, Zoe spins one of her monitors toward me and says, "Oh, look! The cavalry has arrived."

On the screen, I see a team of six or seven CLUE officers in combat gear moving down the hallway on the 45th floor. They walk past the hole I blasted Aaron through earlier.

"This has been amusing," Zoe says with a smirk, "but it's over, Aiden."

My mom and I exchange a glance, unsure of what to do, as loud knocking on the door thunders through the room.

"Commission on Laosi Use Enforcers!" an officer shouts from the other side of the door. "We're coming in!"

CHAPTER 26 – RELEASE

"All of your hard work, only to come up empty-handed. It's regrettable what happened to your friend, by the way, but I told you not to stand in my way," Zoe says, her tone nonchalant.

You... You caused ALL OF THIS! You took advantage of my father's genius and used his work to experiment on my mother. You're the reason my powers were out of control, why I had to settle all of my life. My shame, my insecurity, my wasted potential. It's all YOUR fault! YOU did this to me! And then you sent my own mother to kill me?

My hands and forearms glow with red, purple, and dark grey Laosi.

"Aiden, don't," Mom cautions. "Please. You know what they'll do to you if you do this. If you take that step, you won't be able to turn back!"

"But, Mom," I say, my voice cracking with hot tears streaming down my face. "Because of her... there's nothing for me to go back to."

The energy around my arms swirls with greater ferocity.

Wait for the light!

That sounded like my voice... but I didn't think it.

Nevertheless, the thought silences my mind and resets my Laosi. I stop dead in my tracks. The energy flowing around my arms disappears instantly, snuffed out like a candle on a birthday cake.

Before I can make sense of what just happened, the door flies open, and CLUE officers flood into the room. They move quickly, setting up a formation with energy shields in front of them. After a brief standoff, the squad leader steps forward, making his way toward us.

Zoe's smug grin widens, and my blood starts to boil again. I take a deep breath, steadying myself as the squad leader calls out, "Aiden Lore?"

He raises his hands, palms open, and says, "Ma'am, please stay right there," directing the command toward Leia, who had entered Zoe's office through the hole I blew in the wall.

As the officer approaches, I catch my reflection in the glass visor of his black helmet. My mind's eye envisions the face reflected back at me in a prison jumpsuit, on the cover of the news report, in my coffin, and on my obituary. A shiver races down my spine at the thought of what my future might look like after today.

The officer removes his helmet, revealing a calm, gentle expression. He deactivates the energy shield and lodges its handle back into the holster on his belt. Extending a hand toward me, he says, "Every time my men and I come to work, put this gear on, and respond to a call, we know we might be putting our lives on the line. But what you just did today might be the bravest thing I've seen in my life."

I blink at him, startled and confused. I glance at Mom, hoping for clarity, but she shrugs, just as clueless as I am.

Turning back to the officer, I absentmindedly take his hand and shake it.

"Ma'am," he says, nodding respectfully to my mom before walking past us toward Zoe's desk.

With a more forceful tone, he says, "Zoe Withers, you are under arrest for unlawful use of Laosi of the highest order, the murder of Zane Arroyo of the highest order, murder with the aid of an LET, and conspiracy to commit treason against Tryon United."

My jaw drops as I glance at Mom.

The officer reaches for another compartment on his belt and says, "I am going to attach a Laosi inhibitor bracelet to your arm, or you may choose to do so yourself. Be advised—

failure to comply with this directive will be deemed resisting arrest, and we will use all necessary force, including lethal force, to restrain you."

Zoe glares at him with eyes that could kill. For all her bravado, though, I sense fear in her heart for the first time.

"Give me that," she demands, her tone sharp. "I'll play along for now, but these charges won't stick."

"Oh yeah?" the officer replies. He taps and swipes the touchscreen embedded in the forearm of his uniform, pulling up a holographic image of Zoe. He taps again, and a video starts playing.

Zoe's voice echoes: "Impossible! The ALPHA's control has never been broken before!"

The officer looks at her, waiting for a reaction. She gives none, her jaw tight.

He swipes again, fast-forwarding to another clip.

"Oh, I assure you, he is the only exception," Zoe's voice continues. "This was a cute trial run, by the way. That was the first time I'd ever used any of their powers before. Why don't we play double-or-nothing with someone we're both more familiar with?"

Zoe's composure cracks. "How did you—?!"

"The bracelet!" the officer interrupts, his tone firm.

Zoe sighs, exasperated, before giving in. "Fine."

She grabs the black bracelet, snapping it onto her left wrist. Green lights blink on, one by one, and then turn blue. Her defiance visibly drains away. She just sits still with a blank stare at the officer, completely subdued.

"All clear!" the officer yells to his squad.

The other officers deactivate their shields, their formation relaxing.

"You guys can come in!" one of them calls out into the hallway.

Tirrell, Auriel, Nadia, Arvind, and Elrond burst into the room.

"We did it, man!" Tirrell shouts, pulling me into a

celebratory hug as the others gather around, their voices full of congratulations and relief.

"Let's go, Ms. Withers," the officer says, motioning to Zoe.

She rises silently, walking over to him.

"Take her away," he calls to his team. Zoe walks over to the officers just inside the door. The squad leader stays behind with us.

"Oh, hi, Mrs. Aiden's mom," Elrond says suddenly.

Mom blinks at him, clearly caught off guard. "I'm sorry... Have we met? Probably not if you're calling me Mrs. Aiden's mom."

She turns to me, her expression a mix of confusion and curiosity. "What's going on, son? Who are all these people?"

"Oh... Sorry. Mom, these are my friends... uh... from... the Broken."

"The Broken?" she repeats, her tone cautious. "Oh... um, hi. I'm Jackie."

She extends her hand to El, who shakes it politely.

"I didn't know my son was a member of the Broken," Mom adds, looking between me and the group. "But I suppose there's a lot that's been happening I haven't been aware of."

"Mom," I say, "I promise we're going to have a long conversation, and I'll explain everything. But honestly... I don't really know what's going on myself."

"Aiden, I'm Sergeant Melbourne," the officer says. "My team and I responded to the alarm that went off when your friends got caught on camera in the stairwell. When we got here, we decided to split up to cover all areas affected by the intrusion. We sent a team down to the basement for live footage to figure out what we were up against."

He folds his arms and continues, "I was on my way up to protect Ms. Withers when Officer McClaren told me he found the security team restrained but unharmed—and that he had something I needed to see. Aiden, we heard and saw everything during your encounter with Ms. Withers. I'm not saying everything you did was by the books—or even legal—but in my estimation, all of Tryon owes you and your friends a debt of gratitude for what you accomplished today."

Then he adds, "But she was right about one thing."

"What's that?" I ask cautiously.

"You *are* going to have to pay for that screen you broke," Melbourne replies, his tone firm but amused. "When the investigation gets underway, I might be able to make a case to indemnify you for the windows you flew in and out of—that seemed necessary to stop the conspiracy. But the screen? That was just malicious. ARL will bill you for that."

I blink, caught between disbelief and an urge to laugh.

"But," Melbourne continues, his tone turning thoughtful, "that's assuming there even is an ARL after all this. My colleagues at the office are going to have a field day combing through every bit of ARL's data. We need to track this conspiracy down to the nth degree—no stone unturned. Who knows what Ms. Withers could've done with all the unchecked power she was amassing?"

He shakes his head slightly and looks back at me. "Again, Aiden, you have my thanks."

This is my moment. I... I did something that matters! I made my life count for something! I have to say something heroic and humble.

"Yeah, um... ya know, I was just... It was showtime, I guess..."

Why is that the best I could come up with?

"Hey, speaking of," Tirrell says, looking around. "Where's Zane?"

That's why... Because that's what Zane would have said. If he could speak for himself.

My head drops, and Leia's does too. My mom wraps her arms tightly around herself, holding herself up against the weight of the guilt she feels.

I reach over and pull her into a hug. She clings to me, burying her face into my shoulder.

"It wasn't your fault," I whisper in her ear. Leia places a comforting hand on Mom's back.

"Guys?" El asks.

"No..." Nadia murmurs softly.

Leia glances back through the hole in the wall into my dad's office. "Guys, I'm so sorry... I..."

Tirrell bolts into the office and the rest of us follow. Grief, confusion and fear fill the air.

We find Tirrell standing at the edge of the hole in the floor, staring down. He doesn't say a word, but the tear tracing its way down his cheek speaks volumes.

The rest of the team groans or cries out in their own ways, their sadness pouring out without restraint. But I can't look away from Tirrell's tear.

He notices me staring. He opens his mouth to speak, but no words come out—just the quiet struggle to push through the lump in his throat. His tears fall freely now.

He clears his throat, trying again.

"Zane was the heart and soul of the Broken for me," he begins, his voice cracking with emotion. "His energy, his... enthusiasm, it... ya know, it was Zane that really made me believe in the Broken."

I tilt my head toward him, silently urging him to say more.

"Yeah, he, uh..." Tirrell starts, his voice heavy. "Well, I mean, I grew up in the Broken, right? It was all I ever knew. I did and believed what I was told to do and believe, but... it wasn't *mine*, if that makes any sense. Not until I met Zane."

"Yeah?" I ask gently. "What made the difference?"

"It was seeing the change in him. When he came to us, he was hotheaded, angry, and stubborn as all get out. And I know some of y'all are thinking, 'That doesn't sound like much of a change.'" A small chuckle escapes him. "Trust me—he was on another level back then. But I watched him, day after day, week after week, month after month, struggling to apply the Six in his life."

Tirrell's voice steadies as he continues. "At first, we would call him out on something, and he'd defend himself —argue like crazy or just walk out. Then, little by little, he started owning up to his mistakes when we challenged him. Eventually, he'd call *himself* out, making amends before anyone else could say a word. He literally changed. The man we call Zane today is *not* the young guy I met a few years ago."

Tirrell glances at all of us. "That's when I knew Tessa and the Broken were a force for good. I'm sure Tessa's proud of him... giving his life for the cause."

"Makes you wonder, though," Arvind says thoughtfully, "if Tessa knew this would happen."

"How could she?" Leia asks. "It's not like she can see the future... right?"

"Well," I say, "*she* can't actually see it. But there's a girl in the group who dreams about it sometimes."

Elrond chimes in. "I'm just wondering about what happened. I mean, how did he...?"

I sigh. "Guys, you deserve an explana—"

"I already know how this happened," Auriel interrupts, her voice sharp. "You all thought it would be a good idea to send *me* to the ALPHA with Arvind while sending a rookie to the biggest fight we've ever faced. No offense, Leia, but how many fights have you ever been in?"

Leia hesitates, caught off guard. "What? Oh, um... well, none, really. Not since tertiary..."

Auriel's frustration bubbles over. "Exactly my point. I *told* you all that I should've gone with Aiden and Zane, didn't I?"

"Yeah, but we—" Elrond starts to reply but stops abruptly. I catch the subtle signal Tirrell gives him to let Auriel keep going.

Everybody's going to grieve their own way. Tirrell must know that the worst thing we can do is interrupt that process. Clearly, Auriel's in the anger stage. What about me? Probably denial... and Tirrell? He looks almost like he's smiling. Definitely denial. And Mom...?

Auriel's voice rises as she says, "So I'm not wondering *how* it happened. What I don't understand is *why*. Why didn't anyone listen to me? I knew it was a bad plan, but I was taught to respect leadership, so I just went along with it. But I told you all—it didn't make sense!"

Her final exclamation is punctuated by an explosion of energy as a tornado erupts around her, spinning so fast it feels like the entire office—maybe the whole building—is shaking.

The roar of wind is deafening, mingling with what sounds like an electrical storm raging overhead. I stagger and look around for something to hold onto in case I lose my footing. Looking behind me, through the swirling chaos, I see shards of glass flowing upward and chunks of wall rearranging themselves, returning to their original positions.

A loud rumble draws my attention forward. A thick, black aura forms, streams of transparent energy swirling around it violently, dispersing it bit by bit. As the storm settles, the aura disintegrates completely, and we see what lies beneath.

The floor is whole again. And lying on it is Zane, clutching at the instrument still lodged in his chest cavity.

"Leia!" I scream, the force of my voice ripping through the stunned silence.

Leia scrambles to Zane, dropping to her hands and knees. She places her hands on his stomach and closes her eyes. The rest of us hold our breath, watching intently as Leia's LET activates. White light grows from her hands, radiating outward until it's so intense that shielding our eyes no longer works. One by one, we all look away to avoid being blinded.

But when I hear the thud as that chair leg hits the floor, I look back and see Zane sitting up, trying to regulate his breathing. He glances around, his eyes landing on my mom. In an instant, he's on his feet, assuming a ready stance.

"Whoa, whoa! Zane, chill, bro!" I say quickly, holding up my hands in a calming gesture. "We're good, man! We got her.

We beat Zoe!"

He looks at me, then at Mom, then at everyone else. "What happened?" he asks, his voice shaky.

"A *lot*, bro!" I say with a heavy sigh. "But Auriel and Leia just saved your life, man!"

"Th... thank you," he says, the words coming out slowly, like he's still processing everything. He hesitates, then asks, "Yo... was I, like... dead?"

"Actually..." I say with a small smile, "You were."

"Really? For how long?!" he asks, his eyes wide.

"About 15 minutes? Maybe more? It's hard to say—there were a lot of moving pieces," I explain.

"Zane," Mom says, stepping forward cautiously. "I want you to know I am so sorry. I only barely remember doing it. I don't remember much of anything except standing here, looking at Aiden. I've never seen him so grieved, so angry, so... distraught."

Her voice wavers as she continues. "I turned around and saw you down there, and there was blood on my hands... and without understanding how or when or why, I *knew* I had done it. It was like waking up from a dream and then going right back to sleep. I just... I want you to know how sorry I am."

"It's all good, Mrs. Lore," Zane replies, his tone surprisingly light. "It's nice to actually meet you. And, honestly? I wouldn't mind sparring with you in the future. I was all cocky until you started kicking my butt!"

"Oh, I could never..." Mom says, flustered.

"Zane," Auriel says weakly from her spot on the floor, "you're back... I'm so glad..." She collapses onto her side before she can say anything else.

"Auriel!" a few of us yell in unison.

Arvind reaches her first, kneeling down to check her pulse. We all wait, holding our breath, until he smiles and says, "I think she's fine. Poor girl probably just overexerted herself."

Astonished, Tirrell shakes his head. "I've never seen her do anything like that before. She compressed 15 minutes of time into a 20-second bubble! But more than that—she reached into death and pulled Zane back out! She's gonna need more than just rest to recover."

"Should we take her to a hospital?" I ask, glancing between her and Tirrell.

"Unfortunately, Aiden," Officer Melbourne interjects, "you all aren't going to be able to take her anywhere."

A panicked hush falls over the room.

Melbourne raises a hand, his tone reassuring. "I gotta bring you all in for questioning. But I wouldn't worry too much if I were any of you. You did what needed to be done. This isn't about incriminating you—it's about starting the investigation into what Ms. Withers and ARL have been up to."

He nods toward the hallway, where Zoe is being escorted away by his men. "I'll personally vouch for each of you as a character reference."

"So, what's gonna happen to Auriel? She's got a kid to look after," Elrond pleads with the officer.

"We've already called in med support. They should be here any second."

"I think we should probably get her looked at, too, right?" Zane asks, pointing to the girl he knocked out earlier.

"And him," Leia adds, motioning toward the holes in the walls where Aaron lies crumpled.

"Absolutely. You guys made a bit of a mess, " Melbourne says with a chuckle. "We'll make sure everyone here gets patched up."

"Then... it's over," I say, hardly believing my own words. "I mean, the Collective, the attacks on TU, Zoe's mind control over who knows how many people. We... we did it. And we're not going to jail for it!" I add, drawing some snickers from my battered but triumphant teammates.

"Just about," Melbourne says, nodding. "Let's get you all down to the office to take your statements. With any luck, we'll have you home by nightfall."

"Party at HQ?!" Zane blurts out, grinning wide.

"I'm down!" Tirrell says, immediately catching the mood.

"Me, too!" Arvind chimes in.

"That way, we can talk about who did what," Zane teases. "Tirrell, I *have* to know what you were thinking when these guys showed up!"

"Maaaaan, I was sweating bullets!" Tirrell laughs.

"We can thank Elrond for that!" Arvind jokes, slapping El on the back.

"So, who else is coming to the party?" Zane asks, clearly energized despite everything.

"Count me out on this one," Nadia says. "I'm gonna check on Brice and then stay with Auriel at the hospital."

"Same here," El says. "But y'all enjoy yourselves."

As we walk out of my dad's office toward the elevator, I take in the pride, accomplishment, and camaraderie radiating from my people. It's infectious, and I feel it, too... mostly. But there's still this nagging uncertainty gnawing at the edge of my mind.

As the others leave and a couple of officers come in to prep Auriel for transport, I hang back with Officer Melbourne.

"Are you sure there won't be any charges pressed against us?" I ask, keeping my voice low so the others won't overhear. "Just so you know, my friends and I... we're the ones who fought Zoe's dragon at the Felicity station."

Melbourne raises an eyebrow but doesn't seem surprised. "Not if I have anything to say about it. Some people might not love that you took matters into your own hands, but with everything we now know, it looks to me like you all were just defending yourselves. Besides, you've got more allies in uniform than you realize. Officer Daniel Emmaus, for one, wanted his team to take this call to make sure you were all right. But, well, it's best to keep personal feelings out of a high-stakes situation like this."

"Okay," I say, nodding slowly. "I'll take your word for it."

As we walk out together, Melbourne pauses and points

back toward Zoe's office with a sly smirk. "You really should thank your friend who pulled off that time reversal trick," he says. "I guess you won't be paying for that screen after all."

End Part 5

CHAPTER 27 – ZOE

"Can I just say I have the best big sister on the entire planet?! You didn't have to do that for me, Sissy," Nick says, grinning from ear to ear.

"Oh, but of course I did," I reply, thrilled at his excitement. "You know me, Nick. When I say I'm going to do something, I'm going to do it."

"Yeah, but, Zoe," my little brother says, "you really went all out for this one! How did you even manage to get this? And in perfect condition? That's insane! This is probably the last paper copy of *GlobalMan* Volume 1 that exists!" he shrieks, clutching the comic book to his chest.

"Let's just leave the details to your imagination," I tease. "Otherwise, you might start wanting me to use my powers for evil!"

He laughs and says, "You must be using some kind of powers. Either that, or you've been lying all this time about being a broke college student!"

"The less you know, the better. I'm trying to protect you," I counter, trying to keep a straight face but failing miserably as a smile creeps in. I hold his holographic gaze for a moment before letting my eyes wander around his room. *GlobalMan* and *GlobalWoman* posters cover nearly every inch of wall space.

"You're a rare breed," I say, my tone softening.

"Whaddya mean?" he asks.

"You're the only person I know who still reads paper comic books or has paper posters on their walls," I point out with mock accusation.

"What can I say? I just love vintage stuff," he says, practically glowing.

"Which is so weird because—remind me again, how old are you? Five?"

"I'm nine, Zoe. You know that! I was six when you moved to Sanctuary, so how could I be five now?" he shoots back, pulling off his exaggerated pout, which he perfected through years of trying to get his way with Dad.

Completely ignoring his logic, I add, "You're also the only person I know in this century who's into *GlobalMan*."

"What's not to love? A man without LETs hunting down his best friend's killer while falling in love with his childhood sweetheart, only to find out she was the one who killed him because she was under the mind control of a freedom fighter tearing down the national crime syndicate that the best friend was second-in-command of? How do they come up with this stuff?"

"Nicholas Sheridan Withers, did you just say all that in one breath?" I ask, genuinely concerned.

"Maybe," he says with a shrug. "And don't use my middle name! You know I hate the name Sheridan. It sounds like an old person's name."

"I have to use it to remind you to take the choices you make more seriously! How's your breathing now?" I ask, raising an eyebrow.

"I'm fine, I'm fine," he says, brushing the topic off quickly. "Why are you always so worried about something?"

I let out a deep breath, but I can't stop smiling at him. "I guess that's just what big sisters do."

He makes a goofy face, another one of his signature moves, and we both burst into laughter. Once we settle down, I ask, "Do you feel like you relate to GlobalMan? Is that why you like him so much?"

"Kinda… I mean, I know what it's like to be the little guy nobody really pays attention to… feeling like you can't do much but still trying to overcome the odds, I guess. But, honestly, I think he reminds me more of you than me," he says thoughtfully.

"Me? How so?"

"Well, just look at you. Whether you admit it or not, you're a country girl from somewhere nobody expects much from," he starts, and I am admittedly not flattered with his setup. "But you made it to the big city on a full scholarship! They're actually paying *you* to learn how to make stuff better in the world. You don't have any powers or anything that makes you really stand out, but you're making a difference. You're... my hero, Zoe."

"Wow..." I say. "I don't really know how to respond to that, Nick. That's... literally the nicest thing you've ever said to me. I didn't know I meant—"

"If you repeat that to anyone, I'll completely deny it," Nick says. But the sentiment he shared can't easily be suppressed. I let the moment linger until he starts blushing and scrambles to change the subject. "So, uh, who do you feel like you'd be in *GlobalMan* comics?"

"That's a good question... I think I'd relate to Globalwoman. I'd love to marry a man with ambition. I love that they're a power couple and how she supports him without losing herself. She's still a hero in her own right, too, ya know?"

"You? Getting married? Ew!" Nick says, pretending to gag.

"Did you say you were Nine? Or four?" I ask, trying not to sound too annoyed.

"How could I be four?!" he protests.

"I don't know. I heard Tryon United's getting close to perfecting their teleportation portals near the house. I thought maybe they accidentally sent you back in time."

"It seems like you went back in time. How are there *less* decorations on your dorm walls than the last time we talked?" he counters.

"It's called efficiency," I fire back at him sharply.

"That... doesn't even make sense," he says, rolling his eyes.

"Maybe not to you. But my roommate, Jackie, wasn't

a fan of all the pictures of people's internal organs. She said they made her queasy during dinner, so I took them down," I explain, dejected.

"They weren't really good decorations anyway," he says.

"Of course they were! Wall coverings that also help me study just by coming home? Now *that* was efficient."

"You're weird," he says. "I still don't know how you find all that nasty stuff interesting."

"What's interesting to me is understanding 'all that nasty stuff' well enough to help people. You've got *GlobalMan*, and I've got becoming a doctor. Everyone's got their thing, I guess."

"Your thing is gross," he says flatly.

You know I'm doing this... for you, right? Or maybe because of you?

Deciding not to weigh him down with thoughts like that, I just shoot back, "Your thing has a really terrible and uncreative name," and stick my tongue out at him.

"Oh, yeah—that's real mature, big sis," he teases.

"That's what I was going for," I reply. "Speaking of going, Little One, I need to get going. Especially if you want this other surprise, I've got planned for you."

"Another surprise?" he asks, his face lighting up.

"Yup! Should be arriving in about five hours."

"Ooooh, I can't wait! Your surprises are the best!" he says, bouncing in his chair.

"What was that?" I ask suddenly.

"What was what?" Nick asks, confused.

"Really, Nick? How did *I* hear something from your side of the Solo that *you* didn't hear?"

"I don't know. I just didn't hear anything. What did it sound like?"

"It sounded like... scraping. It was—just go ask Dad what it was. I bet he heard it."

"He's asleep," Nick says.

"Well, go stay close to him anyway... I don't want..."

"Don't want what?" Nick asks.

"Um, don't want... you to get into any trouble while he's sleeping."

Maybe it was just some kids down the street playing with some new toys. Maybe it was construction in the neighborhood. Maybe it was... It could've been anything, right? There's no point in getting worked up. If Dad slept through it, I'm sure everything's fine.

"You're 200 miles away and still worrying about me getting in trouble? Good luck marrying GlobalMan!" Nick laughs.

"Oh, be quiet," I say, rolling my eyes. "Anyway, I'll talk to you later, okay, Little One?"

"Okay, Sissy. But when?" he asks, his voice softening.

"I guess you'll just have to wait and see. My study schedule is quite demanding these days, but hopefully, by the time you finish reading all those *GlobalMan* comics I sent, I'll be free for you to tell me all about them," I say, smiling.

"I'm gonna start reading right now! Bye!"

"Wait! That's not what I—"

"Call ended. Would you like to call Nicholas back?" Zoe 2.0 asks.

"No, that little runt did that on purpose," I grumble, tossing my Solo onto the bed.

I flop onto my back and stare up at the plain gray walls of my dorm.

He's not wrong, though. Maybe when I visit, I'll take some photos to get a big hologram projector for the wall. Jackie can't complain about family... I smile softly to myself. *Family is everything.*

A rumble in my stomach reminds me I haven't eaten since breakfast.

I don't want to travel on an empty stomach. Monorail food is more expensive than my budget can handle at the moment. When I'm Dr. Withers, that won't be an issue. Dr. Withers won't even need the monorail. Maybe I'll have my own personal helijet!

I pull myself out of bed and walk out my dorm room door. I stroll to the Cube in the center of the hallway, a sleek 10-by-10-feet glass hub connecting residents to every on-campus function available to us. I press my finger to the smooth surface, holding it there until it recognizes me.

The screen lights up with a soothing royal blue glow, matched by a cheerful AI voice. "Hi, Zoe! What can I help you with?"

"Food options," I reply. As the virtual menus appear before me, I swipe until I find Gibb's Court.

Let's see... What will it be today? A spherra sandwich? No, the meat was bland and undercooked last time. Maybe a vegetarian option? Something filling but light enough to travel on.

Oh? A roasted bolena bulb plate? Seasoned with caydor root and a side of Nardin grass?

I bite my lip, debating.

It's okay to splurge this time, right? Bolena is brain food, and they say the orange glow of Nardin grass works wonders for skin clarity and elasticity. My skin has seemed a bit lifeless as of late.

I tap my selection to the pleasure of the Cube's AI. "Excellent choice! I'll have the cooks begin preparations immediately. Is there anything else I can do?"

"Yes. Please hail a carrier for me in front of Demetrious Hall and send the elevator up. That will suffice."

"Yes, ma'am! Please do enjoy your meal and your ride!"

I walk over to the elevator as it opens and two of my hallmates exit.

"Hey, Zoe!"

"Hey, ladies!"

"What ya got going on tonight?"

"I'm headed home to surprise my little brother for his birthday."

"Oh, cool! How old is he now?"

"Nine, but it's giving three," I say, eliciting a laugh from my counterparts.

"Okay, well, have fun with your family! We were just thinking about inviting you to play some glade with us tonight, but I guess you're tied up."

"That would've been great!" I say. "But I need to go home. We don't have long—" I say as I dash onto the elevator.

"I understand," one of the girls says. "Have a safe trip!"

"Thanks!"

The elevator doors close, and I turn around to look outside the glass walls of the elevator.

What a rainy day... I wonder what the weather's like in Reality.

I arrive in the lobby and walk over to the pickup section outside of Gibb's Court. The bioscanner reads me and opens the metal encasement surrounding my to-go plate. I grab the plate and walk out the front door of Demetrious Hall to the carrier waiting for me at the sidewalk. I scurry out of the rain and into the carrier, instructing it to take me to the monorail station.

As the carrier takes off, I open my plate of food and begin to consume it. I engross myself so deeply into eating that I don't realize that I've arrived at the monorail station until I find my plate empty. I hop out and run up the stairs to get to the front door.

An unusually high number of travelers stand and sit around, and the ambient noise of their conversations seems tense. I ignore all that, though, because I've got a train to catch and a little brother to surprise.

At the security station, the Solo reader says, "Zoe Withers. One ticket for Reality - Alabast District. Departure station - Gate 72. Departure time - delayed. To be determined."

Delayed?

I make the arduous walk over to Gate 72 and find a few agitated patrons sharing less-than-pleasant words with one of the administrators. Rather than add fuel to the fire, I decide to simply listen and gain what information I can about this unusual turn of events.

"I want my credits back!"

"That's not going to help me! I have a contract signing that must take place today! I don't have time for a delay!"

"Can you at least tell us what's causing the delay?"

"Ladies and gentlemen," the administrator says, addressing the crowd. "Tryon United apologizes for the inconvenience, but the monorail train departing for Alabast has been delayed indefinitely. No information has been provided to us yet as to what has caused this delay, but as soon as an update is available, we will share that information with you."

The patrons all groan collectively, but the administrator continues to speak the words he was obviously given.

"A full refund is available to you at this time, or you may choose to upgrade your seating at no additional cost on a train headed to another destination in Reality. Again, we apologize for the inconvenience and invite you to head back to the ticket kiosk at the front to make your refund or upgrade selections. Thank you!"

With that, the man quickly scurries away from the crowd and into his office. I continue to observe the reactions of other patrons to make sense of the situation.

"A free upgrade does sound nice," a man says.

"Yeah, but what's going on with the train?" his friend asks.

"Probably just routine maintenance they forgot to schedule properly, as usual," an older woman grumbles. "TU's been pulling stunts like this for decades. These bloodsuckers will do anything to cut costs once they've got your credits."

"I heard about a rail line that snapped while carrying passengers," a young man adds excitedly. "Luckily, nobody got hurt, thanks to the conductor's quick thinking. But honestly, I'd rather be stuck here than stranded in the middle of nowhere like that!"

"Yeah, but if that's the case, why not just tell us?" a frustrated traveler snaps. "All they had to do was come out and say, 'Hey, folks, damaged rail—give us a minute.' End of story!"

Their theories abound, but none satisfy. I decide to stop speculating and try to get some real answers. Taking a seat on the edge of a bench away from the crowd, I pull out my Solo.

"2.0, call Dad," I command.

"Calling Adam Withers."

"Zoe? Zoe, I'm scared!"

"Nick? Hey, where's Dad, Little One?"

"He's right here!" Nick cries. "He's lying down next to me, but... but he's not moving, Zoe! Why won't he wake up? Dad! Dad, wake up!"

No, no, no... What's going on? Okay, stay calm, Zoe. Don't overreact. You're training for this.

"Nick, is Dad breathing?" I ask, forcing my voice to stay steady.

"I don't know, I—" Nick breaks into sobs. "He's not waking up, and there are these men outside in weird yellow suits! They keep knocking on the door—"

"Hey, buddy. One thing at a time, okay? Hey, I'm here with you, okay? Let's slow down, Little One. I need you to focus on your breathing. Take a deep breath in and let it out slow, like this." I exaggerate a calming breath loud enough for him to hear. "Can you do that?"

"O... okay," he says shakily.

"Good, Nick. That's better... Yeah, take some slow deep breaths. You're doing great," I encourage, listening as he takes slower, fuller breaths. " Okay, I need you to lay your head on dad's chest on his left side and see if you can hear his heart beating. Think you can do that?"

"Mm-hmm," Nick mumbles, his voice tight with fear.

What if there's no heartbeat? He's going to lose it if there's no heartbeat!

"I hear it! I hear it beating!" he exclaims.

"Oh, thank goodness," I say, releasing the breath I'd been holding subconsciously. "Okay, and is his chest moving? Even just a little bit?"

"Yeah, it's moving," Nick confirms.

"All right. So dad's not dead, which means you're not alone. But dad must be really tired, so now we need you to help take care of him. Think of it like paying him back for all those Smackers he bought you, okay?" I smile as I hear Nick giggle softly between sniffles, and I breathe out another sigh of relief. "I'll help you, but I need you to tell me everything you see and hear. Where are you guys?"

"We're at home."

"Right, but where in the house?" I press, keeping my tone even to hold his focus.

"Oh, I came into his room because I had been reading about GlobalMan for a long time, and I think I finally heard that thing you were talking about. So, I just went to Dad because the noises kept getting louder, and I thought he would've woken up, but he didn't. And I started calling him because people were knocking on the door saying, 'Mr. Withers, please open up.' But he didn't."

"You're doing great, Nick. What can you tell me about the people outside? You said they had yellow suits?"

"Yeah, they do. They're wearing these funny-looking yellow suits that are like plastic or rubber or something. You can't see anything but their faces behind the plastic. They're—what do you call them?"

I lower my head and softly say, "Hazmat suits."

"Yeah, those! Why are they wearing those out in the street? I've only seen those in the movies," he says.

"I'm not sure... Is anyone at the door now? If so, I'd like to speak wi—"

"No, they left when they saw no one was coming to the door."

"That makes sense. Well, can you look outside and tell me what was making that loud noise?" I ask.

"Hold on, one sec!"

I hear his feet plodding on the stairs as he runs down to the first floor.

"Hey, slow down, Nick. Be careful!"

"I'm good, I'm good," he says.

Stubborn brat.

"Hold on," he says as I hear the door opening. "It looks like the hazmat people have been leaving papers on people's doors."

"Oh yeah? What does it say?"

"It says... hold on. Something about ray-dee... It has a lot of big words. I'll just send a picture of it to you. I can see what that noise was now."

"Yeah? What was it?" I ask eagerly and fearfully.

"It's like... a... fence or something. Yeah, it looks like an energy fence. It's pretty far away, so it's hard to tell, but it looks like a really tall fence. Hang on," he says. I hear the door close and then more footsteps. The footsteps stop, and I hear some heavy breathing.

"Hey, Nick... what are you—?"

"I'm good, I told you!" More footsteps, and then latches opening.

"What are you doing on the roof?"

"I'm trying to see everything. Okay, yeah. It's definitely an energy fence! It's really long. It goes all the way out to the park and all the way around to the forest. I think it's got all of Adarria inside all the way to the Kerioth River!"

What!? The whole community is behind a fence being patrolled by people with hazmat suits? What's going on?

"Did you send that picture yet?"

"Oh... sorry! Yeah, I'm gonna send it! I'm just... I'm feeling kinda tired."

"I told you to be careful! You know better than to do all that running!" I scold.

"I know, I just... I'm gonna go to my room and lay down."

His is strength waning.

"That's probably a good idea," I say much more tenderly. "Hey... I wasn't going to tell you this, but do you know what your other birthday surprise was going to be?"

"No... What was it?" he says weakly.

"Me!" I say, trying to encourage a flicker of enthusiasm in him. "I'm at the monorail station now. There was a delay in the train to Alabast, but I'm going to get upgraded to one of the luxury cabins for my train ride into the capital! Isn't that cool? I can't wait to get there and tell you all about it!"

"That sounds great, Sissy. So, I'll see you soon?" he says with all the vigor he can muster.

"Yeah, I'll see you real soon. If you want to take a nap until I get there, then go ahead and get some rest, okay? I only have to wait about eight hours before the next train leaves here for the capital, and then I'll jump on a few carriers and get right there to you... I'll tell you about all the cool sights I see, and you'll tell me about the GlobalMan comics... That will be our deal... And you'll see. When I get there and talk to those people in the suits... I'm gonna make things right."

At this point, I'm only talking to fill the silence on the other side of the Solo. My mind races to try to find more words to say rather than give in to that awful silence. But eventually, I decide to let him rest.

Those were the last words my brother and I ever spoke to each other. My dad never woke up. When I arrived at the quarantine zone outside my neighborhood twelve hours and forty-eight minutes later, they were both gone.

Based on the autopsy, my little brother really put up a fight. He most likely took his last breath an hour and a half before I got there. He really wanted to see me, but he just...

That was the day I lost the only family I had left. It was also the day I gained my power and my purpose. I made a promise to my brother to make everything right, to get justice for him and for all the people Tryon United hurt. And I've lived every day of my life since then for that purpose.

My one regret is that the only promise I've made over the years that I won't see through to fulfillment is the promise I made to Nick.

PART 6 - KNOW THYSELF

CHAPTER 28 – SELF-CONTROL

"I am... *so* sorry to hear... what you went through. I can't imagine what it feels like to lose so much, so suddenly. Just hearing you tell me that now, some 30 years later... Even without my empathic Laosi, the grief you feel is *crushing*," I say, choosing my words carefully. "But... why are you telling me this now? As bad as what you went through was... Zoe, you can't be expecting that to justify what you've done since then."

Zoe looks at me from across the table in the visitation room. She raises her cuffed hands and points up at the silver, pulsating anti-Laosi lights beaming down on us. "Aiden, I accepted a while ago that we're beyond forgiveness. I made my choices, and these are the consequences." Looking up again, she says, more to herself than to me, "I never thought I'd be restrained by the technology I helped develop, though."

"Okay, so if not forgiveness or pity or some hope for a second chance, then why are you telling me this?" I ask. "Why waste one of your three Final Conversations on me?"

"Waste?" Zoe chuckles. "No, this isn't a waste. You're the only person I chose to have a Final with."

"What? Why?"

Zoe straightens the collar of her all-white jumpsuit and says, "To be honest, as lamentable as it is to say this... you're the closest thing to family I have, Aiden."

Family?! She's GOT to be kidding me.

"As you heard in my story," she continues, "the last of my blood relatives with whom I had any relationship died a long time ago. So, I devoted myself to my newly discovered purpose at the expense of building new relationships. The closest I came to making friends was when your mother became my roommate and your father became a co-researcher. In hindsight, it was actually both selfish and self-sabotaging, but the connection I felt to the Lores was the real reason I wanted you to leave the Broken and join the Collective. It was never really about how powerful you are."

"Self-sabotaging?" I ask, raising an eyebrow.

"Yeah... If I had killed you in the station, your friends would never have picked up my scent until I was done," she says, looking down at the floor. "It was my unspoken—actually, subconscious—desire for a family, after all these years, that led to my failure. It's also what led me to call for you on my last day here on Tryon. I called you because I just wanted you to understand. And because I think you want to understand. I wanted to answer any questions you might have."

"Okay... I think the biggest question I have is... Like, you wouldn't tell me before, but it seems like you wanted to destroy Tryon United, right?" I ask.

"Absolutely!" she says confidently.

"But... why?"

"They took my brother from me. That would be reason enough, would it not? If someone killed Candace, Jack, or Leia and no one did anything about it, wouldn't you want to make sure that person couldn't hurt anyone else?" she snaps.

"Maybe I missed something... You blame Tryon United for your brother's death?"

"Of course I do. They are the ones responsible," she says with absolute certainty. "The notices they left on everyone's doors mentioned radiation, which they explained to the rest of the world as some type of cosmic phenomenon—a rare type of solar wind that happened to break through a weak point in Tryon's atmosphere and hurt certain people who seemed to be highly susceptible to it." She scowls.

"I take it that's not what you think happened."

She turns her head to the side and says, "I'm disappointed that so few people thought it strange that this *rare phenomenon* just happened to do its worst a stone's throw away from TU's experiments with tearing through space. Additionally, it just so happened that all the records concerning these experiments were heavily redacted or lost entirely to the public."

I sigh. "You sound like a conspiracy theorist..."

Zoe looks at me, her eyes sparkling. "But you know I'm not wrong, don't you? Your people pulled together the data off the jump drive, didn't they?" she says with zeal in her voice.

I roll my eyes and look away from her, but I nod.

"Oh! Then, this is not the end! I was so sure of myself that I almost dismissed the notion of needing a contingency plan. And then I got arrested... but Aiden, you can finish my work!"

"What work?" I exclaim. "You want me to carry out your revenge mission? Is that what this has all been about? Revenge?"

"Some may see it that way, but no," she says pensively. "No, my brother had a degenerative heart disease. We all knew he was on borrowed time. The doctors told us he wouldn't make it to his 12th birthday. And my father and I had a very strained relationship. The man had an insufferable knack for burning bridges! When my mom passed, and none of her family wanted anything to do with us because of him, I gave up on him, too. So no, it wasn't revenge."

"What was it, then?"

"Weren't you listening? Aiden, Tryon United is a governing body funded by the people they're commissioned to protect, and yet they can kill anyone at any time with no accountability! Don't you understand how dangerous that is?" she cries out.

"I do," I say firmly, "but..."

She's doing that thing again where I know she's wrong, but I think I agree with her!

"But aren't you the same one who just accepts that everyone is going to die? Whether a TU accident, disease, solar flare—'death always wins,' right?" I ask.

"I'm flattered, Aiden... you remembered! But what else did I say? I said *'Death is not the enemy,'* right? So what is?" she asks, staring right back at me.

"... You said something like 'anyone who will keep you from being able to live,'" I mumble.

She slaps the table between us and leans forward, exclaiming, "Exactly!" Then, regaining her composure, she says, "It shouldn't have taken me twelve hours and forty-eight minutes to get to my little brother. It should have taken four—at most, five. I should have been able to get to the quarantine zone, put on a hazmat suit, and spend that time with my brother while he breathed his last. But because of them, my sickly, nine-year-old little brother died scared and all alone because they took away my right to make my own choice."

"So all of this boils down to you being mad at them for delaying your train ride? You wanted them to send you and a couple hundred people through a field of deadly radiation? It seems like they were trying to protect everyone else," I rebut.

"When will you stop being so naive?" Zoe asks, exasperated. "The path of the monorail was only close enough to Adarria for the passengers to see what was happening, not to be affected by it."

"You don't know that for sure," I protest.

"You forget... I was studying to be a doctor. I researched the range and effects of the radiation when I got back on campus. We would have been out of harm's way. More to the point, if they were that worried about my safety, they should have given me a hazmat suit!" she says, standing her ground.

"But... but what if they didn't have any extra suits?"

"Even if they didn't have a hazmat suit for me, it would have been *my choice* to go into that radiation and march right into my house and hold my brother. I don't need the people who killed my brother to try to protect me.

"Besides, their top concern was clearly protecting themselves from me and people like me. That's why, rather than being accountable for their actions and explaining to everyone what happened, they just blamed the cosmos and told everyone to stay away while the neighborhood I used to play in turned into an uninhabitable swamp. They're cowards, Aiden. And you understand that now, don't you?"

"I'm not going to argue with you anymore, Zoe," I say, reclaiming myself. "I didn't have to come here, so I certainly will not use this time in a debate I don't want to participate in."

"I... wouldn't want you to," she replies. "I didn't mean to upset you. That's not why I asked you to come... You put your life and the lives of your friends on the line in a fight that you didn't even understand. I've had a lot of time to think, as you can imagine."

Tapping the currently inactive Laosi inhibitor around her neck, she says, "It is the most surreal experience to have one of these things on. You still see, hear, and feel the world around you. You still retain all your thoughts, your feelings, and your desires. But your conscious mind has no ability to influence your body. Your body is on autopilot, doing only what it has been told or trained to do.

"The inability to make my own decisions... the powerlessness... that which I fought hardest to overthrow, I have been subject to every day for the last eight months. The only sounds I hear—in the solitude of my cell and when my fellow inmates and I quietly shuffle past each other—are the echoes of choices I made during what feels like a lifetime ago."

She stands up and walks around the room, stretching her legs in her last moments.

"We can't undo what we've done, right?" I ask. I feel for her more than I want to, so I try to move the conversation along. "Someone much wiser than me once said, 'We can choose our sins, but we can't choose their consequences.'"

Zoe stops, nods respectfully with a smirk, and says, "That's pretty good. It's been eight months since our last heart-to-heart, right before you made the decision that brought us here. I'm all out of appeals. These are the last 39 minutes I have on Tryon, the last page in the story of my life. But you—you're fresh off your honeymoon with your lovely bride, starting a brand-new chapter. Thank you for taking the time to answer my call and talk with me. Like I said—I didn't want to argue. I just wanted someone to understand, and now I think you do. That's all I could ask for. You gave me the last thing I wanted, and I'm grateful. I'll let you get back to your story."

She breathes a heavy, relieved sigh, and that somehow makes me happy for her. In a strange way, I'm glad I could provide a sense of closure to what must have been a very troubled life. I feel darkness in my soul as well, but it seems to be the residue of the burning sadness Zoe has carried all these years. I plan to leave all that with her when I walk out of here. But there's one thing I'm still curious about.

"Hey, so... you mentioned twice to me that you have an active LET... What exactly was your talent?" I ask as I rise to my feet.

"Intelligence," she says in a friendly tone.

I laugh as that was not the answer I was expecting, and it makes her laugh, too.

"Okay, that probably sounds like I'm saying I think I'm the smartest person ever. Sorry. Maybe a better word to use is consciousness. No one even knew I had a talent, so I've never had to explain it," she says, almost bashfully.

"Well, ya do now," I say. "Consciousness? Meaning...?"

"Meaning I can communicate my consciousness to other vessels that are receptive to it."

"Oh, so is that how you controlled the Collective?"

"Yes, but not in the way you might think. It has more to do with computers than anything. We developed artificial intelligence a long time ago, but computers are still essentially logic machines. Everything is ones and zeros to them. The human consciousness has a lot more to do with intuition, instinct, and even spirituality—things that can't be programmed. Well, I can communicate all of that to a machine effortlessly. I can program any computer to do whatever I want it to do. If I can think or even *feel* it, I can make a computer do it."

"So that's why ARL always had such cutting-edge technology," I say.

"Right. That's why Richard and I were such a dynamic duo. As we both learned about the nature of the soul, he designed more precise tools for detecting Laosi while I used what he developed to create the programming," Zoe says, embracing her last moments as a woman of science.

"That actually sounds pretty cool... in a 'let's not use it to take over the world' kind of way," I say, causing us both to laugh.

"I told you... I never wanted to take over the world. I just... needed to make something right." She pauses, then asks, "Have you ever read a *GlobalMan* comic?"

"The name was a big turnoff for me," I say, laughing again.

"I can't tell you how many times I said that to Nick," she says. "But then I understood why they called him that. He had no powers, but he fought against people who could turn invisible, triplicate themselves, and stop time... and he always won. It was because he always found a way to use what he had to his advantage. It's like the *world* was his power. At least, I think that's what they were going for with his name."

"Ah, I see," I say, stroking my chin. "And so when Nicholas said you reminded him of *GlobalMan*..."

"And then I found my power... As I said before, it's not very flashy, destructive, or intimidating... but I found a way to use it for my objective. I found a way to alter the frequency of someone's Laosi and harmonize it with a frequency that the ALPHA could broadcast all over the world. And since I could communicate my consciousness with the ALPHA, and the ALPHA could alter a person's Laosi, I could communicate my consciousness onto anyone who went through LIST."

"I see... It kinda makes me wonder, though... What would your power have been if you were born before the invention of computers? Like, I would have thought that Laosi would have a more natural base of influence... How did yours give you the ability to affect something so artificial... so external to the human makeup?"

"Maybe the real question is this: would I have had powers at all if I had been born before computers?' I think maybe yes and no. There would have been no TU and thus no purpose of mine for which to manifest these powers. But, I suppose there might have been any number of other stimuli to precipitate an imbalance in my Laosi.

"But, as far as my connection to computers goes, I think we as a species have become so integrated with our technology that it's only natural that LETs have evolved along with that integration. I'm the closest thing to a real cyborg this world has ever seen so far. Give it another hundred years or so, and cyborgs will probably be normal. And what kinds of LETs might a cyborg manifest?" she says, her excitement breaking through.

"Zoe... you're such a brilliant scientist. Who knows how much more you could have done for the world, how many other ways you might have advanced healthcare technology! I wish you could have met Tessa when you were my age..." I say, unable to hide the sadness in my voice.

"Tessa... the woman who oversees the Broken? My archnemesis?" she says with a forced laugh. "We've had a few run-ins, believe it or not... By the time we met, it was too late. She knew I wouldn't yield to anyone for any reason. I didn't know she was building an army of followers. But, in retrospect, I bet she always knew she would win, one way or the other."

"She always does, doesn't she?" I say, partly amazed and partly frustrated.

"Yeah... Well, Aiden, I won't tell you what to do about this TU cover-up situation. A choice like that will have consequences for the rest of your life. My hope is that you'll bring it to the surface because you know it's the right thing to do. But, obviously, I can't make you. Even if I could, that wouldn't be my style, now would it?" she asks with a wink.

She reaches her hands across the table for a handshake. I smile faintly and take her hand. "May you be free to make your own choices, and may you be satisfied by the harmony of the echoes they produce all the days of your life. Thank you, again. Truly."

What do you say to someone as the last friendly face they'll see before they die?

"We obviously didn't agree on everything. And to be honest, from the moment I knew it was you pulling the strings of the Collective, I really thought you were a cold-hearted psycho."

I'm not quite sure this is going the way I intended...

"And I wanted to kill you when Zane died... In fact, I had made up my mind that I was gonna do it. I honestly still don't know what stopped me."

Come on, Aiden! Say something helpful!

"I mean, come on, Zoe... You were about to make my mom—your former roommate and friend—throw her son out of a window that was 450 feet high! I really don't have words for how messed up that is..."

She winces, her gaze dropping to the floor. Looking at her face, I see an emotion I'm all too familiar with creeping across it.

I guess that's what shame looks like.

She struggles mightily to raise her eyes back to mine, and a forlornness welling up as tears streams down her face.

"I... can you tell Jackie..." she starts, her voice barely louder than a whisper. It cracks as she says, "Can you tell her that I'm... I'm sorry? Can you tell her that for me?"

She looks into my eyes, but I can tell she's not looking for forgiveness. As I look back into hers, I see desperation. And I pity her because after hearing her story, I understand why she doesn't have any peace right now. Mom was the closest thing to a friend Zoe ever had, and she *needs* to know that her remorse will be expressed to Mom. She brings her cuffed hands to her cheeks to wipe the tears, but her gaze never leaves mine.

"I'll tell her," I say softly.

She closes her eyes and exhales sharply through her nose. When she reopens her eyes, she looks down at the white tiled floor for a moment before meeting my eyes again. "I didn't bring her there to fight. I knew you'd get cold feet, so I brought her there to talk you back into accepting the procedure through her. Richard would have told you to do what felt best, so I scheduled your appointment for a day I knew he wouldn't be able to do that."

She sighs reminiscently and adds, "I was so close. I came up with this plan when we started developing the ALPHA."

That probably explains why she feels so connected to me—I was born right after the technology she needed to keep her promise to her brother was built.

"My plan went exactly as I expected up until the day I was arrested, primarily because no one knew it was happening. So when you teleported away and came back with all your friends... that was the first time something happened in my plan that I hadn't accounted for. I've had hundreds of people doing what I wanted without resistance for decades, thanks to the ALPHA and ARL's influence. To be this close to the finish line, only to have you fight back—I just... I snapped. I sent your mom in to forcefully get what I wanted from you. It was a child's temper tantrum, backed by the strength of the world's most powerful woman. I became what I hated most in that moment, using strength to oppress others for my own gain and wounded pride.

"It was never part of my design to pit your mother and you against each other... I know she won't forgive me—how could she? I wish I could do so much more than apologize..."

"I know," I say. "You wish you could make this right."

Almost mystified, she says, "Yeah..."

I know you do, Zoe.

I scratch the top of my head and say, "It's probably not the most gratifying thing to hear someone talk about how they wanted to kill you and how screwed up the things you did were... especially not right before you... ya know."

She smiles at me and says, "There's no way to dress it up, Aiden. I'm going to die. I've accepted it."

"Death always wins, doesn't it?" I say, and she chuckles. "But, you know, maybe it's the certainty of death that gives life its beauty. Knowing you don't have forever makes each moment count... wouldn't you say?"

"Indeed, I would," she says almost triumphantly, respectfully engaging my banter.

"I was just gonna say that, in this moment... I don't feel any of that hatred or desire to see you harmed. I don't even know where it went. I'm grateful and honored that you chose to tell me your story. I think it's giving us both closure. It makes me glad but also sad to see there was so much love in your heart. And I want you to know that I know the sincerity in Nick's heart when he said you're the world's greatest big sister."

Tears begin to well up in Zoe's eyes again, but she deflects to hold the emotion at bay. "You'd better not let Candace hear you say that." She laughs but then sniffles as one of those tears escapes.

"These walls are soundproof, right? No recordings?" I ask, joking along with her. "But seriously... You spent your whole life fighting to honor his memory, validating his life even though he only had a few years left to live. A lot of people aren't lucky enough to have someone who cares about them that much. It'll look different, but I think I'll continue the fight you started. I won't try to overthrow Tryon United or kill anyone... but I do believe in accountability. I'm going to talk to Tessa about all of this and see what she thinks we should do to make it right."

Choking back the tears, Zoe says, "Then I can go on to die at peace. Thank you for your authenticity and your kind words..." She pauses, looking at me with pleading eyes. The vulnerability of this moment causes my breath to catch in my chest. It's uncomfortable, but I decide to stay with her as long as she needs me to. She studies me, but then her face softens. With acceptance and resolve, she says, "Farewell, Aiden."

"Ms. Withers... I don't rea—"

Smiling, she interrupts me, jovially asking, "You still can't bring yourself to just call me Zoe?"

"No, I could call you 'Zoe' if that's what you'd prefer. It's just... this is how I was raised to address someone I respect."

Her smile deepens. "If after all this, you still consider me worthy of respect, then I'd be honored to hear 'Ms. Withers' here at the end."

I gaze at her gently, genuinely amazed that I never caught even a glimpse of all the hurt, anger, and isolation she carried when I saw her before everything escalated. As I study her smile, memories of different moments flash through my mind: my 10th birthday party, the time she picked me up from school because Mrs. Gloria got sick suddenly, and even when I saw her at my graduation ceremony. I find myself lost in wonder at the fact that, even though my empathy was online from my earliest memories, I never sensed any of the pain she just shared with me.

Zoe, you kept that hurt bottled up all this time, not wanting one drop of it to spill on anyone who didn't deserve it. But I'm glad you got to pour it out the way you did with me today... It really is the certainty of your death that has given these last moments their beauty. Thank you for inviting me to witness this.

"Goodbye, Ms. Withers."

CHAPTER 29 – SELF-IMAGE

"Right this way, Mr. Lore. Please retrieve your Solo and any other personal belongings surrendered upon your arrival. Thank you for visiting Atheria Correctional, and enjoy the rest of your evening!" the prison escort says as we exit the labyrinth of hallways designed to prevent breakouts.

"Thank you. Have a good one!" I call back through the red energy shield activated by the guard.

I grab my Solo and my belt from the locker assigned to me and head toward the sliding door.

"Lil' A, how are we looking?" I ask as I step out into the evening air. Glancing back, I take in the grey stone fortress towering against the navy blue sky. The air is muggy and still.

"Your hair's a little messy, and you've got something green stuck in your teeth that I was going to tell you about before you put me down. Plus, when was the last time you went to the gym, sir?" Lil' A asks.

"I'm asking if there were any missed calls or messages, and you knew that!" I fire back.

"I mean... did I, though?" Lil' A asks innocently.

"Answer the question," I say while using my pinky fingernail to pick between my teeth.

"Yeah, Tessa asked if you had time to come by Otto's Autos alone today."

Alone?

"Um... yeah, tell her I'll come by after dinner if she'll still be there."

"I'm down for the cause!" Lil' A reports back.

I guess that means he'll send the message? Why is my AI like this?

"Did you order that carrier I asked you about?" I ask,

checking the time.

"Uh, sir? It's right in front of you. Do you need to get your eyes checked? I can schedule an appointment with your optometrist if you want."

"Lil' A! All you had to do was say, 'The carrier ten yards ahead is the one you requested,' or something like that," I growl as I walk down the stairs to street level.

"My sensors detect elevated stress patterns in your voice. Diagnosis: hurt feelings. Remedy: affection and reassurance. Would you like a hug, Sarge?"

As I approach the carrier and get in, I say, "I would like you to call Leia."

"Holo or audio?" Lil' A asks.

"Audio is fine," I say.

"Very well! Connecting to Leia Lore in 3... 2..."

"Hey, baby!" Leia says.

"Hey, boo. I'm just leaving Atheria, so I'll be home in about ten minutes. Will you be ready in ten?"

"I'll have you know that I'm already ready, Mr. Lore," she says.

"Impressive... I guess there's a first time for everything," I say.

"Whatever," she says, laughing. "So... how was it?"

"Not really what I was expecting."

"You wanna tell me about it?"

"Nah... I mean, I'm sure my parents will wanna hear, too, so I'll just wait until we're eating dinner."

"Fair enough," she concedes.

"Hey, speaking of dinner... Tessa said she wanted me to go to Otto's alone after dinner. I don't know why."

"Hmmm... Maybe she wants to hear about your talk with Zoe, too?"

"I thought about that, but she could've just read my mind if that was what she wanted," I reply.

"Good point," she says.

"So I have no idea what it is," I confess. "Well, anyway, I

just wanted to let you know I'm on the way! See you soon."

"Bye, baby! End call," Leia says.

As the carrier hovers down the street, I reflect on the conversation with Zoe.

So she named the ARL building after her brother's middle name... Why did she say she used that name? To make him pay attention to his choices and their consequences? I guess going to work every day was a reminder to her about the choice she didn't get to make.

That's probably why she was so laser-focused on her objective. I don't know if I've ever met anyone so devoted to their purpose, so willing to sacrifice everything. But then again, maybe she didn't have anything left to sacrifice. What was she living for? To settle the score? It seems hard to live a healthy life if that's what gets you outta bed every morning.

But, no... she said it wasn't about revenge. It sounded like it was more so about accountability. Or freedom. Somehow, in her mind, she felt she was going to work each day to fight for freedom. Her brand of freedom was worth living, dying, and killing for to Zoe.

I can't get behind that purpose, especially the way she went about it. But what am I living for? I'm still not sure I've found that purpose Tirrell was saying I should have to get me out of bed. I do enjoy leading Dynamics discussions and helping people through those first couple months of transition. Helping them learn about their soul streams and applying the Six and stuff like that...

Do any of the Six apply to Tryon United? I know we have to hold them blameless. But we also have to help when we can, right? Demanding accountability from those with power is helping... I think.

But is that our fight? Are we supposed to be getting involved with political issues, or do we just help people learn to manage their LETs? Is that what Tessa wants to talk to me about? Maybe she already read my mind... But why would she need me to be physically present at Otto's if she can talk to me from anywhere?

"You have arrived!" the carrier announces.

I pull out my Solo and send a message to Leia: "I'm here. You can start heading to the loading zone."

Okay, I'm in too deep. Time to shake that off so we can just enjoy the evening.

The carrier rises to the 12th floor, and the loading zone double doors slide open, revealing the hallway where my wife is waiting. When she steps into the carrier and sits next to me, I wink at her.

"Hey, good lookin'."

"You are so corny," she laughs.

"And you aren't?" I tease back. "See, I was going to kiss you, but no! You hurt my feelings."

"Leia, please give this man a hug," Lil' A chimes in.

"All right. That's enough. Off you go!" I say, shutting down my Solo.

"No! Wait!" Lil' A yells. The Solo gives its familiar Tryon United jingle before powering off as I slide it into my pocket.

"Don't be mean to him!" Leia says. She reaches into my pocket, pulls my Solo back out, and turns it on again.

"Seriously? You're taking up for my avatar?" I say, unamused.

"Hey, how long was I out?" Lil' A asks, sounding breathless.

"He is so dramatic!" I blurt out.

"I wonder where he got it from," Leia says sarcastically.

"I don't like what you're implying," I say, narrowing my eyes at her.

"Hey, Aiden, your mom's calling!" Lil' A announces. "Here she is!"

"Wai— uh, hey, Mom! What's up?" I ask, flustered.

"Hey, son! I'm just trying to get an estimate of when you guys think you'll be arriving. The food's almost ready, so—"

"Okay, so spin around counterclockwise three times, count to 19, say the ABCs backwards, and—"

"I ain't doing all that, boy!" my mom says firmly, then chuckles.

"You play too much," Leia mutters under her breath.

"Nah, I'm just messing with you. It looks like we'll be there in 13 minutes."

"Sounds good! I'm looking forward to seeing y'all!" she says cheerily.

"Us, too! Bye, Ma. End call, Lil' A."

Leia's hand finds mine, resting on the cushioned seat between us. She looks at me and says, "You're bothered by something."

"I am?" I ask.

"Yeah. You get... more playful when there's something on your mind. Something that you've dealt with as much as you wanted to but not as much as you needed to," she says softly.

I love being known by you.

"Oh, I have a tell?"

"Mm hmm," she says gently, moving her hand to the back of my neck and stroking it tenderly.

"For years, my tell was my LET activating. Without any fireworks going off, it's easy for me to assume I must be fine."

"That may be true... but now, we don't blow stuff up. Now, we talk stuff out," she says with a smirk. "Besides, it doesn't seem like something really intense is going on. More like something just didn't sit well with you or is nagging at you."

"Yeah... it's kinda weird. After all that we've done, after all that we've been through, it still feels like I'm just trying to find my place in this world. Does that make sense?"

She nods reassuringly. "It does. As long as I've known you—and I'm sure it was true before we met—you've been trying to find a sense of purpose."

She slides closer, leaning her head on my shoulder. "I think you haven't found it because you don't know what you're looking for. It's almost like you have this expectation that living out your purpose means you'll wake up every day feeling a certain way, like everything in life will just flow smoothly and easily. It's like you think fulfillment is something you'll feel all day, every day, and if you don't feel that, then you're not living out your purpose."

She pauses, placing her palm on the back of my hand and interlacing her fingers with mine. "But I don't think life works that way. We find things we're good at and love doing, and we do them as often as we can. For the rest of the time, we just maintain through the mundane parts. We never really arrive at this ideal state of living. We solve a problem, and the next day there's another one. All we can do is make the most of the moments we have with the things and people we care about."

"So what you're saying is I need to get my head outta the clouds."

"Hey, if that's what you heard, then that's what I said," she says with a shrug.

"Okay, okay. That's fair..." I respond.

"But not satisfying?"

"It's just... Zoe told me what it was that got her out of bed every morning. What drove her, what she had to accomplish. And I guess that just stuck with me," I say with a sigh.

"You taking life lessons from a psychopath now?"

I snicker. "Shut up!"

"Just let me know now. Just because I said 'I do' doesn't mean 'I will' if that's how you want to live your life."

"Wait... for real though?"

"Oh, look! We're here!" she says abruptly, batting her eyes at me.

Nah, she wouldn't leave me. Not after all we've been through. Not after all I've done for her.

"You know I love you, Aiden Lore. Just don't go trying to take over Tryon, and we're good."

"Ha ha," I say with emphatic sarcasm. "Anyway, let's go eat. You hungry?"

"I am! I wonder what Mom cooked!"

We get out of the carrier and walk up the stairs to my parents' house. They meet us at the door. My mom gives me the warmest hug I've ever felt—not just from her, but from anybody—and says, "It's so good to see you!"

"It's good to see you, too, Mom."

"It's been way too long, son," my dad adds.

Leia clears her throat.

"And you, too, daughter!" my dad says, laughing.

"Come in, come in," my mom says. After we all exchange hugs inside the doorway, Mom ushers us through the kitchen and into the dining room to take our seats.

"Smells great!" Leia says.

"Thank ya kindly," my mom says.

"What did you cook?" I ask.

"It's a surprise! This time, I decided to cook *my* favorite."

"Good for you!" Leia says, and Mom winks at her.

I guess I can start getting to know my mom for who she really is now.

"It's an old recipe. Something your grandma taught me when I was a little girl," Mom adds.

"Oh, really?" I ask. I pause, then ask, "How come we never talked much about your parents or how you grew up, Mom?"

"Oh, I don't know. I guess I never thought you all would find that interesting," she says dismissively. "Is that what you wanted to talk about after all this time?"

"I think I'd rather hear about the honeymoon first," my dad says as we all find our seats. "That was your first time seeing Eternity with your own eyes, wasn't it, Aiden? How was it?"

"I was really amazed by all the natural beauty," I say, holding Leia's hand and looking into her eyes. "The beach was nice, too." My dad grins as Leia pretends to blush. "But seriously, the landscapes in Eternity are the most amazing images my eyes have ever taken in. Thanks for the recommendation! Aaaand the extra credits."

"It was our pleasure," Mom says. "You know, that's where we went on our honeymoon, too. Same resort and everything."

"After the year we've had, I think we should take another trip," Dad says, looking at Mom.

"Ooh, just say when!" Mom says, swaying her hips side to side in her chair.

"Hold on, Mom... There was a little too much friskiness in that body language right there," I comment.

"There's nothing wrong with a little frisk," Dad says, putting his arm around Mom.

"How do you think you got here?" Mom asks.

I don't think I want to know her for who she really is anymore. This is so uncomfortable.

"Sorry to change the subject—" Leia starts.

"Please change the subject," I say, garnering laughter.

"I just wanted to know how you all have been holding up," Leia continues. "Aiden got a new job, we got married, and went on a honeymoon since all of that craziness happened, but... how have you two been? Our part in the investigation was pretty quick, but I think I heard they're still going through all the records at ARL. How has that been for you?"

My dad takes a deep breath and then says, "Not too, too bad, I guess. You can't be mad at an eight-month sabbatical, can you?"

"No, honey... It's okay," Mom says, looking deep into his eyes. "You can tell them how it's really been."

"Yeah," Dad says. Then, with difficulty, he adds, "To be honest, I still don't quite know what to make of all this. One minute, I'm just pursuing my life's work, trying to find a... ya know, new applications for it, and the next minute, I learn that all of that work has been used in a global conspiracy."

There it is again—that same shame in his heart when he stumbled over his words.

"The flood of reporters always showing up at the house. The detectives asking all their questions, trying to get me to remember statements from 20 years ago, and the threat of facing charges just for doing my research. Receiving death threats and being assigned a sentry detail because I'm a critical informant... It's been... hard."

"Hold up—death threats?" I ask.

"Nothing serious," Dad says. "Angry, misinformed former patients and family members lashing out because they felt violated. Their bark was always much worse than their bite. But it was still just a lot."

"I can't imagine," Leia says, slowing down the pace. Turning to Mom, she says, "How's it been for you? Are your powers back online?"

"They are," she says, looking down at her hands. She pauses for a moment, closes her eyes, and shudders. When she reopens them, she says, "I'm sorry. I don't seem to have gotten over 'waking up' and seeing your friend's blood on my hands... How's he doing these days?"

"Who, Zane? That clown is completely back to normal. He keeps saying, 'Yo, Aiden, man... I'm just saying... Tell your mom that if she wants to spar, I'm down.' So now I've told you, so I can tell him I told you, and he can leave me alone," I say.

Leia laughs and says, "That was pretty good! You sounded just like him. I'm impressed."

"That's why they're called 'impressions,'" I say with a smirk.

Mom rolls her eyes. Dad mutters, "Oh boy," under his breath, and Leia looks at me, shaking her head.

"He wants to be a comedian so bad! I keep telling him to stick to his day job," Leia laughs.

"Sound advice," my dad affirms.

"Anyway, can you tell Zane I said, 'No thank you'?" Mom says gently. "I'm not interested in using my powers, especially against him."

"That's understandable," I say. "Have you—"

DING!!

"I'm sorry. That means the food is ready... Honey, can

you go get it? I think Aiden was about to ask me something," Mom says.

"Sure thing, dear, but I might need a little help," Dad says.

"You got this. I believe in you," Mom says, her lack of sincerity barely masked.

"Oh, brother," Dad says before walking out.

I laugh at their playfulness. "Yeah, I was going to ask if you've used your LET since we broke the ALPHA. Like, were your powers ever out of control like mine?"

"It's kinda hard to say with me," she replies. "My talent isn't external like yours. So, when I pick up something heavy, was that Laosi strength or natural? When I strain my eyes and see something that others can't, is that LET vision? It's hard to say."

"That makes sense... But Leia taught me that Laosi has a sound that I've learned to hear when someone uses a talent. I could help you learn to hear it if you want, or—"

"I wish I heard someone using a talent to help me carry all this food in here," Dad calls from the kitchen. "Aiden, can you teleport a pot from here to there?"

"Coming, dear!" Mom calls into the kitchen. She starts to stand up, but I wave her back down.

"You've been up in that kitchen for who knows how long making that food. The men can take it from here," I say.

"You better know it!" Mom says, giving Leia a high five across the table.

I stand up and walk into the kitchen.

Has she always been this sassy? Also...

"Dad... was that a LET joke you just made?" I ask.

"Yeah...? Was that bad?" he asks.

"No, not at all," I say. Then, timidly, I add, "I'm just surprised to hear you joke about it... I honestly thought you hated LETs. I mean, most of your life's work was all about getting rid of them."

"Aiden, I'm a scientist. My life's work is about

understanding nature and finding ways to adapt it into something people can benefit from. It's not personal. I'm not 'for or against' LETs. I just want to help people."

I reach down to grab a saucepan and a couple serving utensils.

"Besides, ARL used LIST for way more than just suppressing LETs. We've helped people resolve traumas, reduce anxieties, curb depression, and even regain suppressed memories. If it has to do with a person's soul, LIST was designed to help it."

Honest conversation, right, Tessa? Here goes...

"Yeah, but... Dad, you know I'm an empath, right? If it's not personal, how come I always felt so much shame in you toward me whenever my powers came up in the past? And even just a few minutes ago?"

He puts the pot in his hand down on the counter and turns to face me. "Is that what you thought all this time? That I was ashamed of you because you had active LETs?"

"Yeah, I... And that's why I never really... Dad, I don't know how to tell you this, but I never really, really felt like I belonged with you guys. Because Candace and Jack went through LIST and never had any powers. But whenever we talked about mine, I just sensed so much shame in you."

By this point, the words I want to use to express myself become harder to force out, but I've learned from Tessa that they have to be released.

I have to accept and be honest about what I truly feel. Otherwise, I'll never be reintegrated.

"And then, you were so happy when you developed the second-gen LIST... Even Mom said she hadn't seen you that happy in a long time. But it was because you could finally *cure* me of my powers."

Has Dad ever seen me cry like this before?

"So please don't try to tell me it wasn't personal. Just be honest. I'm sorry you couldn't fix me, but I didn't want you to be ashamed of me."

"Aiden, you're right. In some respects, it was personal. And I did feel shame about your struggle. But I was never ashamed of you or your powers, son. I was ashamed of myself for not being able to help you," he says, walking over and giving me a hug.

I place the contents of my hands on the breakfast nook table behind me and hold him back.

Have I ever seen my dad cry like this before?

"Son, whether you have LETs or not, you will always be my son, and I will always be proud of you," he says into my ear as he holds me. "I just felt ashamed because here I am, supposedly this big-name scientist helping people all around the world accomplish their goals, but I can't even help my own flesh and blood?"

He pulls back from the hug and looks me in the face. His eyes hold a pure compassion.

"One day, if you and Leia have kids, you will love those kids more than you can stand it sometimes. You'll be willing to do anything to help them. I know I feel like that with you three a lot. So, to see my son struggle so desperately with something, to have the answer to help so many others struggling with this same issue, but not to be able to figure out how to help my son? That's what I was ashamed of. Never you, Aiden. I'm so sorry you felt I was ashamed of you. Please hear me say that that was *never* the case."

I look at him for just a second longer and then pull him back into the hug. I sob softly into his shoulder, embracing the catharsis. That is, until we hear, "It seems like it really *will* require some talent to get that dinner on the table!"

"Hush, Jackie! We're having a moment here," my dad snaps back.

I laugh as we pull out of the hug, and he looks at me with a broad smile. "Son, please don't ever doubt how proud I am of you for being the man that you are... I mean that."

"So, you're not mad at me for... kinda destroying your company and all your work?" I ask, treading carefully.

"If I'm mad, I'm mad at myself for working so closely with someone capable of the things Zoe did and not seeing it. I'm mad my work was used to help her do it! But I couldn't be happier with you for doing what you knew to be right. That's all a father can ask for. I love you, son... Now let's get this food out here before the women get hangry!"

We carry all the food back to the dining room and lay it out on the table. Then, we take turns passing around the meat and vegetables until everyone has a full plate. My dad offers a word of gratitude, and we all start digging in.

Amid the sounds of chewing, burps, and compliments to Mom for outdoing herself with this feast, Leia leans over and asks under her breath, "Hey, everything okay?"

"Better than ever," I say back, smiling.

As we all reach that point where we're moaning from our overly full bellies, Mom says, "So, Aiden, how was your day? You two left us in here so long, I've heard Leia's whole life story *twice!*"

"Y'all are *so* hilarious today," I say. "Anyway, my day was very interesting. Zoe—Ms. Withers—called me. I was her Final."

"Oh..." my dad says, and the mood of the room darkens by about three shades. "I knew today was the day for..." His words trail off as sadness pierces his heart. "So, um... what did she want to talk about?"

"I think she just wanted me to understand why she did everything she did... or what she was trying to do," I say.

"What *was* she trying to do?" Mom asks.

"She would say you have the right to know that, Mom. She was trying to dismantle Tryon United."

"Why?" Dad asks, bewildered.

"Did she ever talk to either of you about her upbringing, her family, or anything like that?" I ask.

"No... Now that you mention it, that was a bit odd," Dad says. "I talked her ears off about how much I love my family."

"She didn't have anything left to talk about. They died

just before she met you, Dad. It was the end of that semester when she was your roommate, Mom."

"Yeah, I do remember that weekend... She was never the same after that," Mom comments.

"That sounds awful," Leia says.

"It was... She told me the whole story. But she blames Tryon United for their deaths."

"What? Why?" Mom asks.

"I won't say too much now, but... keep watching the news," I say.

"Do we have to?" Mom groans. "It feels like the whole world is spinning out of control right now, and the news just keeps broadcasting the chaos with catchy headlines. People whose LETs were in remission for years suddenly reactivating... Second-generation LISTers manifesting multiple powers... User vigilantism on the rise... Cultists and radicals call for the general populace to kill all Users... Public trust in authority figures at an all-time low... Mental health concerns at an all-time high. I can't handle another 'breaking news' headline. Zoe really left her mark on this world."

"Then I guess she's winning after all..." I say, lost in thought.

"What do you mean?" Leia asks.

"Well, at first, I thought overthrowing TU was just a quest for vengeance. But more than that, Zoe was... basically an anarchist. She was opposed to people putting restraints on how others live their lives in the limited amount of time they have. She wanted people to be able to make their own choices and find their own meaning in life."

"Interesting philosophy from a person who controlled people's minds," Leia muses.

"That's what I said! But I believe her, though, when she said that once she did what she felt she needed to do to TU... if she had succeeded, she would have stopped using the ALPHA in that way. I mean, who knows? She might have just been blowing smoke in my face to get me to join her... She might have been many things, but she didn't strike me as a liar," I conclude.

"She definitely wasn't a liar. That's one of the things so many of us respected her for. She kept her secrets, clearly... but she also kept her promises," Dad adds.

I clear my throat and say, "Mom, Zoe wanted me to tell you that she's sorry. She didn't intend for you to fight against us. She just wanted to use you to talk me into joining her by going through LIST again. When I turned the tables on her, she just kinda... lost it."

"She's sorry, huh?" my mom says dryly. "I wake up in the middle of the night screaming because of a nightmare I keep having where I throw my own son out of a window to his death, and she's 'sorry?' My husband's good name is tarnished, and all the decades of his hard work taken away because she was using it to hurt people without his knowledge, and she's 'sorry?' We were friends, and she nearly destroyed my family, and she's just *sorry?!* When I came to, and you burst through the wall into her office, I wanted to kill her just as bad as you did."

"It's still a miracle I didn't do it myself," I say.

"I'm so glad you didn't, though," Dad says.

"Are you taking up for her?" Mom asks, her tone mostly intrigued but slightly offended.

"No, I'm glad for Aiden's sake. If he would've killed her, we wouldn't have been able to argue self-defense, and lack of intent would be out the window. We would have lost our son, and whatever impact she's made on this world would still have been left," Dad reasons.

"So... all of that to stop her, but maybe she still gets what she wanted?" Leia challenges. "That doesn't seem right. What do you think we should do?"

I look at my wife and ask, "You think this is our fight?"

"I don't know... but I can't imagine Tessa won't respond to all this... or that she hasn't already," Leia says.

"Tessa? Who's that?" Dad asks.

"She's the lady over the Broken," I explain.

"The User group?" he asks. "You're going to keep hanging out with them?"

"Dad, most likely, the only reason one or more people at this table aren't dead is that I've been hanging out with the Broken."

"Okay, I hear you. And I trust you. We didn't raise you to be crazy," he says with a laugh.

"Absolutely not," I say, affirming their parenting. "Yeah, I'm sure Tessa will have a lot to say about everything going on. I don't think I want to get too involved, though."

"I don't think you should," Mom says.

"Yeah," Dad agrees. I can tell Leia isn't convinced, though.

"Tessa told me early on to stop carrying this weight on my shoulders like I'm the hero or something," I recall. "All we can do is all we can do, ya know?"

Is it bad that I want Zoe to win? Not in the way she was trying to go about it… but that's messed up what they did to her neighborhood. I feel like they can't be trusted with the power to make our choices for us. But… who can?

"Speaking of Tessa," Leia says, looking at me.

"Yeah, it's getting late. I told Tessa I'd meet with her after dinner. This has been great!" I say. "I hate to rush out like this, but it seemed like something important."

"We understand," Mom says. "I'm glad you enjoyed the food! Take some to-go plates for CounterAid to wrap up if you'd like. There's plenty left. We should do this again… real soon. Ahem, ahem, Leia, ahem."

"I got you, Mama Lore."

"Guys… I'm right here!"

"We know," they say in unison. I look at Dad for backup, but he just throws up his hands.

"Anyway… since it is so late, do y'all think Leia can ride in your carrier so I can get my own? I'd rather she could go straight home instead of having to drop me off, and I'd really prefer not to pay for two carriers," I plea with my parents.

"What, you think that just because we bought our own carrier, that means we don't have to pay for it?" Mom asks sternly.

"That... is what it means, isn't it?" I ask back.

"Richard, did you tell him that?"

"I'm sure I did at some point," he says nonchalantly.

"Why would you do that? I was trying to get paid back for all those diapers we bought for him!"

"Sometimes, it's your own people," I say to Leia.

"I'm just teasing. Of course she can use ours," Mom says as she rises to give me a hug. Everyone follows suit, and we all exchange our goodbyes.

As we walk to the door, I stop and say, "There were a lot of things that you guys didn't know and a lot that was outside of your control... but I'm glad to have you two as my parents. I love y'all."

"Aw, so sweet," Leia says.

"We love you, too, son. Goodnight!"

"Goodnight."

Leia and I step out into the warm night air and make our way over to my parents' carrier. I open the door for her, and the AI immediately recognizes my SOLO and fingerprints. It activates and says, "Where to, Aiden?"

"City Sector AL, apartment building 106, floor 12."

"Very good, sir!"

"See you soon," I say to Leia as she sits down in the carrier.

"Don't wake me up if you stay out too late," she warns playfully.

"You're trying to limit my time with Tessa?"

"You heard what I said, mister," she says with a smirk.

I lean into the carrier to give her a kiss and say, "Bye, Leia!" Then, I stand back up and close the door. I watch the carrier silently float off into the night, the mild hum of its engine fading as it disappears from sight.

For a moment, I stand there, letting the stillness of the night settle over me. The sounds of the city buzz faintly in the background.

Okay... Let's go see what Tessa wants!

CHAPTER 30 – SELF-ACCEPTANCE

"Hello, Aiden! I'm glad you decided to come. I trust that you enjoyed your honeymoon getaway? Do you mind if I...?" Tessa taps her finger on her temple.

"No, go right ahead," I say. "Oh, but wait... It *was* our honeymoon, so..."

"Aiden, I've been reading people's minds for longer than you've been alive. I know how to see only what I'm looking for. The real question is whether or not you trust me," she says, her tone gently inquisitive.

"I'm used to feeling naked around you," I say with a laugh, shoving my hands in my pockets. "I trust that you're not going to see anything more embarrassing than what you've already seen."

"Which is different from saying that you trust me..." she says, squinting her eyes at me to make her point. "Interesting."

She's... not wrong. But I really hope this doesn't turn into another teachable moment.

"I have a question for you," she says.

Incoming teachable moment in 5... 4...

I glance around her office and preemptively say, "I feel a bit frustrated because I did—"

"Not that question," she interrupts, smiling. "You'll notice I don't ask you that as much anymore. You've become significantly more aware of your emotional state. You know how to hear your heart's voice now. Whether you will listen to it is up to you, but you've learned to dignify it. You've done well with this first step in reintegration work, so we won't be spending as much time working on identifying feelings in the future. That's for you to do on your own now."

My heart flutters a bit. "So... you really feel like I'm making progress? Thanks, Tessa! Sorry, though. What were you actually going to ask?"

"Who in your life do you actually trust?"

The question causes my mind to go blank.

I want to say, "Everyone"... but if that were true, she wouldn't be asking me that. But I don't have a better answer, either.

"I think I pretty much trust everyone," I say. When she doesn't change her gaze, I feel the need to defend my answer. "I'm pretty much an open book with everybody. I don't have secrets that I haven't shared with anyone. So I think I trust everyone. At least, all the people I know who care about me. Like you, Tirrell, Leia, my parents, Zane..."

"So you believe that you trust us because you are so transparent with us?" she asks.

"Right!" I say, feeling understood.

"Transparency involves little more than the relaying of facts or the refusal to withhold them. News reporters do this all day, but that doesn't mean they are very trusting people. Admittedly, reporters aren't typically relaying facts about themselves, but it's the *attitude* that I'd like to draw your attention to more so than the content."

"I don't follow, Tessa. Help me out here," I say.

"There's a big difference between transparency and vulnerability. Transparency says, 'This is how things are.' Vulnerability might say, 'This is how things are, and I don't like it, but I don't know what to do about it. I don't have the answers or the solution. Will you take the reins for me and not judge me for my inadequacy?' See the difference?"

I nod.

"So, who in your life are you regularly vulnerable with?"

"Well... Oh, I was vulnerable with you that first day I met you."

"You were," she says with a smile. "And do you remember how freeing that felt? You put your trust in me, you let me take the reins, you believed I would accept you, and the next thing you knew, you were flying around the showroom!"

"Yeah..." I say. "It felt great!"

"Okay, and what about since then? Did you trust Tirrell, Zane, or Auriel when you knocked Elon down and wanted to keep fighting him?"

I lower my eyes. "No," I admit, my tone full of lament.

So much for my progress...

"What about when I told you to go apologize to Leia?"

"Yeah, I did trust you. I didn't want to apologize to her, but I did, and it went great!"

"Mm hmm," she says. "Progress isn't a linear pursuit like people assume. It's not like you reach a certain milestone and never look back in any respect. It's much more complex than that. Rather than worry about overall progress, you should just focus on one decision at a time. Who did you decide to trust when you went to destroy the ALPHA?"

"Hmmm," I say, folding my arms. "I guess no one. But you said yourself that I put together a solid plan. So I didn't need to trust anybody... right?"

"Didn't need to trust anybody," she repeats slowly, emphasizing a point I haven't understood. "You say that as if trusting is a thing you do only when needed... as if the better alternative is to have all the answers yourself. You'd rather not ask others for compassion towards your weaknesses and to lend you their strength to use as your own. You admitted that a *moment* of vulnerability was freeing, but a *life* of vulnerability... how does that sound to you?"

"Scary," I say glibly.

"Why?"

I sigh. "Because what if they don't show compassion? What if my weaknesses end up being too much to cover because I'm not doing enough to make it worth their while? If I'm always asking for help, then I'm just gonna be a burden. So it's better to have the answers myself and to make sure people see me as someone who has what it takes."

Though I turned my eyes away from her a while ago, Tessa looks at me tenderly and waits for me to lift my gaze back to hers. "And in your fear of being left alone, you keep your heart to yourself. Because being alone hurts less than being abandoned. Fear, loneliness, and self-reliance... What does that sound like to you?"

Sounds like home to me...

Wait, what did I mean by that?

"I don't know," I say. "I'm actually kinda confused. How did we get here? Weren't we talking about my honeymoon just a while ago?"

She laughs. "We were."

"Right, so did you call me over here just to ask if I trusted you enough to let you look at my memories of my honeymoon?"

"Not exactly... but since you brought it back up!" Her eyes glow blue as she tilts her head to the side. Two seconds later, her eyes return to normal, and she says, "Yeah, it looks like you guys really did have a great time! I'm happy for you, Aiden!"

I scrunch my eyebrows. "Really?"

"Yes, really," she says.

"I can tell you're being genuine, but I don't understand how that could be... since you wouldn't give your blessing to our marriage and everything."

"My commitment to you is not based on yours to me. My interest and desire for your well-being is not based on how well you perform or follow the Six," she says, remarkably unbothered. "Also, you'll find that rejoicing with others who rejoice helps cultivate humility while staving off bitterness and jealousy for social beings like us.

"Besides all that, I wasn't saying I didn't think you and Leia should get married. I love your friendship and connection. It wasn't the principle—it was the timing. You're still not ready yet. There's something very important you need to grapple with. Let's go out to the showroom."

As I follow her out of her office, I say, "I didn't understand that then, and I don't understand it now."

"I know," she says simply.

"But what's done is done, right?"

"That's right."

The showroom's emptiness heightens my self-consciousness.

I'm flattered by the individual attention, but I still don't understand why I'm here!

I follow Tessa to the middle of the showroom floor, and she says, "Sit here."

"Okay," I say. "Do you mind if I ask why?"

"I find that the exercise we're about to engage in works best in an open space."

She sits down in front of me with her legs crossed and motions for me to imitate her posture.

"You didn't answer my question earlier about what fear, isolation, and self-reliance sound like to you. That's okay. I imagine you don't remember the first time we talked about it. That was a long while ago, and a lot has happened since then. Close your eyes."

I follow her instructions as she continues. "You probably don't even know why you changed the subject like that when I asked. That's also okay. I called you here to help you find the answer to some questions you've been asking lately but not thinking about nearly as much as you should. For instance, why couldn't you stop attacking Elon? What was it that made you stop short of killing Zoe? And why did you think isolation sounds like home?

"And maybe more telling than all these: why did you never ask me any of these questions or the others I know have crossed your mind?

"This exercise will answer all of those. It will even tell you why Leia broke up with you and got back with you, as well as why I couldn't give my blessing yet. I can't just explain it to you, though. Technically, I could, but it would likely do more harm than good unless you experience it. I will warn you, though—this will be the hardest lesson you'll ever have to grapple with. I would ask you if you're ready, but you're not."

Sounds promising.

"You're going to go on a psychic journey with me, so I will need you to stay as close to me as possible."

With my eyes still closed, I say, "Tessa, if we were any closer, I'd be in your lap."

"The physical proximity supports the psychic connection," she says, clearly unamused by my joke. "I need you to focus, Aiden. Use your empathy. What am I feeling right now? Your empathy is usually a passive trait, but I want you to tap into it and push it as far as it can go. Be as precise as you can be."

"Okay... You are feeling... concern. Not fear, but deep concern."

"That's very good. And what else?"

"I recognize your affection. Yours is different. It's... clearer? It's not tainted by the leftovers of disappointment you've felt because of the other person's shortcomings. You were disappointed that I didn't wait to get married like you said, but that doesn't affect your affection."

Most people aren't like that.

"What else?"

"There's peace... and joy... I don't understand how they correlate with the level of concern you feel, but they're all there!"

"Wonderful... Now, we will push a little farther. I want you to try to see what I'm thinking."

You mean I'll learn how to read people's minds?

No, this will only work with me, and only because I'm extending my mind to you. But I want you to start with the feelings and work your way in towards what I might be thinking.

Umm.. The peace and joy come... from a place of... maybe...

confidence? Like... You know this will work or be for my good or something. I WILL learn the lesson.

You're doing great. And the affection?

The affection... You are thinking... that you know... this will be hard... but it will be worth it.

That's it! Keep going.

The concern... The deep concern... It's coming from a place of... a very dark place. A place of pain and... Like an ACTUAL place of— uhh, Tessa, what's happening?

Suddenly, my body feels like it's dropping, even though I know it can't be—I'm sitting on the floor. Or maybe I'm floating away from my body?

You're coming with me on a psychic journey, is the sense I get from Tessa. I no longer hear her voice or even her thoughts. None of my senses are active anymore. Everything is raw instinct, impulse, intent, and impression. There's no more understanding of up or down, left or right. Everything is everywhere. Yet nowhere.

Stay with me.

I'm scared! I don't know what's happening!

Stay with me.

The impression I have of her weakens.

Am I dead? Is this what it feels like to die?

Staaay with meee...

Okay, right. Physical proximity, psychic connection. Tessa... Tessa... Tessa!

I reach out to her as best I can until her presence starts to become clearer. Even with my eyes closed and no senses active, I "see" her!

Good... Come with me.

I have so many questions but the intent is telling me they won't be answered. It's like I can feel the intent of other people in this space... Unfulfilled desires, fear... Loneliness... Anger, pain... Greed, lust, envy... They seem so familiar. I can't quite tell how I know them, but I know the people who felt these things... I can almost see them... but there isn't anyone else here. Just Tessa and me in this space.

Am I feeling the residue of what others left behind in this space?

Stay with me.

Suddenly, everything is clear. Even though I can't see anything, I know exactly where I am.

This is familiar.

But there's someone else here... bound and motionless. Floating in this endless nothingness, just barely able to move, barely even conscious.

Aiden... This... is the Gaius Realm. It's time for you to meet the other you.

Her voice sounds like it's echoing through water.

Why is he bound?

Set him free and he'll tell you.

Set him free? Set him free?! I don't want to! I'm scared! If he's bound, that means I'm in control, right? I don't wanna set him free! No! I need to be in control! Don't make me set him free! You hear me?

I won't make you do anything. But remember—acceptance is the key to reintegration, reintegration precedes alignment, and alignment is necessary for fulfillment. If he stays bound, then you'll never attain fulfillment, and our work together will end here because there's no further progress to be made.

Nooo... don't abandon me. I don't want it to end.

Then set him free.

Okay... I will. How do I do it?

You must choose to accept... and love him.

After some time (or maybe no time—it's hard to tell how time passes here) the bonds disintegrate, and Ithe other consciousness grows in that freedom until the space feels overcrowded.

I sense Tessa saying, *Aiden, meet the Gaius version of you. I imagine this must be quite confusing for you, but I'm here to answer any questions you have.*

That's when you said, *Am I... free?! Am I FINALLY...?*

Thank you! Thank you so much! I had almost given up on freedom. Thank you so much, Tessa!

Fear and anger rose within me as I focused more and more on you; I was not at all excited about the existence—let alone the *presence*—of the other me. Having seen what Alexi could do, I grew very tense and wanted to withdraw from you as much as possible. I couldn't make sense of Tessa's words when she said I needed to accept you, especially when the more I tried to do that, the more suffocated I felt.

Accept you? How could I accept someone who represents everything that could get in the way of what I want and need?

But you weren't concerned with my reaction. *Ummm… as far as questions go, how long ago was it that Leia made it out?*

It's been about ten months.

You exclaimed, *10 months?! I've been down here for that long?* Then, with sadness, you added, *How much trouble did he… did we cause?*

I could fill you in. But it would be more beneficial for your self-acceptance to let your Gaius self explain everything that's happened lately. That is, once he's ready.

You said, *The last thing I fully remember is the radius blast that put Leia in her coma. Everything is fuzzy for me after that. Going back and forth to work and the hospital… waiting for her to wake up… Yes, I'd like to hear what has happened since then.*

I felt your focus shift to me, as you expressed. *Please tell me.*

Tessa also turned her intentions to me and said, *Very well. Please fill him in from there.*

That's when I thought, *I don't need him to explain anything to me. What are you talking about, Tessa?*

To which you replied, *No, she… she… wasn't talking to you. Wait, did you… You thought you were the conscious self all this time? You really didn't know that you're our Gaius? How is that even possible?*

I pushed back on the notion that I'm the Gaius Aiden, and

you and Tessa said all that you said to convince me otherwise. Next, our memories appeared all around us, the same way they did right before we flew around the showroom, and I walked you through each incident that led us to this point.

And now, we're here. I've told you everything. So, you're caught up now? Are you satisfied?

I am. Thank you.

Great. I did my part. But what are we going to do now?

We both know that only one of us is leaving the Gaius Realm.

ABOUT THE AUTHORS

J. W. Frederick has always been fascinated by stories about people with superhuman abilities. Drawing from his background as a Licensed Professional Counselor, Frederick develops relatable characters with larger-than-life powers that struggle to navigate real-world issues like love, regret, self-image, and purpose. He aims to tell stories that entertain readers and create safe spaces for them to explore these issues in their own lives.

T. L. Hughes grew up on Saturday morning cartoons, watching superheroes battle against villains. Watching their creative uses of abilities inspired a passion for developing superpowers, action sequences, and fantasy worlds with limitless imagination.

The two have been best friends since 2003. Echoes of Choice is the first of many stories that they have co-created and that they're excited to share with the rest of the world.